# MISSION: NUTCRACKER

## A THRILLING HOLIDAY STEAMPUNK ROMANCE

## CECILIA DOMINIC

# ABOUT MISSION: NUTCRACKER

She dreams of joining the scientific elite. He's desperate to save his business and his sister. Together, they may hold the turnkey to adventure...

Terminus, 1871. Fiona Telfair won't give up her gears and gadgets for the ball and chain of marriage. But her future as a tinkerer comes under attack when nutcracker automatons raid the trade hall masquerade party and kidnap her fellow inventors. With her brilliant engineer father among those taken, Fiona's only hope of rescuing him lies with the captivating rail baron who rescued her from the fray.

Devon Meriweather can only keep his train empire on track if he marries into an influential family. Plus, he needs the connections to make certain his chronically ill sibling is taken care of. So no matter how engaging and beautiful the firmly working-class Fiona may be, he knows she'll only ever be a partner in solving crimes.

As they work closely hunting for clues to the strange aether-powered apparatus and magical mice, the intrepid duo can't deny their budding feelings. But neither can afford a distracting courtship with the growing threat of the nutcrackers and their deadly chompers.

Can Fiona and Devon expose the menacing mastermind behind the machines and make their passion run like clockwork?

*Mission: Nutcracker* is the second book in the charming Inspector Davidson Mysteries steampunk romance series and can be read as a standalone novel. If you like plucky heroines, nineteenth-century mystique, and unusual Christmas fairytale retellings, then you'll love Cecilia Dominic's yuletide triumph.

Buy *Mission: Nutcracker* to steam headlong into holiday fun today!

# LOOK FOR THESE TITLES BY CECILIA DOMINIC:

*Steampunk Series:*

*The Aether Psychics*
Noble Secrets
Eros Element
Clockwork Phantom
Aether Spirit
Aether Rising

*The Inspector Davidson Mysteries*
The Art of Piracy
Mission: Nutcracker

*Urban Fantasy Series:*

*The Lycanthropy Files*
The Mountain's Shadow
Long Shadows
Blood's Shadow

*Dream Weavers & Truth Seekers*
Perchance to Dream
Truth Seeker
Tangled Dreams
Web of Truth

1

———

*erminus, 16 December 1871*
Fiona pulled on her old gloves, which were already dingy but now made more so by a liberal application of coal dust. She smeared some of the dark gray matter on her cheeks, distributing it so it would draw the viewer's gaze to her sparkling blue eyes. Her mask and headpiece with round ears in place, she stepped back from the mirror to check out her costume. Yes, in spite of the mask having a pointed nose with ridiculous whiskers, she made quite the fetching mouse. And the best part—the costume, which consisted of a simple gray dress she'd worn as part of her half-mourning—had been made of salvaged clothing and parts. She hadn't spent any of the money set aside for her upcoming debut season, so her mother couldn't argue with her desire or right to go to the Tinkerer's Holiday Masquerade Ball.

Well, not unless her mother found out Fiona had been one of the few unattached females invited. But she didn't need to know that. Fiona trusted her father not to tell, although he'd been known to slip.

A knock on the door startled her out of her thoughts, which

had started to creep toward old, familiar territory. How could her brother have gotten himself killed and left her alone to manage her mother? Connor had been her mother's favorite child. Fiona had never measured up.

"Are you ready, Pet?"

Fiona smiled at her father's voice. "Yes, Papa. Be right out."

She gave herself one more look from the front, and then another from the back. Good, her dress showed off her small waist and the white skin of her neck, and the dim light would keep anyone from noticing the freckles that popped out no matter what she did to get rid of them. Her dark red hair would shine like burnished copper in the candlelight, and what better to attract a handsome young inventor than copper? And her mind, which several of the tinkerers had said they admired. Granted, they hadn't been *looking* at her mind at the time, but they shifted their gazes upward when they started discussing aether theory...

Another knock brought her back to herself. Then her father's voice. "The steamcart is here."

Again, her thoughts had run away with her. Her father laughed when that happened. Her mother sniffed disapprovingly.

"There's nothing wrong with a girl with a quick mind," her father would say.

"Not unless it keeps her from catching a rich husband." *Sniff.* The sound made Fiona cringe every time. It even followed her into her dreams. Ever since Connor had died, that had become her mother's refrain—catch a rich husband. Maybe then Fiona would finally earn her approval.

Well, Fiona was on the hunt tonight, but for brains, not money. She had faith that the latter would come from the former. Education could be bought. Intelligence could not.

Fiona walked out of her bedroom to find her father hilariously dressed as a cat. His gray mask had black tabby stripes painted on it, and he'd used kohl to continue the stripes on the side of his face. He'd even fixed pointed ears into his curly gray-specked black hair. His bright blue eyes—the same as Fiona's—twinkled behind the mask. Otherwise, he wore all black evening dress with an emerald pin—his one piece left from his Irish father—in his cravat.

He kissed her cheek. "You look lovely, Miss Mouse."

She giggled. "And you look ridiculous, Professor Cat."

"That's my job, Pet. To bring attention to the belle of the ball. And I have something for you." He brought out a small box and gave it to her. Inside, nestled in cotton fluff, lay a dark gray chain with a pendant shaped like a cross between a walnut and a macadamia nut.

"What is it?" Fiona asked. "And what is the material?"

"A krakatuk nut locket. It's an old family heirloom, and I don't know about the metal. Your mother wanted me to wait until Christmas, but I thought I should give it to you now. Why don't you hide it in your room so she doesn't know?"

"Thank you. It's lovely." Fiona took one last look at it and stuck it in the drawer of her dressing table.

They descended the stairs of their modest townhouse. Fiona's mother waited at the bottom.

*Sniff.* "Well, you're a fine pair." She crossed her arms over the black mourning dress she still wore. Her perpetual frown had drawn lines beside her lips, but otherwise she looked like an older, heavier version of Fiona. "Don't be out too late."

"Yes, Mother."

Fiona's father kissed his wife on the cheek, and Fiona smirked to see a little of the coal dust had rubbed on to him, and therefore on to her mother. Or maybe he'd smudged a stripe.

"I'll have her back before midnight. It would be awkward for her to turn into a pumpkin, after all."

Another sniff and not the faintest hint of a smile, although

Fiona grinned at his joke. She'd thought about dressing as a pumpkin, but she didn't have anything orange, as it was not a flattering color on her.

They almost ran out of the door and into the steamcart. Had this been a ball at one of the fine houses, they might have rented a carriage with real horses. But mechanical conveyance fit this particular party.

Once he'd confirmed Fiona was comfortable, her father lapsed into silence. He gazed out of the window, his hairline tight above his mask and his lips pursed below it, so she didn't disturb him. Instead, she followed her own mental meanderings. One more check of the contents of her reticule, then back to the mathematical problem she'd been attempting to solve all week.

When the steamcart drew up to the door, Fiona's father paid the driver and instructed him to return at eleven-thirty. The Tinkerer's Guild Hall had been decorated in reds and greens. No religious imagery—they tended to shy away from objects that would remind the members of the long war they'd just come through and the losses they'd each experienced. No one wanted to think of funerals or discord as they all struggled to make sense of their new world.

Fiona and her father walked through the ballroom and nodded to acquaintances they recognized. Some wore costumes that covered their heads and all or part of their faces, making it more difficult for Fiona to identify them. The costumes ranged from scientific concepts and tools to animals or characters. One commonality—they all wore a concerned expression that would appear between words and smiles, reminding Fiona that some of their number had been disappearing. Indeed, the ball seemed less crowded than she'd expected. But at least they were all safe here among their own kind, weren't they?

"Oh, there's Thaddeus." Fiona's father veered to the right

toward an older gentleman who, along with Fiona's father, was a Master Tinkerer. "Will you be all right on your own for a bit? I have some things I need to ask him."

"Yes, Papa. I'm going to get some punch."

His smile gave him the look of a mischievous cat. "Don't drink too much. Some young buck always adds spirits to it before the night is over."

"Yes, Papa." She wandered around the periphery of the ballroom. A chamber group played on a small stage between decorated trees, which held flickering candles and strings of popcorn. The gas sconces along the wall provided dim light. During meetings, the flames would be turned to medium or high so the members could see the books and papers being discussed, but tonight the lamps gave the room a warm, lovely glow. Fiona smiled—no seeing her freckles here! Some people danced, but tinkerers preferred to talk—well, argue—hence the limited number of musicians.

The sparkling of cut glass cups and a ladle in a stand beside a large crystal bowl drew her attention to the punch table. As she moved closer, the rosy concoction's apple and cherry scents made her mouth water.. Ah, yes, the famed Tinkerer Hall punch, only served once a year at the holiday ball. Who had lent the family crystal to the party?

"May I pour you some punch?" A man's deep voice resonated through her, and Fiona turned and stifled a gasp. Of course Devon Meriweather hadn't bothered with any sort of costume, merely a plain black mask over the top half of his face. Still, she'd recognize him anywhere.

Fiona opened her mouth to speak, but only a squeak came out. Surely her face must be turning red beneath her mask.

"Ah, I admire your staying in character." He grinned and picked up a cup and the ladle. "I'll take that as a yes."

She nodded. For some reason, she could converse comfortably with any of the other young men who had returned after the war ended, but she couldn't string more than a few words together for the handsome but arrogant Meriweather.

He handed her the punch, and she did manage a, "Thank you."

"You're very welcome. Have you read anything good lately?"

Fiona hid her jaw drop by sipping the punch. No heat to indicate it had been tampered with—yet. She'd mentioned once that she liked Edgar Allan Poe—one of her few moderately successful and brief conversations with Meriweather—but he'd teased her about her morbid tastes.

She shook her head and took another sip, the words she wanted fleeing her brain like, well, mice before a cat.

"Ah, too bad. I've twisted my ankle and have been laid up, so I've been seeking recommendations."

"Is that why you're not dancing?" she blurted. *Right, go for the inappropriate, almost personal question.* She didn't even know if he danced.

"Well, that and I hadn't yet found a partner who interested me enough to give it a try." He sipped his own punch, but the look he gave her over the glass made her cheeks heat again. Was he asking her to dance? What if he was? If it was hard to talk to him, how much worse would it be to dance?

Why didn't he leave her alone?

The questions flew so fast through her brain she tried to swallow and breathe at the same time, and she went into a coughing fit. He guided her hand to put her cup down. "Here, let me find you some water."

She nodded and tried to melt into the shadows, as her coughing had attracted the curious and concerned looks of the people around her. Coils, what had been in that punch?

When she finally got her breath back without any help from Meriweather, who had disappeared, Fiona took a couple of sips from her punch glass, which had stayed where she left it. People had returned to their conversations—thank goodness.

But then the murmuring faded to whispers. The small hairs on her arms raised, and the temperature in the room dropped as the shadows along the edge deepened. She found the source of the disturbance—someone had come dressed as the Masque of the Red Death. They strode to the center of the room.

Fiona took in the physique of the person. Tall, thin, with dark wavy hair—or at least, so she thought. Why did it relieve her that the person looked too gaunt to be Devon?

Her father rushed to her side. "Fiona, we have to go. Now."

She didn't argue, but when they turned toward the exit and joined the flow of the crowd, who had been edging toward the door, automatons clanged through the one entrance. They looked like giant German nutcracker dolls with white breeches and red jackets. But not benign ones—their eyes glowed over their painted-on rictus grins.

Curses from the men and shrieks from the women joined the roar of fire as the sconces on the walls turned sideways and shot flames out of both sides. Curtains, picture frames, and anything else flammable moved from smoldering to burning in mere seconds, and smoke joined the darkness in the air. Fiona coughed again.

Fiona's father tugged on her arm. "This way." He pulled her behind the punch table and pressed on a section of molding. Part of the wall folded inward. "Secret entrance for servants to replenish the refreshments without being seen," he explained. "We can get out through the back."

"Fiona! And Bryan. Thank God you have her." Devon Meriweather appeared, followed closely by his doppelganger. No, his cousin Pierce, whom Fiona had only met once. If possible, he was even more arrogant than Devon.

"I need to find Thaddeus and Hollowell," Fiona's father said. "Can you get her out of here?"

"Yes. Let's go." Devon placed Fiona's hand on his arm, and they ducked into the passage and descended a staircase. Light shone at the end of it—the kitchens, which were in a state of panic as servants had managed to escape from the ballroom and tell the others what was happening.

"Everyone, get out." Devon didn't need to shout—his voice carried enough for people to hear him. "The hall is on fire. Where's the way out?"

"This way, Sir." One of the waiters who had been carrying champagne through the ballroom gestured for Devon to follow, and Fiona was swept along with him. She kept looking back for her father.

Once outside, they met up with a group of partygoers. They huddled at the far end of the lawn in a copse of trees, where they could observe but not be seen too easily. Or maybe their curiosity overcame their senses of preservation—tinkerers could be like that.

Fiona pulled away from Devon and joined her friends Lucy and Posey Lillet, who, fortunately this time, arrived late for everything.

"Fiona, are you all right? Were you in the fire?" one woman asked. Fiona recognized Lucy's mother. A pang of jealousy joined Fiona's anxiety. What must it be like to have a mother who supported her daughter's dreams?

Right, she had coal on her face. "No, I'm fine. Where is everyone? Did they get out?"

"Maybe." Fiona's anxiety flared like the fire when the woman gestured upward.

Orange and yellow flames illuminated the black balloon and gondola of the airship that hovered over the roof. Fiona could barely make out automatons, which shone with reflected flickering, herding darker shapes on to a gangplank that led inside. Then they, too, disappeared, and the vehicle took off, almost mocking in its slowness. It faded into the night sky.

The fire brigade had arrived and attempted to douse the flames, but soon it became apparent that all they could do was keep the blaze from spreading. The strength left Fiona's legs, and she leaned against Devon.

Where was her father? Had he been taken in the airship? A certain sense—the same one that indicated to Fiona when she was close to the answer of a stubborn problem—told her yes.

She had to find him before they hurt him, but how? And why hadn't she insisted he come with her? Dread joined the fear that tightened her chest—she'd have to manage her mother before she could do anything else.

**2**

———

*erminus, 16 December 1871*

Devon didn't mind supporting Fiona Telfair's weight as they all gazed at the spot where the airship had vanished into the night sky. He bet that the scientists in the ballroom and their families had been rounded up and taken, leaving...

The servants. Devon had only been in Terminus a short time but knew that no one would think to check on them. He needed to make sure they were all right, that everyone had gotten out and would get the necessary medical attention. He turned to the best logistical mind he knew.

"Pierce, the servants."

Pierce turned to look at him, his expression strangely blank...or was it satisfied? Then he blinked. "Oh, right, they weren't taken."

Devon wanted to say something to comfort him—Pierce loved the Tinkerer's Guild—but he couldn't find the words. He felt other eyes on him, and his skin heated from his chest up. Right, he still supported Fiona. And he'd run from danger again. He tensed, waiting for the typical whispers.

He cleared his throat. "Please go around back and check on the situation there. If anyone needs help, arrange it."

"Right, Cousin." Pierce mock-saluted and hurried away.

Devon turned his attention to Fiona. He'd go help Pierce, but he needed to ensure Fiona's comfort. "Will you be all right?"

"I'll be fine." Fiona pulled away, but he didn't let go of her until he knew she'd be steady on her feet. "I'm more worried about my father. And my mother. Her health is fragile."

"We'll take her home." A young woman with dark brown hair and dressed in a shimmery blue dress with a matching mask smiled at him, then gave him a coy look. "Unless you'd rather?"

"Lucy!" Fiona jerked her arm away from Devon's. "I'll go with you."

Devon knew Fiona had just rejected the thought of accepting a ride from him—even though he hadn't offered—out of propriety, but still, it stung. Or maybe she truly didn't want to spend more time with him. He knew she would be aware of the grumblings against the "cowardly cousins," as Terminus society called him and Pierce.

She looked at the sky, then at Lucy, who nodded. Devon relaxed slightly. She was likely still focused on her father, who'd been taken gods-knew-where. He didn't know what the girls communicated with each other, but they piqued his curiosity. Were they already coming up with a plan to find and retrieve the missing Guild members?

"Thank you for your assistance," Fiona said and held out a hand.

Devon gave her what he hoped was an appropriately serious smile. He admired the confidence with which she shook his hand. Right, in the Tinkerer's Guild, men and women were treated as equals, at least socially if not with regard to Guild business itself. He'd heard some rumblings from the older members. But now they all had bigger problems.

"You're welcome," he told her.

"Will you let me know if you find out anything about what happened?" She glanced toward the roof of Tinkerer Hall again. "We need to find them."

He tried not to grin at her use of *we*. What in blazes was happening to him? "Yes. Of course."

Once she'd joined her friends in their carriage, Devon looked for the medical team that often accompanied the fire brigade. The war had been good for one thing—they'd all gotten much more prepared for disasters. He found them packing up their things and loading the stretchers, which they hadn't used, into the carriage.

"What are you doing?" he asked. "There are more people around the back."

Two of the men exchanged glances.

One of them squinted at him. "Oh, Mister Meriweather. You're concerned about the coloreds?"

Devon didn't miss the man's disrespectful tone. "Yes. They may need help."

They hesitated, and Devon clenched his jaw, trying to find the words that would get through to them.

Finally, one of them said, "Let's check them out. Don't want to piss off the tinkerers. I don't want clockwork critters sneaking into my house making mischief."

"What?" But Devon didn't want to waste time listening to their explanations.

He led the medics around to the back of the house, where the servants huddled together by the outer kitchen. His ankle throbbed with every step. The bandage keeping it stable had come loose with the rush out of the hall.

He quickly found Pierce, who arched an eyebrow at Devon's limp and handed him his flask. "Laudanum," he mouthed before turning to one of the waiters. "So you said you were in one of the guest rooms upstairs when you heard something on the roof?"

Devon hated the stuff, which Pierce kept on hand in case his back pain flared, but he took a swig. The warmth from the alcohol slithered into his stomach, and fog swallowed the ankle pain without reaching his brain. Or perhaps not—his thoughts seemed to slow. What the heck kind of opium was his cousin getting? With effort, he turned his attention to the server's words.

"Yes, a thump. Then footsteps. I thought at first someone had activated the Santa Claus protocol as a joke, but they were too heavy."

Devon nodded as the man described running out of the room and seeing the first of the automatons descending the stairs that led from the observation deck, where the tinkerers engaged in telescope experimentation and development.

"I was so scared I yelled for people to get out and came flying down the stairs and warned the people in the front hall to go back outside. But those things—they moved fast. I barely got out the front door ahead of them. One caught my jacket." He turned, and Devon saw a piece had been torn from the man's black uniform.

"Is the door to the roof typically locked?" Pierce asked.

"Yes, but they got it open."

"Did they force it?"

The man frowned. "Now that I think about it, no. There was no bang. It was like it had been unlocked or they had a key." He shook his head. "I know I'd've heard it if they'd picked the lock or broken it. The room I was in was right under the entrance to the stairs. It's a heavy-duty door. High security so no one comes in stealin' guild secrets."

Devon and Pierce exchanged a glance. "Was anyone upstairs?" Devon asked. "Besides you?"

He nodded. "My wife and daughter. They were getting some of the ladies' rooms ready." He looked around, then spoke quietly. "I've been lookin' for them, but I haven't seen them."

"We'll do what we can," Devon said. "Thank you for telling us what you saw. If you think of anything else, let us know."

"There was one more thing…" He held out a mass of wire. "I found these all over the roof."

Devon took it, wrapped it loosely in a handkerchief, and stuck it in his dinner jacket pocket. "Do you know what it is?"

"No, haven't had the chance to look."

"Thank you, we'll look at it. And thanks for your help."

"Name's Thom." The man shook hands with both of them. "Let me help you if I can."

"We'll let you know."

Pierce murmured some sort of condolence, and Devon cursed under his breath. What were those nutcracker things?

When he turned, the device he'd put in his pocket moved and stuck an appendage through his clothes into his side. Devon hissed.

"What is it?" Pierce asked.

Devon pulled the bundle of wires out and held it gingerly. He hoped he wasn't bleeding. "Do you know what this is?"

Pierce shook his head. "Can't tell in the dark. Let's have a look when we get home. Here." He picked up a blanket from the ground, where someone had dropped it. "Wrap it in that. Is there anyone else you want to talk to?"

Devon took the cloth and looked around to make sure no one needed it. People stood together comforting each other. They all had blankets, and it looked like they were being taken care of. He wrapped the offending device tightly enough for it to not stick him again and—hopefully—loosely enough not to damage it.

"Not this evening. Let's not intrude on their grief and worry."

"Right. So," Pierce asked as they walked away, "who was the attractive mouse you were talking to?"

"Oh, just one of the tinkerer's daughters. Smart girl." He didn't want to say too much. Now another chilling thought born of his time engaged in espionage overseas occurred to him —what if she was still in danger?

TYPICALLY AFTER THEY left a party together—the few times Fiona's mother had allowed her to go home with her friends— Fiona, Lucy, and Jane would spend the ride deconstructing the evening, both in terms of typical female talk but also the technological advances on display. New methods of lighting, ways of keeping food warm or cold, and other new ideas brought on by the forced ingenuity of a long war would all be topics of conversation. But they remained silent for this ride, caught up in the horror of the evening. Lucy held Fiona's hand, and Fiona appreciated the small comfort it gave her. She also had faith that her friend—more qualified than she to extrapolate the direction the airship had taken—was working on the problem. More than anything else, she feared for her father...and herself. She'd failed so badly with handling things after her brother's death. And now it would just be her and her mother.

Fiona's heartbeat accelerated, and the fickle organ felt like it crept higher and higher in her chest until, by the time they'd reached her house, it had firmly lodged itself in her throat. She could barely speak when Mrs. Lillet asked if she would like for them to accompany her in.

"No, thank you. I had better handle this alone." Her mother had accepted condolence callers after Connor had been killed, but then had faded out of society. Fiona didn't know how she'd respond now.

The driver helped Fiona out of the carriage and walked her to the door. Once inside the house, Fiona paused to listen to determine where her mother could be. The household had taken on a certain hush after Connor had left, his quick male footsteps no longer echoing through the rooms, and their father's heavier ones not making up the tempo. Then after Connor had died, the silence had thickened for a time, stifling sound and thought. Tonight it lay over the house like a winter shroud.

*No. I will not allow myself to fall into despair. Father is still alive.* For if the automatons had wanted the tinkerers dead, they would have killed them all on the spot, not taken them. She had to believe her father had been one of those kidnapped and wasn't lying dead on the ballroom floor.

"Fiona? Bryan?" Her mother's voice floated through the quiet, as wispy as candle smoke.

"Mother?" Fiona's voice cracked—from smoke or unshed tears? She could be strong for a few more minutes. She had to be.

She always had to be. And then a few more minutes would turn into a few more days, and months, and then she would find herself unable to shed tears after years. At only seventeen, she had already discovered one of the dark secrets of womanhood—how not to cry.

"In the parlor."

Her mother's favorite room. A portrait of Connor in his Union uniform hung over the fireplace. She'd had it commissioned after he died, and the painter had used old photographs to create a decent, although stiff image. Fiona remembered Connor as always moving and laughing, not this grim-faced person whose face looked like it had been stuck on someone else's body. Indeed, his portrait seemed to frown at her when she entered.

Margaret Telfair, once known as Margie to her friends, sat in her favorite armchair, the one that faced the fireplace and the portrait. She held a cup of tea, no doubt brewed from the same leaves she'd been using all day.

"Oh." She looked up at Fiona. "What happened to you? You smell like smoke and look like you've been through a fire." She leaned forward and looked around. "Where's your father?"

"There *was* a fire, Mother." She wouldn't tell her of the sconces that had turned and set the place ablaze. "And I don't know where Father is. He and several of the others were kidnapped."

"Kidnapped?" The teacup rattled as it met the saucer. "By whom?"

"I... I don't know."

"Well?" Margie frowned and leaned forward, her disapproval almost tangible, like an invisible wall pushing Fiona backward. "Why don't you? Why did he get taken and not you?"

Fiona blinked so she wouldn't crack in front of her mother. No tears now. "He showed me a secret exit, and I got out with the help of Devon Meriweather." She hoped dangling the name of the bachelor everyone was curious about would distract her mother.

"And why didn't you force your father to go with you?"

Fiona didn't say she'd been asking herself the same question. "He ran back inside to save others. I couldn't."

Margie slumped back. "And now we are doomed."

"Doomed?" While Fiona knew her mother was prone to drama, she felt that was a bit much. "No, we'll find him, and everything will be fine." But she knew from before that nothing would be fine. Not after something like this. She hadn't felt so helpless since Connor—

Her mother's voice broke into her memories. "We spent all our savings on gowns and other fripperies for your debut. Your father had some jobs lined up so we could pay off the last of the debts. And to bring in income again. But now that he's gone..."

She wiped her eyes with the handkerchief she always carried. "We'll have to fend off creditors. Perhaps end up in prison."

Sorrow might have overtaken her mother, but a hot flood of anger spread from Fiona's gut to her extremities, and she found herself clenching her fists and even her toes. "What? I didn't ask for you to do that, to spend all our money! How could you do something so stupid?"

"Because it's the best gift we could give you, ungrateful child." Now her mother's words hissed from within the shadows between the chair's wings. "You have this foolish dream of being a tinkerer, to spend your life with objects and puzzles, but that's not the way of the world. Not now. Do you think anyone will pay you, a girl, to build things for them? Maybe if they think it's your husband's work."

Fiona stepped back. Could that be true? Even if she convinced the Tinkerer's Guild to allow her to access the traditional training path from apprentice to master? She'd hoped the world would be changed, more open to female commerce now that so many of the men had been wounded or killed. But if she couldn't even convince her own mother...

"So this is our last hope," Fiona said, the words emerging like slugs. "For me to marry well?"

"Yes. Else we'll be on the street. Or worse."

Fiona said nothing else. She turned and pushed through the silence, which had thickened again, and crept up to her room. The tears pricked at the backs of her eyes, and she thought she would be able to release them, but then she saw it.

A small nutcracker doll stood in the middle of the room. Its grin mocked her.

If she'd had the choice between crying or fainting, she would have cried, but blackness overtook her.


WHEN DEVON and Pierce arrived at their house, they proceeded into a room in the basement that Pierce had converted to a laboratory. He had progressed immensely in his tinkering education and talent while Devon had been abroad, and although proud of his cousin, Devon couldn't help but feel jealous. Also while Devon was away, Pierce had moved the household to one of the larger estates north of downtown, abandoned by its previous owners when the Confederates had surrendered. He'd argued that being out of the city would be better for Therese's lungs, and Devon couldn't disagree. His sister seemed to be maintaining her improvement better than she ever had previously after a trip abroad.

No, Devon couldn't complain. It had been a mild winter, and the almanac said the weather would hold, which bode well for them getting started on expanding and repairing the rail system through Terminus and beyond, and would be healthier for Therese. As much as he'd enjoyed talking to Fiona, he had to remember his responsibilities. Alas, she was not in a position to enhance his social cachet through marriage, and while he didn't need to secure another fortune in order to maintain his upward trajectory, he would have to marry strategically to achieve his legacy and goals for Terminus' progress. And to allow his sister to be in the best position when she wanted to marry.

Pierce cleared off a space on his long workbench. "Do you have it?"

"Yes." Devon handed Pierce the bundled-up blanket with the device inside it. He took the opportunity to pull his shirtsleeve from his pants and peek at his side, which showed a small cut, but nothing too deep. Good. He didn't need additional discomfort. His ankle throbbed in time with his heartbeat.

Pierce unwrapped the device, his brows drawn in concentration. He and Devon looked enough alike that people who didn't know the family often mixed them up or thought they were brothers, one reason Therese said she didn't want to marry Pierce, who had been attempting to court her since they returned home. Did Devon tighten his mouth like Pierce currently did when he focused hard on something?

As if Devon's thoughts had summoned her, Therese appeared at the top of the stairs. An extraordinarily clever girl, of course she'd have figured out there was something up when they came straight to the laboratory after the ball. She and Devon shared the same reddish-brown hair, hazel eyes, and curiosity about the world, but it would be obvious to anyone who saw them that he'd gotten the healthy constitution.

"How was the ball—oh!" Her eyes widened, and Devon realized that he and Pierce must be smudged from the fire.

"Don't get too close," Pierce told her without taking his attention from the crushed clockwork. "We still reek of smoke."

Devon leaned over to get a better look, but Pierce waved him back.

"Light," Pierce snapped.

"Right." Devon stepped back. He shouldn't be surprised that Pierce took command in this realm. Pierce couldn't always be expected to defer to him. That's what made them a good team—they each respected the other's strengths.

Pierce poked and prodded at the object, turning it and looking at it from every angle. From what Devon could tell, the black wire cage had once been an oblong shape, and the inner clockworks, now half-disassembled by someone's foot, still had an elegant delicacy. Then Pierce dropped the device and sucked on his finger.

"It has a defense that's triggered when two of the outer parts are squeezed together. It ejects a wire that pokes at whatever is closest."

"Are you all right?" Therese asked. "I'll get one of the maids to bring something to clean the wound with."

"Thank you," Devon told her. "Please ask her to bring double. It got me, too."

"Oh, Devon," she sighed, and her light footsteps ascended the stairs.

"Oh, Devon," Pierce mocked in a falsetto voice. Devon punched his arm. "But did you see that?" Pierce asked. "She's worried about me."

Devon shrugged noncommittally. "She'd take care of anyone who's injured."

"Right." Pierce cleared his throat. "From what I can see, this was once some sort of clockwork bug."

Devon walked to the other side of his cousin so he wouldn't cast a shadow on the workbench. "Reminds me of a cockroach with its shape. Can you determine its purpose?"

Pierce turned it over again, careful not to compress it. "Perhaps. It has a wax cylinder as though for recording sounds. Not that it could hold much data with the size of it. Mostly volume, if anything."

"So something loud coming close." Devon frowned. "And then what?"

"That's the ingenious part. If the needle scores the cylinder deeply enough, it causes a lighting mechanism to set the wick here on fire."

"So a crawling, noise-triggered flare."

"Yes." Pierce demonstrated by pressing the tip of a knife into the cylinder, and they both shielded their eyes against the bright flash, which subsided into a glow. "That could be seen from a ways off."

Devon thought through the possibilities. "What if some of these had been on the roof of the hall? When the party reached a loud enough volume, they'd trigger..."

"...and light up to show the automaton airship it was time to descend..."

"...to grab the maximum number of tinkerers," Devon

finished. "Someone finally figured out how to tell when parties really get started."

Therese arrived and directed a maid and a valet down to the two men. Pierce covered the now dark clockwork creature with a rag. They didn't speak of it again in front of Therese. Devon didn't know how the excitement would affect her delicate constitution. Besides, he needed time to think and plan. As if the automatons weren't enough evidence, he now knew without a doubt that they were dealing with a master tinkerer, perhaps even a Clockwork Guild mason. He'd only heard of one so talented while he was abroad, a man who had haunted a theatre and escaped during the Prussian siege of Paris—Paul Farrell.

And if Farrell was involved, it meant the situation held more peril than he'd originally thought. How had the clockwork bugs been placed on the roof? Their location pointed to the involvement of someone at Tinkerer Hall.

His butler and former valet, Crenshaw, met him at the top of the stairs.

"Good," Devon said. "I need you to go into town and send a telegram."

Crenshaw didn't question or object to it being the middle of the night. "Yes, sir. To whom?"

Devon sighed. He'd hoped he was done with foreign service, but he'd been warned it wouldn't be that easy to leave. "To my contacts at the bureau."

Crenshaw nodded. "Very good, sir. And what should I tell them?"

"That I have a lead on the man who got away."

## 3

<br>

B*oston, 17 December 1871*

The summons crinkled in the pocket of Henry's trousers, and the months-old injury in his leg throbbed to the rhythm of his steps. Known as Inspector Davidson to some, as Agent Davidson to others, and as words he couldn't repeat in polite company to yet more, he kept his gaze on the rain-slick cobblestones. He'd been trained to better monitor his surroundings, and a fall wouldn't kill him, but he didn't need any more pain—physical or mental. And if he'd guessed correctly about the summons, he'd soon experience plenty of the latter.

This time, Violet and Hobbes had chosen a teahouse that was tucked in a neighborhood, indistinguishable from the residences around it except for a discreet sign advertising high tea by reservation only. The garden in front would have been lovely in spring or summer. Henry almost smiled at the thought of taking tea with a certain hazel-eyed woman who would be likely to drop into the place from an airship, her trousers keeping anyone from a scandalous view of her legs but giving anyone watching more than a hint of her slender waist and muscular build. Or she might surprise him and walk in from the road like a normal person.

Henry shook his head and smiled, but barely. He didn't associate with normal people. Nor did he smile much. And he had no time to dwell on old mistakes.

The wooden door, swollen with the damp, took an extra tug to open. A blast of warm air smelling of fresh-baked scones and the bitter green of wilted watercress greeted him. In the late afternoon light, candles flickered on the tables, and lamps along the wall did their best to defend against the sodden gloom. Henry almost felt the chill melting off him, and he paused to soak in the heat. But he knew he stalled to avoid the biggest challenge that was yet to come. He could face down villains and their nefarious intentions and inventions, but he feared his superiors and what they would tell him to do.

No, this time he would take the upper hand, insist on his retirement. He'd been in Her Majesty's service for twenty years, ten of them with an organization so secret he wouldn't ever be able to be honest about what he did. And now he had this annoying leg injury. But he also knew agents in his field rarely retired. They were more likely to be killed, and according to rumor, eliminated by their own bosses.

But hadn't he earned his rest?

"This way, sir." A server dressed impeccably in tails and a white tie—fancy even for a teahouse—took Henry's overcoat and hat. He led Henry through the front room and a hall, into which other rooms opened. He caught glimpses of staid matrons and young ladies sipping tea out of delicate cups in a parlor and drawing room. At the end of the hall, a curlicued sign pointed to the Private Rooms. Its tilt told Henry stairs— and pain—lay around the corner.

Henry suppressed the grimace that wanted to emerge whenever he had to step up with his bad leg. The cold damp had settled into it, and the stiffness refused to leave his thigh muscles in spite of the teahouse's comfortable warmth. He paused at the landing, but not for too long. Alas, they'd not yet reached their destination. The second set of stairs led to a wider hall, which opened on to bigger, airier rooms, probably former bedrooms.

The waiter paused in front of the only closed door and knocked. After a soft, "Come in!" floated through the wood, the man opened it with a bow.

Blue-and-white striped wallpaper with pink roses rivaled the tan-bricked fireplace for its air of forced cheeriness. Henry didn't attempt to hide his limp when he walked in, but he didn't stand in front of the fire, as he would have liked. Instead he bowed to his handlers. Violet somehow managed to appear brighter than the decor in her yellow dress and hat, and her blonde hair and blue eyes shone. Dark-haired Hobbes wore a gray suit, remarkable only for its elegant simplicity—but then, he never tried to stand out. He left that to Violet, whom Henry had long ago surmised was his partner in more than a professional sense.

"Ah, Henry, come in." Hobbes rose and shook his hand.

"Thank you."

Henry finally made himself look at the table. Just one teapot and plate of pastries. He didn't know whether to be relieved or disappointed he wouldn't have to play their old game of, *Is the second teapot poisoned?*

Violet smiled but didn't rise. "It's a new world, Henry. And a new game. But we have exciting news. Please, have a seat."

Henry did so, and Hobbes poured him some tea. Henry helped himself to cucumber and watercress sandwiches and an iced cranberry scone. There was a second plate of little cakes in dainty paper wrappers, but they hadn't been touched, and Henry didn't dare. A new world and new games, indeed. And new threats.

"What news, Violet?" Henry asked after tasting his scone, which had the exact right balance of butter and sugar.

Violet leaned forward and put her teacup on its saucer. With the wide-eyed delight of a matron sharing a juicy tidbit of gossip, she said, "Paul Farrell has been spotted in Terminus." She paused, her expression eager.

Henry sighed, feeling the figurative bonds tighten on his wrists.

Violet drew back and cocked her head at him. "What? Aren't you excited? You hate loose ends."

Henry tried to figure out how to tell her he didn't care about Paul Farrell anymore, but in a nice way. "I can't help but feel there are others who are better suited for tracking him down, Madame." He found himself massaging his leg over the injury. "And I have no desire to return to Terminus."

"Right, that's where you were injured. Too bad." She snapped her fingers. "Hobbes, the file."

Henry hadn't expected sympathy, nor was he surprised when Hobbes reached into his ever-present briefcase and brought forth a folder, which he handed to Violet, who, in turn, gave it to Henry.

Henry took a bite of a cucumber-dill sandwich—again, perfectly made—and studied the contents of the dossier on Paul Farrell. He skimmed over the line, "Allowed to escape by H. Davidson in Boston" and returned to the latest information, which he found himself drawn to in spite of his desired disinterest. Farrell, a damned fine inventor, had always come up with creative ways to not only skirt, but challenge the law. But this time...

"So there are rumors of him using aether to build some sort of automaton army?" he asked. The idea, while not out of the realm of possibility, seemed farfetched, even for the mad inventor. "The Clockwork Guild, as always, comes up with creative means of mayhem."

Hobbes replied, his soft voice too low for a woman but too high for a man, "With the War Between the States just over, several factions with different motivations are jockeying for position. We think he's going to sell his services to the highest bidder. And maybe start another war."

"It wouldn't be the first time he colluded with someone with dangerous ambition." And Henry had no doubt that some of the former Confederate planters could match or exceed his old foe Parnaby Cobb in nefarious schemes. Cobb had almost sacrificed his own stepdaughter.

Henry suppressed a shudder. His superiors might take such a reaction as a sign of weakness...or interest.

Violet helped herself to one of the small cakes and held the plate up for Henry to take one. Rather than choose the one closest to him, he took one from the middle. Violet winked. Hobbes, however, took one from the edge that had just been offered to Henry, and heat that had nothing to do with the rapidly warming room lit Henry's cheeks. He'd just demonstrated a certain degree of paranoia. Warranted, assuredly, but had he failed at the game? At least the petit four was good, its frosting hard but not too much so, and the layers of cake and soft icing inside practically melted on his tongue. Was that arsenic he tasted, or almond extract?

Did he care anymore?

"Plus there is another interesting wrinkle," Violet said. "Tinkerers and other mechanical-makers have been disappearing, along with members of their families."

"Disappearing? Including children? And are there any leads?" Now this piqued Henry's interest. Of course innocent lives would be involved somehow. His mother had long-ago joked he must have some Round Table knight blood in him since he couldn't resist the chance to jump in and defend the helpless.

"Yes, women and children. They've been simply vanishing

from their homes. No sign of forced entry or exit, no blood or signs of struggle. They're just gone." Violet lowered her voice and her lashes. "Our contact in Terminus told us that clothing has been found rumpled on the floor like the bodies have somehow come out of them without undressing. And it's both colored and white families, although the police only investigate the white kidnappings. And then this morning, this..." She laid a newspaper on the table, the afternoon edition of the Boston Times. *TINKERERS TAKEN BY AUTOMATONS*, the headline blared with a subheadline, *Nutcrackers gone amok.*

Henry put his teacup, which had been raised halfway to his lips, back on its saucer, and scanned the article. A mass kidnapping by automatons. Damn, that *was* intriguing. "Are there traces of aether or other substances?"

"Our contact unfortunately doesn't have the equipment to test for that, but your clever Professor Bailey and Mister O'Connell should by now."

Henry neither confirmed nor denied the implied query as to his team's progress. He only sipped his tea. Its bitterness was well-balanced with floral notes, unlike the bitterness in his gut. They'd roped him in again. But perhaps if he could capture Paul Farrell and find the missing tinkerers, they'd agree he had earned the right to retire.

"I believe they are working on it as we speak."

"Good." Violet nibbled on a cucumber sandwich. "We've arranged for you and your staff to be embedded as a security team in the home of one Devon Meriweather. He's been abroad with his sister, ostensibly due to her poor health. But you've probably guessed he had a greater role in managing perceptions of the war abroad."

Henry's mind ticked through the scenario. "Right, a rich young man escaping a horrible war abroad to protect his ill sister would draw sympathy. I assume he was working for the Union?"

"You assume correctly," Hobbes told him and took another cake, this one next to the spot where the one Henry had eaten had been. Was Hobbes taunting Henry in his own subtle way? "Although France supported the South, the people didn't like how it drained their treasury. Meriweather helped that perception. His parents moved south about twenty years ago, but he was born in the North and has always identified more with that part of the country."

"And now he needs security?"

Violet spoke. "He has returned to Terminus to take advantage of the opportunity to help rebuild and expand the infrastructure, specifically the railways. Some are happier about this than others. Plus his cousin Pierce is a talented tinkerer, and with men like that disappearing, there is added concern. So..." She raised the pink and white teacup to her lips, her eyes sparkling. "What do you think?"

Henry sighed, realizing he had been doubly trapped, both by his superiors and his own curiosity and hatred of loose ends. "When do we leave?"

RURAL MASSACHUSETTS, 17 December 1871

LIEUTENANT DAVINIA CROW—VINNI for short—placed the last of her uniform shirts in her valise. Outside the window, the rain and wind danced in a swirling, howling frenzy that rattled the casements. Raindrops—or maybe sleet—tapped against the windowpanes like insistent fingers. No matter how many times the rattling and tapping ebbed, the noise startled her when it resumed with the next gust of wind. But not in a frightening way, more like the surprise kiss of a lover on the back of her neck.

She walked to the window and pressed her hand against

the pane. "I'll be with you soon," she promised the sky she couldn't see. Was it her imagination, or did the wind pause as if to acknowledge her words?

It would be a miserable day to travel, but she didn't care. Soon she'd be rising above it all, back as first officer of the Sun Dog, a passenger airship but also one of the many sky-level eyes of the neo-Pythagoreans, the religious organization that had raised and sheltered her. And who now tried to smother her. Grounding and coming "home" threatened Vinni's sanity. Being in the air freed her, especially since the crack in her faith from the events of the previous spring had turned into a fissure.

But would she claim the freedom of the skies soon? She'd woken with her nerves alert. The crackling, electric feeling reminded her of when she encountered danger while engaged in her ground-level "work." And told her to be ready for a change of plans.

The rap on her bedroom door made her jump higher than the weather had.

"Come in!"

Cat, Vinni's partner, filled the door. On first glance, many mistook her for a man with her short haircut and square jaw, but Vinni knew her softness. It came out occasionally, but not today. Vinni looked for the rueful smile that Cat typically wore when it was time for them to leave, but instead her lips pressed together in a grim line.

"Uncle Dross wants to see you."

Uncle Dross—their leader, and not anyone's uncle, although there was speculation that he may be a few of the children's father—rarely summoned someone as junior as Vinni. Her shoulders straightened with the tension that gripped her upper back and neck. She breathed against her heartbeat, which accelerated like a runaway train's wheels.

"What does he want?"

"Dunno." But Cat wouldn't meet her gaze. Then Vinni

remembered—Cat was older than she, and she'd been summoned the year before and had refused to talk about what had happened. In fact, since then, she'd not spoken much at all, only uttering words that were absolutely necessary.

Cat jerked her head, and Vinni followed. She thought about running, but after a prisoner had escaped the year before on horseback, security around the perimeter had become tighter. She knew better than to press for more about what to expect. While the airship corps had Vinni's loyalty, the neo-Pythagoreans had Cat's.

They wound through the estate house, past cold spots that Vinni had always suspected were ghosts. She didn't have the talent for seeing them, thank goodness. Nor did she have any ability for predicting the future, manipulating aether, or any of the other so-called high callings. No, she'd only demonstrated mild precognitive abilities and the keen powers of observation that a child abandoned to the hands of a cult needed, and sometimes she suspected she'd seen too much. Hence why she'd been sent to the airship corps, her main mission being to look for signs of their rival organization, the Clockwork Guild, in the sky.

Vinni followed Cat into the basement and the tunnels to the temple complex and Uncle's offices. As per usual, the stone and dirt walls felt like they pressed in on her, and she sensed the weight of the earth above them, each ton a barrier that separated her from the freedom of her beloved sky. She didn't take a full breath until they emerged above ground-level, the gray walls drab in the rain-drenched light. The lamps flickered in their sconces, but their glow turned from warm to *why bother?* in a few feet and barely touched the shadows.

They ascended the steps through the gloom to the offices, and Cat gestured for Vinni to precede her on the landing.

"He only wants you," Cat said, her tone grim.

Vinni couldn't resist a nervous look at the two guards outside of the dark wooden office door. "Oh?"

Cat shook her head. "Watch out. See you at the carriage. I'll load it."

"Thanks. For both the warning and the packing."

Cat nodded once, a jerk. She never wasted a movement, either.

Vinni took a deep breath and knocked on the dark wooden door.

## 4

*erminus, 17 December, 1871*

The next morning, Fiona picked herself up from the floor where she'd landed in a faint, thankful that she hadn't bruised herself. What had made her...

*Oh!* She slowly lifted her gaze until she focused on the middle of the room, where the nutcracker doll no longer stood. She looked around for the small intruder, but she only found dust bunnies and discarded ribbons, her familiar girlish furniture, the lace and frill her mother thought she should appreciate, and the scattering of tools and devices her father had given her.

Her father...

The memories of the previous evening rushed in, and after a brief stab of panic at the recollection of those *things* coming after her, filled her with the bubbling energy of anger and the cool steel of determination. They were only automatons, after all. She rose, her jaw firm—she would figure out who had kidnapped the tinkerers the night before, and she would find her father. Never mind her sex and societal limitations—she had brains, and she would use them. She'd rescue her father *and* she would prove herself worthy of a place in the Tinkerer's Guild.

A glimpse of her reflection reminded her that she still wore her costume, but without her mask, which lay forlorn on the ground beside where she'd fainted. She shook her head—she hadn't been feeling ill, and she didn't consider herself to be the fainting type. What had happened? And had the doll been there, or had she imagined it? She'd dreamed strange things after her brother's death, his voice calling for her outside her window, and she'd thought she'd seen him once, but the young man had turned away before she'd gotten a longer, second look.

So she knew her mind could play tricks on her. But she could still rely on it to help her mission.

A quick wash restored her face to its usual non-sooty color and removed the lingering odors of stress and exertion from the rest of her. Her hair still smelled of smoke, but faintly. She'd have the maid help her wash it later. If they still had a maid. Ugh, she didn't want to have to ask her mother to help her dress —she wouldn't be able to breathe against her mother's tight lacing.

"Fee-OH-na!" Sniff.

Fiona cringed. Her mother couldn't have possibly known Fiona had been thinking about her. Fiona closed her eyes and counted to ten before calling back, "Yes, Mama?"

"You have a visitor." The breathless excitement in her mother's voice told Fiona the visitor must be a young man of means. She sighed, her jaw now fully clenched. Probably a curiosity-seeker, not someone who was actually interested in her. Word would have gotten out about the strange events at the ball, and the men would be pursued by the press...

Or would they? Who had made it out besides her and the Meriweather cousins?

Fiona's shiver had less to do with the cold of the room and more to do with the memories she tried to push away. In spite of her best efforts, the thoughts—like her mother's insistence on Fiona's marrying—crowded back in. Not that there was much of a chance of that after the removal of yet more men from the population. The sheer inconsiderateness of the kidnappings warmed her again with indignation, easier to deal with than fear for her father. Hadn't they suffered enough?

But some women had found happiness with each other. Fiona shook her head—that path was not for her. She didn't need a partner of either sex, just her inventions.

"Oh, Fee-oh-NAAA..."

The shrill call ended with a knock on the door, and Fiona took a deep breath. She cracked the door open to see the housemaid, Tessa, standing there. Her pink eyelids and nose showed she'd been crying—had she already been sacked? Or was she upset about Bryan's disappearance? Fiona would have to find out later once the two of them could sit and have a good chat. But first they had to deal with Margie.

"Oh, good, you're still here." Fiona let her in. "Who's got Mother in such a snit?"

"A young man, Miss." Tessa guided Fiona to her dressing table. "I'm glad you're cleaned up. We'll make you look beautiful."

"Did he say his name?"

Tessa grinned. "Your mother said I'm not to tell you."

"Great." Fiona sighed. Likely that meant it was someone she wouldn't want to see, someone particularly obnoxious. And, judging from her mother's volume, rich. But she looked up at Tessa's determined expression. Could Fiona stand to see the servants—maid and cook—turned out? They'd have good references, of course, but with so many families struggling after the war and the new competition with former enslaved servants, would they be able to find work?

*Silly me. I thought our sacrifices would end with the war.* She felt the weight of something new—could it be the meaning of womanhood?—settle around her chest. Tessa gave her a quizzical look, but Fiona shook her head. She'd puzzle it out later.

After helping Fiona into one of the dresses they'd had made for afternoon teas—a lovely light green silk with pink roses embroidered around the sleeves and bodice—Tessa tied a matching ribbon around Fiona's slender throat. Fiona kept herself from clawing at it, the chokehold of female responsibility.

Tessa stepped back. "There. You look lovely."

"Thank you." Fiona barely recognized the young woman in the mirror with her hair up and her skin pale in the watery morning light. The color of the dress accentuated her hair —"more gold than copper," her mother liked to say, even though Fiona found copper the more useful of the two—and made her eyes blaze.

"Now go impress the young gentleman." Tessa winked. "It shouldn't be hard. He seemed quite eager to see you."

"Right." Fiona took a deep breath and walked out of the bedroom and into her uncertain future.




"Thank you." Devon resisted the urge to stick his finger in his ear after Margie Telfair's screech to call Fiona. No wonder the poor girl barely spoke. She probably couldn't get a word in with her talkative mother, who still prattled on.

"She's a smart girl, so brilliant, her father always says." A sniff and a dab at her eyes with a handkerchief. "Do you think you'll be able to find him? The authorities don't seem to be much help. I sent a message to Jim Blair, but he told me to sit tight."

Devon refrained from saying his first thought, which was that Jim Blair couldn't find a cow patty in his own pasture. The sheriff was next to useless, often looking the other way when violence was committed toward formerly enslaved people. The attitude Devon had seen from the so-called public servant ambulance staff was a direct result of Blair's prejudice, which infected all the government departments. And where prejudice came, laziness followed as brains became locked into one narrow way of thinking, keeping them from finding solutions to important problems.

"That's why I'm here," Devon told her, hoping she would get the hint that he wasn't there to talk to Fiona about marriage. He opened his mouth to add, *"This isn't a courting call,"* but then Fiona emerged from the hallway at the top of the stairs, and he had to struggle not to let his jaw drop.

She wore a light green gown that was too flimsy for the chilly weather, but which brought out the green in her eyes and almost turned them emerald. Her dark copper hair shone burnished in the sunbeams she passed through. How could a woman's face have such delicacy while still showing strength and determination? What had been going through her mind that morning? Had she been crying? If so, her face didn't show it. She nodded to him when she reached the bottom of the staircase and held out a hand, which he bowed over.

"Miss Telfair," he said. "'Tis a pleasure to see you this fine morning."

She gave him a small smile. Had she lost the ability to speak to him again? Apparently so.

"Fiona, greet the gentleman." Mrs. Telfair snapped. She clenched her fists, and Fiona flinched. Had Fiona ever been hit by her mother? He couldn't imagine her father doing so, and he had to hold back from putting himself between Fiona and Margie.

Fiona opened her mouth, but no sound emerged. Mrs. Telfair, apparently not one to be dissuaded by any awkwardness, gestured toward the parlor.

"Go have some tea. That will loosen your tongue." She turned to Devon and wrung her hands. "The poor girl has been unable to speak since her father was taken. You're her only hope for a normal life."

Was that a devious glint in her eyes? Devon knew that Margie lied—should he be alone with Fiona? He wouldn't put it past her mother to lay a marriage trap. She seemed ruthless enough to sacrifice her daughter's reputation to do so.

Devon almost sighed. His enemies piled up in all areas, but at least he didn't live with one of them.

"Tessa will chaperon you," the woman added, perhaps sensing Devon's hesitation.

"Thank you. Shall we?" He held his arm out to Fiona, who hesitated before taking it. Right, the last time he'd done that had been before their mad dash from the ballroom the night before. But he intended to talk to her about the incident—indeed, that was the purpose for his visit—so while he wanted to be considerate of her feelings, he couldn't encourage her to avoid the topic.

He did turn to her mother and ask, purely for politeness' sake, "Would you care to join us?"

"Oh, no," Mrs. Telfair dabbed at her eyes again. "I'm too distraught, and I'd only be a distraction."

"I understand," Devon said. With Fiona still on his arm, he followed the maid into the parlor. The first thing he noticed was the portrait of a young man hanging over the fireplace mantle. The soldier wore a Union uniform—good—and resembled Fiona in the shape of his face and coloring. However, he looked sternly down upon the two of them. Devon guessed this was Fiona's brother, who had been killed. There had been some sort of rumor about the boy's death, although Devon couldn't remember what, that cast the young man in a poor light. And now tragedy and scandal had visited the household again.

Fiona removed her hand from his arm, leaving a cold spot,

and gestured for him to take a seat in one of the maroon-damask upholstered wingback chairs that sat before the fire, which had been built to the barest comfortable level. A small pile of sticks barely thicker than Devon's thumb sat in the metal basket beside it. The intricacy of the basket's ironwork almost distracted him from the pitiful condition and size of the wood.

"Shall I build up the fire?" he asked. "You must be chilly."

Her lips thinned, and she shook her head. She motioned again for him to sit, and he did. She didn't seem to be cold, so he didn't press the matter. Perhaps she had developed a thick skin during her tinkering work.

The maid poured the tea, and Fiona lifted her cup to her face. She took a long sniff before drinking it, her eyes closing in pleasure. Devon sipped his own tea, which was on the weak side. The maid retreated to the far side of the room, where she sat in a sunbeam and took out some mending. None of the lamps had been lit, so Devon speculated the maid's position had a more practical reason than giving the two of them space to talk. Indeed, the whole house spoke of financial peril, now that he noticed it. What had happened to put the family in such a position? He'd never gotten a hint from Bryan, although the man could easily be swayed by stronger personalities in arguments that didn't involve mechanical or other topics. Bryan Telfair knew his stuff when it came to tinkering, but he lacked the ability to manage people.

But Devon didn't.

"Tes-SA!"

All three occupants of the room cringed.

"I need my smelling salts." Margie's voice carried even when it didn't sound like she was nearby.

"Excuse me, Miss," Tessa said. "I'll be back shortly." And with a look that told Devon she would personally relieve him of his balls if he so much as thought about deflowering her young mistress, she left the two of them alone.

**5**

———

*ural Massachusetts, 17 December 1871*

R    "Come in, come in!" Uncle Dross's tone sounded too jovial. It was only nine o'clock in the morning, but he could have been drinking early again. Vinni had heard that alcoholism claimed all of the cult leaders eventually. She pushed through the door.

Her nose twitched, and she stifled a sneeze. The office looked neat and tidy as it always did, but it hadn't been dusted in at least a month. The gray film lay undisturbed on the bookshelves. Whatever Uncle did in there, it wasn't reading.

"Davinia, there you are."

"You summoned me, Sir?" She forced herself to look at him, to meet his gaze with the confidence she'd learned in the airship corps.

He looked her down and then up with his ice-gray eyes, and she stifled a shiver. He'd lost more hair since the last time she'd seen him, or maybe it had transferred to his eyebrows, which met over the bridge of his sharp nose. His smile looked more like a leer. And his erection showed under his robe. She turned to leave, but he snapped his fingers, and the door locked behind her.

Vinni recognized this game. She'd worked with enough males who thought that, as one of the few females in the corps, she'd be easy prey. The bastard wanted her to try to run, to escape, which would inflame his arousal. Vinni resisted the urge to turn and force the door open. Instead she planted her feet. Outside the window, the wind's velocity picked up, and it shook the frame like an angry animal trying to get in.

When Uncle spoke, his voice was gentle. "You've been a ward of the neo-Pythagoreans since you were what, three? Four?"

"Four, Sir."

He walked around the desk, and she stiffened. But he didn't touch her, only circled her. She found herself glad she'd worn her travel skirt, not her trousers, which would have hugged her hips and legs, showing more than she wanted to. Still, she felt his gaze as though he ran invisible hands over her. Then a hand that wasn't invisible reached around and cupped her right breast. She stifled a snarl.

"You've been with us for twenty years, and yet I don't feel that I know you." His breath came hot and acrid on her neck, and she smelled alcohol, the sickly sweet odor of the bourbon he favored.

She jerked away from him. "You know me well enough. And I will not violate our principles to allow you to know me better."

"Our principles dictate that your body is mine to do what I please with." He laughed. "And you are spirited, as always. I have a mission for you, Davinia." He advanced, and the only place she could back up was behind his desk. She realized too late that she was cornered, the desk too close to the book-shelves on the other side for her to get around.

"What is the mission?" she asked and looked around for

something she could defend herself with. But the surface of the desk was clear—not even a pen or letter opener. The only thing she could think to do was unlatch the window, which she did with a quick movement when he focused on her bosom. Not that she knew what good that would do. Her stomach dropped like when the airship lost latitude. She was well and truly trapped.

"Our seers have detected a fluctuation in the aether sphere." He walked slowly toward her, his hands behind his back.

"Where?" She had to keep him talking, give herself time to figure out how to escape.

*Oh, gods, is this what happened to Cat?*

"Somewhere north of Terminus."

"In the South." Vinni braced her fingers against the cold windowpanes and sent a silent prayer for help.

"Yes." Now he stood in front of her.

She reminded herself to stand strong, to not seem like prey.

He placed his hands on either side of her. "And I want you to check it out. Find out what's going on. Our seers have also seen someone who looks like Farrell."

"What about my commission?" *My salvation?*

"I have arranged for your furlough to be renewed once you arrive in Terminus." He leaned forward. "This is important, Davinia. We made a bargain to obtain Farrell's freedom, and he turned and betrayed us to the Clockwork Guild. I want my revenge."

As his face came closer to hers, she flashed through her options. Head-butt him and break his nose? No, he'd yell and bring his guards in here, and she'd be hauled into a dungeon and never seen or heard from again. Distract him and try to get around him? No, that would only inflame his predatory lust more. Allow him to kiss her?

*Oh, hell, no.*

As though the wind heard her thoughts, the howl outside built into a crescendo. Something crashed against the window to her left, and Uncle paused, his glance reflexive.

Distract and go, it was. She ducked under his arms and darted past him. He turned, his smile wider, but he'd only taken a step toward her when the window flew open, and the leaded glass casement bashed him in the face. He fell, and Vinni didn't wait to see what had happened. She unlocked the door and ran into the hallway.

"There's been an accident," she gasped in her best distressed damsel voice to the guards. She pressed a hand to her chest, her eyes wide. "The storm blew one of the windows open, and Uncle Dross has been hurt."

Then she darted down the stairs and found Cat waiting for her outside.

"Are you all right?" Cat took her hands and studied her face.

The horrible suspicion punched Vinni in the gut—had Cat known what Uncle would try to do? He must have done it to Cat, so why had Cat brought Vinni into the same trap?

Because Cat didn't question the cult. Or its leader.

"I'm fine. The wind..." She stopped, not sure what to say. If she voiced her suspicions, she would sound crazy. "It blew the window open and knocked him out."

Cat's grin wasn't pleasant, confirming Vinni's speculations. "Thank the gods."

"Yes." Vinni looked over her shoulder at the lightening sky. She couldn't wait until she could escape to the clouds again. "Yes. Thank the gods."

WHEN HENRY ARRIVED at his team headquarters at the Cobb mansion—now presided over by Louisa Cobb—he decided to stop by the basement laboratory. Renowned aetherist Edward Bailey and less renowned but somewhat notorious Patrick

O'Connell worked on what they were calling an aetherometer, or a device to measure levels of concentrated aether. Aether—the substance that light passes through—was always present, but Edward had figured out how to stabilize it. And in doing so, he unlocked its potential uses. Not as an energy source, although Henry had no doubt that would come eventually, but as a manipulator of other things, specifically human emotions, and by extension, behavior. And, in a concentrated form, as a weapon—the one that had ended the War Between the States.

When Henry rounded the corner of the basement stairs, a loud bang and then a flash greeted him. He covered his mouth and nose against the acrid smoke that billowed forth and thankfully dissipated.

"I told you to hold the fecking needle still!" There was no mistaking Patrick's Irish brogue. Or his annoyance.

"I did. You're the one who didn't adjust it right." And that was Edward's English accent, which became more clipped with his exasperation. "According to the theory—"

"The theory isn't working. You need a better one."

"We need tea," Edward said gently. Henry mentally applauded him. Not that Patrick typically had any trouble holding his temper, despite his red hair, but they'd all been working long hours.

"You can come down now, Henry," Patrick said. "I heard you come in. No mistaking that limp of yours on the stairs."

Henry ignored the barb and descended just far enough for him to see the two of them. "How's it going, gentlemen?"

The electric light overhead—a luxury they might have to do without in Terminus, but standard for Parnaby Cobb's former residence—illuminated Patrick's red hair and beard and Edward's dark hair. They wore protective goggles and had various mechanical parts spread out on the table in front of them. Henry had a rudimentary knowledge of machines, or as he'd found in the past, just enough to be dangerous, but he could only admire how the two geniuses in front of him managed to figure out the problems set to them.

Edward pushed his goggles up, revealing indentations around his bright blue eyes. "We're having an academic disagreement as to which frequency range will work best in our device." He used a handkerchief to blot perspiration from his face. "But we'll work through it. We just need more tests."

"Aye," Patrick said and wiped his forehead on his sleeve and admitted grudgingly, "But we've been at this for a while. Perhaps it is time for a break."

Henry admired how the two of them eventually came to agreements, even if only about refreshments. But he'd seen them work before and knew they could come up with brilliant inventions. "I'll have the maid set out tea, then."

"Thank you." Edward's expression always brightened at the mention of tea. "We'll be up as soon as we can clean up."

Henry nodded and turned to ascend the stairs. Why were there so many steps today? He'd have to put heat on his leg that evening.

He found tea already set out in the drawing room and two women chatting. Louisa Cobb played hostess, which made sense since it was her house, after all. As Boston's richest heiress, the only reason potential suitors hadn't flocked to her door was because the mourning period for her late stepfather hadn't passed yet. It had been six months since the disastrous party that had claimed Parnaby Cobb's soul and body, so she'd gone from heavy into light mourning. The lavender gown set off her rich black curls and sky blue eyes that only lit up when Patrick O'Connell entered the room. Henry guessed they'd make their arrangement formal when Louisa had completed her year of mourning and disappointed Boston's eligible bachelors.

The other woman, Iris Bailey, Edward's wife and a talented archaeologist, wore royal blue and had her white-blond hair pulled back in a chignon. She turned and smiled when she saw Henry. At one time, her smile would have warmed his heart more than was appropriate, but thankfully he'd gotten past that. Now he admired the strength and intelligence in her deceptively petite frame. But he wondered at the sadness that haunted her dark blue eyes lately.

"Ah, Henry, have you seen the boys?" Iris asked. "We dare not disturb them to tell them tea is ready."

"I've just informed them, Mrs. Bailey." He bowed over her and Louisa's hands. While they'd agreed that since they were on a team now, they could address each other less formally, he preferred to keep some semblance of propriety. And he was glad he had—it would be useful in the more formal South.

"Excellent." Louisa held up the teapot. "May I pour you a cup?"

Henry shook his head. "No, but thank you. I've just come from tea."

"Ah, right, your mysterious meeting." Iris leaned forward. "What news? Do we have an assignment?"

The team didn't know who Henry's superiors were, only that they issued orders during mysterious meetings. The separation was mutually beneficial. The less the team knew, the less they could divulge if ever captured and tortured, which put them in less danger. They could also part ways with Henry and the organization with fewer repercussions. At least that's what Henry had tried to negotiate for them. He stuffed the shard of guilt that stabbed his gut at the thought of putting these people, whom he'd come to count as friends in spite of his best efforts not to, in danger.

He didn't feel like sharing the news in stages, so he suggested, "Let's wait for the others to come so I can tell all of you at once."

"That's fine. Marie and Johann should be down soon." But Iris didn't seem excited at the thought of tea with her best friend. Rather, she looked like she could barely contain her curiosity. Henry made a note to himself not to touch anything she could then "read" and spoil the surprise before he had the chance to tell them.

Louisa rose. "I'll send a tube to the clinic and summon the Doctors Radcliffe."

"Ah, right, I'd forgotten they were working today." Henry motioned for her to resume her seat. Acutely aware of the imposition housing the team had made on her in spite of her protestations to the contrary, and not wanting to ask one more thing of her, he said, "Don't disturb them. I can tell them tonight."

"Don't be ridiculous. They'll want to hear." She disappeared into the next room, leaving Henry with Iris.

"Is it somewhere exotic?" Iris asked. "Boston is lovely, but I do miss the sands and the ruins of the Ottoman Empire."

Henry laughed. She was one of the few women who could coax a true smile from him. "It depends on how you define exotic. Definitely someplace with vast swaths of uninhabited land."

"Hmm." She put a gloved finger to her lips. "I shall have to ponder that delightfully vague answer."

Edward and Patrick arrived, and so did Johann and Marie Bledsoe. They both looked somewhat sleep-deprived since their baby daughter had arrived the month before, and Marie had refused to hand the infant over to a nanny or nurse. Henry didn't blame her. They all watched the girl for signs that something had happened when Marie had temporarily been possessed by a goddess during the pregnancy.

Chadwick and Claire, the doctors Radcliffe, soon returned from their clinic, and Henry looked around the room at his team of eight. It was time to let them know what their first assignment would be.

. . .

VINNI DIDN'T STOP TREMBLING until after they'd driven down the long gravel path that led from the side road to the complex, and then along the side road on to the main road. While the driver was employed by the neo-Pythagorean temple, Uncle didn't welcome the staff, the menial class, into the cult, and so Vinni didn't worry that the man's motivation included anything but a paycheck. But now that her thoughts could turn from escape from the complex—a false freedom, but better than being there—she found them going in a disturbing direction.

"You knew what he was going to try to do," she said to Cat. It wasn't a question, and so Cat didn't answer her. Or deny anything. Vinni tried again. "When you summoned me, did you know that Uncle Dross had impure intentions?"

Cat, who sat across from her, gazed out of the window. "I didn't *know*."

"But you suspected?" Vinni leaned forward and put her hand on Cat's knee. "Did that bastard hurt you? In the past?"

Cat looked at Vinni, but her eyes were as flat as a dead fish's. "He did what he needed for the good of the temple. Sometimes sacrifices must be made."

Vinni drew her hand back like it had been burned, and she swallowed against the nausea that threatened to overwhelm her. "Do you really believe that? That he can take advantage of women and it's good for the organization?"

Cat shrugged. "What should I believe? That I allowed a man to take advantage of me? *Me*?" She gestured to herself. Most men wouldn't try to fight her, much less rape her.

Vinni clenched her fists. "Yes, because then perhaps you won't be so quick to draw others into his snare."

Now Cat narrowed her eyes, and an angry spark came to them. At least it helped them to look alive. "But you escaped. I knew you would. You're too clever to be trapped by him."

"But you didn't know that!" Vinni wanted to take Cat by the shoulders and shake some sense into her. Or do something else to ensure she wouldn't be betrayed again by her best friend, her lover. "If it hadn't been storming, I don't know what I would have done."

"You would have figured out something." Cat leaned forward and tried to take Vinni's hand, but Vinni snatched it back. "C'mon, Vin, don't be like that. We're not all as strong and smart as you are."

"You're as strong as a man," Vinni snapped. She folded her arms, drawing in on herself, and muttered, "And about as dumb as one, too."

Cat's face crumpled, and she sat back but didn't say anything.

Vinni wished she could take back her last words. "I'm sorry, Cat. You're not stupid. And it's not your fault that Uncle Dross took advantage of you. There's more than one way to trap a person."

Cat wiped something from her cheek, and regret squeezed Vinni's chest tighter. She'd only seen Cat cry once, after her naming ceremony.

"We need to figure out a way out," Vinni said. "Don't you see what being part of the temple is doing? It's skewing your —*my*—sense of reality, of who or what we can trust. It's isolating."

"And go where?" Cat closed her eyes and rested her forehead on the window. "Our airship corps commissions are tied to the temple. What would we do for work?"

Vinni looked through the window at the sky, which had started to show patches of blue. She could almost feel the lightening of the liftoff, the sense of falling up and away from the earth and all her problems. She would hate to give that up, but... "We'll figure something out. Maybe we could hire out as private crew."

Cat snorted. "A couple of women? You know that wouldn't happen."

"We'll have to look out for opportunities. Terminus and the South in general should be full of them."

"Right. Keep believing that."

"Maybe I will."

Cat turned to her own window with a huff.

Vinni swallowed her growl of frustration. "If you're not going to help me, I'll find something on my own."

"And I'll stop you. You belong with me. With the temple."

"No, I don't." Then, with sickening certainty, the words came to her mind—*I don't think I ever have.*

Cat returned to her silence, and Vinni's mind whirled with plans. The first question would be how she'd get away from Cat. The second—what would she do? Then, the third and hardest—how could she stay hidden from the cult?

6

T*erminus, 17 December 1871*

    Fiona watched helplessly as Tessa left. She had no doubt her mother had manufactured some sort of complaint to make sure she and Devon ended up alone. But to what end? There was no one around to spread the gossip that they'd been in each other's company, much less without a chaperon. Was she hoping Fiona would throw herself at Devon? Hardly. Fiona could hardly talk, as much as she wanted to. She wanted to know why Devon had come to see her, so she gave him her most inquisitive, *"Now that the niceties are over, and you can speak openly, why are you here?"* look.

And if he didn't read her mind, he at least read her look.

"You're probably wondering why I've come."

Fiona kept herself from spreading her hands in an exasperated, "of course" motion. She simply nodded and put on her most polite smile.

"I needed to talk to someone else who had witnessed last night's events from inside the house." He rubbed the back of his neck, and she noticed that he'd not gotten his hair cut recently. She refused to notice, however, how it curled charmingly at the nape of his neck over his collar. "As you can imagine, those people are in short supply at the moment, most of them having been taken. Oh—I'm sorry."

At the mention of the kidnapped tinkerers, Fiona's hands had started shaking, and tea spilled onto the saucer. She leaned forward to put the cup down, and he took it from her. She almost grabbed it back but thought better. No reason to cause more of a mess. He placed it on the small table between them.

"So I needed someone besides Pierce to corroborate my observations. You have a good eye and a talent for tinkering, so I thought you may be use—er—amenable to helping me."

Had he been about to say useful? Fiona arched an eyebrow.

"Can you help me?" Devon asked.

Fiona nodded. She closed her eyes, and her skin heated, and her heart rate increased as she recalled the fire and the confusion. And the automatons. Something bothered her about them... "They moved like men. Not at all stiffly or artificially." The voice was hers, and her eyes flew open. She found he'd leaned closer to make out her words, and he jerked back as though she'd tried to steal a kiss. Humph. She had no reason to be embarrassed, but the fire beneath her skin flared even more.

"Do you know of any advances that have been made with limb articulation recently?" Devon asked.

"N-no." Now the lump had returned to her throat, but she was able to speak around it. "Machines mimicking human movement? Acting independently? The technology hasn't advanced that far. Although..."

"What?" Now he leaned forward again, and her wicked side imagined what he'd do if she pressed her lips to his.

"Father did know of some colleagues who were experimenting with aether and mechanisms to see if they could use a combination of the two to motivate objects, like dolls, to do simple tasks. He said it had to do with finding the right frequencies, and the mathematical formulas were extremely complicated. So much so that only the most talented tinkerers and aetherists were up to the tasks."

"So life is reduced to formulas." Devon shook his head. "And those reserved for machines."

"Not life. Just a more-complex-than-usual machine. They still don't have free will."

Speaking of free will and less than noble motivations, where was Tessa? She should have delivered the smelling salts by now. Fiona swallowed.

When Devon asked, "Do you believe life requires free will? What about base animals who are motivated by one thing, survival?" Fiona could only shake her head. Apparently she was limited to only speaking comfortably of tinkering subjects. Philosophy clammed her up.

She looked down and picked up her teacup and saucer again. Devon ran his hands through his hair.

"Did she do this to you?" he asked. "Your mother?"

Fiona looked up, wide-eyed, and shook her head. She couldn't make herself tell him, *"No, you do."* Especially since she couldn't figure out why herself.

"Would it help to know that I have no intention of marrying you?"

Fiona reeled back as though he'd slapped her. Sure, his statement brought some relief, but he didn't have to be so blunt.

"I wasn't asking you to marry me!" But why wouldn't he want to? She wanted to curl in on herself—perhaps her mother was right.

"Oh, good, I can shock you out of silence."

The heat beneath Fiona's skin had nothing to do with his flirting with her and everything to do with her own anger. "Shock me? Are you a neuroticist now?" She set her teacup back on the small table between them and stood, her hands on her hips. "You're an arrogant, selfish..." Coils, she needed a better insult vocabulary.

"Go on." He leaned back and had the audacity to look amused.

"Dandy." Was the best she could come up with.

"But you need my help to get your father back."

There was no retort to that. She resumed her seat and primly poured more tea. Once she sat, her anger faded, and the block in her throat returned. She looked around for something to write with and on, but the only paper she knew of was in her mother's writing desk in her bedroom, and she wasn't about to go into her mother's bedroom. And her father's workshop was locked, the key likely still with him.

Devon thankfully picked up the previous thread of their conversation. "Our best bet for finding them is to figure out who made the automatons. Especially since we don't know why they were taken."

"Do you think they were really machines?" Fiona asked, curiosity again overwhelming her reticence.

"I don't know. All I do know is that we're dealing with someone very sophisticated and deadly."

Now a chill flushed out the heat that had sustained Fiona. "Do you think they'll hurt them?" she whispered with the last of her voice.

Devon didn't offer false comfort. "I don't know. It depends on what they wanted them for."

Fiona swallowed, the lump in her throat now multifaceted with worry. Surely no one would kidnap tinkerers just to turn them into something awful, would they? She'd heard rumors of some ethics-challenged inventors trying to incorporate flesh into machines, specifically limbs taken from wounded soldiers. But then anyone would do, and there were plenty of displaced people to choose from. Not that she condoned it in any case. No one deserved to be turned into a machine.

She looked up from her teacup, surprised Devon hadn't interrupted her thoughts.

"Did you come to any interesting conclusions on your mental wander?" he asked. His tone teased, but the weight of his eyebrows over his hazel eyes made his expression serious.

Fiona shook her head. She didn't know if she could have said anything, and she didn't want to. Why put such a horrible idea into the world?

He stood, and she did as well.

"I should be going," he said. "I got word this morning that I'm expecting company, so I need to prepare my household."

Fiona put her fists on her hips and frowned. *Company now?*

"Don't think I'm shirking my duties or that I don't want to help." His grin could only be described as smug. "It's quite likely that my company could prove to be very helpful. I'll keep you posted."

Tessa ran into the room, breathless, and stopped when she saw them standing, the tea table between them. Was that disappointment on her face? Fiona resisted the urge to groan.

"Everything all right, Miss?" the maid asked.

Fiona nodded.

"I was just taking my leave. Please let me know if you remember any other interesting details," Devon said to Fiona. "You know Sheriff Blair is useless, so it's going to be up to us."

Fiona nodded again.

Tessa brought Devon his cloak and hat, and he bowed to Fiona, then left.

"Well, Miss?" Tessa looked like she could barely contain herself once she'd let him out. "Is he courting you?"

"No, not at all." Fiona grabbed a shawl that had been lying over the arm of one of the chairs. It smelled like her mother's perfume, but she didn't care. The whole encounter had made her flush hot and cold so much that she felt devoid of energy. But at least he wasn't thinking marriage. She could deal with their relationship being strictly professional. That way he wouldn't realize that love wasn't for her, and she was too poor to be of interest to him strategically.

Coils, she hated it when her mother was right.

WHEN DEVON ARRIVED BACK at his house—mansion, he corrected himself—he decided to go in the side door in case someone waited for him in the front parlor. He needed a few minutes to settle into his office, get his bearings, and write down his thoughts after meeting with Fiona. Well, his thoughts beyond how pretty she looked in that shade of green and what had happened to bring the household to such ruin. The last Devon had heard, Bryan Telfair had a thriving business making custom dolls that displayed a limited range of behaviors depending on how their limbs were moved or what lever was flipped. It all sounded creepy to him, but then, he had never liked dolls—a childhood leftover from his parents not wanting Therese to have them since they gathered dust and seemed to make her breathing problems worse. But he couldn't respect a man who had let his business lapse, and he guessed that Bryan, like many tinkerers, had gotten distracted by a New Shiny Thing. He'd seen many an NST derail a clever mind, which tended to crave novelty. But still...didn't family responsibilities matter?

He directed the carriage driver to go straight to the stable, and took the opportunity on the walk back to the main house to stretch his legs and ponder through the events of the night before and the morning. Luckily the place where the clockwork cockroach had poked him had healed well after being cleaned, and there was barely a scratch. His ankle, however, had not fared so well, and he pondered taking something when he got inside. Then he shook his head. He needed to be mentally clear for the day, not muddled by laudanum. So, he'd deal with the pain. It wasn't so bad if he remained sitting.

After crossing the drive and walking around the back lawn, he arrived at the delivery entrance. A small part of him thrilled at his petite rebellion and subterfuge. Sometimes a man needed a break. He'd become accustomed to being accosted when he arrived home from meetings and errands and he had to admit, he didn't mind overmuch. The attention meant he was making a name for himself and moving beyond being the useless "cowardly cousin."

So why didn't he ever feel like he did enough?

When Devon opened the door, he found himself face-to-face with the last person he expected—or wanted—to see there. He knew Layla Bollington from the occasional interview she'd done with him after he'd returned and then once he'd re-started his family business interests. She stepped back, seemingly as surprised to see him as he was her, but then her lips split with a grin that shone against her dark brown face. Devon simultaneously cringed and admired the woman. The daughter of formerly enslaved people, she had fought with all her might for her current position as a reporter for the Atlanta Journal, and he knew she would not miss an opportunity for a scoop.

"Why, Devon Meriweather," she said, and her lilting accent made the syllables of his name bounce. "Just the man I wanted to see." She stepped back and gestured for him to enter his own home.

Shaking his head with amusement and rueful acceptance, Devon complied. "What can I do for you today, Miss Bollington?"

"I was hoping to talk to you about what happened last night at the Tinkerer's Ball. Of course Jim Blair—who's waiting out front for you, by the way—wants the official statement, but I know there are more interesting facts about what happened than the law wants to know about."

Devon smiled. "It all happened so fast I can barely recall the order, much less the details. Why don't you come back in a couple of days after I've gotten my head straight, and you can do an official interview?"

Surprisingly, Layla looked relieved. "I'll do that. How's ten o'clock?"

"That will be fine. I'll have coffee waiting for you."

"You know the way to a girl's heart." She dropped a quick curtsy and swept out of the door.

Devon shook his head again, this time with bewilderment. What was happening in his own home? Had someone tipped Bollington off to something? She could have interviewed any of the attendees of the party, at least the ones who had made it out. But then he realized—he didn't know how many had escaped. He and Fiona had joined a group on the lawn, but they hadn't gone in to begin with. And he hadn't seen if the door had closed behind them or if anyone had followed them besides the servants. He added to his mental list—talk to Thom to see if anyone else was missing besides the two upstairs attendants and find out exactly who had been taken.

He walked as quietly as he could to his office, taking the servants' hallway. He slipped into the office via a space that looked like a closet but served as a way for the maid and butler to enter and leave the office without being observed from the receiving parlor. As much as he had objected to Pierce's extravagance in buying the place, he could appreciate the perks of a large house with secret passages. There must be others they hadn't discovered yet. He'd heard that many of the larger Southern houses had had them installed in anticipation of a Yankee invasion, which thankfully hadn't happened. He cringed to think at how the beautiful city would have burned at the hands of unsympathetic invaders.

A folded slip of paper on his desk caught his attention—a telegram. He swallowed against the anxiety that rose in his throat. When he read the telegram, his suspicions were confirmed.

*Help on the way. Expect investigative team Dec 18.*

He stifled a groan—he didn't want an investigative *team*, a government-sponsored committee to muddle facts with opinions. He needed someone with creativity and guts to help him find the missing tinkerers. Ah, well, he'd deal with them when they arrived.

But first he had to find out what Sheriff Blair knew. Perhaps the man had stumbled upon leads worth following.

**7**

———

*T*erminus, *17 December 1871*

After Devon left, Fiona helped Tessa clean up the tea, or what remained of it, but rather than allowing her to throw out the rest of the now-lukewarm pot, Fiona took it and her cup to her room. Tessa arrived soon after and helped Fiona change into one of her work dresses, a plain gray wool serge she had left over from partial mourning. Not that she really wanted to be reminded of Connor and everything they'd lost, but she also knew her father's workshop—one of the few places in the house only he was allowed—would likely not be clean.

"Is she asleep?" Fiona asked as Tessa took down her hair and wove it into a plain braid, which she then coiled and pinned in place. Fiona preferred her hair out of her face if she was to be working. Or searching.

"Yes, although she made me give her a detailed recounting of the visit, at least while I was there."

What would Fiona's mother have thought of Devon's pronouncement that he had no intention of marrying her? She probably would have emerged from her bedroom and chased the poor man out with a broom. And then gone out to the street and found another eligible-looking young man and chased him inside with the same implement.

Fiona caught the quirk of her lips, a small smile, in the mirror, and banished it. She didn't need to entertain herself with flights of fancy, as funny as they may be. She had work to do.

Tessa left Fiona alone, and Fiona counted to a hundred before peering out of her bedroom. She knew she had chores, but they could wait.

She slipped down the stairs and to a room behind the kitchen, which had steam pipes running through it. She was surprised when the door opened easily. Her father never left his office unlocked, but she wouldn't question the gift of the opportunity to peek inside. Although small, it held a workbench, a stool, and several lengths of pipe that screwed into the steam and gas systems on the wall, which resembled a network of tubes of varying metals. Terminus had been outfitted with steam and gas systems during the war in preparation for the Southern states to take their place as a technologically progressive and socially conservative country once the war was over. Never mind that since they'd been installed, there was no guarantee they'd actually work.

Meanwhile, the South had fallen behind in weaponry. Fiona's greatest dream was to meet Claire McPhee, the woman behind La Reine, the weapon that had ended the war. While her neighbors, most of whom had sympathized with the South, moaned and groaned, Fiona had inwardly cheered. Of course a woman would be required to birth peace. Men had been mucking it up for a decade.

Fiona set her teacup and pot on the workbench and looked around. Where had the nutcracker doll gone? Or, again, had she even seen it to begin with? There were certainly plenty of places for something that size to hide here. Wooden shelves and cubbies along the red brick walls were filled with barely organized odds and ends, or at least that's how it looked.

Fiona frowned, trying to remember who had been at the party. It had been difficult to tell with everyone in costume and masked. She picked up a teacup from the other set the family used. It had been there a while—the brown liquid at the bottom had congealed and then dried, and a few flecks of leaf remained stuck to it. It was the set that her father used when working with his friends, who didn't seem to mind the weak tea.

Right, his friends. The previous week, Bryan Telfair had welcomed two other tinkerers into his home for a meeting, and they'd come straight back to the workshop. She could hardly imagine more than one person in the room—her father was not a skinny man—but sometimes they required darkness and relative quiet, and the Telfair kitchen didn't get much demand with just the three of them. Not like when Connor had been home with his teenage boy appetite.

And now there were two. What had Bryan been doing with the other two tinkerers? They'd been whispering frantically as Bryan had brought them in, and Fiona had caught a few words. *Aether, frequency, animation...* All as expected, but had there been something else? Her own thoughts of how unfair it had been for her to be shut out had kept interfering with her determined eavesdropping, but he'd said it was too dangerous for her to be involved yet.

*Dangerous.* That was the other word. But how? Sure, aether had plenty of not-so-nice uses such as concentrated as a weapon, but what else?

*Emotion.* They had said something about emotion.

Fiona rubbed her eyes, but the memory dissipated like the heat from her tea. Emotion. What did feelings have to do with anything? Machines didn't have them. She clenched her fist— why hadn't she thought of that when Devon had asked her about life? Or teased her, rather? She could never tell with him whether their conversation was serious or a jest. Well, not most of the time. He'd seemed serious enough about recovering the lost tinkerers.

So who had her father been meeting with? The leader of the Tinkerer's Guild, Master Thaddeus Lillet, and his assistant, who had been freed with the peace, Hollowell. He hadn't chosen a second name yet. Fiona liked both men, although she was intimidated by Master Lillet.

And she was pretty sure she'd seen each of them at the ball. Master Lillet was easy to spot due to his tall, gaunt physique, and Hollowell because he was never far away.

Fiona looked through drawers and the one small cabinet in the room for notes, drawings, or anything else that would give her a clue as to what they'd been working on but turned up nothing. If her father had kept any notes, he'd hidden them well.

She drummed her fingers on the table. She needed to talk to the Lillet household to see if she could look at Thaddeus's work, although she doubted he'd been careless with it. To ask for access to his notes would be presumptuous—she wasn't even an apprentice yet. Or maybe she could have Devon help her.

No, she couldn't rely on him for help. If the recent experience with her father's poor judgment and family finances showed anything, it was that she couldn't rely on men to aid her and keep her best interests at heart. She would tell Devon afterward and see what he came up with on his end. They ran in different circles, so they could use that to their advantage.

And if she wasn't marriage material, that was all for the better. She didn't need—or want—someone to stand up for her, worry about her, or otherwise inhibit her ability to be an independent woman. Her mother wouldn't be cooperative, so Fiona knew she had to find her father.

Worry stabbed her through the chest every time she thought about his perilous situation, but there was always an echo of frustration at losing the one parent who understood and supported her.

She decided her next step should be a visit to the Lillet household. Even if they couldn't get to Thaddeus's and Hollowell's notes, perhaps Lucy could shed some light on Fiona's father's work and collaborations.

DEVON TUCKED the telegram into his pocket and stiffened at a knock on the door. Crenshaw poked his head around before Devon could respond.

"Sir? Ah, good, you're home. Did you manage to evade Miss Bollington?"

"No." Devon placed his hands palm-down on the table. "What in the deuces was she doing here? I saw the article in the paper this morning. It was full of fluff and nonsense, so I'm guessing she wanted the real story."

Crenshaw shrugged. "I don't know, Sir, but I'm sorry. I sent her out of the servants' delivery exit so she wouldn't waylay you."

Devon sighed. He didn't want to give away that he'd been using that exit to evade the family and upstairs servants, but he suspected that the butler knew better. Had he been in on the arrangement for Devon to encounter Bollington?

Devon rubbed his eyes. Now he was getting paranoid about his own household. "What business awaits me today?"

"The sheriff is in the receiving parlor. Says he wants a statement from last night. He also wishes to discuss a personal matter." Crenshaw raised an eyebrow.

"I don't know what that could be." And indeed Devon didn't. "Give me ten minutes, oh, and a cup of coffee, and I'll see him"

"Yes, sir."

The butler disappeared, shutting the door behind him without a sound. Devon couldn't complain. The man ran the household with such amazing efficiency that they hadn't had to hire a maid. Or, rather, under Crenshaw's capable direction, his wife served well enough as head maid even though she hadn't ever held such a position before.

So now it was time to face the sheriff. The thought gave Devon some worry, although he hadn't done anything wrong. But he knew Jim Blair from other arenas of his life. Jim had his own estate and fortune, but he'd decided to run for sheriff after the war to help ensure that things wouldn't change too much. And he was one of the planters who thought Devon and Pierce were cowards, Devon more so than Pierce, who at least had returned to run the family business. Although Devon didn't like Blair, he knew what to expect.

Unlike from Fiona. Every time he thought he knew what she would do or say, she surprised him. An admirable trait in a woman. Too bad they couldn't ever make a match.

Suddenly Devon wondered if that personal matter could have something to do with Jim Blair's oldest daughter Meribelle, who was of marriageable age. She had the connections... But she also had no spark. He shook his head. Spark didn't matter. His legacy and his sister's welfare did.

Soon Crenshaw had brought Devon some coffee and "a teaspoon of laudanum, courtesy of Master Pierce." Pierce had guessed Devon's ankle may be bothering him after his errands. Indeed it did, but Devon didn't put the laudanum, measured in a thimble-sized glass, into his coffee. Although Pierce's stuff seemed to not cloud his judgment, he dared not test its merits or demerits, as the case may be.

A sharp rap heralded the appearance of Jim Blair. His belly, which strained the buttons of his waistcoat, preceded him into the room, and his pocket watch draped with tight desperation.

Was the man ill? Devon had encountered some people whose large guts were a sign of ill health rather than prosperity, and Jim's round face appeared flushed under his light brown hair, of which much had fled. He wore the star on his coat and kept running his thumbnail over one corner of it.

Devon wanted to ask him to stop, but instead said, "Good morning, Sheriff. I guess I know what brings you here."

Blair half-grinned as though moving his jowls was too much of an effort. "Part of it, I reckon. But yes, what is your recollection of last night's events at the Tinkerer's Ball?" He shook his head. "I warned them that they'd been getting too uppity with their inventions and that they'd attract the wrong sort of attention."

"The wrong sort of attention from whom?" Devon asked, concealing the excitement behind his words. This was what he and Fiona had been talking about.

"From the wrong sort of people." Blair hooked his thumbs into his waistcoat pockets. "Now, what do you remember about the ball last night?"

Resigned that the direct approach wouldn't work to get the information he wanted, Devon gave him the sparse but strictly factual account of the ball. Blair listened and nodded, seemingly bored until Devon got to the part about escorting Fiona out.

"And so you ran from the danger?"

Devon bit back the defensive comment he wanted to make. Instead, he took a deep breath and said, "I helped others from the burning room."

"And who was that young lady, again?" Blair interrupted.

"Fiona Telfair, daughter of Bryan Telfair. I believe he held some sort of office in the Guild. Holds rather—I'm assuming he's not dead."

"We're not assuming anything," Blair said vaguely. "But yes, we hope those who were kidnapped are still alive."

"I'm sure their families would be happy to have them back," Devon agreed, careful to appear as harmless as he could. "There had to be what, a dozen?"

"Two dozen, most like." Blair's nod said he enjoyed correcting Devon. "At least that we know of. We're still talking to the servants of the house."

"Right." Two dozen? What did the kidnappers want with all those tinkerers and their families?

"But getting back to Miss Telfair... Was her father there?"

"Yes, but he said he had to get back to a couple of the other men and find them. I don't remember who," he added before Blair could ask. He would ask Fiona—after the astute observations she'd shared, he guessed she remembered the incident much better than he. And he also wanted to punch Blair in the face when he thought of the odious sheriff interviewing her. He had no doubt she could hold her own, but—

"So then what happened?"

Devon related their flight and leaving Fiona with some of the latecomers. He thought he'd seen Thaddeus Lillet's wife and daughters, although why they'd arrived after he did...

Wait, Thaddeus was the Guildmaster, so it made sense that he'd have to be there early and would have gone ahead to allow his womenfolk to have more time to prepare. He then told Blair about going to talk to the servants after ensuring that they'd have the medical help they needed.

"You didn't trust the ambulance men?" Blair asked, his jaw hardening.

Devon tried to think of a way to answer the question without alienating the sheriff. "They were exhausted and overwhelmed," he said. "I'm sure they were about to go back there when I encouraged them."

Blair nodded, but his eyes remained narrowed. "Did you see or find anything suspicious after you walked around the house?"

Devon sat back and steepled his fingers. Could the sheriff know about the clockwork creature? Or had someone seen Thom giving it to him and Pierce? Impossible—it had been too dark.

"No, only a bunch of distressed people."

Blair nodded again, a jerk of his head up and down once. "Good. Thank you. This has been helpful."

"I wish I could give you more," Devon said and spread his hands, again trying to convey a helpful and harmless impression. "I just wish I knew who would do such a brazen and hurtful thing. So many of the families have already lost so much." He thought about the portrait of the young man over the fireplace in Fiona's parlor.

Blair's face closed like a mask, and Devon realized he'd gone too far.

"We're following every lead we can. I'm going to talk to Miss Telfair next. Do you have any advice on getting her to talk? I understand she's very shy."

"Go through her mother. They're very close." Devon hid his smile at the thought of the encounter. All right, perhaps that was mean of him, but he would pay to see Jim Blair versus Margie Telfair in a battle of words and wits. He honestly didn't know who was the thicker-headed.

"All right, thank you for that." Blair rocked on his feet, and for the first time, he looked anxious. "Now, I have something else I'd like to ask you about."

"Ask away." Devon made an expansive gesture. "I'm all ears."

Blair sat for the first time during the interview and put himself eye-to-eye with Devon. "Well, as you know, I have a couple of daughters."

"I knew of one of them. What's her name, Meribelle?"

The sheriff gave Devon what looked like a genuine smile. "Yes, and Meribelle is getting to be of an age where she's thinking of finding a nice young man. Settling down, you know."

Devon nodded. He wasn't going to appear too eager, but could this be his chance to be redeemed in the face of Southern hostility?

"And anyways," Blair said and ran a finger under his collar, "you're a nice young man, making a good living, and I'm thinking you must be considering something similar, a wife and family, like."

Devon smiled. After what felt like months of effort—all right, it had only been weeks—the marriage mart was opening to him. He didn't think that Meribelle Blair was his type, and he definitely couldn't imagine sitting across from Jim Blair during holidays and Sunday dinners, but he hoped this would be the first of many hopeful fathers bringing potential suits and feeling him out.

"It's crossed my mind, "Devon admitted. "But I hadn't gotten as far as thinking about which young lady would suit me best."

"Well, when you do, I think you should consider my Meribelle." Blair made his decisive head-jerk motion again, as though his chin could stamp approval on his idea. "She's sweet, pretty—takes after her mother, thank goodness—and knows how to run a large household." He waved his hand, and Devon could practically see him salivating at the thought of his daughter as mistress of the unnamed mansion. Devon had hesitated to give the estate a new name, knowing that the opportunity to name the place would be a way to attract interest in potential wives. His wayward mind questioned what Fiona would call it. Not that she was the type of woman he'd consider, either. No dowry or connections to think of.

Blair continued, "Well, I'll leave you to think on it. And let me know if you recall anything else about the ball and the kidnappings. Even if you don't think it's relevant, don't worry.

Just tell me, and I'll determine whether it's useful. Oh, and let me give you a warning—stay away from the Telfair family."

Devon's eyebrows slid up his forehead before he could rein in his surprise. "Excuse me?"

"Saw you coming from their house this morning. I can't tell you much, just that Bryan Telfair was mixed up in some things he oughtn't have been."

"What things?" Devon clenched his fists beneath his desk. He understood taking risks for one's business, but not if it endangered one's family. Was that how the Telfair household had fallen into poverty?

"Can't say. Government business. Not the sort of thing I could share with an acquaintance." He winked, and Devon got the gist. While Blair may not share confidences with someone he didn't know well, he'd be more open with a son-in-law.

"Thank you for your visit," Devon said and stood. Blair did likewise. "I'll have Crenshaw see you out."

"Thank you for your time," Blair, ever the Southern gentleman, drawled. "And let me know once you've made a decision on my offer. You'll find that we're not the wealthiest family in town, but I've made generous arrangements for my daughters, and everybody likes them. You won't lack for invitations."

"I'll consider it. Thank you again."

Crenshaw appeared, and Devon watched the back of Jim Blair vanish through the door with relief. A sheriff shouldn't be sharing information with anyone outside the investigation— another reason Devon didn't like him—but what had Blair been hinting at? Or had he been making vague accusations to keep Devon from being distracted by Fiona, who was definitely the prettiest girl he'd seen in Terminus thus far? Hence why he'd kept trying to talk to her even though she seemed unable or unwilling to talk to him. At least not until the talk turned to technical matters. But still, what kind of life would that be, only speaking of puzzles and problems?

Devon put his head in his hands. He didn't need to be thinking about Fiona. He needed to find the missing tinkerers and get his own household in order.

But still, a little spark of hope made his heart feel lighter—could the Southern planters finally be forgiving him?

## 8

-------

*Terminus, 18 December 1871*

*Progress through unity. Remember your legacy.*

Devon Meriweather knew he should be pondering more immediate questions instead of the stamp he wanted to leave on this new era of Terminus, but his eyes stung from studying the documents on the table in front of him. Admittedly, the piles had shrunk since he'd forced himself to go through them for several hours each day since returning from France, but they seemed to grow again overnight and when he wasn't looking. He rubbed his eyes. Everything appeared in order. Pierce had done well during Devon's absence, even with the War raging around Terminus and disrupting trade.

"The vultures are circling," Pierce said from where he stood by the window, waiting to answer any questions Devon might have. Sometimes people mistook one for the other due to their dark hair that shone red in the sun and dark hazel eyes, and Devon suspected Pierce had used that to his advantage.

Devon shook his head and recognized the thoughts as

coming from his irritable disposition since that morning, when he'd woken with what he thought may be the start of a sick headache.

It didn't help that the light blue of the sky beyond Pierce made the room almost unbearably bright and mocked the heaviness of Devon's mood. While the open lawn in front of the house allowed more natural light into the office, Devon missed the old townhouse, which was both cozy and in the middle of things.

"Whose carriage do you see?" Devon didn't bother to get up. His left ankle ached and added to his foul mood.

"A steamcart. One of the newfangled ones." Pierce looked over his shoulder and wrinkled his nose. "I can almost smell the charcoal from here."

Devon bit back the reply that burning coal was preferable to horse shit stench, but he and Pierce didn't disagree on much, so he didn't make anything of it. And in his current mood, if he started arguing, he might not be able to stop himself. Therese had gotten their mother's calm temperament, Devon their father's passion and temper.

"Whose steamcart?" Devon persisted.

"A tall gentleman. He has a limp."

"Just one person?" That didn't sound like a team. Perhaps his silent prayers to the gods of efficiency had been answered.

"Yes, why?"

Devon sat back in his father's old chair. Although he had his father's height, the chair felt too big for him, even beyond the fact that he lacked his father's bulk. Or absolute honesty. The lie he'd concocted slid easily off his tongue. "After the incident at the ball, I decided to hire a security team."

"Oh?" Pierce raised his eyebrows. "You didn't tell me about this."

"It's something I've been thinking about for a while. I want to keep you and Therese safe." Devon shrugged with apparent regret but thrilled that he'd at least kept his cousin out of one aspect of his life. It wasn't that he didn't like or trust Pierce. He just liked having things for himself as well. And secrets. Like how part of the reason he'd been in France was to make reports back to Washington as to how the war was perceived there, and to monitor who was supporting whom. And if he managed to sway some opinions, he was doing his part to help the war effort at home.

Pierce simply grinned, again surprising Devon with how someone with such good business sense could also have such an easygoing nature. "Probably not a bad idea, considering..."

"Considering what?"

Pierce's smile vanished. "How many of the planters still don't care for us, the 'coward cousins,' although you did seem to make some headway with Sheriff Blair." Then he sighed. "I do wish you trusted me more, Cousin."

Devon wondered how Pierce had known about Blair's visit, but he first had to deal with the many levels of his cousin's complaint. Pierce had been making a suit for Therese's hand, but Devon hadn't given his blessing. Mostly because Therese hadn't given hers. Although of marriageable age, her health problems had kept her off the market, and Devon didn't want to force her into anything that would jeopardize her happiness or health. And he worried that childbirth would kill her.

"I'll try to do better at keeping you involved in household decisions. Meanwhile..." Devon cocked his head at the office door.

"Your wish is my command." Now back to his easygoing self, Pierce mock-bowed and left. Devon took the opportunity to rub his burning eyes again. He'd never been able to sleep when there was a storm coming, and he'd had the feeling for over a month.

"Sir?" Crenshaw knocked on the door a few minutes later.

"Yes, come in."

Crenshaw held a tray upon which sat a glass that held an amber liquid. "Mister Pierce said you were having a headache again, so I brought you some whiskey with laudanum."

Devon hesitated before accepting the cure. But a stabbing pain behind his right eyeball heralded the next stage of his sick headache, which would send him to bed for the rest of the afternoon.

"Thank you." He took a sip, and the pain receded slightly. With the next sip, the tension in his neck relaxed, and the stabbing subsided to a dull ache.

"Also, there's a chap outside by the name of Davidson. Says you're expecting him?"

Devon nodded. "Please send him in. And some tea."

"Yes, sir."

Crenshaw held the door open for the man Devon had been told to expect—Henry Davidson. The man himself walked through the door, and his direct gaze took in everything before settling on Devon. "Mister Meriweather, I presume." He spoke in a soft English accent.

Devon rose, wincing when he put weight on his ankle. Was that a sympathetic glint in Davidson's eyes? "And you must be the head of my investigative team. Please, have a seat."

After resuming his seat, Devon took a moment to study Henry Davidson. Tall and thin with a smattering of freckles and hair somewhere between dark red and medium brown, he had an unassuming air until one looked more closely. Then Devon took in the way he sat, straight but slightly forward as though ready to spring up at a moment's notice, and how he also studied Devon with more than mild curiosity.

Davidson spoke first. "Who was that young man out there? I see a family resemblance."

"My cousin Pierce. He helps me to manage things while I'm away."

Davidson nodded. "And I assume he will also need my firm's protection?" He pulled a notepad from his pocket. "I have written that your household consists of you, your sister Therese, and several servants. Formerly enslaved people, I presume."

"You presume incorrectly." Devon almost grinned. "My family, being from the North, never owned slaves. Those who work for us have always been free. And paid."

"Noted." Davidson made a mark in his notebook.

Devon felt that Davidson had let him have a victory. "As for Pierce needing protection, let's be straight with each other. He can handle himself, but I am concerned for him, considering how tinkerers have been vanishing."

"As well you should be." Somehow Davidson managed to convey both approval and censure, and it hit Devon who he was really talking to.

A wave of exhaustion overtook Devon, and he remembered why he'd hated the foreign service work—all the deception. "Look, let's drop the pretense. I know you're not in charge of a security firm. I heard of you while I was abroad, Inspector Davidson."

Davidson raised his eyebrows and put his notebook away. He studied Devon for so long that Devon speculated he'd just made a horrible mistake and revealed too much about his own secret work. He pushed the half-finished whiskey with laudanum away.

"And is your sister truly fragile?" Davidson—or whoever he was—finally asked. But he didn't say yes or no to Devon's implied questions.

Devon sighed. "Unfortunately, that much is not a cover-up. She's been ill since childhood. My parents pursued many treatments for her before they died, and I after, but while we've managed to keep her alive, she is still unwell."

"Very well." Davidson nodded. "Since you know this is more than a security arrangement, please tell me how you would like it to work. You and your family are in danger, and so my purpose for being here is twofold, and I would like to help as much as I can."

Devon heard the words that weren't said—*whether you like it or not.* He relaxed slightly as the warmth of the alcohol and opium continued to spread through him. How had the glass ended up in his hand again? "I have told the household that there is a security team coming. And that you will be staying as we implement the first stage of railroad reconstruction to guard against sabotage."

The pad of paper appeared again. "Anything else?" He inclined his head to the office door, through which the ebb and flow of an intense discussion could be heard, although not the words. Devon recognized Pierce's and Crenshaw's voices.

"In the interest of being completely honest, I'm also looking for a strategic marriage. But I don't want to jump in blindly."

"Then perhaps now would be a good time for you to introduce me as your new head of security. It sounds like you could use some protection with all these people who want to use you."

Devon nodded, but he stifled another sigh. Wasn't Davidson also using him? At least Devon could do the same.

"How many are on your team?" Devon asked.

Davidson paused for a second too long before answering, "Five, including myself. And two more who may join us, but who will not be staying here."

"And when do I get to meet them?"

"They will be arriving in a few days with equipment."

Devon stood, as did Davidson, and said, "I look forward to

it." Another lie. Why had he allowed his life to get so complicated?

Typically Vinni enjoyed the landing of the airships, the gentle almost-kiss when machine descended to hover above the earth, but not today.

"I hope your uncle recovers soon," Captain Andrews told her once they'd done their final check of the instruments. "It's a shame there isn't any other family to help out." He shook his head. "But then, some people aren't lucky enough to have lots of relatives to help care for them."

"Thank you," she told the captain. "I'll be back as soon as I can. Again, I'm sorry." Sorry for having to go on leave again so soon. Sorry for lying to him. Sorry for not being able to fulfill her duties and follow her dreams because she was too far embedded in an organization that demanded her life and her soul.

The captain had told her once she boarded that he'd gotten the message about her sick uncle, so of course she'd been granted leave to care for him. Then he'd confided in her that he feared he would end up in the same situation, being a man with no wife or family himself, and an orphan to boot. She'd never asked, but she had no doubt the neo-Pythagoreans had ferreted out his formerly secret insecurity and used that to their advantage.

As for the plausibility of an uncle in Terminus, she had a Southern drawl that came out occasionally, although she had no idea where it originated. Had her parents been Southern? She couldn't remember. And anyone she'd talked to at the temple had only said she'd been found wandering near the property when she was about four years old, and they had no idea where her parents were. They swore they'd looked, but she'd often suspected they hadn't put too much effort into the search. At least her burning desire to find her parents had diminished to an occasional sting, which stuck her heart at times like this.

Would this enforced leave be an opportunity to find out more about her own past? It might not be so bad after all.

The captain shook her hand. "You'll always be welcome back. Regardless of where you disappear to when you're not flying." With that odd statement, he exited the bridge.

Vinni shook her head. Had Captain Andrews guessed she was involved in something? His superiors might know of her connections to the neo-Pythagoreans, but he shouldn't. But like her, he was a shrewd observer, which made him a good captain. She was pretty sure she hadn't slipped. She kept the tattoo of a circle inside a square on the inside of her left wrist covered by both a watch and her sleeve.

She gathered the few belongings she kept with her on the bridge and waited for the passengers who were getting off in Terminus to disembark. She and Cat had agreed to meet once the crowd thinned. Cat would have Vinni's luggage, and they'd go to the apartment in the city that had been rented for them.

Vinni sighed. It all seemed to be nicely planned and laid out for them, but she knew that things could easily go awry. Like they had in the spring, when she'd failed her assignment, been betrayed by Paul Farrell, and lost her faith.

Cat waved her over, and they took a carriage from the airship field south of the city to an apartment downtown.

Two hours later, Vinni stood by the window and watched the hustle and bustle on the street below—carts and carriages, driven and ridden in and unloaded by people with a range of skin tones. She envied their easy manners and warmth. Could she disappear into the chaos? Or would she stand out?

She kept one ear on Cat, who sat on a cushion in front of the fireplace—not burning since the chilly morning had turned into a balmy day—and closed her eyes, seeking the signature of the aether. Or that's what she'd told Vinni. Vinni wondered if that was the case because every time she'd tried to sneak out the door, Cat had caught her and had fixed her with a look that said, *Don't you even think of it, Missy.* Now all Vinni could do was wish Cat would fall asleep so Vinni could slip out.

Vinni regretted confiding her plans—well, desire—to escape to Cat. She hadn't been allowed to go anywhere alone, and Cat felt more like a jailer than a lover.

"That's it!" Cat opened her eyes. "I've found something."

"Where?" Vinni walked to the dining room table, which had a map of the city spread on it. She tried not to be jealous of Cat's abilities, but sometimes it was difficult. Vinni didn't like feeling useless.

Cat closed her eyes and hummed, which she'd told Vinni helped her to block out distractions. Her fingertips traced over the map, finally landing on a block that Vinni knew to be warehouses. "There."

"When do we go?" Vinni asked. Being out would give her the chance to run—more of a chance than she'd had previously, anyway.

"Now." Cat grinned, some of the tension of the past two days melting from her broad cheeks. "Let's check it out."

"Now?" Vinni tried not to show her shock at Cat wanting to leave the apartment so soon.

"Yes. But Vin?" Cat put a hand on Vinni's shoulder.

"Yes?"

"You won't leave me, will you?"

Vinni hated lying to Cat's face, but she smiled and tried to allow the remnants of the love they'd once shared to shine through her eyes. "Why would I do that?"

"Why wouldn't you?" Cat turned and wiped something from her cheek. "I'm sorry for bringing you to Uncle."

Vinni couldn't tell Cat it was all right. It wasn't. "I'm sorry we're both in this situation," she said softly.

Cat nodded, and to Vinni's relief, didn't say anything. Maybe she didn't want to pile more lies between them on top of everything else.

Vinni went to check her gear and make her preparations—to find the source of the aether, and to be alert for any opportunity to make a run for it.

**9**

———

*erminus, 18 December 1871*

After taking care of the morning's business, Devon joined Therese and Pierce for lunch in the informal dining room. He thought it silly to have a formal dining room that could seat two dozen at least and an informal one that could accommodate a more intimate party of ten or so. He certainly hadn't thought about hosting any balls before the winter was over, but now that the marriage mart had opened to him, perhaps it wouldn't be a bad idea to see who was interested enough to come.

Or, more likely, who wanted free food, drink, and an opportunity to show off.

Well, whatever their motivation, they'd be in his home, and he'd be working toward his legacy.

He was shaking his head at his cynicism when Therese touched his arm.

"What are you pondering with such a twist to your mouth, brother mine?" she teased. "You look like you've kissed a goat and found it tastes of grass."

"Therese!" Pierce looked at her with an amused glitter in his eyes. "Where did you come up with that horrid expression?"

Therese laughed, and Devon relaxed at the sound. She must be feeling better. She wouldn't be laughing if she wasn't. But then, she'd seemed gayer since that morning, when he'd said a quick hello before leaving to talk to Fiona.

"Say," he said and picked up his fork, "Layla Bollington cornered me when I got in yesterday. Do either of you know what she was doing here?"

A quick flush came to Therese's cheeks, and she shook her head, but without meeting his gaze. "I wasn't aware she'd been here."

And Devon wasn't aware his sister was a liar, and a poor one at that, but he elected not to confront her until he could do so when they were alone. Had she been entertaining the journalist? But to what end?

"No idea," Pierce added. "Probably here to talk to us about the disaster that was the Tinkerer's Masquerade Ball." He shuddered. "Beastly automatons."

Therese looked up. "Automatons? Did they have something to do with the clockwork you were looking at the other night?" She crossed her arms. "You can tell me. I've read the article in the paper about the ball, but it just mentioned cloaked men, not machines."

"Yes." Pierce described the scene in excited tones. "They invaded the ball and rounded up the tinkerers. Only a few escaped. Your brother and I helped the survivors and the servants."

"With help," Devon added, not wanting for him or Pierce to take credit they didn't deserve. He might be called a coward, but he wouldn't be called a liar.

"Right, with the useless fire and medical brigades. They didn't want to help the Negroes."

"And you said the automatons were beastly." Therese's mouth thinned to a line before she asked, "Were many hurt?"

"We don't know." Devon rotated his ankle, which throbbed at the very memory of the escape and the walking around after. "I should have asked Blair, but he seemed to be treating the thing as a kidnapping, not a murder, so perhaps the ones who didn't escape were taken."

"We can hope, at least." Pierce dabbed at his upper lip, where sweat beaded. Devon hoped he wasn't being taken by a fever.

"Are you all right, Cousin?" Devon asked.

"Just fine. I think perhaps I need to take a turn outside, cool off a bit. This house is less drafty than the townhouse, and I fear I'm still adjusting." He stood and pushed back his chair. "Would you care to join me, Therese?"

She shook her head. "I'm going to lie down for a bit, clear my own head." She stood, and Devon did likewise.

"I'll walk you up."

"No, no, stay here, dear brother. I fear my head is trying to develop an ache, so I'm going to go up as quickly as I can, and I don't feel up for conversation." She fled the room.

"Strange," Pierce said.

"You think she's acting strangely?" Devon gestured to Pierce's napkin. "Since when do you have problems with the heat in the house? It's barely adequate."

Pierce shrugged. "She's hardly spoken to me today." He gestured to the door where Therese had just left. "I have a lot on my mind, so I'm going to go for a walk. Any chance you'd like to come along?"

"No, I have some thinking to do as well."

"You're not keeping anything from me, are you?" Pierce's expression fell. "You are. I can tell."

"We'll go shooting later," Devon promised. If he got invited on any hunting trips, he'd need to brush up his marksmanship, and that was something the two cousins had always enjoyed doing. It was also the one technical skill in which Devon outshone Pierce.

"Good." Pierce smiled and stood. "I'll see you later, then."

Devon watched Pierce leave, then decided to go in the lab to take another look at the clockwork creature he'd found. And to not get poked by it again.

He found the door to the cellar locked, but his key opened it. Strange—they didn't usually keep it locked. Perhaps Pierce was feeling protective of his work, although he never had before.

Light through the high windows, which the servants opened on dry days, allowed Devon to see to get down the stairs. He turned one of the lamps they'd had installed to low flame so he could make out the objects on the workbenches. While Pierce usually kept his workshop in some sort of order, today it appeared to be jumbled. It looked like someone had gone through and rifled for something. Had Pierce lost something? Or maybe Devon wasn't remembering correctly.

He walked to the clockwork creature and was just reaching to light the table lamp when someone knocked into him. He hit the ground with an "Oof!" and tried to roll away from his robed attacker. The odors of sweat and something chemical wafted over him. Even if he'd had enough light to see the person's face, Devon wouldn't have been able to because the man punched Devon in the side where the clockwork had gotten him, sending a jolt of pain through his torso. He curled up and tried to breathe deeply. His attacker got to his feet and stood over him, and Devon found himself staring into the face of a nutcracker—just like the automatons.

He kicked the thing in the knee, or tried to, but it jumped over Devon's foot. Then it grabbed something from the table and ran. Devon rolled to his knees, clutching his side, and unsteadily got to his feet. He tried to follow where he thought the mysterious attacker had gone but found nothing but a red brick basement wall. Then he returned to the workbench and groaned. The clockwork bug had gone missing. Of course. The kidnappers wouldn't want anything that could be traced to them left out in the world at large. But how had they known Devon and Pierce had it? Did it send some sort of signal through the aether to its makers?

He grabbed the lamp from the table, lit it, and brought it to the wall where he thought his attacker had disappeared. Sure enough, streaks showed in the dust on the floor. He traced a crack in the mortar to find a vaguely door-shaped outline. Another secret passage. Would this house never cease to surprise him? Or dismay him? He hated the idea that someone could come and go as they pleased, and how many more were there?

And did Pierce know?

Devon tried pushing, tapping, and otherwise bruising and roughing his fingers on the bricks and mortar in an effort to open the secret door, but to no avail. With a sigh, he stepped back and decided to return to the puzzle later. He would also have to ask Pierce if anything else had gone missing from the workshop, but he suspected not. And he'd inquire whether Pierce had noticed anyone else on the grounds during his walk. Not that Pierce might have seen anything—Devon had no idea how far the passage went. It could come out in the middle of Terminus for all he knew. Or into the woods north of the house, which would be impossible to search. That was the more likely scenario—that the passage had been built so the inhabitants could escape during an invasion.

What in the blazes was going on in his house?

WHEN TESSA BROUGHT Fiona the note saying the Lillet sisters would be delighted to receive her, Fiona quickly got ready. She then rushed out of her room and straight into Tessa, who'd just come up the stairs with a load of linens. She stepped back, but not before the pile shifted, and clean towels ended up strewn all over the floor.

"Oh, I'm so sorry!" Fiona bent to help the maid gather them. "I'll help you wash them later."

Tessa looked up, a grateful expression on her face. "Thank you, Miss, but I'll do it. Keeping busy makes me not worry so much."

Fiona smiled and squeezed the girl's shoulder. "Me too. I find myself worrying about Papa every minute my mind is idle."

"Do you think he'll be all right?"

"I have to believe so. They wouldn't have taken him to harm him, would they?"

"I hope not, Miss."

"How is Mama holding up?" Fiona glanced over Tessa's head as though her thoughts would summon her mother.

"She's asleep, Miss. I think that's how she keeps from worrying."

And how her mother kept from doing anything helpful. Fiona stifled a sigh weighted with frustration—and guilt. She needed to be more understanding—if she had a husband whom she loved, she would definitely need to be distracted if he went missing. Or off to war like Connor had. It seemed that the household had snapped back into its old way of handling things while in crisis, which was to say, not well.

"I'm going to go out for a bit. Are you available to accompany me?"

Tessa looked down at the now dirty linens in her arms. "Not right now, Miss. Please don't go. I can't handle worrying about someone else."

"Don't worry about me, I'm not going far. Just over to the Lillet house. I want to check on Lucy, Posey, and their mother."

"That's right nice of you, Miss. I wish I could go with you.

Their cook always has extra for..." She put a hand over her mouth.

"For visiting servants. I know." Fiona sighed. "I wish we had more for us to eat, too. But at least we're keeping our slim figures."

"Yes, Miss. And I think Mister Meriweather noticed yours. He certainly gave you an interesting look when you came down the stairs yesterday."

"Oh, stop." Her cheeks bloomed with heat again. Stupid blood vessels. Her pale skin gave everything away.

"Maybe he'll be the one to help us."

"Or at least the one to find out where Papa went." Fiona descended the stairs. She knew she shouldn't go out on her own, but the importance of her errand outweighed her need for propriety. She grabbed her bonnet off the peg by the back door and her cloak from the hook beside it. "I won't be gone long. Please don't tell Mama. If she asks for me, please tell her I'm asleep after all of yesterday's excitement. That should make her happy."

"Yes, Miss."

Walking into the chilly air made Fiona feel more herself. It seemed that the kidnappers had also taken the strange winter balminess, and now the world felt different. Or maybe that was just her fancy. Would it be possible to control weather if one could figure out a way to change the concentration of air molecules on a large scale? What sort of device could handle such a thing? And would aether have an application, being the substance light traveled through but apparently connected to so much more?

When Fiona arrived at the Lillet household, she found it in a stir. Whereas her own house had been silent as though her father's death was a foregone conclusion, the Lillet girls had a map spread out on the dining room table, and they chattered away under the patient gaze of their mother. The maid showed

Fiona in, and all three Lillet women surrounded her in an embrace.

"Oh, Fiona, what are we to do?" Lucy asked. "Our fathers have been taken somewhere into the wild."

"You have some idea as to where they've gone?" Fiona asked. The map showed Terminus, but also the mountain range and lake north, and the flat areas to the south and west. The rolling hills to the east, blanketed with forest between Terminus and Athens, had been folded back to make room for the rest of the giant map to lie on the table. "And where did you get such an amazing map?" She hadn't ever seen one on such a large scale.

"Father had it commissioned, but he wouldn't say why," Lucy said and tapped her lip with a pen.

Lucy's sister Posey, who looked similar to her except blond, gently pulled the pen away. "You're going to get ink on your collar. Stop that. And he said we'd learn when it was time."

"Well, it's time, at least I think so." Lucy walked around to the other side of the map. "Now Fiona, do you remember what direction the airship was going when it left? We have somewhat of a debate going on. I think it was north. Posey said it looked more east to her. Mother says somewhere in the middle, but even the slightest miscalculation could make the difference of hundreds of miles."

That was Lucy's specialty—navigation calculations for airships and, on a smaller scale, clockwork messenger pigeons which were reliable, provided they were pointed in the exact right direction. Indeed, a push-pin over Terminus had several strings radiating out from it leading to other pins, some in the mountains, and some in other directions.

"Why did you not consider Athens a possibility?" Fiona asked. "The university may harbor a scientist clever enough to make the..." She shut her mouth. She couldn't say it.

"The what, Fifi?" Lucy regarded Fiona shrewdly.

"The nutcracker men," was the best Fiona could come up with.

"Right. The wind wasn't strong enough that night for the balloon to get back to Athens, at least not with the weight it must have been carrying, and without having to refuel somewhere nearby. As for the direction, please help us to settle this debate. You're the best observer of all of us."

Fiona closed her eyes, and just remembering the sight of the dirigible carrying her father off made her throat close and her eyes sting. It had risen from its position on the roof, its balloon seemingly parallel with the line of the house. But had it been exactly parallel? The dark balloon against the dark sky had been difficult to make out, even with flames flickering underneath it to illuminate it.

Then it had made a quarter turn and headed into the night.

"It was a fifteen-degree turn from its original position," Fiona said. "But it could have adjusted its trajectory once out of sight. They're quite clever—surely they would have thought to mislead whoever may be watching. And there was a breeze that night, too, which they would have corrected for." That Lucy hadn't thought of those facts made Fiona's hopes dissipate like steam on a warm day. They must be truly panicked over their father, which likely meant that Lucy hadn't discovered anything.

"Oh." Lucy and Posey's faces fell. "That's a good point."

Lucy sighed and started pulling the pins up off the map, leaving tiny holes all over it. Fiona hoped their father would be so happy at their attempts to rescue him that he would forgive them for the damage.

"Where did you think it went?" Fiona asked. She saw the tears in Lucy's eyes, and her own burned in response. If her friend hadn't any better ideas than she...

"It must have gone into the mountains. That's what I keep thinking. It would be harder to get to than the forested flatter areas west of town, which means it would make for a perfect hideout, and there are plenty of old mines." Lucy's shoulders slumped. "But to what end, I don't know."

"Do you know what your father was working on?" Fiona helped her friends to roll up the map. She winced whenever her fingers found a hole in the paper from their pins.

"No," Posey piped up. Her voice was higher and thinner than her sister's. "He was always very secretive about his projects. But he was excited about something recently, wasn't he, Lulu?"

Lucy nodded. "Yes, quite. But he wouldn't tell us no matter how much we begged." She lowered her voice and glanced at her mother. "And I did look through his workshop last night after the ball but didn't find anything."

"That's what I feared." Fiona allowed her shoulders to slump.

"And what about your father?" Lucy asked.

Fiona sighed. "Same. I remembered our fathers meeting with Hollowell not too long before the party, like in the last week or so, and—oh!" She spied something on the shelf by the mantel. "How long have you had that?" She pointed to the small nutcracker doll. It looked like the one that had appeared and then vanished from her room.

Lucy picked it up and held it out to Fiona, who backed away. "What? It's just Mama's old doll. She brought it with her from Germany. It comes out every Christmas."

Now that Fiona could see the doll closer, she noticed its scuffs and scratches. She'd only had the barest glimpse of the interloper in her room, but she thought she remembered it being brand new and in pristine condition. Or maybe she'd been mistaken altogether, and nothing had been there except the frightened workings of a young tinkerer's mind. She'd heard madness was a risk of the profession when one spent too much time thinking about objects and not enough around people.

"Thank you, I don't think that's the one I remember."

"From what?" Polly asked. "Do you have one, too?"

Fiona shook her head. "It's nothing. Thank you for having me this afternoon, but I really should get going." Since her friends didn't know what their fathers had been working on, she needed to return home and compile her notes on what she did know. She took her leave of the Lillets, who were holding up much better than Mrs. Telfair, and walked into the afternoon sunshine, which had tilted toward fading. When she rounded the corner, a flash of white under a dark cloak caught her attention. A man crossed the street just in front of her, his white pants and black boots obvious under his billowing robe.

Fiona frowned. No one in their right mind would wear white pants on the streets of Terminus, especially not in the winter.

But the automatons had worn them, as had Lucy's mother's nutcracker. Could this be one of the kidnappers?

Fiona looked around, gathered her cloak, and followed the man in the white pants.

**10**

———

Terminus, *18 December 1871*

Fiona stepped in a puddle of something and cursed in words her mother would not have approved of as she extracted herself. When she looked up, she found she'd gone off the sidewalk and stood on a corner that at first seemed unfamiliar. She hadn't been that lost in thought, had she? She looked around to get her bearings and realized she'd wandered into the airfield warehouse district, and with it being after lunch, the afternoon ships were flying in. She looked around, her senses prickling. Someone was watching her.

Fiona searched as best she could, but the edges of the bonnet kept her from being able to see as far as she would like, and she didn't want to be obvious about her being lost. Coils. She shouldn't have followed the mysterious figure, but she needed to find out where her father was. And it would make sense for the kidnappers to be somewhere near the airfields since the airship had taken them away.

The hiss of a blade being drawn made her whirl around, and there he was, his face under the hood of the cloak a rictus of a grin. No, a nutcracker mask. A face that could be removed and stowed in the pocket of his cloak after he committed whatever violence he wanted against her.

She backed away, wishing she'd stuck to the crowded streets. Now she recognized her stupidity—she'd been drawn into a trap. And soon she would join the many young women who had died in Terminus's back alleys, her life and reputation lost.

But she wasn't going to go down without a fight. She pulled out her electric zap gun—named because of the sound—and flicked on the switch, which ignited a small coal and a simple battery of a wire between two magnets. It would take a few moments to charge—again, she should have thought better—but at least it was something. If nothing else, she could hold the wires and sling it.

"You think your little toy is going to help you?" The voice growled and grated along through the air between them. Curiosity nudged at the sharp edges of Fiona's panic. Could the automatons talk? Or was this a man speaking through some sort of device to disguise his voice?

"I don't want to hurt you," Fiona said in her bravest tone. She lifted her chin and stood as straight as she could to give herself more strength behind her throw.

The creature—man?—machine?—laughed. "But I want to hurt you. Put dark bruises all over your pretty skin. Stick my—"

He flew backward. Fiona had discharged the zap gun, its wires stretched out ahead of her. But they were slack. She'd missed.

"There are some things no young lady needs to hear."

Fiona wheeled around to see a young dark-haired woman armed with a pistol, from which she unscrewed a silencing tube.

"Well, he's dead. If you don't mind getting your pretty shoes dirty, you can search him to see if he's carrying anything that will tell you why he targeted you specifically. Well, other than you wandering into somewhere you shouldn't."

Fiona had no intention to stand there and be insulted. But she also didn't want to miss the opportunity to get a closer look at the automaton.

"What about you?" she asked.

"I'll stand guard and make sure no one bothers you. And if someone comes close, I'll warn you."

Fiona wanted to ask why she should trust the woman, but then again, the strange person had saved her life, or at least kept her from being raped.

"Are you sure it's dead?" she asked.

The woman sighed, rolled her eyes, and walked over to the prone body on the ground. She gave it a hard kick. Fiona covered her mouth so she wouldn't cry out, but the thing didn't move or react.

"I think you're safe. Now come on, you don't have all day."

Fiona nodded and tried not to stare at the woman's trousers. She didn't want to approach the dead body—she'd never seen a dead body before—but she didn't want this strange and brave rescuer to think less of her.

Careful to step over and around the rivulets of blood on the ground, Fiona found a spot where her skirts and cloak wouldn't trail in the muck, or at least not more than they already had, and, with hands trembling so hard she could barely grasp the edges of the mask, lifted it from the thing's face. Was it a thing? No, the dead eyes of a young man stared up at her. He had a sneer, and she almost reeled back at the lascivious expression on his face. Instead, she dropped the mask back on his face, where it lay crooked and mocking her.

She had to sternly tell herself to pretend it was an automaton before she could force herself to touch it again. A quick search of his pockets didn't reveal anything, but she noticed the buttons on his uniform. She couldn't place why they looked odd.

"So they weren't automatons," Fiona murmured and stood. "But where did he come from?"

A stain on the man's white trousers caught her attention. It shone green along the right cuff. "That looks like grass, but where is it still green this time of year?" All the lawns she knew of were brown, including the one surrounding the Tinkerer Hall.

"Got what you needed?" the strange woman asked. She leaned out of the alleyway and looked back and forth.

"Vinni!" The word made Fiona's protector jump back into the alley. "Where the hell have you been?"

"Damn and triple damn," the woman, who must be named Vinni, muttered. She turned to Fiona with a look of stark despair. "You owe me big, Girlie. Now get back out to the street and get yourself home."

"Wait! Will you be all right?" Fiona walked over to the woman, who squeezed Fiona's hand.

"I will be soon. Now shoo." She stepped out into the street. "Cat, what do you mean, where have I been? I've been right here all along."

Fiona pulled her bonnet tight around her head and slipped into the street, where she allowed the foot traffic to pull her along. Who was that strange woman? Worse—or curiouser— who was the young man, and why had he lured her into a trap? He'd definitely meant her harm.

Once she'd gone a few blocks, Fiona pressed her still-shaking hand to the pocket where she'd placed the zap gun, but she experienced her own jolt of nasty surprise when she found it missing. It must have tipped out while she'd been examining the body. But she couldn't return. By the time she got there, the sheriff's men would have found the man, or someone else would have. She had to hope that no one would be able to associate it to her, but she also knew she had a reputation for inventing and assembling such things.

She'd managed to escape from the erstwhile rapist —*murderer*, her mind added with a twist to her stomach—but what would Sheriff Blair do to her if he connected her to him? The chill along her spine had nothing to do with the breeze that flowed along the edge of the airfield and teased the small hairs on her neck.

Vinni watched the girl slip into the crowds and didn't look away until she'd disappeared.

"Found a new toy?" Cat growled.

Vinni sighed. "No, just someone toying with something she shouldn't. Did you pick up the signal again?"

Cat half-lidded her eyes and took a deep breath.

"Yes and no. It's faint, like whatever it was is moving away."

"Damn," Vinni swore on the exhale of another sigh. "I suspect our attacker in the alley may have been the source."

Cat glanced behind them and moved slightly closer to the alley until she nodded. "He practically reeks of aether residue."

How Cat could tell, Vinni didn't know, only that her peculiar talent had manifested in the neo-Pythagoreans. Vinni had thought for a few thrilling moments that Cat had gone on to follow a different trail. Something had told Vinni that there was trouble in the alley, and Vinni had the possible chance to escape. No such luck. Cat had found her again.

They walked back to their flat in silence, agreeing without saying to halt the search for the source of the spike in aether energy. They'd only arrived that morning, after all. Vinni loved flying by the stars, but she was ready for some sleep.

Once they'd returned, Cat went into another room to meditate while Vinni assembled a simple soup on the stove. Someone had been kind enough to leave supplies for them including vegetables that had long since been frozen out or buried by the winter weather in New England.

She'd just set the vegetable stew to simmer on the gas stove when a hand cupped her waist, and someone's presence warmed her back. Acid rose to her mouth along with the fear that Uncle Dross had come down to finish what he'd tried to start.

"How long does the soup have?" Cat asked into Vinni's hair.

Vinni spoke around the heartbeat that fluttered in her throat. "About half an hour of simmering." She turned and found herself pinned to the counter. *Don't panic, don't panic.*

Cat brought her face closer to Vinni's, and the air supply around her thinned.

The words Vinni wanted to hear didn't come. She wanted Cat to beg forgiveness, but Cat simply closed the kiss.

Vinni's lips tightened as the contents of her stomach—not much, admittedly—rose, and she lunged to the side, holding a hand over her mouth and trying not to retch.

Cat stepped back and folded her arms. "Is that how you feel about me now?"

Vinni straightened and wiped the back of her hand across her mouth. Not that anything had come up, but she couldn't help the motion, or wanting to wipe the kiss away.

"You set me up. You sent me in there to Uncle Dross knowing what he wanted to do to me." The time since they'd first had the conversation had only made her anger grow.

"He does it to all the women. And some of the boys. It's part of the initiation into the full mysteries." Again, a longer than usual string of words from Cat. "How do you think I can find the aether?"

"Because you were raped?" Vinni shook her head. "No gift is worth that." And she'd also heard the self-justification in Cat's tone. "How do you know that's what did it? Would you have come into your talent anyway?"

"I don't know." Cat's shoulders slumped. "But you haven't come into any power, only the basics that they teach."

What was Cat getting at? "What if I don't want power?"

"As a foundling, you need to have some. Else the Goddess will destroy you."

"She had her chance." And had destroyed an evil man instead. Vinni wondered why the Goddess hadn't done anything to punish Dross for what he did, had tried to do. But then, she didn't understand divine logic or plans.

Again, she questioned why she'd been left in the countryside near the compound and who her parents really were. The curiosity around where she came from never sank out of her mind for long, especially not in Terminus. Being in the Southern States had brought little tickles of memory, but nothing she could put words to, only the preverbal impressions that a very young child or infant might have.

"You got lucky." Cat poked a finger into Vinni's chest and brought her back to the conversation. Vinni backed up.

"Or the Goddess decided I wasn't worthy of her notice. And that's how I like it. Lying low and not allowing trouble to find me."

"Trouble certainly found you this afternoon with that young redhead."

"We found her. She was following that man like we were." Vinni admired the girl's pluck, as stupid as it had been for her to follow him into that alley. She had met others who had that single-minded focus. Like Henry Davidson. She still felt badly about helping Paul Farrell escape. It would have been the prize to define Davidson's career. But she'd had her orders, and she dared not oppose the neo-Pythagoreans *and* the Clockwork Guild.

Cat seemed to want to say more, but then shook her head. "The landlord brought a paper by while you were in here. You might want to see this."

She grabbed a newspaper off the kitchen counter where she'd left it—how focused had Vinni been on her soup preparation?—and handed it over. The headline on the front page blared, "Tinkerers Kidnapped from Ball. Mysterious Airship Observed. Automatons Run Amok."

Vinni raised her eyebrows. "Automatons?" She scanned the article. "Nutcracker automatons? Who would have come up with those?"

Cat shrugged. "Prussians?"

"They're too busy torturing the French with reparations. Perhaps they're trying to gain some sort of influence here. But why tinkerers?" All that inventiveness and brainpower in one place would be a good asset for someone, but tinkerers were notoriously secretive, at least with others outside their little circles. The ones she'd known, like Paul Farrell, preferred to work alone on their devices and inventions, only talking to others when they had something to show off. An active Guild like the one in Terminus seemed to be the exception rather than the rule.

"And the man you killed was dressed like one of the automatons in the article." Vinni tapped a finger against her lips. "Perhaps they weren't automatons after all, but someone wants to build an army of them. Hence why they'd want the tinkerers—they need their brains."

Cat nodded. "And their technical skills." She wiggled her fingers.

Vinni almost smiled. Cat had never excelled with delicate work, like that required for clockworks or other mechanical inventions. She preferred to smash things, not put them together.

"So now we have another mystery. Maybe. I bet if we find the source of the aether spikes, we'll find the tinkerers."

"Assuming no one interferes," Cat growled.

"Right. Well, the girl left her little toy at the scene, and I didn't grab it, so the authorities should be focused on her."

"You think they'll connect it to her?"

Vinni nodded. "Devices like that aren't commonplace. She also had the curiosity of a tinkerer. I'm guessing that she has a reputation for delicate little inventions like that."

"Good point."

A delicious smell filled the air, and Vinni turned to the soup. "Dinner's ready."

But when she approached the stove, her shoulders stiffened. For a few moments, it had seemed like before—the two of them discussing their missions. But nothing would ever be as it was before. She needed to get out of there, but would she get another opportunity?

If fate didn't give her one, she'd make it. Meanwhile, she wished she'd thought to ask the girl why she'd gotten herself in the predicament in the alley. Were they investigating the same case?

**11**

───────

T*erminus, 18 December 1871*

The farther away Fiona got from the scene of her almost-rape, the more she trembled, the images from the ball intruding and imposing themselves on the memories of the afternoon's experiences. When she arrived home, Fiona paused at the side door and took a few deep breaths, seeking comfort in the familiarity. She would be safe there, right? She wanted to go to her mother, but she knew the consequences if Margie found out what had happened.

She opened the door as quietly as she could and tried to sneak upstairs, but she heard the dreaded sniff followed by, "Fi-OH-na!"

"Yes, Mother?"

Margie sat on her chair in front of the fire. "Oh, you were out? Tessa said you were napping."

"I couldn't sleep, so I popped over to see Lucy and Posey. They and Mrs. Lillet send their regards."

"Good, same to them." She leaned forward, and Fiona knew her mother had other things on her mind. "How did your meeting with Mister Meriweather go? He certainly is handsome, isn't he?" Her eyes glowed with hope.

She wanted to ask if her mother even saw her as a person, but instead, with a sigh, she said, "It went well. We discussed how to find Father and the other tinkerers who have gone missing."

Margie drew back. "Why did you do that, you silly girl? You can't show a man how smart you are. You'll drive him away if he thinks you're trying to make him feel like he's less intelligent than you."

Not the men Fiona was interested in, but she knew that line of conversation wouldn't get her anywhere. She decided to throw her mother a bone. Well, a sliver.

"We'll be meeting again to discuss our findings." At least she hoped they would. They hadn't exactly set a meeting time or place, just promised to be in touch, but that was close enough. She wondered if he'd had any luck with Jim Blair.

A knock on the door made Fiona jump and her mother still. Did the same recollection jump to her mother's mind—the knock when the army sergeant, a young man the same age as Connor, had come to give them the news? Connor had been killed in one of the final major battles of the war before both sides had retreated to their respective fronts and the entire war into the stalemate. How many knocks had happened after the final battle?

Tessa answered the door and appeared in the parlor. "It's the sheriff," she said and twisted her cap in her hands. "He says he has some questions for Miss Fiona about—"

"Yes, about the infernal ball," Margie finished with a sniff. "I know, I've heard enough about it."

"No, ma'am," Tessa said, then gave Fiona a regretful look. "About something that happened this afternoon."

Fiona's stomach clenched, and she went cold from the inside out. Her hand went to her pocket where she'd kept the zap gun. Anyone in the Tinkerer's Guild would have been able to point to her as the owner and inventor of the device.

"She'll see him in here," Margie said. "With me present."

"Yes, ma'am." Tessa curtsied and dashed out, soon to return followed by Blair. He carried something wrapped in brown paper, and Fiona feared it was the correct size for her zap gun. Was it covered in the man's blood? Or, worst horror, was she? She glanced down at her skirts to see if any incriminating red stained the hem, but thankfully—for once—the only spots and smears came from what one would expect for a muddy street in the middle of winter in Terminus.

"Afternoon, Missus Telfair. Miss Telfair." Blair took his hat off. His balding head reflected the watery sunlight.

"Good afternoon, Sheriff Blair," Margie said and held out a hand. "Please forgive me, but I'm too distraught over the disappearance of my husband to stand. My knees simply won't have it. Please tell me you've made some progress in finding him and the others."

Blair wiped his head with a white handkerchief that had seen cleaner days. "No, ma'am, but it's still early. My best men are on it. In fact, they've found a suspect in an alley near the airfields."

"Oh, thank goodness!" Margie clasped her hands. "I'm sure he will give you all the information you need."

Blair shook his head. "Can't get information from a dead man, ma'am." He looked at Fiona. "That's what I need to talk to your daughter about."

"What in the world would my Fiona have to do with a dead kidnapper?"

Fiona had to give her mother credit—she played the incredulous woman perfectly. She tended to forget that her mother had been an actress before she'd married Fiona's father. The thought of her father made Fiona's chest tighten.

"Well, that's what I'm hoping she'll be able to tell me," Blair drawled. He unwrapped the package he held. "Does this look familiar?"

It was Fiona's zap gun. The wires had been wrapped around it, not drawn back into it, and the grime they'd lain in made reddish-brown streaks on the paper. The metallic smell of blood wafted through the air, and Fiona fought to not gag as the sense of danger—and indignation—returned. She wanted to tell Blair off. How dare he come in here and confront her like some criminal when she'd only been defending her virtue? Oh, and by the way, when she'd gotten closer to catching one of the kidnappers than Blair and his incompetent men.

But she didn't get the chance to speak. Margie leaned over, wrinkled her nose, and said, "Yes, that's Fiona's, but she told me she lost it last week. Didn't you, darling?"

Fiona didn't have to force the tears out. She was so shocked, they immediately came to her eyes. "I was so upset to have lost it," she said, which wasn't a lie, since she had been.

Margie nodded, encouraging Fiona in her sin of omission. She'd have to add that to her confession list. Both of them would.

"It's one of my favorite devices," Fiona told Blair and wiped her cheeks with her hands as more tears slid out. "I had been working to perfect it. You see, it doesn't do much for defense other than shock the attacker rather than actually harming them." For that, someone would need a pistol like the woman in uniform had had.

Blair sighed and wrapped it back up. "Well, it's covered in filth, so I'll just take it with me and dispose of it for you."

"If you're interested in the design, we'll sell the rights to the department once Bryan has returned." Margie gave Fiona a shrewd glance that stifled Fiona's objection, which teetered at the edge of her tongue.

"I'll consider that, Ma'am. Thank you."

"It would be a good way for women to defend themselves.

The streets aren't safe with all the newcomers, you know." Margie looked to the left and right as though criminals lurked in the corners of the parlor, waiting to pounce. "Especially all those Yankees coming down seeking opportunity, vultures circling our phoenix trying to rise from the ashes of the war."

Fiona was pretty sure a phoenix could take out a few vultures, but she again decided to hold her tongue, as difficult as that was. She could only stand there and watch, incredulous, as her mother charmed Blair into leaving before he'd had any tea. Which was a good thing since they didn't have much left, having given Devon Meriweather most of the leaves during his visit. Fiona had enjoyed her cup of mostly strong tea, or at least stronger than the tea-water they'd been drinking.

Once Blair had been shown out, Margie turned to Fiona.

*Uh oh, here it comes.*

Sure enough, Margie narrowed her eyes, put her hands on her hips, and fixed Fiona with the stare Fiona had come to associate with a tongue lashing. She cringed.

"I don't know what you're up to, young lady, but whatever it is, it has to stop. The police have enough on their plate without you going and messing things up."

"Do you think I killed someone?" Fiona asked, horrified that her mother was more concerned for what Fiona had done than for the dead man.

"Of course not. You're not a killer. Anyone who looks at you can see that. But you have to be more careful with your toys."

"Toys? That's a legitimate weapon."

"That can only shock people." Margie huffed. "Your father was so proud of you for inventing it, but he assured me you wouldn't be able to truly harm anyone. That it was just to stun so you could run away." Then she paused as though an idea had hit her. "You are all right, aren't you? Did that man hurt you?"

Fiona took a deep breath. "No, but thank you for asking. I was able to get away."

"Good, so your device worked. Something else must have killed him."

She waved a hand, and Fiona marveled at how her mother could hang on tightly to her own version of reality, the one where there was no room for her daughter to seriously hurt anyone. Fiona didn't want to hurt people, but perversely she wanted her mother to appreciate that she could pose a threat if she wanted to.

"Wait—who was chaperoning you?" Margie asked and glared between Fiona and Tessa, who rushed to straighten up some cushions. Tessa sent Fiona a frightened look.

Fiona swallowed. "No one."

"No one? Do you not care about your reputation? *Our* reputation? That's it." Margie stood and stomped her foot, an affectation that had held over from when she needed to make a point on the stage. "You will not be allowed to leave the house without an escort whom I approve of. And Tessa has enough to do."

Fiona sank to the chair beside her. "But then how can I manage to find Papa? You know the police aren't capable of it."

Margie again dismissed Fiona's concerns with a wave.

"The police are working on it, dear."

"Like they worked on Connor's death," Fiona muttered.

Margie's slap came so quickly that Fiona couldn't duck.

"Don't say that. He was killed in battle."

"Right." Fiona stood and rubbed her cheek. "He was killed in battle," She repeated dully, the family's mantra that protected her perfect brother's reputation from sullying. She moved toward the door.

"Where are you going?"

"To my room. Like a good child. Don't worry, I don't expect any supper."

Margie winced, and guild twinged in Fiona's gut. They didn't have much to eat, anyway. Perhaps the gnawing in her stomach would keep her from being too upset about her father and the progress—or lack thereof—that the police seemed to be making.

She trudged up to her room, and there again stood the small nutcracker doll.

"Not today, you little..." Once again, insults failed Fiona. But she didn't faint. She picked up the doll, and her hand tingled like it had when her father had shown her an experiment with static electricity. She set the nutcracker down and watched it for a few minutes, but when it didn't do anything, she examined it, ignoring the strange feeling in her hands.

Although money was scarce, including for lamp oil, she lit her lamp and let out the wick as far as it would go to make the room as bright as possible. She took the doll to her small workbench, which her father had insisted she have in her room over her mother's objections. Fiona didn't care, and neither did her father.

"Oh, Papa," she whispered and put the doll down so she could wipe the tears that had leaked from her eyes again. "Where are you? Are you safe? Why did they take you?" She turned back to the doll. "And why did someone leave this?" Had it been the man she'd followed? Had he been following *her*? The thought sent a cold shiver, like a raindrop in one's collar, down her spine. She needed to be more aware of her surroundings, a familiar self-scold. But why would he? Were they rounding up people who had somehow escaped from the party? To do what, give them dolls?

She shook her head. None of it made sense, but she dreaded to think what someone could do with all the brainpower and creativity they now had at their disposal. And since the man in the white pants had been a man and not a machine, she now questioned her memory of the ones she'd seen at the party. They hadn't moved like machines, as she'd told Devon. Now that she'd seen one, she was convinced that they had been men in masks whose clothing had been coated with some sort of reflective material to make them stiff and seem like painted wood.

She turned the doll over. Aside from the glowing eyes, she found it to be a rather normal nutcracker doll, designed more for decoration than for cracking nuts. No little warrior here as in the legend. Not that she feared it would battle any mice or whisk her away to a magical place made of candy.

Candy. Her stomach growled. What were they to do about food? She hated to do it, but she would have to ask Lucy Lillet if she could sneak her some from their pantry. Fiona wished she were more practical, or her mother more industrious, to have canned and put away some of the food from their summer garden. Not that they'd gotten much from it. It had been a rainy summer, and many of their vegetables had rotted or split.

Back to the doll. She grabbed her smallest screwdriver and unscrewed the tiny fastenings, then pried the thing apart to find a minuscule aether stabilizing and frequency system inside. A magnet battery powered a wheel that didn't seem to do anything to the glass globe that contained stabilized aether. Ah, right, the little magnet fed a frequency to the aether with the speed of the spinning. Ingenious, really.

When Fiona stopped the magnet, the aether turned from golden to its typical opalescent color, and she could barely make out its ouroboros shape, a tiny opal snake biting its own tail and writhing. But what was the purpose of the aether other than to make the little man have creepy glowing eyes?

She shook her head again. She'd reassemble it in the morning, but she wished she'd thought to count the frequency of the turns before stopping the magnet battery's wheel. Oh, well—it had been turning too fast for her to see. She'd try to see if she could get it to spin at the proper frequency to make the aether peach-gold again. There was something about that frequency, but she couldn't remember what. Her father had the paper.

She continued to think about the puzzle as she undressed, hung her dress up for Tessa to try to clean in the morning, and went to bed. She darted under the covers as soon as she'd put on her nightdress due to the chill in the air.

She didn't think she would, but she fell asleep right away and dreamed that she was a mouse racing around and exploring her room from an interesting new and tiny perspective. The dream was so vivid she could even smell the muck and dirt on the hem of her dress, which now looked monochromatic with her limited vision. She'd even found a piece of bread, a leftover from the small sandwich she'd eaten the day of the ball, under her workbench. The crust had been small enough to hide behind one of the legs, but to her mouse self, it felt like a feast.

And then when Tessa came in to wake her, Fiona stretched, her nightdress somehow on backward.

**12**

---

T*erminus, 19 December 1871*

Devon sat at his desk after breakfast and pondered his legacy. Dinner the night before and breakfast had been the same as always with the cousins bickering as only old friends could, and Pierce's dark mood seemed to have lifted. Devon had asked him to accompany him to the office after breakfast, but Pierce said he had an errand to run and would come see him later. Devon had wanted to make sure Pierce was in a better frame of mind before he told him that the little clockwork had been stolen.

Meanwhile, Devon had alerted the servants that there had been an intruder in the house. He asked about the odd door in the basement, but either they didn't know anything about it or didn't want to discuss it. Finally, one of the valets who had been with the house when they'd acquired it had said he remembered something about a secret passage. Then, when pressed, he'd admitted that he and his wife had helped people through it as part of the Underground Railroad, the former owners of the plantation having been sympathetic to the plight of the slaves. Once the war was over and movement was allowed between the Southern and Northern states again, the previous owners had sold the house and moved away from the bad memories, including that of their own son's death. Devon couldn't blame them. He still couldn't go to the airfield where his parents had been killed in a fiery crash.

And there went his thoughts in directions he didn't need for them to go. He checked the time—9:45. Layla Bollington would be there at ten, and at eleven he'd be meeting with Pierce and would introduce him to Henry Davidson.

Crenshaw showed Layla in right on time and brought Devon some coffee.

"Thank you." He looked at Crenshaw inquisitively, and the older man shook his head. Good. Devon didn't want the temptation of the laudanum although the damp weather made his ankle ache. Why wouldn't the damn thing heal? Well, scuffling with a stranger in the basement had likely not helped.

Crenshaw offered Layla Bollington some coffee, but she declined. Finally, when she was alone with Devon—a privilege afforded to female journalists, but not other women—she took out her pad and smiled. Devon knew that look. Women wore it when they thought they had him at a disadvantage.

"Tell me what you remember about the party."

"It's pretty much as you described it in the article in yesterday's paper," he said. "Nicely done, by the way. The servants?"

She didn't look down demurely as other women would have at the compliment. "Thank you. And yes, the poor and service class are often the most overlooked but best witnesses. Some of them said you tried to help them."

Now Devon's cheeks heated, although he wasn't sure why. Perhaps an angry memory at the firemen's initial refusal to help them. "Yes. It seemed they were being overlooked, as you said. I'm sure they saw much more than we." In fact, he wanted to know what.

"Right, but I want *your* impressions. What I wrote was an aggregate, not a single eyewitness account." She shrugged. "I feel it's fair to say this to you since you have a sympathetic ear and heart to them. People are interested in what the rich and powerful have to say, not the poor and non-influential."

Devon nodded and identified the source of his earlier blush—he was one of those readers who looked for the name, the headline trumpeting the opinion of someone who others listened to because they had money. And he was comfortable, but he didn't think he could play in their league.

Or—remembering Jim Blair's proposition—could he? A wife of some influence would help.

And here he was pondering his ambitions again. Had it been only himself he was responsible for, it wouldn't matter so much, but he needed to make sure Pierce and Therese were taken care of. And so far Therese hadn't shown the slightest inclination toward marriage.

"So, Mister Meriweather..." Bollington called him back to the moment. "Tell me about the party. When did you arrive?"

"At around seven o'clock. Pierce, my cousin, and I were two of the first to get there. We spoke to the Guild officers and then made the rounds, looking at the decorations and mingling." During that time he'd noticed Fiona and her father walk in, she dressed charmingly as a mouse and he as a cat.

"Which costumes did you notice?" she prompted. "I imagine the tinkerers came up with some creative ones. And were you wearing one?"

"No, sadly. Pierce is a member of the Guild and had secured an invitation for me, but I wasn't sure if I was going to go. My ankle has been bothering me since I sprained it in France."

She nodded. "That sounds like a story for a different time. I hope it doesn't pain you too much."

He shrugged, and the offending joint gave a throb. "It depends on the day and the weather, I suppose. I haven't found a doctor I trust to look at it here. The one in France said to keep it wrapped and to elevate it, but I re-injured it by walking on the rolling boat deck on our journey back to the States." The weather hadn't been great at sea, but he couldn't stay cooped up in the cabin. "But yes, that's a story for another day, and not a terribly interesting one."

"Costumes?" Bollington prompted. She'd arched one eyebrow.

"There were some elements. A few people dressed as famous inventors. A dueling Tesla and Edison—those were my favorites." His favorite had actually been Fiona-mouse, but he didn't want to say so. She'd drawn enough attention from Jim Blair that he didn't want to bring her into the spotlight again. But she'd looked so adorable and sweet he had to approach her.

Bollington's lips lifted in a small smile. "Did they duel?"

"No, they behaved."

Her expression turned serious. "And then the trouble started. What did you see and do? What did you first notice?"

Devon took a moment to collect his thoughts, and he shivered like the heat had left his body through the conduit of his spine. "I heard a roaring sound, and the lamps on the walls rotated, spewing flames sideways."

"That's quite a trick."

"I believe they'd been constructed to be either vertical single flame or horizontal dual-flame lamps, but they shouldn't have been able to spew fire like that. Did any of the servants say anything?"

"Only that some of the guild members had been talking about special effects they wanted to rig up for the party, but nothing like that. It sounds like they got too enthusiastic with their flames."

"Yes, the lamps caught curtains and picture frames on fire. People panicked, rushing toward the exit, but they were blocked." He swallowed, still questioning his memory. "By giant nutcracker dolls. But they moved like no automatons I've ever seen. Typically machines like that are slow, clunky almost. Even the more advanced ones lack a smoothness in their movements that humans have. These were too real to be machines."

"So you think they were humans in costume?"

"Possibly. And they were fast. They rounded up partygoers like a well-trained military unit. Thankfully one of the guests knew of a secret entrance behind the punch table that the servants used to refill refreshments, and some of us escaped that way. I also alerted the kitchen about what was going on." He looked at Bollington, who furiously scribbled notes. "Were any of the servants taken?"

"Yes. A man named Hollowell, who worked for Thaddeus Devine, and two upstairs maids." She pressed her lips together in a line.

"Right, Pierce and I talked to their father and husband." Devon couldn't believe someone would be so cruel as to take a child. Well, he could, but he didn't want to. He'd learned on his travels that there was no end to human cruelty, but having it so close to his experience always made him feel like he stood just on the other side of an inferno of ice waiting to swallow all those who looked on it in despair.

"Thankfully the fire brigade doused the flames in the ballroom quickly," Layla said, "Sparing the servants who were hiding in other parts of the house. Tinkerers aren't stupid— they built their building to not burn quickly in case experiments went awry."

Devon could appreciate the wisdom in that. "So there were no deaths?"

"No, assuming that all those taken are still alive."

That was a big assumption. Would the kidnappers pick off the least important and influential to make the others work harder? "Do you have a list of those who were kidnapped?" Devon asked.

"As you can imagine, Jim Blair has not been terribly helpful with my investigation." Bollington flipped her notebook closed. "I have a preliminary list based on some interviews I've done. If you could add to it, I'd be much obliged."

"I'll try, but as I said, I'm not a member. I can talk to someone who is, though."

"And who wasn't taken? Some escaped, but I haven't managed to track them all down."

"There was a group on the lawn after the party, some who had escaped the ballroom and some who had arrived late and who hadn't gone in yet when all the trouble started."

"Do you have names?"

Devon hesitated, again not wishing to give Fiona up. He would leave that up to her. "I'll speak with my contact and let you know if they'll talk to you."

"Fair enough. I can understand how some people may not want to have their name in the press. And at the same time how others crave it."

Devon arched his eyebrow now. Was she insulting him? Or teasing him?

Her grin lit her face. "Obviously not you. I asked you for this interview."

"Right." He felt foolish, but something about the woman threw him off. He hadn't heard of her pursuing marriage, but then, many professional women—those who had stepped in when the supply of men went to the front and dwindled—didn't. They liked their freedom.

"Thank you for your time, Mister Meriwether. You can reach me through..." She paused and blinked, then recovered. "I'll leave you a card. You can reach me at the paper, but I'll check in with you if I haven't heard from you in the next few days."

"I'll talk to my contact today." In fact, he realized he hadn't yet heard from Fiona. He'd thought she was going to talk to her friends who'd arrived late and who had taken her home, and they had agreed to exchange information.

"Perfect. I look forward to hearing from you."

They both stood, and Devon bowed as she curtsied. As if he'd been listening—and indeed, he might have been—Crenshaw opened the door for her and showed her out.

His and Layla Bollington's conversation prompted Devon to ponder which of his servants he'd overlooked and who may have seen or heard something interesting. Again, what trouble had he overlooked in his household?

AFTER HIS INTERVIEW with Layla Bollington, Devon turned his attention to the documents on his desk. Contracts, proposals, agreements... The letters of the business swam before his eyes, and a headache threatened to bloom behind his right temple. He recalled a conversation he'd had with his father soon before his parents had taken their last airship flight, the one that had ended in flames and disaster. It seemed that fire and loss followed him everywhere, although it had been a miracle that no one had died at Tinkerer Hall.

"Devon, son, you need to ponder your legacy." Arnold Meriweather had stood behind this desk, and Devon in front of it. Pierce had just left for university to study engineering, and Devon had stayed behind to learn the business. He'd missed his cousin, who had been like a brother to him since Pierce's parents had been killed by a yellow fever epidemic when the two of them were twelve.

"My legacy?" Devon had gestured around the office, which was lined with books and pictures of various ships and trains, all part of Meriweather Shipping Enterprises.

"Yes, your legacy goes beyond all this. These are objects and money. When I die, they'll pass to you if you want them. But I sometimes wonder if I've made a damn bit of difference in the world." Arnold had been in a strangely pensive state of mind. With the war looming on the horizon, they'd all been pondering their fates and the future. "If we go to war, and that's looking more and more like *when* we go to war, our family will be on the wrong side of the battle for this part of the country. You know this."

"Yes." Devon had hated the idea of leaving their townhouse in Terminus, which he'd grown up in. His parents had never tried to buy a bigger estate, his father being more interested in reinvesting in the business. Not that they'd wanted for anything, but they'd all come up with a disdain for the material. Well, besides Pierce. His father had been a notorious spendthrift, which was why the family had been in Florida when the fever had hit. Tamany Meriweather's latest aim to make money had been land speculation, and they'd been touring the area.

Pierce had always liked the nicest clothing and had bought the newest steamcart. His father had left him a little money, and Arnold and Pierce had had some arguments about how much of it would be left for Pierce's education. Apparently enough if he was going to be educated at Harvard.

Meanwhile, Devon had been stuck in Terminus, although it seemed more and more likely he would be shipped away soon, and his father was babbling on about legacy and making a difference. What sort of difference could one make when there was a war about to start and everything they'd worked for could be confiscated or destroyed?

"So I want you to join the foreign service," Arnold had told him. "I've already secured you a spot to go to France."

"But I don't want to go to France. I want to stay here. With you. And Mother and Therese."

"Your mother and Therese will be going with you." Arnold

had pulled a drawer open and extracted an envelope. "Here. Look through these."

Devon had looked at the stack of papers. One had been a letter of acceptance for him to attend Foreign Service Academy in New York before being stationed in Paris. The other had been a deed to a townhouse in a small town in the French countryside. There had been others, but Devon had shaken his head.

"I can't go. I can't abandon my country."

"You'll be doing what you can for it by spreading the word that the North is on the right side of the war and the South is in the wrong. Think of the enslaved peoples. This is really a fight over what happens to them."

Devon had nodded. "Is that my legacy, then? To become a glorified public relations person while my friends die?"

"No, your legacy is to be your choice after it's all over. Come now, you know the Northern States have superior weapons and the moral right. This conflict shouldn't last more than a year, two at most. But you can't define your legacy if you're not alive to do so."

Devon thought back to his father's words, now more than a decade later. He'd done as his father had asked, and had it not been for Therese, he might have backed out and decided to enlist as a soldier after all. And many of his friends had died or come back from the conflict badly injured. The fact that he'd been away and not actively fighting against the Southern States had given him some entree back into Southern society, even if they considered him cowardly. Every time he heard someone talk about the glory days before the war, he wanted to retch.

But what was his legacy to be? At first, when he'd rejoined Pierce at this monstrosity of a house, he thought he'd be buried in paperwork—a legacy of papercuts. His eyes stung from studying the documents and organizing them for hours each day. Admittedly the piles had shrunk, but they seemed to grow again overnight when no one was looking.

He rubbed his eyes. At least Pierce seemed to have done well with the family coffers during Devon's absence, even with the war raging around Terminus and trade disrupted through it.

Pierce knocked on the door and entered without waiting for Devon to invite him in. Devon caught the sharp response to his cousin's invasion before it could leave his mouth. Pierce had been in enough of a mood that there was no point in making it worse. Besides, Devon needed to give him the bad news.

"Have you looked at the clockwork we found lately?" Devon asked.

"No." Pierce frowned. "Damn thing seems to have reassembled itself and crawled off."

"Or someone took it."

Pierce's frown deepened. "Took it? How? No one can get into the basement laboratory besides us."

Devon told him about the intruder from the day before, and Pierce cursed. Devon found himself to be relieved at Pierce's surprise.

"Did you know there's a door to a secret passage down there?" Devon finished.

"Yes, but I can't for the life of me figure out how to get it open. But this person did?"

Devon nodded.

Pierce rubbed his eyes. "I'll ask the servants again, but the ones who came with the house didn't know anything about it." He shot a sideways glance at Devon. "They may tell you, though. They like you better."

Devon frowned. "That's ridiculous. Of course they like you."

"No, I'm not Mister Popular like you are. I don't have your charm, your fortune, your..." He waved his hands. "*Je ne sais quoi.*' I also don't have proud papas who swore they wouldn't have anything to do with traitor families who fled to the wrong side during the war throwing their daughters at me."

Now Devon's eyebrows reversed direction in surprise. "How did you hear about that?"

Pierce smiled, but like he knew a secret. "I may not know about where to find the key for the secret passage in the basement, but I do know how sound carries in the house. Tell me, are you at all interested in Miss Blair?"

Devon leaned back. "No. You want a shot at her?"

Pierce shook his head, his nose wrinkled. "Can you imagine having to sit across from him on Sundays and holidays? No, no thank you. I'll take my chances with your sister. At least I know the company will be good."

Devon released the tension that had gathered in his belly at Pierce's attempt at humor. If he was joking, he was in a better mood. Sometimes Devon felt like he didn't know his cousin anymore. He'd become mercurial at times, and at others, maintained the same humor as he had before. Or perhaps Devon hadn't ever known him.

"Again, the decision is hers." But would Therese ever say yes or no to Pierce? Wouldn't it be fairer to cut him loose? He made a mental note to talk to Therese about it soon so Pierce could set his romantic sights on someone else. Devon hated to see his cousin unhappy, and in truth, having the affair settled either way would release some of the tension in the household.

"You know what you need to do?" Pierce asked.

"What?" Devon grinned. "Let me have your advice, o expert on women and society."

"Remember, dear cousin, I've been here longer than you since the war ended. These people are hungry for things to be as they were before. It's the holiday season, and you know what would make things better? A ball."

"A ball." Devon's stomach sank like a stone through water,

landing with a thud somewhere around his pelvis. "Where? Here?"

"Yes, you know they've been dying with curiosity to see the house since we've moved in." Pierce looked around, his nose wrinkled. "Not that we've done much to it other than bring in our furniture. But yes, a ball."

Devon nodded, the plans spinning in his mind and weaving themselves into a coherent whole. "Mamas could bring their eligible daughters, and proud papas could come and discuss business in drawing rooms. I could make sure to have eyes and ears everywhere."

"Now you're getting it." Pierce clapped him on the back. "The servants like you, as I said. They'll be happy to report whatever they happen to overhear. Stupid former Confederates still haven't learned that they have eyes and ears...and mouths that pass along information."

"Right." Devon recognized he shouldn't want to spy on his guests, but if it would give him an edge in knowing what deals to pursue and who was open to doing business with him—and which marriage would be more advantageous—it could be worth it.

"Brilliant. I'll work on a list, and I'll bring it to you for approval and additions. I've already got some ideas."

"Thank you." Again, Devon thanked whichever divine being had arranged for his cousin to have the inventive head and the connections in the community, and that Pierce was on his side. And whatever Pierce thought, he wasn't at all unpopular among the gentlemen of the society. Together they made a good team.

"Plus it will help to move the community past the disaster of the Tinkerer's Ball." Pierce shuddered. "The sight of those automatons..."

"Do you think they were truly machines?" Devon asked. "They moved so smoothly."

Pierce considered the question for a moment. "You're right, I should have thought of that. No, they seemed to be more human than machine. So unless someone has gotten very clever, I don't think they were automatons. But that clockwork still indicates we're dealing with a dashedly clever inventor."

"That we are. So we should still proceed with caution. Do you know of anyone with that sort of talent? Whether in the Guild or not."

Again, Pierce paused, his brows drawn together in thought. "I'll have to get back to you on that. There are a few possibilities, but they were in attendance. Not that that means anything."

"Right." Devon stopped speaking and moving, hoping Pierce would get the hint and leave him to his papers.

Finally, Pierce did.

"All right, I'll put that list together for you and then ponder clever tinkerers. Anything else?"

"No, but thank you."

With a nod, Pierce left. Devon turned back to his papers, grinning at the idea of a ball. Not that he could marry her, but he imagined Fiona Telfair smiling when she got the invitation. Or should he invite her? Blair had warned him away from the family, after all. But her father had been taken, and he did need her cooperation in his own investigation into the kidnappings.

Speaking of whom, he needed to give her an update. He dashed off a quick note and asked Crenshaw to send a boy to the Telfair townhouse to ask Fiona to come 'round to lunch with him and Therese. He had no doubt his sister and Fiona would get on well, as similar as they were in temperament and interest. He ignored the nagging voice in his head that said *his* interests aligned quite well with Fiona's, too, and he would be particularly interested in exploring their connection further.

"Wife with money and connections, wife with money and connections," he murmured to himself, but the words had begun to sound hollow. Then he heard Therese's cough—she seemed to have worsened again with the return of the cool weather—and his resolve strengthened.

When Crenshaw came to get the note, he informed Devon that Henry Davidson's team had arrived.

## 13

---

*erminus, 19 December 1871*

The crust she'd found during her mouse dream seemed to hold Fiona, and she watched as her mother ate the last of their bread with the tail end of the preserves in the jar.

"Are you sure you're not hungry?" Margie asked for the tenth time. "You don't need to be any thinner. You'll never catch a husband if you're too skinny."

Fiona shook her head. She couldn't tell her mother she'd dreamed her hunger away, so she simply said, "I'm still upset over Sheriff Blair's visit. Imagine thinking that I could have killed someone." She shuddered visibly, which didn't take too much effort, as the memory of what had happened still disturbed her. "Excuse me, I feel as though I could faint at the thought."

"Yes, go lie down if you need to. But don't forget to practice your violin. A young lady must keep up her skills, and I let you off yesterday since you'd had such a rough day."

Of course her father's place sat empty, glaringly so.

"Have you heard anything from the police?" Fiona asked. "Any news?"

"No, but I'm sure they're working very hard on it." Margie's eyes grew hard. "Now go either lie down or play the violin. I won't tolerate any more impertinence from you."

"Yes, Mother."

Fiona went up to her room and found her violin. The family hadn't been able to afford a piano, but her father had brought the instrument over from Ireland and taught her to play, mostly reels, folk songs, and other things proper young ladies shouldn't know. Fiona caressed the wood. She loved classical music, and she dreamed of playing the scandalous melodies of contemporary composers like Brahms and Berlioz, but she would always find comfort in her father's home's songs. What would Ireland, where red hair would be the norm rather than a novelty, be like? She'd heard there were pockets of Irish people in Georgia in the mountains north of the city, but her mother would never allow her to go visit them. Yet another area where Fiona's curiosity outstripped her ability to go explore it. Damn womanhood.

Thinking the curse word made her feel better, and Fiona went into a melody she'd never heard before, something simultaneously plaintive and angry, but with the technical complication of an elegant clockwork.

"Fee-OH-na!" Sniff. "Stick with the melodies you're supposed to play."

Of course her mother wouldn't let her have that, either. She'd once upon a time encouraged Fiona in her composition, but after Connor had died...

Fiona remembered when the sergeant had brought the news. She'd been in her room practicing, as she was now, but playing her own variations on a theme by Mozart. There had been a knock, and somehow Fiona knew that it was bad news. Something about the sound had echoed through her soul, three raps that brought her farther away from the life she'd known, the comfortable familiarity of her brother being gone but still somewhere, his homecoming assured.

She'd put her violin down and listened with her entire body, praying it wasn't what she thought. But when she'd heard her mother's wail, she knew what it was, that life had ceased to be the same and that no one she loved was safe. She'd placed her violin and bow in the case as though by putting them in their proper place she could put her entire life back where it should be. She'd then opened the door and crept down the stairs.

The young man who had brought the news had stood in the parlor and twisted his hat in his hands. He hadn't worn a uniform, but a brown suit that looked like it had belonged to an older and slightly larger brother. None of the Union soldiers who braved the journey South to bring families the news dared to wear their uniforms, but something about how they carried themselves allowed Fiona to spot them. She simultaneously hated to see him but was also relieved that there wouldn't be any ambiguity like there could possibly be with a letter or telegram, both of which could have been intercepted. As far as their neighbors knew, Connor had been at University and had been unreachable to the Southern States' increasingly insistent attempts to conscript him into the Confederate army.

Of course later, they'd found out that Connor hadn't been killed in battle, but rather had ended his life at the hands of a jealous husband. Then the leash had tightened on Fiona to a stifling degree, and it was only through her father's intercession that she'd been allowed to leave the house at all. And now she didn't even have that.

"Where are you, Papa?" she whispered beneath the music, a minuet by Strauss that was on her mother's approved list. Fiona hated Strauss, but she could admit to herself that part of the reason was that she'd never been asked to waltz, not even by the boys at the Tinkerer's Guild, what few of them were left. She wished she didn't care, but she did. She'd learned her lessons too well—her brother, the favorite child, had failed to live an honorable life. Fiona, the less favored one, had no chance at redemption except to catch a husband. And none of them had wanted her, which hadn't surprised her mother at all. Too skinny, too tall, too smart... her *toos* went on and on.

When Fiona put the bow down, she had to wipe tears off the instrument. Too weepy. She wished Connor was still alive. He'd be home by now and taking the attention and pressure off her. But he'd sacrificed her welfare for his selfishness, and his footsteps wouldn't sound through the house again. And it was up to Fiona to get her father back.

She needed to talk to Devon, to tell him about the previous day's events. And see if he knew where there may still be green grass growing. All she'd seen was brown and dry and unhappy with the winter.

She summoned Tessa and penned a quick note to Devon to please come call on her. Then she sent Tessa off to give the note with a penny to a boy to take it for her. While she waited for a reply, she freshened up and was surprised when Tessa returned quicker than anticipated.

"A different boy brought a message for you, Miss. Devon Meriweather has invited you to his estate to have lunch with him and his sister." Tessa dropped her voice. "Your mother is in a right tizzy about it, particularly since she wasn't invited. She said I'm to go with you to chaperon."

"Very well." Fiona straightened. The part about the sister was for propriety's sake, she was sure. Devon had made his intentions quite clear—their alliance was to be professional to secure the tinkerers' return, nothing more. But she couldn't help a thrill of excitement at the thought of an intimate lunch with him and his sister.

. . .

After breakfast in the kitchen with the servants, Henry made his way out of the house and back to the former slave quarters, which the Meriweathers had gutted and refurbished as a workshop and guest quarters for visiting artisans. Crenshaw, who had greeted Henry upon his arrival, had said that Devon wanted someplace close by for special projects, and that the basement laboratory wouldn't be big enough for the ideas he had. After meeting Devon, Henry wondered if the young man had any fixed ideas or acted on hope and instinct. Henry hoped for the former.

His team's train had been scheduled to arrive at ten past nine, and indeed, he found them unloading when he walked up to them. Two Negroes stood at the ready, but they didn't do anything.

"They said they'd handle it, Sir," one of them told Henry.

"Thank you," Henry replied, "but we won't require any assistance."

Indeed, Patrick O'Connell and Edward Bailey lifted and moved crates from the first wagon. Likely they wanted to handle the materials for their workshop themselves. Johann Bledsoe and Chadwick Radcliffe went back and forth with luggage, and Henry heard Iris Bailey inside giving instructions with the occasional comment from Claire Radcliffe. Chadwick and Claire would move on to their clinic later.

Devon, noticeably limping, huffed down the drive, and Henry waved to him.

"Who have we here?" Devon asked when he arrived at Henry's side. Henry called the team.

"Mister Devon Meriweather, please allow me to introduce my associates. First, renowned aetherist Edward Bailey." Henry gestured to the lanky scientist, whose dark blue eyes looked Devon over with curiosity.

"It's an honor," Devon said and shook Edward's hand. "My

cousin Pierce will be excited to meet you. He's grown very interested in aetherics lately."

Henry filed that away for future reference. He gestured to the petite blonde woman beside Edward. "And this is Mrs. Iris Bailey, archaeologist."

Devon nodded to her and said, "I'm charmed to make your acquaintance, ma'am."

Henry continued down the line. "The tall redheaded fellow is Patrick O'Connell, tinkerer extraordinaire."

"Welcome. Pierce will be excited to see you as well. Is that Claire McPhee?" Devon asked. "The two inventors of La Reine here? This is truly an honor."

"Yes," Henry said as Claire blushed as redheads do when suddenly the focus of attention. "And the gentleman beside her is her husband."

"I'm Claire Radcliffe now," she said. "This is Chadwick. We're physicians." She emphasized the last word. Henry hoped Devon would take the hint—she didn't want to be associated with war, but with healing.

"And finally, the blond fellow is musician Johann Bledsoe."

"Please to meet you all." Devon shook each man's hand and nodded to the women. "I'm glad you're here, especially you Maestro Bledsoe, in light of what I've decided this morning. We'll be holding a holiday ball on Saturday, and it would greatly honor me if you were to play for us."

Henry wanted to ask if that was wise considering what had just happened at the Tinkerer's Ball, but he kept his mouth shut. His directive had been to investigate, not influence. And perhaps it would flush out some of the villains, although this group of attendees would be different. And it would be a good chance to test out his team.

"Please give me the guest list once you have it," Henry said. "And the layout, and we'll work on a security plan."

"With interesting devices, I hope," Devon said. Henry caught more than boyish enthusiasm in his tone.

"We'll see," Henry told him. "Team, as you were."

They resumed unloading, and Henry caught Patrick's grumble, "Feel like a fecking dog and pony show." He hoped Devon hadn't heard the Irishman's complaint, but when he turned to Devon, he found the young man had an amused expression.

"Interesting group of professions for a security team," Devon said. "But I won't ask."

"It's probably best you don't. I'm sure you came across odder during your foreign service."

"Yes." But he didn't take Henry's implied invitation to elaborate. "Please let me know if I can give you any more assistance."

"Thank you."

Devon limped back up the drive, and Henry almost offered the assistance of the Doctors Radcliffe but refrained. Investigate, not influence, he reminded himself. But how long would he be able to hold that line?

DEVON THOUGHT he'd seen Layla Bollingon slipping out the servants' entrance. He checked his watch—they'd finished their conversation an hour ago. What was she doing here still? He decided he needed to ask the servants about it. He didn't need someone lurking about, especially not a member of the press. If the person who'd tackled him in the workshop the previous day hadn't been of significantly larger build, he'd suspect Bollington of being the assailant. But she was too tiny. So was she snooping around for stories? He shook his head. There were too many things to think about these days, and he needed to focus on his lunch with Fiona.

Who had trouble talking to him. He shook his head again. He didn't think himself to be so intimidating, but perhaps for someone like Fiona, of modest means, the idea of a rich man paralyzed her tongue. He wished he'd better thought through inviting her to his house. If she'd been flustered in her own home, how much more would she be so here, surrounded by luxury? But he needed to get her away from her mother so they could talk frankly.

He encountered Therese coming out of her suite. Her cheeks looked flushed, and her lips slightly swollen. He'd become so attuned to every nuance of her appearance that each little change stood out like a beacon.

"Are you well, dear sister?" he asked.

"Oh!" She put a hand to her lips, and the color in her cheeks deepened. "Yes, quite well, thank you. Do I not look so?"

"You look feverish," he said and put a hand on her forehead.

She batted it away. "I'm perfectly fine. What can I do for you, dear brother?"

Devon studied her. He didn't know if he believed her, but her eyes were bright, perhaps even sparkling, and her voice strong. "I have invited a young lady for lunch. No, not like that." He added when she put both hands to her mouth, which had formed a surprised and delighted *o*. "She's a professional contact. We're working together on finding the tinkerers, the ones who were kidnapped from the ball."

"Right. The ball. I was thinking I'd like to have another look at that odd device you found," she said. "There was something familiar about it, but I can't tease what from my addled brain."

"Your brain is far from addled," Devon said. "You're smarter than me and Pierce put together. As for the clockwork, it's gone missing." He didn't want to alarm her by telling her about the attack.

"Did it crawl off?" she asked.

"Not exactly. I'll have to tell you later." He pulled her aside into one of the unused drawing rooms, then regretted it when he saw the dust on the surfaces. What would such a mess do to her delicate lungs? He spoke quickly. "The young woman has a strange reaction to me. She seems unable to speak to me when we're together. I'm hoping that having you there will help her be at ease. Please?"

"Are you bringing me into the investigation?" Therese asked.

"Yes, but only as an adviser. I can't risk you being hurt."

She pondered for a moment, then nodded. "I'll see what I can do to help you with your young lady. Whatever did you do to her to make her not want to speak in front of you?"

"I'm afraid I don't know," he confessed. "The first time I met her, I thought I was making charming conversation, but when I thought through it later, I'm afraid I came off as a cad." He thought back but still couldn't understand why she'd initially reacted to him so coolly or why she still couldn't speak to him. "Go and tell her I've been caught up with something important and warm her up."

She crossed her arms and gave him a stern look.

"Right. Please?"

"That's better." She swept out of the room. Devon glanced at his pocket watch. How long would it be permissible to keep Therese and Fiona waiting? He instructed the kitchen to go ahead and start serving lunch, which would hopefully put them further at ease. He guessed from the state of the tea at the Telfair house that food wasn't plentiful. He'd be damned if Fiona went hungry while under his protection. A hungry thinker was a poor thinker, and he needed her mind sharp.

Not that he would be able to do anything for her once she left. He would have to speak with his steward to see what they could work out.

Devon paced the kitchen for ten minutes, then went into the dining room.

**14**

———

Terminus, *19 December 1871*

Fiona and Tessa left the Telfair house at half-past eleven. Thankfully Devon had sent a carriage to collect them in case Fiona should acquiesce to lunch, and she enjoyed watching the scenery pass from inside a relatively warm space. The cool breeze had turned into a sharp wind under leaden clouds, and she suspected it would be one of those winter days that grew colder rather than warmer as it went on. Father had called it a ghost day, a backward weather day. When they'd had money, he would send Tessa or the cook out for cider, and they'd sit in the parlor and laugh and talk in front of a roaring fire.

What would the Meriweather mansion feel like? From what she'd heard, Devon's sister Therese was delicate, so Fiona eagerly anticipated fully built fires and warm food and drink. She was happy Tessa had accompanied her so the maid would be fed as well.

The carriage took them north of downtown along a winding road, and soon the city buildings gave way to estates that grew farther and farther apart and soon disappeared behind gates and trees and other barriers that said *Keep Out, Poor People*. Fiona and Tessa exchanged a grin. They'd often talked about moats and other ways the inhabitants of castles kept others at bay. This was no different, except this time the target had been slave uprisings or, as the war drew to a close, a Yankee invasion.

Once they reached the Meriweather Mansion, which had not been renamed after Pierce Meriweather had bought it, they got out of the carriage and stretched. It had taken them a good three-quarters of an hour to reach it, and Fiona felt far away from home. She noticed that the grass on the expansive lawn was brown like the rest of the stuff in Terminus, which relieved her. Not that she thought Devon or Pierce had anything to do with the automaton men, as she'd started thinking of them, but somehow nothing would surprise her.

A tall, dark-skinned butler let them in and led them to a formal dining room. The walls were hung with a burgundy damask wallpaper above the dark wood chair rail. Under it, wood molding protected the bottom part of the walls from scuffs and other damage. The walls were noticeable for the lack of art or portraiture. Did the Meriweathers like classical art, or did their tastes run to more modern paintings of landscapes with big open skies? Or, as Lucy's cousin Veronica had told them, the strange, electricity and aether-inspired patterns that were all the rage in Europe. Fiona guessed they were still deciding how to decorate.

Indeed, the entire house lacked that certain identity that came with a place's owners. It felt like a rented property, like the Meriweathers only slept there but didn't really *live* there. She'd heard that they'd only bought it that summer, so that would explain it. And if Devon was in the market for a wife, he'd be waiting for her to put her touch on it.

If Fiona were interested in such things, she would be jealous, and she admitted that her mind was doing what it shouldn't—placing art and decorations on the walls and shelves, painting the walls a less somber tone, otherwise turning the dining room into a happy, calming place rather than a red-walled dungeon. But he'd said he had no intention of marrying her, and even if he did, she had no intention of saying yes. There was too much she wanted to do to put herself in a prison, even if she got to decorate it herself.

The butler led Tessa to the kitchen, leaving Fiona to herself with a glass of cordial, which she didn't sip since she'd not eaten since the day before, and that not much. She tried not to resent the difference between her lifestyle and that of the Meriweathers. Getting her father back was a matter of survival for Fiona, but an intellectual exercise for Devon.

The smells that came from the kitchen made her stomach growl, and she caught her thoughts wandering in an impatient direction.

Her feet wandered along with her thoughts, and she found a grate in the floor. It smelled of fresh wood shavings and the tang of oil. The Meriweathers must have been putting in a furnace heating system. She bent to take a closer look and see if she could detect any of the inner workings, but instead of piping, she found voices.

"I don't want you to go," one said, petulant and frustrated. "Our moments together are too few as they are."

Fiona raised her eyebrows. She didn't want to eavesdrop on a private conversation, but the woman's tone drew her in. A lovers' quarrel?

"I have to." Oh! That was another woman. "He'll see me on my way out if I don't go before he leaves his office."

Fiona's eyebrows rose higher. If she wasn't mistaken, the second voice sounded like that of a female Negro journalist she'd heard speak at the Tinkerer Guild's monthly meeting, on the intersection of press and invention in the aftermath of war. That was before people had started disappearing. Fiona had held on to every word, both because of what the woman said and to see if she could glean a hint of what she did to be able to live and act so independently.

And who was the *he* she was talking about?

"Very well," the first voice said. "But come back tomorrow."

"I will. I've given myself a reason to. Your brother is getting some information for me."

Ah, so the first voice must be Therese Meriweather, Devon's sister. What information was he going to find? Did it have something to do with their case?

Kissing sounds floated through, so, cheeks burning, Fiona straightened and wandered back to the sideboard where the bottle of cordial and glasses stood. She didn't need to listen in on lovemaking, but now she had a secret in her pocket— Therese Meriweather was having some sort of affair with the lady journalist. How did she manage it? Surely the pressure on someone of that station to marry would be huge.

A few minutes later, a soft voice asked, "Miss Telfair?"

Fiona whirled around to see a young woman with the same coloring as Devon, mahogany hair and hazel eyes, and a slight spattering of freckles along her nose and cheekbones. The spots were so faint as to hardly be seen, but Fiona noticed freckles, having fought against her own for so long. She'd chosen to wear a nice gray-blue dress with small bustle and white piping along the sleeves and bodice, but the young woman, who must be Therese, put her gown to shame with the elegant simplicity of her copper-colored satin day dress. Who had the money to spend on satin for day clothes? Of course the Meriweathers did.

"Miss Meriweather, I presume?" Fiona said and held out her hand. The other woman took it by the fingertips and gave her a slight squeeze. Fiona wondered what she looked like to Therese. A city mouse come to the home of the cat? Or a fellow young woman striving to live as she pleased?

"Yes, I'm Therese Meriweather. Please pardon my brother for his tardiness. He got caught by a pressing matter." Therese smiled, but Fiona could tell the other woman sized her up. While Therese and she shared slender frames, she could see that Therese's was more due to a delicate constitution than hunger. Right, that's why they'd been in France during the war—the stress and bustle of Terminus had been too wearing for her. Or at least that's what the gossip mill had said.

"I understand. He must be quite busy with everything going on." Fiona wasn't sure what, exactly, she meant by that, but she'd felt the need to say something. She hoped her cheeks weren't so red as to give away her eavesdropping.

Footmen appeared and pulled out two chairs. Four places had been set in total, and Fiona and Therese sat across from each other.

"Devon said for us to start without him. He'll be with us momentarily." Therese smiled, and some of the anxiety in Fiona's chest melted away.

"Thank you. Who is the fourth place set for?"

"Oh." A shadow flickered across Therese's face. "That's for Pierce, should he decide to join us. He often doesn't since he spends much of his time in the city, but we keep a place for him in case he's home for meals."

"That's kind of you." What happened to the fourth portion that wouldn't be eaten? Would the servants get it? The dogs? All large houses like this had dogs, didn't they?

"So Devon tells me that you're a talented tinkerer." Therese murmured her thanks to the footman, who set a plate of orange soup in front of her.

Fiona was so distracted by the savory, earthy smells she almost forgot to answer, but recovered herself. "I'm a tinkerer, yes. I'm not sure how talented I am."

Therese grinned. "Well, don't worry, I'm sure you are. What's your specialty?"

Fiona took a spoonful of the soup and almost allowed her eyes to roll back in bliss. Some sort of squash—pumpkin, maybe?—with warm spices. Perfect for a chilly winter day. She swallowed before she said, "Clockworks, mostly tiny ones for ladies, like brooches, hand sculptures, that sort of thing."

"Brilliant. You must show me your work sometime." Therese lowered her voice. "By the way, the soup is one of our chef's specialties. I'll ask for seconds if you're up for having them."

Fiona nodded. "Thank you."

"And where were you educated?" Therese continued her interrogation in her normal tone. She asked for more soup, and the footmen complied by bringing out two more bowls rather than topping off what they were eating out of. Therese barely touched her second helping while Fiona wolfed hers down. In a perfectly acceptable, ladylike way, of course. She could practically hear her mother behind her admonishing her to make a good impression.

Fiona realized she'd never answered the question. "I had private tutors while—while my brother was with us. Then the war started, and I mostly learned from my father and whoever would let me observe at the Tinkerer's Guild." She had almost said *while we could afford them*. Again, the pendulum of her emotions swung between worry for her father and anger that he'd mismanaged their finances so badly. Fiona was pretty sure she could've had them stick to a budget. At least they wouldn't have spent money on dresses for a coming out that would only end in disaster.

"Sometimes informal educations are the best ones. Ah, there's my brother."

Fiona looked toward the entrance to the dining room from the back of the house, and there stood Devon. She could definitely see the resemblance. Which parent had given them their coloring? She knew better than to ask, both of them being deceased in a tragic manner. But worse, whereas she and Therese had been conversing easily, once Devon walked in, Fiona found herself once again unable to speak. She opened her mouth to greet him, and the only sound that came forth was a mouse-like squeak.

WHEN DEVON ENTERED the dining room, Fiona looked up, smiled when she saw him, and mouthed the word, "Hello," but all that came out was a squeak. Her eyes widened in horror, and her face went pale. When she looked down at her plate, his heart almost broke.

"It's all right," he said and slid into the seat beside Therese's. "We'll get you warmed up talking about technical matters."

Therese cocked her head. "Have you spoken to a neuroticist about that, Dear? They can work miracles with puzzles of the mind, or so I hear."

Fiona shook her head. Devon nudged Therese with his foot to drop that line of questioning. He doubted the Telfairs could afford a regular physician, much less a neuroticist. Perhaps he could enlist Claire Radcliffe's help.

Devon waved away the soup the footman presented to him. "Please bring the next course," he said. He smiled at Fiona. "Our cook does wonders with chicken."

Fiona gave him a small smile, and he saw the tease in her eyes.

Therese said, "I told her the same about the soup. She's going to think our chef is a wizard."

"He is," Devon said. "And his wife is an amazing pastry chef. By the way, Pierce had an interesting idea." He felt himself wading into dangerous waters but couldn't hold his tongue. "He suggested I give a ball to introduce us to the rest of society and to see who's on the marriage mart. For me," he added, seeing Therese's stricken look. "Not for you. You still have a year or two yet, no marriage considerations until you're better."

Therese nodded, seemingly relieved. Fiona grinned and looked down at the lovely brown-crusted chicken with green beans and mashed potatoes that had been set before her, but Devon had the sense that her amusement was not due to the food. What could she possibly know about his household and situation? Not that she could tell him, anyway.

"By the way," he said, "I've come to realize after talking with Pierce that it's impossible that the automatons who committed the kidnappings were machines. The technology just doesn't exist yet, and they moved too smoothly."

"I noticed that as well," Fiona replied. "The joint articulation was simply wrong for machines. Plus, I was attacked by one yesterday."

"What?" both Devon and Therese said. Devon clenched his fist beneath the table so hard that his fingers caught the table-cloth, and his plate shifted. He fought the wave of rage that welled up at the thought of anyone trying to harm Fiona.

"What happened?" Therese asked and put a hand on Devon's other arm. He relaxed slightly. Fiona had come through unharmed, but as she relayed her tale, primarily to Therese, he found his mood darkening again. He wished she'd look at him, but he guessed that if she did, she would clam up again, her words not exactly having anything to do with the technicalities of tinkering.

"Who was the mysterious woman who helped you?" Therese asked.

Devon forced himself to keep listening around the rush that filled his ears at the idea of the filthy things the man had said to Fiona. He admired her frank storytelling and her courage, if it could be called that and not foolhardiness, but he wanted to tell her never ever to put herself at risk again.

"She wore an Airship Corps uniform with trousers," Fiona

said. "She didn't seem afraid at all," she added with admiration. "In fact, she was the one who told me to search the man's cloak and pockets."

"Did you find anything?" Devon asked. He couldn't help it —he couldn't remain silent any longer.

Fiona shook her head. Damn, she'd gone mute again.

"But you said he had on white pants and a uniform like the nutcracker kidnappers," Therese said.

Devon wanted to ask Fiona a million questions about the man who had lured and then insulted her, but he allowed Therese to take the lead so Fiona wouldn't clam up. Why couldn't she talk to him? What had at first been a charming demure characteristic had taken on a sort of hurtful insult quality—perhaps he didn't intimidate her, but rather some part of her considered him beneath her notice. It was not a comfortable thought. Nor was his speculation that perhaps that's what he believed, that her intelligence and simple life put into sharp relief the shallowness of his own marital quest, for money and power, rather than that which mattered.

But Therese mattered, and he needed them to be in a position for her to be taken care of should she decide not to marry. That was the other thing about being with Fiona and watching the two women. He'd known his sister was smart, but he'd underestimated how dashedly clever she could be. So if she had the intelligence to manage a deft interrogation, why wasn't she interested in Pierce? There had to be something beyond Pierce and Devon's similarities that drove her away. He wanted to cast his mind about into the past to find a time when Therese had shown interest in a man, but Fiona's words dropping from her seashell pink lips kept him anchored to the present. Where he needed to be. Because someone was after her, it seemed.

"We need to go to Tinkerer Hall and look for evidence," Devon said finally. "If they're men, one of them may have left something behind."

"Machines may drop parts," Fiona pointed out, apparently once again comfortable talking about technical issues. "Gears fall out, screws loosen themselves, even materials from the costumes themselves. Buttons!" She wrinkled her nose. "They love to come loose, especially the expensive ones."

"I don't trust Jim Blair to have made a thorough search," Devon agreed.

"What about the fire damage?" Therese asked. "Is it structurally sound?"

"Layla Bollington said it wasn't too bad. I'll send a message over to the caretaker and ask," Devon said. "Or, better yet, we'll go over there. At the very least we can investigate the yard."

Fiona nodded. "And perhaps they'll let us climb up the side of the building with a ladder and look at the roof."

"That's quite the climb," Devon pointed out. "The hall is, what, four stories?"

"Yes, bedrooms on top, then workshops on two floors, and then the ballroom."

"Perhaps you should stay behind, Fiona," Devon suggested carefully. "It may not be safe." He also didn't want her to ruin her dress, considering the meagerness of the Telfair means. Although the dress she'd worn the day before had been at the height of fashion, at least from what he could tell.

"Don't be ridiculous," Fiona told him. "You won't be able to tell if anything is missing from the workshops."

Therese cleared her throat. "Do you think any of the other tinkerers will have been by?"

"You mean of the ones who are left?" Fiona asked. "Maybe. I can also check the roster, see if I can figure out who's missing."

"Layla Bollington is helping me to compile just such a list, and your help with that would be invaluable," Devon said, noting for the second time how Therese gave him an interesting look when he mentioned the journalist's name. "Very well, if you're done, we can leave as soon as possible."

"But do come back here for teatime," Therese said with a sly smile. "And tell me what you've found. I dare not go with my lungs as they are."

Devon felt a momentary stab of guilt. He'd been so engrossed in Fiona he'd forgotten Therese and her troubles. Or maybe it was because she looked so well and ate with good appetite. She hardly seemed the frail sister he was accustomed to protecting. Dare he hope that she was less dependent on him than he'd thought?

Then she coughed, just a delicate sound, and the little bubble of hope popped. Of course not. And so he'd have to find a suitable wife, after all. Still, it had been nice to hope, even briefly.


AFTER VINNI and Cat had walked through the warehouse district again, looking for the source of the aether vibration, they opted to call it quits. Either Cat's talent wasn't active on that particular day—and it did seem to come and go at its own whims—or the aether signature simply wasn't there.

"I think I'll go to Tinkerer Hall," Vinni said. "Poke around, see what I can find."

"I'll go stand guard," Cat replied.

"I'm sure I'll be fine. It's a standard recon job."

Cat shook her head. "I'll go so you won't be surprised."

"Very well." No escape for her there unless she could somehow manage to shake Cat. But Vinni knew better. Cat wouldn't be thrown off if she didn't want to be, so Vinni decided to tend to the mission at hand and hope for another opportunity. They would likely have to split up at some point, but of course Cat, after their long association, must suspect what Vinni was trying to do.

They donned regular dresses with skirts that could be split and cinched to make pantaloons that wouldn't be as likely to drag or get caught in things, and then cloaks since the air had taken on a definite chill. Vinni hoped that to anyone watching, they'd look like two ordinary women out on an errand. Well, Cat would get glances, as she looked more like a man, but then no one would bother them. Hopefully.

Although the fire at Tinkerer Hall had been two days before, the air around it still smelled of smoke and charred things. But nothing that indicated to Vinni that anyone had been burned alive, or dead, as the case may be. She was relieved at that. She wasn't one to see ghosts as some of her colleagues were, but she did have enough extra sense to know when spirits were near.

No spirits haunted the hall, at least none that she could sense. A policeman stood at the gate to the drive, and a wrought iron fence atop a brick wall surrounded the property, so that was their first obstacle. Another policeman guarded the back gate, which would have been used for deliveries.

Cat sauntered up to him, and Vinni hid a smile. She'd often teased Cat that her sashay was more of a go'way, and indeed the man seemed to recoil from her. A sad expression flitted across Cat's features, and Vinni found herself regretting her smile. She knew Cat wasn't interested in men, but it must hurt to have one shrink away. Vinni never had that problem, as she appealed to and found appeal in both sexes.

Soon Cat led the man away. Vinni slipped through the gate, which stood slightly ajar. She darted into the shadow of the nearest building—some sort of smithy, by what she could tell. Her nose told her the stables were nearby, so that made sense. She made her way up to the main hall, where the absence of a guard struck her as odd. Did that mean that the place was or wasn't safe?

*I'm going to have to use my talent.* The one talent she'd been able to cultivate at the headquarters and temple of the neo-Pythagoreans. The one that had led her into the profession she'd chosen and the side jobs she was assigned. With a sigh, she closed her eyes and grounded herself by focusing on the hard-packed dirt beneath her shoes. Then she visualized a hand, the only part of a figure she could see through a dark mist. It waved in greeting, and then beckoned her forward.

---

*erminus, 19 December 1871*

Fiona and Devon sat facing each other in the carriage. The last time she'd made that trip to Tinkerer Hall, she'd been full of enthusiasm and optimism. Now she shivered, the memory of the fire and her father's kidnapping playing over and over again in her mind. Could she have done something differently to convince him to stay with her? To not rush back to Lillet and Hollowell and therefore get caught up in the fury of the invasion of the fake automatons?

And the imposter automatons were yet one more thing to be angry about. Bryan Telfair had been a proponent of automaton technology, hoping that the uses of aether to enhance emotional experience could somehow be turned to giving devices a sort of will or impetus of their own rather than the mindless motions they already had. Walking, repeating a certain phrase, attacking when a certain stimulus was presented... All were in development, and she'd heard that in England, young ladies had automaton companions that accompanied them. That fashion hadn't made it to the States yet, but she hoped it would. It sounded like a marvelous opportunity for freedom, to go places unaccompanied by a maid or chaperon. Or maybe it would be more stifling.

And there her mind went into a dozen possibilities, all designed to give her more freedom like that which she was enjoying now. Or was she? Devon sat brooding and looking out of the window to his right at the long drives and estates that they passed. Tinkerer Hall had been such an estate until it had been donated to the Guild by an aficionado of the engineering arts, as they called them, much to the chagrin of the widow, who'd had to move to a townhouse. Could the resentful widow be connected to the disaster? She'd spoken many times against the use of machinery...

But those hadn't been machines. And the incident had contributed to the further uproar against the technology, which many were suspicious of. Fiona sighed and drummed her fingers on her knee. She didn't want to follow her thoughts to that direction, to the worst-case scenario of the tinkerers being dead to show that their creations would be harmful, not helpful.

Devon continued to scowl through the window. Fiona dared not speculate what he was thinking about. There was no knowing what was in a man's mind and heart. See: her father, and his ruinous financial decisions. How had he allowed her mother to convince him to spend the family savings on her coming out? Or had there been something else? That was always a possibility. Gambling? Out of the question. An investment gone sour? Goodness knew there had been plenty of those, especially once the war had ended and Confederate money had turned into worthless paper, not even good for burning since the ink made such a smell. So what, then? And if it had been a bad investment, why hadn't they just told her?

The carriage arrived at Tinkerer Hall, and Fiona's heart fell when she saw an armed policeman standing guard at the gate. He stopped them, and Devon peeked out of the window, which he'd lowered. The shade from a large tree dappled through the windows and created dancing shadows on the carriage's inhabitants.

"Oh, Mister Meriweather, you've returned," the guard said. "Did you not find what you were looking for this morning?"

Devon hesitated, and Fiona held her breath. Had he already been there? No, the guard must be talking about Pierce. Indeed, Devon pitched his voice slightly higher when he responded, "Need to take another peek. Sorry to bother."

"No trouble at all, Sir." But the man didn't move. Devon pulled a bill from his wallet and handed it to the guard, who took it, tipped his hat, and opened the gate for them. Devon closed the window and sat back, his expression bewildered.

"If Pierce had been here, he would have told me," he said. "We'd agreed to investigate together."

"Could someone else have been impersonating one of you?" Fiona asked. So apparently curiosity could break through her block.

"Perhaps, but I doubt it. I don't know of anyone who looks like the two of us."

Fiona didn't know what to say to that. "What do you think he was looking for?"

"I don't know, but I'll ask him later. And see if he found anything."

The carriage pulled up to the front of the house, and Fiona swallowed the hot, prickly knot of panic that rose in her throat. She reminded herself that she was safe here, and Devon wouldn't allow anything to happen to her. At least she didn't think so. He'd come for her during the fire, although she didn't know why.

He handed her down, and she forced herself to take deep

breaths as they ascended the stairs. The charred smell of wood and textiles still hung in the air, smoky and chemical, like a barbecue experiment gone horribly wrong. The front hall showed little damage, mostly smoke stains on the white walls. The ballroom, however, was a different scene altogether. The walls had been blackened, the curtains and decorations all burned to ash. Fiona could barely make out the now-melted and twisted frames of the trees.

Debris lay scattered across the floor, and Fiona picked her way through it gingerly. Most of it was unidentifiable, although it appeared that the conflagration had not spread across the carpets. Perhaps the fire brigade had done some good, after all, although the whole place would have to be gutted. It wouldn't take long for mold to set into the wet floor coverings underfoot, the patterns darkened to what looked like a mysterious cipher.

"If you'll start at that end of the room, I'll start here, and then we can go back and forth and meet in the middle," Devon suggested.

Fiona nodded. When would her tongue loosen again? It seemed to tie up at times of its own choosing. Would her ability to speak return when her opinion of him warmed further?

They worked as Devon had suggested, Fiona careful to keep her skirts as above the muck and debris as possible. Occasionally she would find something shiny and stick it in her reticule in a special pocket she'd sewn for her tinkering tools. It kept them and now her finds safe, padded, and away from the purse's main contents. She resisted the urge to examine things too closely, and just made a cursory glance and mental note of where she'd found it.

Silver button—corner of room by former tree decorations.

Brass gear—likely part of a costume, center of outer wall.

Link of copper chain—interesting, by secret door to kitchens under punch table.

The punch table itself had been turned over, and she

nudged through the broken crystal and glassware with the toe of one foot, reluctant to risk being cut. This was no place for an injury, and her family didn't have the money to afford a doctor should it become infected. While the discovery of animalcules had opened up the source of diseases, they still lacked the ability to do much about them.

Twist of wire—center of wall, about ten feet away from the hidden door.

Shoe button—about three feet away from previous.

Brass button that looked like it would have come from a military uniform—interesting, about fifteen feet away from hidden door; right near where Fiona had seen her father for the last time.

"What is it?"

Fiona hadn't noticed that Devon had reached the center of the room and now looked at her from about ten feet away. She held out a button, and he took it, then turned it toward the light from the wall of windows.

"This definitely doesn't look like something from a costume. Do you recall anyone at the ball being in military dress?"

Fiona shook her head.

"Me, neither. And they wouldn't have used their uniforms as a costume anyway. As I recall, the goal was not to call forth memories from the war."

Fiona nodded vigorously.

"So that means this button must have either been from a costume, which is unlikely, or may have come off one of the automatons."

Fiona thought back to the day before and the red coat— with. yes, brass buttons—that the man had worn. And the awful things he'd said. Started to say. Rage loosened the constriction in her throat—barely.

"The fake automaton yesterday," she forced out. "He wore those."

Devon nodded. "So another piece of evidence that our automatons from the party weren't."

"Drop the button!"

Devon and Fiona whirled to face the formerly secret door that had been beyond the punch table. A figure in a nutcracker mask and dark cloak—like the one from the day before—leveled a gun at them.

"Run!" Devon grabbed Fiona's hand and pulled her from the ballroom, pushing her ahead of him even though he had the advantage in speed and length of stride. She tucked the button in her reticule and lifted her skirts so as not to slow him down. A shot blasted behind them, and something whooshed just above Fiona's left ear.

"Don't make me shoot you. That was a warning!"

Another figure came through the front door, and yet another from the kitchens to the back of the building. That left one direction—up the stairs. They didn't waste any time, and the balustrade burst into wooden shards. One of them grazed Fiona's cheek, which only made her hasten her steps. They raced to the second floor, and a shadowy figure gestured for them to run around and keep climbing.

"I'll hold them," she said. When she moved into a gray sunbeam, Fiona saw they were of about the same height, but the woman had dark hair pulled into a bun. Today she wore a dress and cloak, not uniform and trousers.

"You!" Fiona said.

"Why am I not surprised to see you here?" the woman asked. "Now go. I'll join you in a minute."

Fiona didn't wait to ask questions but now led Devon up the stairs.

"Friend of yours?" he asked.

"I don't know yet," she replied. "But I'm guessing we'll find out soon."


Vinni followed her instincts into the ballroom. She wanted to stay and search for clues, but they led her farther up the stairs to the third floor. At that point, the damage was mostly from smoke, and the structure felt sturdier under her feet. Just as she could feel the air currents around her when she flew, she could sense the solidness of the wood and stone around her. She released some of the tension she'd been carrying, that which prepared her to jump out of the way of a falling beam or dodge a hole that may open in the floor.

She wandered along the hallway, ever mindful of the nudge at the base of her skull. Her talents had never manifested so strongly before, so why now? Was it her desperation to get away from Cat and the neo-Pythagoreans? Or was she finally, at twenty-five, figuring them out? And did they have anything to do with the reason she'd been left—abandoned—so near the cult compound? Some might consider her abilities to be from the devil, not from the gods, which those detractors considered to be the same thing. After her experiences of the previous spring, Vinni might not argue.

A groan alerted her to a bedroom, the door of which had been locked. She opened it, or tried to, but found it to be stuck. She pushed harder, and it popped open with a loud crack. She paused, waiting to hear if anyone had overheard it and if she'd drawn attention. She guessed not when no one came, and she pushed her way inside.

A young man lay on the bed, and she hesitated. What if he was armed? Or otherwise intending to hurt her?

"Help," he squeaked out. She rushed to his side and saw he'd been beaten. His lower lip was swollen, as was one eye.

"How long have you been here?" she asked.

"Two sunrises." He coughed, a thick, wet sound. "So... Thirsty."

She pulled her water canteen from her belt and lifted his head gingerly so he could drink.

"What's your name?" she asked.

"Hollowell." He coughed again. "I work for Mister Lillet."

Vinni nodded. She'd find out who that was later. "I have a million more questions, but we need to get help for you."

"Wait. Caprice! Come out."

A little Negro girl of about five emerged from the closet.

"Is she yours?" Vinni asked, then added, "No, don't talk anymore. It doesn't matter. I'll get you both to safety." She helped him to sit, and then to stand. He seemed to breathe better when he was upright. Did that mean more or less damage? She was a pilot, not a medic, for Pete's sake, but she'd help him as best she could.

"What's the easiest way out?"

He had just opened his mouth to reply when they heard gunshots from two floors below. At least that's what Vinni thought.

"What in the hell...?" she asked, then looked at the reproachful expression on the girl's face. "Here, sweetie, do you want some water?"

Caprice nodded, and Vinni handed her the canteen. "Stay here. I'm going to see what's what."

She ran down the stairs and encountered the last person she'd expected to see. Well, maybe not the last since the girl seemed to be very good at getting herself into trouble. And this time she had a young man with her.

"You!" said the redhead who'd confronted the fake automaton the day before.

Vinni grinned. "Why am I not surprised to see you here?"

The wall splintered beside her. "Now go, I'll join you in a minute." They didn't hesitate, and Vinni pulled out her pistol.

She peered around the railing and saw three automatons, or men dressed like them, conferring. They all turned toward her at the same moment, their masks creepy in their blank expressions. She shot one of them in the shoulder, and he crumpled with a cry. The other two pulled out their weapons, and Vinni didn't hesitate—she ran to join the others.

"Come out. There's no escape for you," one of the men called. "If you're cooperative, we may not kill all of you."

"Right," Vinni muttered. She found the redhead and the young man standing in the bedroom with Hollowell and the little girl. The young woman and Hollowell were talking in a familiar manner.

"We can't—it's too experimental," she was saying.

"Fiona, it's our only way out," Hollowell ground out. He clutched his side like he was in a lot of pain.

"Then we need to hurry so it has time to inflate."

They nodded, then turned to Vinni.

"One of the tinkerers was working on a light inflatable craft that can hold four people. We may be able to use it with five since you and I are small, and so is she." Fiona gestured to the little girl, who clutched Vinni's canteen with both hands.

The promise of freedom, the escape from Cat and ability to vanish into a new life, seemed very tempting from Vinni's perspective. Too tempting. Nothing came without a price.


"Where's the airship?" Fiona asked Hollowell as they half-helped, half-dragged him up the stairs. She knew she'd catch hell from her mother for the bloodstains on her dress, but she couldn't help the elation she'd felt at finding him alive, if injured. There hadn't been time to question him, but she desperately wanted to know if he had any idea where the others had gone. Or at least what he knew.

"Top floor. Roof compartment."

"How long will it take to inflate?"

"Dunno. Caprice? Did you start the balloons?"

The little girl nodded, her curls bouncing. "This morning, like you told me to."

Fiona looked at her. "You weren't stuck in the room?"

"No, we'd pulled the door tight so it would be harder for people to come in after us. Caprice is stronger than she looks."

The girl nodded again, her teeth small and bright with a smile. "We were gonna escape today. Hollowell said he needed time to get better before we could."

"So that woman," Devon whispered glancing back to where the dark-haired woman brought up the rear of their little group. "Who is she? The same one who helped you yesterday?"

Fiona nodded, again unable to speak to him. Blast it, why did this keep happening? Hollowell grinned at her, and she wanted to smack him, but dared not in his state.

They finally reached the roof and heard pounding from below. That prompted them to hurry, and Caprice indicated a long door set into the roof's surface. "It's in there."

Devon left Fiona to support Hollowell and opened the door, allowing it to swing up and then back. But it didn't bang. Rather, the joints caught and held it at a forty-five degree angle.

An oblong balloon rose out of the compartment, and then two more, all attached by ropes. Fiona grinned—it looked bizarre, but it should work.

The last thing to rise was the gondola, open, and fitted with benches behind the steering device. Goggles and helmets lay on the benches.

"This is only going to hold four of us," the mysterious woman said. She bit her lip.

"Do you know what to do with this?" Devon asked Fiona.

"No, they only let male apprentices allowed to sit for journeymanship take flying lessons. But I know the theory."

"Then hop in," Fiona's savior said. "I'll quickly show you the basics, and you can handle it with him." She nodded toward Hollowell.

"Yes, Hollowell and I can manage."

But Hollowell's eyes had gone half-lidded.

"Caprice, give him more water."

They got him into the gondola and on to a bench. Fiona put goggles and a helmet on and studied the controls. She knew theoretically how one of these things worked, but she hadn't been able to get any practice. The woman showed her which controls steered it and how to increase and reduce the air in the balloons to make it go up and down. Then she hopped out.

"You go, I'll hold them off."

Caprice held the canteen out to the woman, but she waved her on. "Keep drinking. But slowly. And watch out for those three." With a grin, Caprice nodded.

Heavy steps clomped up the stairs to the roof, and Devon yelled, "We don't have any time left. Casting off!"

He sawed through the mooring rope with a knife he'd found in the bottom of the gondola, and Caprice got the other one. Fiona made sure they all wore goggles and helmets and prayed they wouldn't need the protective gear. She increased the heat to the balloons, and the airship jerked upward, nearly throwing the three standing passengers to the floor.

"Sorry," she said to all of them. "Hang on."

"Bit late for that, don't you think?" Devon asked.

His typical sarcasm made her frustration grow, but instead of clouding her judgment, it sharpened her focus. She saw the schematics in her mind, adjusted dials and the rudder, and cleared the trees. There would be a trail of steam in the cool air behind them, but she couldn't worry about that. She only needed to get them to the carriage. Which she saw galloping off below them pursued by black-cloaked men on horseback. Hopefully that meant the woman on the roof had escaped.

Devon swore, but only loud enough for her to hear the tone and not the specific words. Right, there was a child aboard.

"I instructed the driver to leave if it sounded like there was trouble," he said. "Looks like he waited too long."

"Do you have a weapon?" Hollowell asked, apparently roused by the motion of the airship. Fiona glanced back and saw Caprice sitting beside him.

"A small one. It won't do much damage, but it can at least scare them. I hope."

"I'll follow the carriage," Fiona said.

Devon leaned over the side, holding on to one of the ropes that held the balloons to the gondola, and shot at the cloaked figures. A sound like metal hitting metal reached them, and the men all reined in their horses and looked up, the sunlight glinting off the masks. Fiona shivered.

The men raised their guns. Fiona again pulled the lever for more air and heat, taking them out of range. Plus, their pursuers had lost time they could have used to go after Devon's carriage, which had vanished down the twisting wooden lane. She allowed herself to relax, albeit slightly.

"Nicely done, Fiona," Devon said.

Fiona blushed at his using her given name more than at the compliment. She felt alive, the airship under her command, and its power hers to harness. It again struck her at how unfair it was for women to be barred from the Tinkerer's Guild examinations, but she might be able to change that.

She guessed at the heading for Devon's mansion.

"There's a place to land this thing, right?" she called back, her brain back in problem-solving gear.

"The lawn should be big enough," came his reply. "Or do you think you can't hit that big a target?"

Teasing! He was teasing her. And she liked it. She made the mental calculations. "I think so."

"Good," he said as Hollowell groaned. "And Fiona, you may want to put some speed on this."

Vinni watched the airship—and her hope of immediate escape—lift off. But her instincts had told her she couldn't risk overloading a new inflatable craft. If it crashed, she would be responsible.

The two uninjured nutcracker men stomped up the stairs. Was the slowness in their steps part of the costume's limitations—in which case she could easily outrun them—or a trick to further intimidate her? From what she had seen, she guessed the latter. But, stupid men, it also allowed her time to find a hiding place and take aim when they finally appeared.

They cursed when they saw the airship in the sky. Even though it had moved out of range, they clomped to the edge of the roof and shot at it. She fired at one of them, but the bullet glanced off his back.

Ah, metal plates. Smart move, that.

They turned, and she shot again, and the bullet similarly glanced off the other one's leg. So the costumes were at least partially armored. They'd come ready for battle. But what were they in the house for?

Then she realized—Hollowell. They wanted the Negro. Why else would they be there? The redheaded girl had seemed familiar with him. Had that made her a target of the man who'd followed her the day before?

Armed with that knowledge and a gun with just three bullets left, Vinni checked her escape routes. She ran to the door leading to the upper hallway.

"There she is!"

She darted into the bedroom, yanked the key from the door, and pulled the sheets—bloodstained from Hollowell's injuries—off. The slow tread of the men in the hallway told her she just had a few minutes. She tied one end of the sheet to the bedpost, opened the window, and threw the end out. It was of course way too short to reach the ground. Then she hid in the closet where the little girl had been. It smelled of human waste, but Vinni thought nothing of it. If she'd been forced to hide from metal men, she'd probably soil herself, too.

And that brought back a memory, of hiding in a closet such as this for days.

*"Don't you make a sound, Davinia. Not a sound, you hear me?"*

*Vinni nodded, unwilling to open her mouth and risk a slap. Her papa wasn't normally one to hit, but he'd gotten wild-eyed, and she knew that look. It was either panic or drink, and he hadn't had a drop of liquor for days.*

She felt the coarse fabric of his shirt against her cheek as he carried her to the closet and put her there. She wanted to cast about through the memory, but she had to pay attention to the slow clomp of the nutcrackers.

They arrived at the bedroom door and pushed through it. Seeing the sheet tied to the bed, they walked to the window and looked down. Vinni darted out of the closet and pulled the door to with an extra oomph. A bullet smashed into the other side, but the wood was thick. She turned the key in the lock on the outside and crept down the stairs, alert for sounds of the others.

She opened the front door to find a wide-eyed Cat standing there.

"You all right?" Cat asked.

Vinni nodded. "Right as can be. You take care of the guard?"

Cat's mouth twisted. "Took two hits to knock him out."

Had Cat taking out the rear guard allowed the nutcracker men in? Or had they all been in league with each other? "You're losing your touch. Are *you* all right?"

"Yes. Find anything?"

A pounding noise came from upstairs. If Vinni were to tell

Cat about the young man and woman, as well as Hollowell and the little girl, she would be giving up a potential escape route. She decided to keep the information to herself.

"Just trouble. Let's go."

As they walked around the house and down the drive, Vinni noticed the stream trail left by the miniature airship and its direction. Her talent told her the heading it had taken, which gave her an idea for where to look for them. There was a lot of Terminus to search, but she'd find them, the solution to her mystery, and perhaps even a means of escape.

**16**

———

*erminus, 19 December 1871*

Devon didn't think the path they took through the sky back to his mansion was the straightest, but Fiona got them there. Once he looked up at the sky after they'd landed, he knew there had been some twists and turns, judging from the rapidly vanishing steam trail, but he hoped it had thrown the horsemen off. Although if they'd gotten a good look at him, they might recognize him from the society papers. Unfortunately, photography had progressed to the point that candid shots were more possible than before.

Once they gently bumped to the ground, Devon leaped out and ran to the house, calling for a doctor to be summoned. Henry Davidson rushed out, then back in to send a message to Chadwick Radcliffe, a physician who had treated many men during the long war. He was also half-Negro, and so more likely to treat Hollowell like any other patient. Devon hated that he had to take such things into consideration, and not just because Hollowell had information they needed.

Some of the maids and footmen came out and brought Hollowell into one of the ground-floor rooms, a small study with a sofa, where they made him as comfortable as possible. They wrapped him in blankets and otherwise ministered to him, and Devon did what he could to stay out of the way. Little Caprice managed to observe and also stay back, but never more than ten feet from Hollowell. Finally, one of the maids offered to bring her to the kitchen to feed her.

"No, thank you, I'll stay with him," the little girl said with grave dignity. She spoke like she'd had some education, or at least been around educated people, which made sense if she'd grown up in Tinkerer Hall. Where were her parents? She treated Hollowell more like a friend.

The same maid who had offered to bring her to food instead brought food to her, and Caprice ate, her big dark eyes not leaving Hollowell's pinched face.

Fiona also stood in the room but sat next to Hollowell and held his hand. Devon could tell they were friends, or at least friendly, and he ignored the stab of jealousy at her easy manner with him. She spoke quietly to the injured man, but of good things and happy memories, not the questions Devon—and, he was sure, she—really wanted to ask. They seemed to have an unspoken agreement not to distress the man and worsen his state. The neuroticists had established that mind and body were indeed one, and having a healthy body meant having a healthy mind. Another strange gift from this long war, like better medicine, animalcule theory, and quicker photography.

Finally, Chadwick Radcliffe arrived with Claire. When Fiona saw her, her eyes widened, and she quickly stood and smoothed her dress, leaving bloody fingerprints that she grimaced at. Therese, who had arrived during the commotion and also sat out of the way, went to Fiona and said, "Come on, I'm sure I can find something that will fit you."

She didn't say that between the smoke stains at the hem and Hollowell's blood, Fiona's dress was ruined, but Devon suspected it was.

He shot Therese a grateful look as the two physicians shooed everyone out of the room except for Caprice, who insisted on staying. Chadwick looked like he was about to object. His wife put a hand on his arm and gave him a gentle smile, and so he shrugged and relented.

Devon pondered what it would be like to have someone he could communicate with like that, with a gentle touch and a smile conveying unspoken sentences and complete thought. He'd guessed he'd have to settle for some empty-headed ninny, a daughter of a congressman or businessman who was more concerned with fashion than with matters of the intellect. For the first time, he questioned whether she'd find *him* to be sympathetic and agreeable beyond his position and fortune. And would she find Therese to be a bonus—a ready-made sister—or a burden? He ran a finger around his collar to loosen the anxiety, which of course didn't leave him.

He waited outside the room until the Doctors Radcliffe emerged.

"Well, he's quite dehydrated, starving, and pretty beaten up," Chadwick said. "I think there may be a punctured lung, but it's hard to tell. Just keep him quiet and don't move him."

"Who's the little girl?" Claire asked. "She's precious and so smart. She was able to tell us exactly what happened to them."

Devon tried not to frown, but he clenched his fists behind him in frustration. "What did she say?"

"That they ran from the automatons, who grabbed Hollowell and beat him up to make him cooperate, but he fought back so hard that they had to leave without him or miss the airship. They didn't see Caprice, who'd hidden." Claire cocked her head. "This was at the Tinkerer's Ball?"

"Yes," Devon told her. "Did she say what her relationship is to him?"

"Niece. Her parents work at the hall and were taken, as far as she knows."

Devon nodded. "They were pretty indiscriminate as to who they took, but many of the servants escaped. I'll take her back once we know it's safe and see if we can find other family."

"Thank you, but if you don't mind having her, it's probably best she stay here with him," Claire said. "She let me check her out, and she's merely dehydrated and hungry. It's fine for both of them to eat, but not too much too fast. They can drink as much as they like."

"As for the lung, as I said, try to keep him still. And safe." Chadwick looked at Devon.

Henry, who had been standing nearby, stepped forward. "When do you think he'll be ready for questioning?"

Claire did something surprising—she put a hand on his arm, as though trying to calm him as she had her husband. "Wait until tomorrow, after he's rested and regained some of his strength."

Devon and Henry exchanged an exasperated glance, but both nodded under Claire's stern gaze. She looked like she could be Fiona's older sister, but with darker hair and eyes that had seen too much to ever lose a certain sad look. Did she regret her role in developing La Reine, and the hundreds of men it had killed in a matter of hours? It must be hard for a healer, Devon thought, to turn their skills to destruction. How would Fiona feel if she were ever to be in that role?

Or *had* she caused mortal damage? No, the other woman had killed the nutcracker non-automaton. But were any of them safe? And why was he so concerned with Fiona's feelings?

"Thank you for coming by," he said. "I know it's not the time to discuss such things, but I don't know if I'll get the opportunity to speak with you again, so I'd like to invite you to a holiday ball I'm holding at the end of the week."

"It may be a good idea," Davidson said. "You're already trusted in the community, and your perspective and connections will be invaluable."

"For what?" Devon asked. He wasn't going to be so gauche as to suggest they could help him find a rich, connected wife. In fact, he doubted they could, even with the help of Claire McPhee Radcliffe's celebrity. And in any case, at least half the attendees likely hated her for what she had done in the war.

"Mister Meriweather, surely after all this you can't think you're not somehow connected to the incident at the Tinkerer's Ball?"

It took Devon a moment to untangle Henry's twisting multiple negative. Was that a British thing?

"I'm not connected to it," he said, allowing his shock to show through in his tone. "In fact, I've never encountered a rogue nutcracker in my entire life. I don't even like the things."

"No, but you're familiar with the tinkerers, and you happened to find the young man in the mansion."

"Fiona—Miss Telfair—found him. After we encountered a strange woman on the stairs."

"A strange woman?" Davidson arched an eyebrow. "Now there's a phantom involved."

"No, she was about this high, dark hair, green eyes, and full of grit, I'll give her that." Devon couldn't hide his admiration. "I hope she got out."

"If it's who it sounds like, I'm sure she did." Davidson did something Devon didn't think the dour Englishman was capable of—he chuckled, then added, "I'll assemble the team to sweep Tinkerer's Hall." Now Davidson spoke to the Radcliffes, but he fingered his watch chain as though he was pondering something. The briefest of intrigued and then hopeful expressions had flitted across his face when Devon had mentioned the strange woman. "Be on standby in case there are injuries. I only hope there's still something for us to find."

Once they'd returned to their flat, Vinni excused herself and ran a warm bath. As basic as their lodgings were, at least they had running water that tended to be warm when they wanted it to be. Once she'd cleaned the smell of soot and sweat from her hair and changed into fresh clothing, leaving what she'd been wearing to dry, she walked into the main living area. Cat sat cross-legged on her cushion, her hands palms-up on her knees, and breathed deeply, her eyes closed. Vinni stopped to look at her, a stab of compassion and some of their old attraction flickering through her. Could they get back what they'd had before? Could Vinni convince Cat to leave the cult with her?

"If you look any harder, you'll knock me over," Cat said and opened one eye.

Vinni smirked. "Sorry, it's been a while."

Cat uncurled herself from her cushion with surprising grace for someone of her bulk. Vinni watched the muscles ripple under Cat's forearms—she wore shirtsleeves—and across her broad shoulders. She'd first been attracted to Cat when the two girls had hit puberty, but nothing had happened between them until Cat had consoled Vinni for the ignorant rejection of one of the boys in their cadet class. Then Vinni had found out that Cat had been watching her and wanting her for years. And Vinni had discovered what she had known for a long time—that she liked girls as much as boys.

Vinni and Cat had always been in tune with each other, so maybe, just maybe they could find their connection back. Vinni went to go stand by Cat as she stretched. She smelled of soap and grass and the outdoors. Freedom. Vinni could close her eyes and see them both running away from their current lives on horseback, or in a small airship like the one Fiona and the others had flown off in. What a marvelous thing, the small airship. Vinni added that to her list of things she would like to own someday. When she had left the neo-Pythagoreans and their communal living situation.

Cat paused in her stretching and gave Vinni a wary look.

Vinni had to admit it was well-deserved, as she'd rebuffed Cat's attentions previously. But now she was ready. And perhaps in their post-lovemaking haze, she could convince Cat to come with her. She had to, simply must, leave the organization that had caused her—both of them—so much pain.

Vinni approached Cat with her most seductive smile. The corner of Cat's mouth turned up, and she held out her arms. Vinni walked into them, expecting to find the same warmth and familiarity that they'd had for the last half-decade. But instead, their thickness felt like a prison. Vinni tried not to stiffen, tried not to reveal her racing heart and her panic. She didn't want to see the memory of Cat turning her face away from her in shame in the carriage after Uncle Dross had tried to... Well, do to Vinni what he'd done to Cat and countless others. And that Cat hadn't warned her about but hadn't expressed contrition for, either.

Cat planted a kiss on the top of Vinni's head. "You smell good. Not like smoke."

Vinni turned her face up to Cat's. The combination of the scents of freedom with the restriction of Cat's arms made her dizzy. "You smell like outside, like the wind."

Cat lowered her lips to Vinni's. Vinni fought not to gag as Cat's lips disappeared into the memory of Uncle Dross's. They felt like two worms, or maybe snakes, slithering across her mouth. She stepped back with a gasp.

"What?" Cat asked, her expression hurt. "What did I do?"

Vinni shook her head. "I'm sorry. It's not what you did. It's what you didn't do." She took Cat's hand. "Run away with me. Let's leave all this now. Let the boy and girl from this afternoon sort it all out."

Cat snatched her hand back, and for the first time, Vinni saw fear on her lover's face. "Leave?" Cat asked. "Leave to go where? To a life where people like us"—she gestured between the two of them—"would never be accepted. We're misfits, and the neo-Pythagoreans are all we've got. The only ones who will take us in."

Vinni almost toppled with surprise. She'd lost count of the words. "But at what cost? You think Uncle Dross will be satisfied? What if he runs out of young women? Or—" She waved her previous words away. "We can't just let him continue doing that to them. To us. You don't really think he stops with just one time, do you? You've been around that kind of man enough in the Corps. It's about power, and they don't stop unless they know they've broken your spirit." She realized she had known a man like that once. In her childhood. Her mother had died protecting her.

Acid rose to Vinni's throat, and she ran into the water closet, where she retched into the toilet pot. Another wisp of memory, this time more vivid, came to her. Her father shoved her out of the back door of a wooden house—she still didn't know where —and told her to run far away. Then she didn't remember anything else, only the sense of danger that they needed to get away from the Bad Man who had killed her mother.

Her mother. Vinni squeezed her eyes shut, hoping for a glimpse, even the barest flash that would reveal her mother's face. But nothing came. The past had receded into the mists of memory again, swallowed by tears and fears and regrets. Regret for what, though? Vinni didn't know, only that she felt like she should have *done* something. But what could she have done? She'd barely been a child, old enough to reach her father's thigh, the coarse wool of his homespun pants rough against her cheek.

"What is it?" Cat asked, her eyes wide.

"I remembered something."

"About Uncle Dross?"

Vinni shook her head, then recognized the gesture as a very, very bad idea when her stomach twisted again. "Something about my childhood. There was someone like him. A man who wanted power and killed my mother." She couldn't articulate it any better than that, her mind still half-stuck in child's logic.

"But you don't remember anything about your childhood,' Cat said. "You've said so a thousand times. You've tried before."

"Something about being here makes me remember." Vinni waved her hand, indicating Terminus, perhaps the entirety of the former Confederate states. "But I can't control it." A stabbing pain started behind her right eye. "I need to lie down."

"I'll get water."

And so Cat retreated into her usual stoic self. Vinni wondered what she'd experienced, who else had hurt her and made her feel like she had no choice but to stay with the organization that was led by a power-hungry rapist. It didn't serve as an excuse, at least not enough of one for Vinni. No man should be able to put his hands on a woman without her wanting him to. And no one should stand behind him doing so.

As Vinni's thoughts swirled around her brain, her cheek on the hard pillow, she hoped she would dream of her past—good dreams, not nightmares.

She had just fallen asleep when Cat walked into the room. "I think I've located the signal. It's near where we were yesterday."

"Is he all right?" Fiona's voice made Devon turn. Fiona approached him with Therese, to whom she'd addressed the question, but Devon knew it had been meant for him. Fiona wore one of Therese's old dresses, two seasons out of date, that Therese had gotten in Europe. Whereas the dark green had washed out Therese's complexion, it highlighted Fiona's copper-colored hair and gave a ruddy flush to her cheeks. Or perhaps that was just her. How quickly he'd come to notice the nuances of her expression, how easily her face turned pink when she was angry or excited or otherwise not stuck up in her mind, as she tended to be. The ride to Tinkerer Hall had stretched in awkward silence with them both lost in their thoughts. And who had preceded him to the hall? It must have been Pierce, but he'd left a note saying he would be away hunting on the family's land in North Georgia that day and wouldn't return until the morrow.

"They're saying to keep him quiet," Devon told her. "I noticed you talking to him. Did he say anything to you that could be of help to us?"

Fiona shook her head. "He was mostly concerned about Caprice. But nothing about what had happened or where the others might be."

Devon relayed to her what Mrs. Doctor Radcliffe had told him via Caprice, but they both knew that although the child may be intelligent, she likely lacked the understanding to fully appreciate the situation. So they would have to allow Hollowell to rest and question him on the morrow.

Meanwhile, Devon wanted to tell Fiona how amazing she'd been driving the airship, which was on the lawn, and how much he admired her quick thinking. But she'd clammed up again, and he worried his compliments would embarrass her.

"I'll have the carriage take you home," was all he said. She looked like she wanted to say more, but she stopped and only shrugged. He decided to accompany her, if only to ensure her safety.

Right, that was all.

The carriage had beaten them home, and Devon gave the coachman the rest of the afternoon off after his scare. The grooms changed out the horses, and one of them took the reins. Devon helped Fiona inside, and they bumped down the drive. She hadn't said anything to either him or Therese as they'd watched the carriage's preparations, which Devon had overseen himself. He'd caught the sly grin Therese exchanged with the stable master, but he'd talk to her about it later. There was nothing between him and Fiona other than friendship and the ability to escape from harrowing situations with each other. To her credit, she'd not panicked, screamed, or fainted, but rather gone along with his plans and strategy, stepping in when needed. In fact, she was as capable as Pierce.

Once they'd left the drive, Devon smiled at Fiona with as much warmth as he could—not difficult considering he had started thinking of her fondly. He decided to keep their conversation focused on technical things so she would keep talking. "So those were definitely not automatons this afternoon."

"No," she agreed.

"What do you think their clothing was made of?"

She pondered for a moment. "Some sort of alloy, I would imagine. Bulletproof material is heavy, but if they'd blended it with something lighter but still strong, they could make outfits from it. They were almost like suits of armor."

"With vulnerabilities in the sleeves, or at least the shoulders," he added. "Your friend shot one of them in the arm."

"Right. And she's not my friend."

"Then who is she?"

Fiona looked out of the window again, a line appearing between her brows. "I don't know. A guardian angel of some sort? She does seem to appear when I need her most. Or perhaps she's working on the same puzzle we are."

"I hadn't considered that others besides us and Blair were investigating, but it makes sense." Devon noted that they had strayed from technical matters, but were still discussing the mystery, so she seemed fine. What tied her tongue otherwise? Had someone hurt her, another man, perhaps? The very thought filled him with anger that exploded outward from his stomach.

She turned quickly to the window, and he got himself under control.

*Focus, Devon, focus.*

"So perhaps that's one avenue to consider," he said. "Who else is investigating? It may lead us to the culprits."

"But let's think about the non-automaton nutcrackers," Fiona said. "Who would want tinkerers if they didn't need them, if they could just impersonate automatons? Maybe they want the tinkerers to make real ones for them."

Devon nodded. "That would make sense. But why so many of them? Surely there are men with specialties that would be helpful to our villains."

Fiona's mouth turned up in a half-smile. "Our villains, indeed. Tinkerers, even in the guild, are a secretive lot. They don't like to show what they're working on until it's done and perfect. And only a few of them were working on aether-driven motivation in machines. My father was—is—one of them."

"Do you know who else?"

"Thaddeus Lillet... and Hollowell." She closed her eyes. "I really hope he's all right. He has to be."

"So he's a friend?"

She shrugged. "Not in the acquaintance sense, but more in the sense of an ally in the effort to get the Guild to open its ranks to those it had previously not welcomed, specifically women and Negroes. He's as talented as any of the rest of them, but they won't let him sit for the apprenticeship exams, although he could easily pass the journeyman ones."

"So why didn't they take him?"

"They dismiss him because of the color of his skin." She shook her head. "That's a mistake. The man is brilliant."

"I'll be sure to keep him well-guarded, then."

She paled. "I didn't think of that. Is that why the non-automatons went back? For him? Then they could have followed us."

"Then it's best that you stay away from my house for a while. I'll have one of my men keep an eye on you and your mother." He stopped himself before he offered to allow her and her mother to stay with him. They were in the land of speculation still.

"But then how will I know what Hollowell says when he's able to talk?"

"I'll send you a message. Or, even better, come to the holiday ball I'm throwing. It's on Saturday. I'd love for you to be there."

"Would you—?" She coughed, then shrugged apologetically. Right, they'd strayed off topic, and now she couldn't speak again.

"Would I what?" he asked.

She sighed and looked out of the window. They'd arrived at the Telfair home, and Devon moved to hand her out of the carriage.

"Fi-OH-na, there you are!"

Devon cringed at the sound of Mrs. Telfair's screech, as did Fiona.

"Where did you get that dress?"

Devon stepped from the carriage, and Mrs. Telfair fanned herself when she saw him.

"I'm afraid someone spilled something on Fiona's dress at lunch," he said. "My sister was kind enough to lend one of hers. We'll get Fiona's dress back to her as soon as it's cleaned."

"Oh, I wouldn't want it to be any trouble," Mrs. Telfair said, but her delighted smile told Devon she was happy for the excuse to have more contact with him and his family. "And is your sister a redhead? The color is stunning."

"Her complexion is fair, but her hair is more like mine."

"Oh, she must be beautiful."

Devon couldn't look at Fiona for fear they'd both burst out laughing at Mrs. Telfair's breathless antics.

"Would you like to come in for some tea?" she asked.

Fiona winced, and Devon recalled they didn't have much.

He noted to himself to have someone bring them some food and tea leaves. And he would find a way to help them.

"Did you come to any conclusions about my Bryan?" Mrs. Telfair asked, possibly deliberately ignoring the awkwardness she'd created.

"No, but we did find some more clues," Devon told her. "Would it be all right for me to send Fiona a message tomorrow? Also, I'd love for—" He realized he couldn't invite Fiona and ask her mother's permission without also inviting Margie. "I'd love for the two of you to come to the ball I'm holding on Saturday."

"We'd love to, wouldn't we, Fiona?"

Fiona nodded, her smile strained. Devon shrugged, then, after a wink he hoped only Fiona could see, kissed her hand. Her mother almost fainted but recovered herself.

"I'll see you soon,' he said and watched the two of them make their way up to the house, followed by the maid, who exchanged amused looks with the groom.

"Philip, please have cook pack a basket of victuals and tea, and then please bring it back to this family," Devon said. "And also have one of the other grooms stationed by the house to ensure no harm comes to any of those women."

"Yes, sir."

Devon got into the carriage once he'd watched the door close behind Fiona and her mother. He felt like a heel for not being able to help them more, but he was doing what he could to find Bryan Telfair.

But once he did, would they then separate to their different spheres? He hoped not, but he suspected that whoever his new wife would be would not agree to Devon having an attractive friend like Fiona.

**17**

***

T*erminus, 20 December 1871*

The next morning, the smells of bacon and sausage roused Fiona. She snuggled back into her sheets, thinking they must be a dream, that she'd gotten so hungry she now fantasized about food in her sleep. But then someone knocked at her door.

"Miss Fiona? Breakfast time."

Fiona opened her eyes. The sunlight that filled the room seemed to be real, and the sheets and her night shift lay lightly against her skin. If this was a dream, then it was a darn vivid one.

"Tessa? We have food?" She stretched. "Oh, right, please come in."

Tessa opened the door, her face split with a grin. "We have food, Miss Fiona. From that gentleman of yours. The man who brought it didn't want to say where it came from, only that it was from a friend who wanted to help while they search for your father, but I recognized the groom from the Meriweather place."

"He's not my gentleman," Fiona said. "I don't want a gentleman." It irked her that someone else was able to do what she couldn't—help her family. If only she could join the Guild, even as an apprentice, she could sell her clockworks and make money.

Her stomach growled, a reproach that she should be more grateful. Tessa helped her dress in the gown that Therese had loaned her—more charity, but she had to admit it was the perfect color for her, even if it sat snug across her hips—and put up her hair. She walked downstairs to a feast and her mother's shining countenance.

"He's already providing for you," she said. "What a good match this is! Do you think he'll propose to you at the ball?"

Fiona gritted her teeth. "I'm sure he's just being nice. We barely know each other."

Margie huffed. "A man who isn't interested wouldn't send sausage."

Fiona wasn't sure why, but Tessa turned pink and wheeled around, her shoulders shaking with laughter. Ah, well, they were all giddy with the food. And coffee. Devon had sent both tea and coffee, and Tessa had brewed some of the latter. Fiona couldn't remember the last time she'd had some, and there was even cream and sugar.

After she'd eaten, she went upstairs to practice her violin. When she reached for it, she caught sight of the krakatuk locket.

"That's strange," she murmured. In all the excitement, she'd all but forgotten about it. Or maybe she'd made herself forget so she wouldn't have to consider selling it. But what was it doing out? Hadn't she put it in her dressing table?

She picked it up and opened it, finding not pictures, but a jumble of letters and numbers, A through G and one through eight. What could they mean? With a shrug, she fastened the clasp, allowing the heavy weight of the strange metal to rest against her chest.

*Where are you, Papa?* It was now the third day since the kidnappings. Were the victims being cared for and fed? Why hadn't there been a ransom demand? Or was Jim Blair keeping them in the dark since he, for some reason, didn't like Fiona? And where had their savior, the strange woman from the day before, disappeared to? Fiona hoped she was all right.

She took out her violin and stuck to the repertoire her mother approved of, although she didn't really want to. She wanted to play, to express her emotions. To allow the instrument to sing of her fear and frustration, her terror, and her pride at what she'd accomplished the day before. She'd flown that airship in spite of being kept from lessons and test flights. She'd managed to get her father's friend out of there and navigate to the Meriweather mansion all on her own. She'd had moments of doubt and terror, sure, but she at least had been able to overcome them and do what she needed to do.

"Fee-OH-na!" *Sniff.* Her mother's call cut through the melody, which had gone into her emotions. Fiona sighed.

"Yes, Mother?" She cringed, expecting a reprimand.

"Lucy and Posey are here."

While Fiona's spirits lifted at the thought of seeing the Lillet girls, her shoulders sagged, deflating from the elation of the music. But at least her mother wouldn't fuss at her in front of them. She put her violin back in its case and went downstairs, where her friends waited in the parlor.

"I'll bring some tea," Tessa said, "and some scones if you'd like."

"We don't want to be any trouble," Lucy told her. "We've just had breakfast. Oh, hello, Fiona."

Hospitality warred with pride, so Fiona finally relented, feeling she could be honest with her friends. "It's all right. We have tea." Fiona smiled with what she hoped came across as reassurance.

"Oh?" Lucy asked, her eyebrows raised. "Then a pot would be lovely."

After Tessa left, Lucy took Fiona's hands. "I'm so glad your fortunes have changed. Have they found your father? Is mine with him?"

Fiona shook her head. "No, the Meriweathers sent some supplies to hold us over until the missing tinkerers are found."

"Ohhh..." Lucy drew out the syllable. "The Meriweathers, huh? Would that include the handsome Devon Meriweather?"

"Yes, but not like that. We're simply acquaintances working toward the same goal."

Lucy and Posey exchanged a glance that told Fiona they didn't believe a word she'd said. Oh, well. At least they'd be polite enough to not ask about the dress, which was out of style, so perhaps it looked convincingly hers.

Tessa brought and poured the tea, and the three girls sat in front of the fire, which blazed. Had Devon sent wood, too? Fiona both wanted to thank him and tell him it was too much, and people would talk. Indeed, her friends looked decidedly conspiratorial.

Once Tessa curtsied and left again, Lucy leaned forward, her teacup and saucer in hand. "So since you're on good terms with Devon Meriweather, does that mean you're invited to his ball?"

Fiona nodded. "Yes, are you?"

"Yes," Posey said. "Everyone is talking about it. It's quite the surprise, and it's rumored that he's hunting for a wife there, so all the eligible young women in town who've been invited, which is most of them, are going."

"Including you two."

"Yes," Lucy replied, "though I suspect in our case that it's a pity invite due to our father having been kidnapped. But it appears that your invitation was not out of pity."

"It might be," Fiona assured her. "He announced while

sitting in that very chair that he has no intention of marrying me."

Lucy looked at the chair as though it had offered Fiona an insult, which made Fiona smile. "When was this?"

"When he came two days ago, the morning after..." She swallowed. "After the Tinkerer's Ball."

"He visited you the morning after the ball? Oh, right, he'd escorted you out." Lucy sipped her tea through her grin, making her look like she was scheming.

"Again, he said he's not looking at me as a potential wife," Fiona insisted.

"But that was three days ago. He could change his mind. Men often do in spite of insisting that we're the capricious sex."

Fiona shrugged, not sure what to say. "What are you wearing to the ball?" There. Fashion was often a safe topic of discussion.

Lucy put her cup and saucer on the small table that sat between them. "I'm not here about what I'm wearing. We're here to discuss what to do at the ball. Or, more specifically, what we're going to use the ball for."

Fiona's eyebrows raised with alarm. "Whatever do you mean?"

"Let's be honest. Jim Blair is about as smart as that fireplace poker. And as useful—only for certain and specific things, but not anything that takes much initiative on its own behalf."

Fiona coughed to hide her laugh. She couldn't argue with that. "True. Has he given you any updates on the situation?"

Lucy shook her head. "No. Nor has he communicated anything to any of the other families who had loved ones taken by those awful nutcracker automatons."

Fiona didn't tell her that they hadn't been automatons. She didn't want to get into her adventures of the day before since it would lead to more speculation about Devon. And she definitely didn't want to tell Lucy about the mysterious woman who'd saved them and fought off the non-automatons to help them escape. That would bring up more questions than she could answer.

"That seems rather irresponsible," Fiona said. "He at least needs to tell us what's going on with the investigation."

Posey finished her tea and set her cup and saucer down as well. "Our thoughts exactly. We've taken the heading we extrapolated from all our memories and we came up with a plausible area for where the automatons were heading in their giant dirigible."

"Where?" Fiona had to fold her hands since they'd started trembling. "And did you tell Blair about this?"

"No, but we did talk to a nice lady who works for the paper," Posey said. "Her name is Bollington. Layla Bollington."

"Oh, right. She's a good reporter," Fiona said. "She likes to write about facts, not speculation. So where was the dirigible heading, assuming it didn't change direction?"

"We calculated a margin of error," Lucy said and dismissed Fiona's skepticism with a small wave of one graceful hand. "And guess where it leads?"

"Where?" Fiona didn't sound too eager, stung by her friend's dismissal of her concerns. She thought they all respected each other as scientists, and when one was basing conclusions on weak evidence and speculation, one had to consider the margin of error.

"Straight to the mountains. A little place called Foothills, in fact, where several of Terminus's prominent families have summer homes and hunting lodges."

"So…" Fiona asked, picking up her tea again. "Do you have any other conclusions?" She tried not to sound flippant.

"So," Posey echoed, "yes. We need to find out which of the families have properties and who may want to collect a bunch of tinkerers."

Fiona pondered. "We may want to see who's on the Guild

roster, even if they don't attend meetings. They'd still know what was going on through the newsletter."

"Or," Lucy said, "we could go up there and see for ourselves.'

Fiona nearly dropped her tea service. "What?"

"After the ball, I've arranged for a carriage to take us to Foothills." Lucy clapped her hands. "I've had enough of speculation and Jim Blair's slowness. He has a place up there, too, by the way. He may be in on it."

Fiona simultaneously felt breathless at the idea that they could leave so easily—hadn't she been wanting to do just that?—and stifled by the possibility of everything that could go wrong. But they needed to do *something*. She couldn't depend on the kindness of the Meriweathers forever.

"Tell me more about this plan."


"Penny for your thoughts, dear brother?" Therese gently poked Devon with the tip of her butter knife. It didn't hurt, but it got his attention.

"Nothing, dear sister," he replied, although his thoughts had been far from nothing. He'd been sipping his coffee and imagining Fiona Telfair similarly drinking hers that morning. He hoped her maid had cooked the sausage correctly so it wasn't underdone but also not tough and overdone. Would he think as much about his wife once he'd finally decided on one? He needed to do so quickly—the redheaded tinkerer's daughter was occupying too much of his thoughts. But he couldn't get the image of her flying the mini-airship, the one that still sat on his lawn, out of his head. He'd return it to the Tinkerer's Guild once there were guild members to return it to. Perhaps Hollowell would know how to bring it back and restore it to its hiding place once he'd recovered.

"I think that *nothing* may have copper-colored hair, pretty green eyes, and a smile that lights up your heart," Therese teased. "I like the girl, and I approve of the match."

"Thank you, dear sister. I'm glad to know that you like her. However, I'm afraid I cannot marry her. You know I have to satisfy Father's wishes for our family to establish our legacy in this new era and marry strategically." He didn't add *so you don't have to*, which made him feel slightly better about how pompous his speech must have sounded.

Therese made a distinctly non-ladylike noise with her mouth. "Father would be more concerned about your happiness than our legacy."

"But what if our legacy is my happiness?" he asked. "And my finding a woman with a good dowry and allowance will be good for both of us." He hated to call attention to her frailty, but she was pushing him to do just that. He hoped she'd understand what he was trying so hard not to say.

But she persisted. "Devon, we have plenty of money. And I don't intend to be a burden on you for forever. I have my own plans, although I haven't thought to share them with you. I didn't think it would be necessary. There's something you need to know about me—"

Crenshaw knocked on the door, interrupting Therese's speech, and poked his head around the lintel. "Sir, your cousin has arrived from the hunting lodge, and he's injured."

Devon and Therese both stood with a scraping of their chairs behind them. Devon caught Therese's before it toppled over. "Where is he?"

"They've brought him to his chambers."

"Stay here," Devon told Therese, who had gone pale. Almost laudanum pale, but not quite. It was amazing she'd had the strength to almost knock over her chair. "I'll let you know if he's decent or fit to be seen."

She nodded, her lips pressed in a tight line. Had she been about to tell him that she'd decided to accept Pierce's suit, after all? Or that she'd determined to make a more strategic match? He would be fine either way—he trusted her judgment—although he would miss her quiet presence beside him. But if he were to take a wife, *when* he would take a wife, she would hopefully want to be Devon's adviser and friend.

These thoughts played through his mind as he ascended the stairs and found Pierce in his room, his shoulder bandaged.

"What happened?" Devon asked.

Pierce lay on his bed on top of the covers. His features were crumpled in a grimace as a surgeon worked on his shoulder. Pierce's groom stood beside him.

"We got too close to another hunting party," the groom said, "and Mister Pierce was shot in the shoulder. By the time we made it back to the lodge, it was dark, so we dared not try to travel back until the bleeding slowed down."

"Hurts like the devil," Pierce ground out. "If I ever find out who did this..." He let the threat hang in the air.

Pierce's anger relieved Devon. If he was angry, then he would fight whatever effects the injury might have on him.

"Almost got it, please hold still." It was Chadwick Radcliffe, Henry Davidson's associate. He must have been at Henry's quarters when they'd brought Pierce in, and someone from the house had called for a physician. Indeed, Henry stood in the corner, as unobtrusive as always.

"Got it." Radcliffe pulled out a slug with his forceps. "This doesn't look like hunting ammunition. It's from a handgun."

"People use all sorts of things to shoot at critters," Pierce said. He spoke dreamily, and Devon guessed that they'd dosed him thoroughly with laudanum. "Maybe someone hunting squirrels or possums."

"Right." Devon looked at Henry, who frowned. He would have to ask the man what he was thinking later.

Radcliffe looked at both of them, each in turn. "I need to

cauterize this. It won't be pleasant. I suggest that you wait outside the room."

"Pierce?" Devon asked. He wanted to be there if his cousin needed him.

"Go." Pierce waved Devon off with his other hand. "Do what you need to do, Doctor."

Devon and Henry walked out of the room, but Devon didn't want to go too far.

"What do you think?" Henry asked.

Devon frowned. "What do you mean?"

"Do you think he's telling the truth about how he got injured?" Henry inclined his head toward the room. "It's early for them to have returned all the way from the mountains, especially with him in that state."

"The carriage he used has good cushioning to ensure minimal effect from rough ground. We had it specially made for Therese to travel in." But Devon could see his point. It had been light for two hours, but the journey from their hunting lodge typically took a good five or six. They would have had to have left at four or five o'clock to have made it back. "But there aren't many options for medical treatment up there this time of year."

"Right." Henry looked skeptical. "You trust your cousin?"

Devon nodded. "Yes, I've known him since we were children."

"And you said he bought this house in your absence."

"He was thinking of Therese and her condition. He was right—she's doing much better now that we're out of the city. My father was stubborn in wanting to stay in the townhouse as long as he did."

"I see."

What was Henry thinking? No, he knew, but Devon didn't want to consider the possibility that his cousin could be in league with the kidnappers and had attacked him and Fiona the day before. What would his motivation possibly be? He voiced as much to Henry.

"I don't know, but I have someone looking into it. Do you know much of what he was doing while you were out of the country?"

"He was in school in Massachusetts and then back down here running our family's affairs."

A scream came from inside the room, and Devon felt the agony echo through the center of his body. He found himself perversely angry at Davidson and his questioning.

"Whatever happened, he's certainly paying for it now," he said. "We can discuss this later."

Henry bowed his head and walked down the hall.

Radcliffe emerged and said, "It's done. I've dosed him pretty good with laudanum, but please have someone keep an eye on him and watch him for this list of things." He handed Devon a list of symptoms that would indicate either fever or shock. Devon recognized them from his own training for the foreign service.

"I'll make sure he's watched over," Devon said.

"Good." Radcliffe punctuated his word with a nod. "And call me if anything happens."

"I will."

Devon watched Radcliffe walk away, then turned back to Pierce's room. He hesitated before opening the door. Did Davidson really think his cousin had something to do with the kidnappings, or some other suspicious activity? He needed to sit down with Henry and discuss what he'd found so far and what, exactly, his team was doing. And then perhaps Devon would resign completely from that part of his life that put him too close to international affairs. Except for the business part, at least.

The groom stood by Pierce's bed and watched his master sleeping. Devon couldn't remember from where Pierce had hired the man. Had he been one of the servants who'd opted to stay with the house until they could find something better? Or had Pierce employed him for some other reason? Devon realized he hadn't questioned Pierce or his decisions, just trusted him implicitly.

"How is he?" Devon asked.

The man startled as though waking from a dream. "He's asleep thanks to the laudanum, sir. That was..." He shook his head.

"I know. It's hard to watch. If you need to go get something to fortify yourself, go ahead. I'll wait for you to return or bring someone else in."

"No! I mean, no, thank you." He swallowed, a sickly cast to his brown skin. "Mister Pierce didn't want me to let anyone else watch over him."

"All right, then, I'll send someone up with some food and drink for you. You must be starving and exhausted."

Now relief spread over the man's face. "Thank you." He wiped a hand over his face. "Tea would be good."

Devon nodded, but internally questioned why Pierce only trusted this one valet. "Very well. And please watch him for these symptoms and let me know if he wakes or displays any of them." He handed over the list Radcliffe had given him. "Do you know how to read?"

"Yes, sir. Mister Pierce made sure I learned."

"Good. I'll send someone up in a few minutes."

When Devon left the room, he found Henry waiting for him.

"I'll be with you in a moment," Devon told him. He didn't want to know what Henry had to say, at least not right then. Too many questions swirled around in his brain.

"The man Hollowell has awakened and is asking for you."

**18**

———

*erminus, 20 December 1871*

      After Lucy and Posey left with the strictest—and unnecessary—admonishments to Fiona to not let anyone know their plan, Fiona returned to her room and her violin. She tried to play through a minuet but her mind wouldn't settle on the music. Instead, she kept thinking through the plans—how could they accomplish them? Lucy must have some pull with her family's servants to be able to do such a thing. Fiona didn't think that Mrs. Lillet would approve, and she definitely knew her own mother wouldn't.

Fiona found herself fingering the krakatuk nut pendant, and she unclasped it from her neck. She opened the locket portion again and pondered the letters and number. G7. B5. c2. Then she frowned. The musical scale only went from A to G, and each key had seven chords, major and minor. What if she was looking at a sequence of chords? She put the locket on top of her clothes-press, frowned at it, and picked up her violin. First she played a major G seventh chord, then a fifth in the key of B, and then a minor second chord, which came out very discordant, in C. She played through the listed chords twice. A knock on her door startled her heart into beating at double tempo and stopped her from repeating the chords a third time. Tessa stood in the hallway and twisted her apron.

"What are you playing, Miss Fiona?"

"Oh, nothing. Just doing some experimentation."

"You may want to switch back to your approved music. Your mother's been out, but she'll be back any minute."

Fiona sighed. "Thank you for letting me know. Where did she go?"

"To the dressmakers. She tried on her dress for the ball tomorrow—one of the ones she had made so she could accompany you on your debut rounds—but found it too loose, so she went to see if they could tuck it in."

"Right." Fiona supposed she should be glad, but it was a reminder of how the family's misfortune was partially her fault even though she hadn't asked for all the new clothes. At least she had a dress for the ball the next night. "I'll stop. I'm feeling faint, so perhaps I'll lie down."

"Do you need me to help you?" Tessa's words swam through the air and sounded like they came through water, and Fiona shook her head. What was happening?

"No thank you. I'll let you know if I need anything." She shut the door in Tessa's face—she'd have to apologize for that later—put her violin in its case, and lay on the bed. The room swam around her, swirling like Tessa's words had, and every sound took on a strange echo, not like in a canyon, but more like a tunnel, where they whirled and magnified before coming back to her. She put her hands over her ears to make the noises stop but found her arms didn't want to move, nor did her eyes want to open.

She opened her mouth to cry out, but all that emerged was a squeak. Then her clothing began to move, first her corset loosening itself and then the rest of her clothes sliding around and swallowing her until she found herself encased in a world of cotton, muslin, and whalebone. The smells of perfume, sweat, and the foods she'd eaten while wearing her clothing became as sharp and familiar as the sight of her room used to be. Meanwhile, colors muted and faded until the world turned monochrome and shadowy. She found herself trying to blink with her nose, but when she tried to scratch it, she pulled her hand away with a shriek because tiny claws had poked her. Thankfully she didn't bleed.

There was light up ahead, so she followed it and found herself on a giant bed. Her pillow smelled like the soap she used when she washed her hair and again like the light floral of her perfume, but both so sharp that she could detect the individual ingredients that comprised both. The pillow itself loomed like a hill, and she had to jump and claw her way up it until she stood atop it. From there, she surveyed her room, or tried to, but found her eyesight to be sorely lacking. Furniture appeared as big, dark lumps, and the light from the window barely illuminated the space.

But her nose gave her a clearer picture. She located the pine-herb smell of the rosin from her violin bow, the sharp chemical smells of her oils and metallic odors of her workbench. And a strange smell with a heartbeat pulse, like the petrichor scent of plants when the rain has just started and they've opened their pores to ask for more. But this new smell wasn't tied to anything she could recall in her room.

She followed its trail from the window across her blanket and down to beneath the bed. There she found the source and shrank back. Although the light was dim, she could make out the outline of a nutcracker doll. Twin orbs in its face pulsed, and Fiona hissed at it, wanting it to leave. How dare it be in her room, in *her* space? And what had it done to her?

Vibrations through the floor resolved into familiar patterns, and Fiona realized her mother was home. She would probably want to talk to Fiona about the ball, so Fiona needed to get back to her clothing. She hissed again at the doll for good measure, then scrambled out from under the bed, up the bedskirt, and over the mattress. She had a vague memory of waking up with her nightdress on backward, so she attempted to align herself with her clothing. The scientific part of her brain marveled at the experience, but the human part, the one that often argued her out of wonderment and encouraged her to stick with what was practical, argued that she was having a most enjoyable and interesting dream. And as she woke, her clothing slid over her once more, smells and sounds turned muted, and her eyesight returned so that when she opened her eyes, she found herself lying on her back on her bed. Heavy footsteps stopped just on the other side of her door, and someone knocked.

"Fee-Oh-na, are you awake? We need to talk about the ball." *Sniff.*

"Yes, Mother, I'll be down in a moment."

When she sat, her hair tumbled loose around her shoulders, and she looked back to see the pins that Tessa had so carefully installed in her curls scattered across the pillow. She wanted to look under the bed, but another call from her mother made Fiona twist her hair back in a bun, secure it with a ribbon, and run from the room. She told herself the doll had been part of a dream, and she didn't want to keep her mother waiting.

DEVON FOLLOWED Henry down the stairs to the parlor where Hollowell had been resting. The man lay awake, his bruises still prominent, and he picked at the corner of the blanket that covered him. The smells of sweat, blood, and fear made Devon want to wrinkle his nose, but he refrained. There was no reason for him to make Hollowell feel more uncomfortable than he already did. Devon couldn't imagine what it would be like to wake in a strange place in pain and alone.

The little girl was nowhere to be seen, but Devon thought he'd observed her following the scullery maid about early that morning and chattering about looking for eggs in the henhouse later.

"He said he wouldn't speak unless the master of the house was present," Henry said.

"I appreciate his respecting that I'm in charge here." Devon tried to make his words wry, but it seemed that Henry had slowly tried to take over more than the security functions of the household.

"Of course," Henry murmured, his agreement almost more annoying than an argument would have been. Devon again swore to himself to cut ties with the foreign service, the biggest regret of his life.

"How are you feeling?" he asked Hollowell.

The man shook his head and then grimaced. "Everything hurts."

"Doctor Radcliffe will see you after we talk," Henry said. "Since you said you wanted to report to Mister Meriweather first."

Hollowell ducked his chin like he started to nod, then slowly brought it back up. "Yes," he ground out. "There are some things you need to know."

It was obvious to Devon that each of the man's movements cost him, and he didn't want to harm him further, especially since that would upset Fiona. But he needed answers.

"Was that Miss Fiona yesterday?" Hollowell's face relaxed into a true smile.

Devon tried to ignore the jealousy that lanced through him at the memory of Fiona and Hollowell talking so easily. Why could she speak to the tinkerer, but not to him?

"It was. She flew us out of there in the Guild's mini airship."

It would have been smart to use that machine to pursue the big one, but he supposed the fire had kept people from accessing it. The few people left who could get to it and knew about it, anyway.

"She's amazing," Hollowell said. "Truly, she is. That's why what I have to tell you hurts more than my wounds."

A cold spot started in the pit of Devon's stomach. "Was she involved in the kidnappings?" The words came out before he could stifle them. He couldn't imagine her knowingly harming others, directly or not, but was that why she had such difficulty speaking with him? She was withholding the truth?

"No, no, she didn't know anything. The architects of the plans were her father, Bryan Telfair, and Thaddeus Lillet."

Devon's knees buckled, and he plopped to the armchair behind him. "Telfair and Lillet? Whatever for?"

Hollowell picked at the blanket, and Devon gave him space to think. His own thoughts whirled like the tornadoes that sometimes happened in the countryside around Terminus, funnels of rain and cloud that destroyed everything in their paths. Admittedly, he didn't know Bryan Telfair or Thaddeus Lillet all that well, having mostly spoken to them at the few Guild meetings he'd attended, but they'd seemed like decent sorts.

Hollowell's distress showed in his inability to meet Devon's eyes as he continued speaking.

"They wanted to make automatons, but the other members wouldn't cooperate. Afraid of the machines taking over if they got too much motivation shoved into 'em with the aether."

"So those things at the ball..."

"Weren't machines. They were men dressed up as them."

Devon nodded. He had been ninety percent sure that was the case, but as a non-tinkerer, he'd doubted his own perceptions.

"And what happened to you?" Devon asked.

"I tried to fight them, not let them take me." Now Hollowell looked up at him. "I knew my niece was in the house somewhere. I'd sneaked her in so she could see the ball and the costumes, and I didn't want her coming to harm. They threw me over the rail from the third floor to the second and left me for dead in the hallway."

Henry nodded. "The story is consistent with his injuries."

Hollowell coughed and clutched the side of his chest. "I'll see the doctor now."

"Thank you for your forthrightness," Devon told him. "I'll look further into Telfair and Lillet."

"You do that." His words sounded like a challenge. Devon supposed that if his employer were to betray him and toss him over a stair rail, he'd be resentful, too.

"Did you believe him?" Henry asked once they walked into the hallway. Radcliffe slipped into the room. Devon admired how the man moved like a ghost.

Devon sighed. Of course Davidson would make things more complicated. "Did you?"

Henry looked at him, a line between his brows. "Something doesn't make sense in all this, Mister Meriweather. I feel there are holes in the man's story, and we need to further investigate to see what."

Devon nodded. "I agree." He, too, felt uneasy with what he'd heard, beyond the fact that Fiona's father apparently had engineered the destruction and abduction of his own guild. The facts simply didn't agree with what he'd known of him.

But then, the man had brought his family into financial ruin, so perhaps he had a dark side Devon hadn't detected yet.

Chadwick Radcliffe emerged. "His heart rate was elevated, as was his respiration. You need to keep him quieter. What were you doing to him?"

He leveled an accusing look at Devon, not Henry, which piqued Devon's annoyance.

"He insisted upon telling me who was behind the kidnap-pings," Devon said.

"Oh?"

"Telfair and Lillet." Henry's English accent clipped the names. "I'm going to have the team look into their affairs further and search their houses. Would you happen to know if either of them have property outside the city?"

"I suspect Telfair didn't. He seems barely able to hold on to what he has here. But Lillet might. He's from a very connected family."

Devon recalled that Thaddeus Lillet had two daughters and a niece, Veronica. He'd met the niece during the opening of the Terminus Art Museum. Veronica lived with her husband, a Frenchman with an eyepatch, and the two younger Lillet girls and the wife were still at home. Did any of them know of their father's involvement in illegal activities?

"Would you like to accompany us to Fiona Telfair's residence?" Henry asked. "Since the two of you have a connection, she may be more agreeable to letting you in."

"That's fine. And then perhaps she can help us get into the Lillet house."

**19**

---

Terminus, *20 December 1871*

Vinni lay on her stomach and watched the windows of the warehouse across the street through her binoculars. Fog, or perhaps mold, kept her from seeing inside. Her entire backside had started the day dry, but as the relentless mist fell, her split skirt and pantaloons had become sodden and heavy. And cold. She would be happy to return to the flat, as awkward as things were between her and Cat.

Cat had wandered the street below, first to confirm that her inner sense was correct and had pinpointed the location of the aether energy surge. Then she'd walked around the surrounding area to gauge the energy level of the warehouse. On a Wednesday, it should have been bustling, but the large doors off the alley stayed closed, and all was quiet. Vinni didn't know what that meant, but she hoped she wouldn't have to face down any angry gods or goddesses any time soon.

Now Cat lay a few feet away and looked through her own viewing device.

"See anything?" Vinni asked. Perversely she hoped the

answer would be no because then it would mean she hadn't missed anything.

"No. The windows are all dark. No light at all."

"So perhaps no one's there."

"Or it's aether shadow." Cat rubbed her right thumb over the fingertips of the same hand. "It's so strong over there that my fingers are tingling."

Vinni nodded, wishing she could see or sense what Cat did. She hoped that so close to the aether her own senses would be working, but there was nothing.

"Uncle Dross never told me exactly why it was so important we come here and hunt for the source of the aether surge," Vinni said, voicing the question that had been hiding beneath her disgust for the past few days. "Is he seeking an ally in another powerful priest or priestess?"

Cat shook her head. "More like looking to flush out a rival. Do you remember a priest named Bonclimat?"

"That was when we were in cadet school." And her first taste of freedom from the neo-Pythagoreans. Even better—she'd found her home in the air and her mysterious sense that warned her of danger or told her to go ahead. Sometimes she had to ignore it to follow orders, but she typically regretted it when she did. Or found a better, more nuanced way to use her talent. She'd discovered that life was more than straight yeses and nos.

"Right, he was a young guy, a student at one of the nearby colleges. He came from down here."

Vinni shrugged. She'd not met him, but she remembered Cat talking about him after a trip home. "So you think he's behind this?"

"He had more talent at manipulating aether than Dross, and he was a tinkerer to boot. And Dross trusted him."

"What did he find out?" Vinni found herself only half-watching the blank windows.

"More than Dross wanted him to know. But by the time Dross figured out what had happened, the boy had left."

"Back to school?"

"Graduated and moved back South to run his family's business." Cat grunted. "No one thought much of it. Figured he'd go back to being a rich kid. Then this." She waved toward the building across from them.

"So they think he's decided to do something with the aether."

"And throw it off balance."

"So that's the current theory, that there's a finite amount of it, and isolating too much will leave less available elsewhere." The last Vinni had heard, the amount of aether in the atmosphere was a matter of debate with some espousing the limited theory, and others advocating for a more infinite theory —that aether was like light, both emitting from the sun and not in threat of running out for millions of years. It reminded her of how little anyone truly knew of the substance.

Vinni had always thought the only matter not in danger of running out was scientific speculation, but she didn't say so. She just did her job, flew her airships, and before now had been a good little neo-Pythagorean. If aether were in danger of running out, well, what was one more disappointment to add to her year? It almost paled in comparison to selfish gods and rapist leaders.

"And what theory did Bonclimat follow?"

"Neither. He thought it could be made."

That was interesting. "Can't you track him down and ask him what he's up to?"

Cat grunted. "Tried. That wasn't his real name. He used an alias."

"Figures." Light flashed in one of the windows so briefly Vinni wasn't sure she'd seen it. "Did you catch that?"

"The light? Yes. We need to get in there."

Vinni thought through the possibilities. "Let's see what happens at night, then decide when is the best time."

WHEN FIONA DESCENDED THE STAIRS, she found her mother wasn't alone. Devon stood beside her along with two men. One was a very tall and broad man with red beard and hair. The shorter of the three, although still tall enough, had sandy hair, a narrow face that showed a few freckles, and light hazel eyes that seemed to take in, catalog, and file every detail he observed. Fiona thought she recognized a fellow scientist in the other one, the redheaded fellow, who grinned when he saw her. She smiled back. He held his flat hat in both hands, which were roughened but also possessed of slender fingers. Something told her she was about to make the acquaintance of another Irish tinkerer.

Devon Meriweather's smile showed strain when she returned her gaze to his face, and her own dimmed slightly. What could she have done wrong?

"Miss Telfair, please allow me to present Inspector Henry Davidson and his associate Patrick O'Connell. Gentlemen, this is Fiona Telfair, the daughter of Bryan Telfair."

At the sound of her father's name, Fiona's heart leaped, then plummeted as though it had jumped off a cliff and into the boiling acid of her stomach. "You have news of my father?" she asked, careful to focus on the man with the greatest weight of authority—Inspector Davidson.

Inspector Davidson nodded. "Perhaps it would be better if we were to have a seat?"

"Oh, assuredly," Margie Telfair said and ushered them into the parlor. Fiona followed. She wanted to thank Devon for his generosity but also found herself relieved to not have to acknowledge the charity quite yet. What could they have to tell her about her father? She glanced at the portrait of her brother and hoped they weren't about to hear of Bryan Telfair's death.

Once they'd all been seated and Tessa sent to make tea, Devon looked at Fiona and said, "I'm afraid we don't have good news."

Fiona folded her hands in her lap. She still felt off after her strange nap and hoped they couldn't tell—and that this was perhaps an extension of the dream. The tension in the air made her stomach knot even more than previously, and she regretted having eaten her fill at breakfast.

"Well, out with it," Fiona's mother said. "Waiting is sheer torture. Is he alive?"

"As far as we know, Madame," Davidson told her. "But the problem is that we've had word that he may have been involved in the plot to kidnap his fellow tinkerers and burn Tinkerer Hall."

"What?" Fiona laughed, the tension winding tighter around her stomach in the face of such an absurd accusation. "He couldn't have been. He loved—loves—the Guild."

"Are you aware of any arguments he may have had with other Guild members?" Davidson asked. "Any disagreements, longstanding or recent?"

Fiona shook her head. "None. Everyone loved him." Then she recalled his final words to her. "He and Thaddeus Lillet were working together on something with Hollowell. How is he?" she asked Devon, ashamed to have forgotten her friend in her eagerness to hear news of her father.

"He's well, but he's the one who told us that your father and Lillet were in on the plot together."

Fiona shook her head, anger flooding out the typical block she had when she tried to speak with him. "Impossible. They simply couldn't have."

"Do you mind if we look around, Lass?" The Irishman's brogue, which would have normally soothed Fiona, grated on her nerves.

"Yes, I mind if you take a look around. My father would not like anyone snooping around in his laboratory." Never mind that she'd been doing that the day before.

"Miss Telfair, please," Devon said softly. "It would be helpful."

"You may look around all you please," Margie said. "Fiona, it will help to demonstrate your father is innocent."

Fiona clenched her jaw. She couldn't argue with her mother, but she wanted to protect her father...from what? If he had engineered the kidnapping, then they needed to know, even if it would throw the family into disgrace. If Fiona and Lucy and Posey were to go to North Georgia and find them, they needed to know who they were up against. If their fathers had masterminded it all, they could potentially try to talk some sense into them.

"Fine," she said.

The Irishman reached into the satchel that had been slung over his shoulder and brought out a device. About the size of a brick, it looked like a wooden box with a miniature aether isolater behind a glass plate set into the top.

"What's that?" Fiona asked.

"Told you she was curious," Devon murmured. Fiona shot him a look that she hoped told him he had no right to say anything about her to anyone, especially not strangers who were accusing her father of colluding against his own guild.

"It's an aetherometer. It indicates where there is a concentration of aether. Since your father was working in that area, I thought it might help."

"How... How did you know that?"

O'Connell grinned. "He published some papers. Took

Professor Bailey's work and Doctor Radcliffe's advances in using aether as a treatment for neurosis and put it together beautifully."

Fiona blinked back tears. She hadn't known her father had published. Had professional jealousy alienated him from the Guild? But that was still an assumption.

"Of course," Fiona said. "My father is a brilliant man." If not so great with money, she added in her mind. Part of her wished she'd worn one of her new dresses instead of Therese's hand-me-down, but the other part of her still quivered with fury at the accusations. Oh, and Devon's betrayal didn't help. Didn't he know he could trust her? Why hadn't he asked her—warned her?—before bringing strangers into her home?

O'Connell turned a dial, and the aether in the small chamber glowed brighter. "Shall I show you?" he asked. "This beauty should be able to take me to your pa's workshop."

Fiona sighed. She knew she wouldn't be getting out of this, so she agreed.

Davidson seemed to have gotten the short straw and waited in the parlor with Mrs. Telfair, who soon interrogated him about his marital history and prospects. Fiona could only shake her head. Ah, well, he deserved it.

She followed O'Connell to the kitchen, where he found the door to the workshop beyond without any trouble. The aether in the aetherometer glowed more and more brightly as they approached the small room, then tuned opalescent.

"That's to indicate it's been used for mechanical experiments," he said. "The aether in the chamber is of a small enough amount that it will take on the frequency of the nearer larger source and show what the use is. Your father must have a concentrator around here somewhere."

Fiona nodded. "He keeps it in the bread box." She slid open the lid to reveal a copper globe connected to a glass one, which contained a writhing aether ouroborous. Fiona had to make an effort not to stare. The thing could fascinate her for hours. But then she noticed her fingertips itching as well as her nose, and she stepped back.

Surely her dreams of turning into a mouse were just that —dreams?

They closed the bread box, and O'Connell swept the bottom floor while Davidson, who had extracted himself from Fiona's mother, searched the workroom methodically, careful to replace things as he found them. He glanced through Bryan Telfair's papers, and Fiona watched his face for any sign that he'd found anything incriminating, but the Englishman's expression remained impassive.

"What's upstairs?" he finally asked.

"Just the bedrooms and a water closet," Fiona told him. "Father was one of the first to have one installed."

"We'll need to check up there as well." Davidson's tone—all business—wouldn't allow for argument from either Fiona or her mother, who almost vibrated with the potential scandalous nature of it all. Three strange men in their house was one thing. In their bedrooms? Fiona knew she wouldn't hear the end of the complaints.

"Very well," Mrs. Telfair finally said with a dramatic sigh followed by a sniff. She dabbed the end of her nose with a handkerchief. "But I'm sure you won't find anything. My Bryan is innocent."

"We'll see," Davidson said. His lips twitched—was he trying to hide a smile? Fiona couldn't fault him—her mother could be overly dramatic. But what else could one expect from a former actress?

O'Connell didn't find anything in Fiona's parents' chamber. Nor did Davidson on his quick search through drawers and armoire. Fiona found his method fascinating. First he would survey the furniture from the outside, then look at it from the inside. He'd hold his fingers at a certain width and compare different parts of the furnishings to it. He must have been checking for thicknesses that were unexplained and may indicate hidden compartments. Then he tapped different areas, presumably to do the same. Fiona took mental note—that skill could come in handy. Of course, if she found anything, she'd still have to figure out how to open it.

When they approached Fiona's bedroom, the aetherometer took on a peach glow.

"Emotional aether," O'Connell murmured.

"Please show some propriety and leave my daughter's room be," Margie, who had joined them, huffed. "She certainly has nothing to hide."

"I'm afraid the aetherometer says otherwise," Davidson told her. "The two of you please wait here."

Once they'd gone in the bedroom, Margie whispered to Fiona, "What do you have in there? Have you been tinkering with your father's things again?"

"No, just my clockworks." Fiona hoped they wouldn't have the same argument as previously.

A cry brought their attention back to the men.

"Under the bed," O'Connell said. "Careful, whatever it is, it's a strong concentration."

Someone sneezed. Devon?

Margie shot Fiona an angry look, and Fiona shrugged, but swallowed against rising panic. Her dreams had been just that, right? Just dreams? She hadn't really turned into a mouse, and there couldn't really be a nutcracker doll with glowing eyes under her bed.

But apparently there had been. The three men emerged, and Davidson held the small nutcracker doll with his handkerchief. The object grinned like it thought the situation was the biggest lark, and Fiona wanted to snap its head off.

"Miss Telfair, would you like to explain what this is?" Davidson asked.

"It's sophisticated aether work," O'Connell explained to Margie, who had bristled when they'd come out of the room. "It's on the level of Professor Bailey. If it's hers, she's a genius."

"My daughter is no genius," Margie said.

Fiona wondered when genius had become an insult, but she decided to go with a more logical argument. "Gentlemen, that doll does not belong to me. I don't know how it got in my room. You're welcome to take it." She looked up at Devon, who didn't look angry, merely puzzled. She pleaded with her gaze for him to defend her.

"Are you sure you've never seen it before?" Devon said.

"I've dreamed about stupid nutcracker dolls since the party," she told Inspector Davidson. "And I thought I saw it when I arrived home after, but it disappeared. I fainted." She crossed her arms. She hated to admit to feminine weakness like fainting, but it also seemed a good way to get the men to leave her alone. They tended to run at the sight of a woman crying or passing out. Would pretending to faint work now? She decided against it.

"What is its purpose?" Devon asked.

O'Connell took the doll from Davidson and turned it over. "Doesn't seem to have one other than looking creepy. Miss Telfair, have you noticed anything unusual since it appeared?"

Fiona swallowed, the words choking her. She managed to gasp out, "Strange dreams."

"Oh?" Davidson raised his eyebrows. "Of what kind?"

Now her face heated with a blush. "Of turning into a mouse." It seemed indecent to say so with the three men standing there, and the fact her mother's lips had disappeared into a thin line confirmed her need to be embarrassed.

"Right. Let's bring it back and run some more tests on it," Davidson said. "You said the other young women live nearby?"

"Lillet's daughters? Yes, not too far away. Fiona, would you like to accompany us?" Devon smiled at her.

Fiona shook her head and crossed her arms. She suspected they wanted to use her to gain access to Lucy's house, but she wouldn't agree to it. Let them face down Lucy. And Mrs. Lillet.

**20**

———

T*erminus, 23 December 1871*
Devon checked the ballroom one last time before the servants allowed the guests to enter. He didn't think there was anything amiss, but he didn't want to take any chances that the scene from the Tinkerer's Ball would repeat itself. Never mind that as of yet, no one had heard anything from the missing people, and now they had a complete list. Most of the names were of the tinkerers from the guild's roster, a few servants, and a fair number of wives and daughters. Devon couldn't figure out why they'd all been taken, and it definitely bewildered him that no one had asked for ransom. Certainly there were families willing to pay. He would even chip in for some of them.

The search of the Lillet household hadn't turned up anything, not even an aetherized nutcracker doll. What had the purpose of it been? And how did the aether connect to Fiona's strange dreams? Davidson's team hadn't been able to extrapolate anything beyond some potential emotional manipulation. He would have liked to think the doll was behind the fact that

Fiona couldn't talk to him, but in truth, he had to admit that problem had preceded the appearance of the nutcrackers, both non-automaton and miniature.

"Is everything set?" Devon asked Henry Davidson, who looked dapper in his tuxedo. His cravat had been starched very white, and he pulled on his gloves. Beads of sweat on his upper lip matched those on Devon's. Devon had ordered for the fireplaces to be lit that morning to dispel the chill, and then the day had turned surprisingly warm. He'd forgotten how strange the Southern US weather was since he'd lived for a decade in France. But he couldn't have them douse the fireplaces now or everyone would leave smelling of smoke, so he instructed the servants to not add any wood to them.

"Yes, Patrick has been around the room with the aetherometer, and he hasn't found any evidence of devices, diabolical or otherwise. Edward did the same earlier, so it's been checked over twice."

Devon nodded. He of course had worked with Patrick O'Connell the day before, and he'd been thrilled to meet the infamous Professor Bailey, the genius who had stabilized aether and had led the way to using it in more ways than anyone had dreamed. Devon hoped that perhaps he'd figure out how to use it for energy, specifically on trains, while staying under Devon's roof, but no luck yet. Everyone had been too taken with the kidnappings.

The guests began to arrive. Of course there were plenty of mamas with their debutantes. Devon smiled at each of them, allowed his lips to hover over the young ladies' gloves, and searched their faces for...what? Some spark of intelligence, perhaps? He hoped they were simply nervous, and that's why they only smiled shyly or tittered in the manner only American girls giggled when he made some jest or even complimented them.

Fiona and her mother arrived in blue gowns that were very similar in cut, but Fiona's of a lighter shade. They both wore feathers in their hair, as did many of the other young ladies. Where had they gotten the money to be so stylish? Or had dressing his daughter for her debut driven Bryan Telfair to ruin?

Devon's uncharitable thoughts made him recognize that he tried to justify his behavior from earlier that week. He acknowledged now that he should have given Fiona some warning, but Henry had wanted to surprise her so she couldn't hide anything of her father's. Not that there had been much to find.

Devon greeted both Telfairs, and Margie gave him a bright smile that recalled what she must have looked like on the stage.

"Thank you for inviting us," she said. "I hope all is well with your investigation."

"I'm pleased that you're here." He ignored that Mrs. Telfair squeezed her daughter's hand at his words. "And yes, it proceeds, although nothing conclusive yet."

Mrs. Telfair sniffed. "Well, I'm sure you'll progress quickly now that you've rescued my house from that dreadful doll."

Devon tried not to laugh, and he didn't dare meet Fiona's gaze for a moment. But when he finally did, he only saw coldness, not the answering wit he'd hoped for. As he searched her face for some sign of familiarity or humor, he saw the shadows under her eyes, and alarm jolted through him. Was she unwell? He bowed over her hand, which she took back as quickly as was polite.

"I've a terrible headache," Fiona murmured to her mother as they walked away, her words carrying to Devon. He almost started after them, but a soft touch on his sleeve brought his attention to Therese, who stood there with Lucy and Posey Lillet and their mother. If Fiona had looked unamused, this trio appeared downright angry, but Devon was as polite to them as he could be. He deferred to Therese to welcome them and take them to the punch table.

As soon as all the guests had arrived—surprisingly on time for Terminus—Devon grabbed a glass of punch and gave the signal to the maestro to stop the orchestra from playing after the next song. He checked for his men—Davidson and his team and the extra security detail he'd hired—all stationed around the room, guessing that if something were to happen, it would be when everyone's attention was diverted, in this case, by him. But he needed to say something to his guests.

The music stopped, and Devon walked up to the stage. He looked around for Fiona and her mother and thought he saw her mother's bright blue feather poking up from the crowd, but hers was nowhere to be seen. He hoped she'd found somewhere to rest and vowed to make time to check on her. Even if they could no longer be friends, he at least wanted to make sure of her welfare.

Devon mounted the dais, putting thoughts of Fiona and her mother to the back of his mind. This was the first time he was going to address the *creme de la creme* of Terminus society, the ones he needed to make a good impression on to cement his legacy...and prove he wasn't a coward. He looked over the assembled, the shrewd mothers and the hopeful daughters and the confident fathers, each sure his daughter would win this lottery on the marriage mart. He took a deep breath and focused on his intended legacy—progress through unity.

He started his speech with the words he had prepared, and he was just about to get to the pitch for his legacy when a shriek nearly made him drop the papers he held. The feathers he'd identified as Margie Telfair's swayed once, twice, and then toppled into the crowd. The ladies around her cried out, and Chadwick Radcliffe rushed through the sea of satin and silk to her side.

He shouldn't have lit the damn fireplaces that morning. Devon walked over to where the woman lay in a faint and looked around for Fiona.

"Where's her daughter?"

Claire McPhee, who had just put something in her reticule, shrugged. "I'm sure she's around somewhere. But you need to get this woman to a cooler place."

Devon helped Radcliffe, Davidson, and violinist Johann Bledsoe move Margie Telfair into the green guest bedroom in the southern wing.


FIONA BARELY TOOK note of the ballroom as she passed through it. She murmured a question to a maid, who led her to the ladies' retiring room. Even this early, it was busy with debutantes fixing hems, tucking feathers into hair, and otherwise undoing the small damages that their travel to the Meriweather mansion had caused. None of them took note of Fiona, instead briefly meeting her eyes, then flicking their gazes away to show she was of no consequence.

And indeed, she wasn't. Her family had no money or clout from before the war. They belonged to the merchant class, which, to the high society, was just a step up from paid servants, and those barely a skip up from slaves.

Fiona found a spot at a mirror and sank on to the cushioned chair in front of it. She didn't pretend to apply powder to her face or fix her hair. Her headache pounded like a tiny hammer and anvil behind her right eye, and her shoulders twitched from the tension. She shouldn't have come. She knew this, just as she knew that Devon was no longer worthy of her attention, but her mother had been adamant. She looked at the girls who surrounded her, and snippets of their conversations floated through the air.

"Looking plump since her family's farm started producing again."

"With those teeth? She couldn't snare a horse's interest."

"Too mousy to be of any notice."

That last one made Fiona look around for its source before she realized none of them could be talking about her. Or perhaps they were. One of the girls flounced over, her silver dance card case winking in the light. Fiona stifled a sigh.

Of all the luck, Meribelle Blair had found her.

"What are you doing here, Mouse?" she asked. A sneer ruined her features, which would have been pretty if not for her haughty expression. "I didn't realize the Meriweathers knew such common people."

"I had an invite the same as you, Meribelle," Fiona sighed. "But don't worry, I'm not after Devon."

"I wasn't worried, Mouse. You're no competition for the rest of us. Why would he even look at you with your red hair? Why, it practically screams washerwoman. Irish peasant, even."

Fiona shrugged. She knew from experience that to continue to argue with Meribelle would only prolong the encounter. But then she remembered facing down the non-automaton and how she thought she'd killed him. Meribelle had no weapons besides her tongue, and in a flash, Fiona recognized that Meribelle did what the automatons had done and what her father, Jim Blair, had tried to do—intimidated to imitate power. And to this point, she'd capitulated.

The pounding behind her right eye spread to nausea in her stomach, but she stood. "Well, if there's one thing an Irish peasant isn't afraid of, it's taking down a nobleman by any means necessary. Have you ever killed a man, Meribelle?"

Meribelle's face flashed white, and Fiona knew her father had told her of his suspicions about Fiona.

"I haven't needed to," Meribelle said, but her words lacked her previous swagger.

"Then you don't know about the feeling of complete triumph over someone who was threatening you." Fiona wanted to stop herself from digging herself any deeper, but she couldn't help it. "You don't know what it's like to have true power over someone. Not the feigned influence you so desperately put forth. Oh, I'm sorry. Are the words I'm using too big for you?"

Now Meribelle's face flushed red. "Not at all. I'm not the peasant rat."

"Still, let me spell it out for you. Leave me alone. I know you're faking more than just your swagger." Fiona allowed her gaze to drop to Meribelle's decolletage, which she knew for a fact the girl stuffed. She could recognize structural adjustments in women's clothing.

Meribelle crossed her arms, and Fiona knew she'd won, Pyrrhic though her victory may have been. She guessed some nasty rumor about her would be flying around the ball by the end of the evening, and she would be powerless to defend herself.

She left the retiring room with her head held high, but rather than return to the ballroom with its smells of sweat and food and the pulsing of the music, she turned left and found the library. The barest wisp of a melody caught her attention. It sounded like the one she'd improvised on the violin that afternoon, the one that spoke of longing for a past that hadn't been what she'd thought.

A book with a red leather cover caught her eye. She walked over to it and picked it up. *Aetherics and the Music of the Spheres* shone in golden letters embossed upon the cover.

It seemed somewhat artsy for a scientific book, but not enough to dissuade her from investigating. Indeed, she couldn't resist the urge to pick it up and run her fingers over the indentations of the letters.

"Did you find something you like?"

The words almost made Fiona drop the book, and she wheeled around to see Devon standing in the door. No, not Devon, Pierce. Now that she'd spent so much time in Devon's company, she could tell the two of them apart. Another thought hit her—had the teasing she'd endured from Devon in their earlier acquaintance come from his cousin? Indeed, his next words confirmed her suspicions.

"No good comes to a bookworm," he said. "At least you've found something worthy of reading, not that fictional fluff you were so interested in last summer."

"My reading preferences are not your affair," she said as coolly as possible. "In fact, I don't care whether you approve or not."

He approached her, and while she held the book in front of her like a shield, she refused to back down. His left arm swung naturally in spite of the sling that held it, but he held something behind him. As he got closer, a tingling buzz filled the air and surrounded her.

"But I bet you care if Devon does," he said. "Too bad he'll never know."

Fiona's eyes widened, recalling the mysterious woman's shooting one of the automaton men in the left shoulder. "You were at Tinkerer Hall on Friday," she said. "You chased us and then you got shot."

"Very good, little mouse." He smiled, but without warmth. In fact, he examined Fiona with the eyes of an inventor looking at an object he'd created. Or considered destroying for a fundamental flaw in its design.

Now she did back up, but she didn't have far to go. When her back bumped the bookshelf, he brought out what he'd been holding—a nutcracker doll. But this one was bigger, its eyes brighter.

"Do you know what happens to human flesh when it's exposed to a certain frequency of aether?" he asked and turned the knob on the doll's back. "Especially for hours on end?"

Fiona, her throat too full of panic to answer, shook her head. Her skin felt loose, then tight, then loose again as though it considered sloughing off her, leaving her a creature of naked muscle and bone.

"Well, interesting things happen. Time and space can bend. Laws of conservation of matter suspend, or seem to, as your extra matter is released into the aether. And young women turn into mice."

He gave the knob a final twist and held the doll to Fiona's face. The air around her shimmered and glowed, and she couldn't move. She tried to shut her eyes, but the afterimage of the doll's glowing eyes seared into her brain, and she couldn't escape. Her dress became looser and her corset expanded. She tried to cover herself, but she changed too fast, shrinking into the dress itself, which sank to the floor with a satin *poof!* Gray fur covered her like a cloak, and she pulled it around her until it became part of her. It allowed her to dart through the walls and tunnels of fabric, always seeking a darker spot, a tighter, safer place to hide, especially once the ceiling started to collapse in bursts, then let up, then punch down again.

The part of Fiona's brain that retained its human faculties realized with a jolt of terror that Pierce was trying to catch her. Or kill her. Either way, she didn't want him to succeed.

Curses rained about her like the grabs through the fabric.

"Damnation, she's fast..."

She recognized she would be better off letting instinct take over, so she did so, allowing her little feet to carry her in a zigzag pattern and urging them to stick to places where the fabric made tunnels, and so she would be less visible going through it. Finally she found the spot where her dress ran out, but bookshelf met floor. She didn't know if she would be a copper-colored mouse because of her fur, so she paused to look back at Pierce. He had picked up her dress and shook it, so she moved as quickly and quietly as she could away from him.

The smells of the ballroom drew her, and although she didn't want to go, she couldn't help herself. She had to find her mother, after all. What if something happened to her because she'd been in the house with the doll, too?

Vinni paused on the flimsy catwalk and held up a hand. Cat stopped just in time to not run into her. Vinni could feel Cat at her back, her solid mass both comforting and smothering.

Vinni pushed aside the thoughts. Now that they were on their mission, emotions had no place in her field of awareness. What she needed to focus on was the thick darkness below. Her eyesight had adjusted, and she had excellent night vision, so why couldn't she see what was thirty feet under her? Rafters and other walkways hung around her, but the floor of the warehouse remained shrouded in gloom.

Or was it the absence of light?

"Aether shadow," Cat breathed into her ear, and Vinni nodded. If someone isolated aether and stabilized it long enough, in certain forms it would pull the light from around it and concentrate it, leaving a thick shadow, like a little cloud. But who would be working with enough aether to produce what looked like black smoke?

Yes, they'd found their target. Now they only needed to discover the identity and aim of the aether manipulator.

The catwalk shifted, and the metal ground against stone. Both she and Cat stilled, each of them barely breathing. Vinni looked around for the source of the noise, which had echoed in the cavernous space to the point of obscuring its origin. After what felt like forever, but which only amounted to ten counted breaths, Vinni stepped forward. The catwalk, obviously designed for just one person, slid down a couple of inches.

Vinni and Cat both dropped to their knees so they could hold on to something in the absence of a hand rail.

"Go back," Vinni mouthed. She didn't say Cat was the heavier of the two of them, almost six feet of solid muscle. Cat nodded and retreated until she reached the platform they'd embarked from to get a better look at the warehouse's contents. She backed into the shadows, the only indication she was there the barest glimmer of light reflected in her eyes. Vinni crept forward.

"What are you doing?" The words hissed through the air, imperceptible to anyone who didn't know her and Cat's secret language of breath. Vinni motioned with her hand for Cat to hush. She'd spotted a ladder that would hopefully allow her to climb below the shadow line and peek at what was beneath.

But as she inched forward, the metal bridge dropped another few inches. She looked ahead rather than down, and now that she had reached the midpoint, saw that the bolts had been loosened where the catwalk was supposed to be secured to the wall beside another platform.

No, there were no bolts, and the metal had scratched marks into the concrete of the surface to which it was supposedly attached.

Vinni dug in with her fingers, ignoring the sharp pain, as the brackets continued to slide down the wall with a screech, the metal groaning. While she couldn't claim a lithe debutante figure, Vinni certainly didn't have the sort of bulk to warrant the catwalk's failure, which meant one thing.

She and Cat had walked into a trap. Well, climbed from an alley on to the roof and then into a window of a trap, but still. They were in trouble.

There was no time to turn around, so she pushed herself to her feet and ran as fast as she could, making a leap when she thought she could reach the ladder. The force of her jump made the catwalk finally fail completely, and it crashed to the ground, hitting other objects with a variety of noises that would have delighted her had she not been counting on stealth. She didn't have time to enjoy the jolly smashes. Rather, she reached full-length and got one hand on the ladder. She slammed into it with the weight of her body and hooked an arm over another rung, wrapping her legs around it as well.

The noises from the crash subsided after one more tinkle of something glass, and Vinni hung there, waiting to catch her breath and for her heart to stop pounding in her ears. She guessed some of her fingers had been cut, judging from the wet slickness between her right hand and the rung she clung to, but she kept herself from noticing more. She looked over her shoulder and caught Cat's wide-eyed look. Her partner, too shocked to utter anything, made a hand signal—*what now?*

Vinni shrugged. She had to figure out what direction to take —up, where there was hopefully another way to get to their ropes and therefore their escape, or down, where danger lay.

Or would this be her chance to get away from the neo-Pythagoreans?

Her mind was made up by the crack-whoosh of a door opening below. Of course they wouldn't be lucky enough for the falling catwalk to go unnoticed. At least the aether shadow kept anyone from seeing her. Even without it, she'd be near invisible in her brick-colored jacket, pantaloons, mask, and now-shredded gloves, all designed to camouflage her in dark surroundings made from Terminus's favorite building material.

Up it was, then. She stifled a grunt as her muscles protested moving after having hung so tightly. A glance over her shoulder and down made her climb faster, albeit still silently. Now a glow suffused the edges of the room, pairs of orange splotches at what would be man-height that shone through the aether fog, which—*oh, cripes!*—was dissipating. The edges of the fallen catwalk came into view, and Vinni's right hand met air— the end of the ladder. She jerked her attention away from what was below and hoisted herself on to the platform, barely stopping to catch her breath before crouching and trying the knob of the door in the wall.

*Unlocked!* But if this was a trap, not just another one of several old warehouses, whose owners never bothered to keep in good repair, how smart was it to keep going? Should she find another way across?

She closed her eyes, took a deep breath, and concentrated. The cult had trained her in her one gods-given special ability, but she hated to use it. She'd seen the price extracted by the gods on others who didn't use their gifts wisely—Uncle Dross, for example, who had descended into madness and drink. But this was a case of survival.

*Forgive me,* she thought and stilled her mind, calling forth a vision of a light shining through a gray cloud, like on a rainy day just before the sun breaks through. If it had a feeling, the ability came from the base of her skull, which tightened, inside and outside. The outline of a dark hand appeared in the middle of the cloud and clenched into a fist.

Vinni leaped back as the door was flung open. If she'd been standing where she'd been a moment before, it would've sent her flying off the platform. As it was, she grabbed the person who, not expecting the door to meet no resistance, stumbled out and over the edge of the platform. He clung to the doorknob, his feet in their shiny boots dangling in midair. His black eyes met Vinni's, and she tried not to smile back. No, he grimaced under his white beard.

*Automaton!*

She pulled a large knife from her boot and brought it down on the creature's wrist. The blade severed the cables and passed through the joint. The automaton's eyes glowed orange, and it swung its other arm around to catch her, but its fist met air as it tumbled to the room below.

Vinni hadn't let go of the vision, and now the hand beckoned her forward. She maneuvered around the door and entered a room that looked like an office. She couldn't resist one last look at the floor below. A man's voice floated up to her.

"Good, you got them. Oh, oh no. You lost your hand, you silly creature. No, that's damage from a blade." Then a piercing whistle. "Guards! There's an intruder in the building."

**21**

———

*erminus, 23 December 1871*

"I think the queen is trying to kill me." Henry stuck a finger in his collar and attempted to give his windpipe a bit more air. Not that there was much to be had in the center of the sweltering room.

"Kill you or cook you?" Chadwick Radcliffe fiddled with his gloves, and Henry suspected his friend might eventually be called upon in his capacity as physician when someone fainted. That would make for an interesting turn of events considering that while half the guests had been ministered to by Negro slaves since childhood, they may object to an educated half-Negro's attempt to function as a professional. While freedmen artisans and workers weren't unheard of in the former Confederate states, they had rarely mixed as equals with those who owned their kin.

"Maybe both." Henry again attempted to position himself in the least roasting part of the ballroom. But he stayed as alert as he could to the atmosphere in the entire room, which appeared polite on the surface but pulsed with unresolved tension. Not surprising. With Terminus as part of the Union for the first time in over a decade, no one was sure what to expect. And Henry knew that trouble tended to happen when tempers flared in the heat.

"Anything yet?" he asked Chad's wife Claire, who looked stunning in a royal blue gown that set off the gold in her red hair. She'd just returned from a trip to the powder room. Henry hoped he wasn't taxing her too hard. Claire McPhee Radcliffe, known for being one of the few women neuroticists in the world, could also sense others' emotions. Between her special ability and Chadwick being able to make friends with just about anyone within two minutes of meeting them, they made for valuable members of his recon team.

She wrinkled her nose. "Only what you'd expect from a mix like this. Anxiety, tension, irritation, and hope that Devon will pick one of this crop for his wife by the end of the season, but annoyance that he's so rich that they can't fault him for being a coward."

Henry sighed. He hadn't counted on the single bachelor problem. "There's nothing like a rich unmarried young man to make the hopeful mothers drag their daughters to a mixed event. I only wish he'd not lit the fires." And the dancing flames in the elaborate candelabra and wall sconces took care of any cool eddy that may find its way in along the sides. Henry envied the women in their ball gowns—at least they could expose their shoulders, chests, and upper arms, although every white, tan, and brown bosom and shoulder he spotted glistened with perspiration to match that on the men's foreheads.

The current song ended on a triumphant note, and the equally uncomfortable-looking musicians scattered to take a break. Henry caught the blond head of Johann Bledsoe weaving toward the refreshment table. He'd get Johann's impressions later. Chad and Claire moved off to speak to another couple, and Devon Meriweather ascended the stairs to the dais. He held up his hands, and the murmuring of the crowd ceased.

"Thank you all for coming to this historic event," he said. "I'm honored to open my home to such an esteemed mix of guests, and I hope everyone is having a good time."

A smattering of applause greeted his words. Henry took note of who clapped and who didn't. It didn't surprise him that Jim Blair stood with arms crossed. He'd heard Jim had tried to nip Devon's bachelorhood with a marriage arrangement before anyone else could try. And failed.

Devon continued, "This ball will go down in history as not the only, but the first to mark a new era in Terminus, of mutual understanding and respect, and—"

A shriek from the side of the ballroom made everyone turn. Henry spotted the tall feathered hairdressing of one of the debutante's mothers sway and then disappear as she fell and the blue feathers dropped below his line of vision. He couldn't resist thinking "Timber!"

As he expected, Radcliffe moved quickly, commanding those around her to move aside and give her some air.

Mentally apologizing to the queen for doubting her, Henry pushed his way through the curious crowd and found Chadwick kneeling next to Margie Telfair. Red spots on her cheeks stood out against her otherwise pale face.

"We need to get her out of here," Radcliffe said. "She's overheated and appears to have had a shock."

"We can take her upstairs to one of my guest rooms."

Henry looked up to see the concerned face of Devon Meriweather. A movement at the corner of his eye alerted him to Claire, who wasn't distracted by the drama unfolding around her, picking something up and putting it in her reticule. He suppressed the smile that wanted to emerge as pride for his team swelled in his chest.

With the help of two other men, one of whom happened to

be Johann, they got the matron out of the ballroom and into the blessedly cooler part of the house. Devon led them to a bedroom, and Henry took note of the furniture—light wood—and colors—cream and light green—but mostly looked around to make sure no one hid in the shadows. They laid the woman on the bed, and Radcliffe pulled smelling salts from an inner pocket.

Devon took the man Henry didn't know aside and told him to go downstairs, reassure the other guests, and tell the musicians to start playing again. Johann followed him out, and Henry noted how Radcliffe relaxed a hair, as did he. He guessed none of them were necessarily comfortable with Claire being alone in the ballroom, where she could be faced with hostility at being in a mixed-race marriage, but he also knew she could take care of herself.

The woman woke with a gasp and sat straight up on the bed. "My daughter! Where is she?"

Chadwick patted her hand and gently pushed her back on the bed. "I'm sure she's downstairs, Missus...?"

"Telfair. Margie Telfair. Mister Meriweather knows me," she added with a simper to Devon, then turned back to Chadwick. "Mrs. Bryan Telfair to you."

Although his friend was good at hiding it, Henry could see the barely perceptible disappointment Radcliffe felt whenever he faced racism. "Well, I'm Harvard-trained physician Doctor Chadwick Radcliffe, so now that we know who we are, why don't you tell me why you fainted?"

"Oh, Harvard?" She paused and cocked her head. "Fine. I fainted because it's beastly hot down there, and oh! My daughter Fiona. She was supposed to be back from the powder room by now—then—and hadn't appeared. I thought just after Mister Meriweather's speech would be a good time for them to dance." She looked up through her lashes at their host, whose expression had changed from concern to cool politeness.

"You can lie here for a bit until you cool off, and we'll send your daughter up when we find her," Devon said.

"Good. I'd love for you to spend more time with her." She sighed. "I was even more beautiful than she in my day."

Henry doubted that. The woman had front teeth out of proportion to the rest of her face, which he hadn't noticed until just now.

"By the way, Mr. Meriweather," she said, and she seemed to have difficulty talking. "Did you know your house has mice? I saw one in the ballroom just before I fainted." She gave him a shrewd glance, which made her look even more rodent-like. "I'd hate for that fact to get out. That you had a rodent at your ball." Her eyes rolled back in her head, and she fainted again.

"Odious woman," Radcliffe muttered but applied the smelling salts again. They didn't rouse her. He took her pulse. "It's very high," he said and asked Devon, "Do you have any pharmaceuticals?"

"I'll check." Devon left, and Radcliffe stood.

"Let's dim the lights and leave her for a moment. She's had a shock to her nervous system. Perhaps giving her time to sleep peacefully—and finding her daughter—will help her to recover. If not, she may need the hospital."

"Or Claire," Henry said, holding the door open for Radcliffe to precede him. Radcliffe turned down the flame on the bedside lamp, and they both left. Henry reached behind him to close the door, and a bright flash of peach-colored light almost blinded him. The door slammed, pushing him into the hall.

"What the bloody...?" he asked, but no matter how hard he and Radcliffe pushed, they couldn't get the door open again. When they paused in their efforts, the sound of small clawed feet scrabbling through the room could be heard.


Fiona skirted the edges of the party. She had to find her

mother. Her stomach pained her terribly, and she needed to go home and rest. Why had she come? The more she thought, the harder it was to think. Plus, it had been a decidedly strange evening.

First, she had lost her dress, but she found herself unconcerned, having instead a lovely gray fur coat.

Second, she now ran on all fours, but again, it seemed to make sense. That was the easiest way of getting around, after all. Four feet took her around much more easily than two.

Third, everything had gotten large. Very large. Like, the claw feet of the ballroom refreshment tables stood as tall as she, and the legs reached out of sight into the gloom under the tablecloths. She'd figured out to stick to under furniture. Otherwise large, cruel shoes tried to smash and step on her, or she got knocked about by moving walls of fabric. Thankfully no one had noticed her yet.

The smells of food and alcohol tempted her to stop and investigate a fallen morsel here, a splash of something sweet there, but she had honed in on her mother's unique combination scent of perfume and the chemicals from her father's workshop.

*There!* Fiona had to look up, but she was pretty sure the wall of satin belonged to her mother. She'd been wearing blue, hadn't she? Fiona had been finding it difficult to keep her focus on just one thing, but whenever her mind wandered, her stomach pain kept her alert on the goal.

Her mother looked down, and, head craned back as much as possible, Fiona stood on her hind legs, waving. But instead of being happy to see her, her mother's eyes had grown large in horror. Then she shrieked and fainted.

Fiona tried to run to her, but something caught her by her tail, then by the loose skin at the back of her neck. The floor fell away, and Fiona plopped into something dark and filled with strange objects. The opening closed above her, and she squeaked in panic.

"Hush, little mouse," a woman's voice said. "There's something odd about you, and I want to help, but I can't get you out of here if we're caught."

Her words made sense, but Fiona still burrowed as low as she could go and, finding a tear in the reticule's—that's what her brain said—lining, she snuggled between the layers of soft fabric so she wouldn't be poked by the things around her. While the gentle rocking as they moved may have put her to sleep ordinarily—she had a dickens of a time staying awake in carriages—she remained alert. Where was the woman taking her?

The noise of the ballroom rose, and glad to be hidden, but still not relaxed, Fiona attempted to use her nose to determine their progress.

Ah, there were the cucumber and cream cheese sandwiches. Then the savory cheese balls. And the little sandwiches with the smoked meat. The punch table, the last station before the door that led to the hallway she'd gone down to find the powder room, smelled of fruit and the effervescent alcohol that had been added to it to make the intoxicating beverage. But Fiona never partook of the punch—she'd seen how alcohol made her friends' cheeks rosy and dulled their intellect—and she had no desire for that to happen to her.

The reticule's motion included some vertical jerks as they ascended some stairs, and an odd but familiar noise made Fiona curl up tighter. The singing—she'd heard it before. Then the world had gone all wrong. But it had all started when she'd heard what sounded like a choir made up of only sopranos or children, their harmonies beautiful yet mathematical. She didn't know how she heard the math, just that it was the only way she could describe it that made sense to her.

"Claire, stay back." A man's voice stabbed through the ethereal sounds. Fiona caught his tension, but also the tenderness. This one and the woman who had captured her—Claire?—must have some sort of romantic relationship. She folded her paws, er, hands over her chest and sighed. She might be on her way to being a scientist, but Fiona Telfair would always be a romantic.

Oh, right, she needed to pay attention to her captor.

Another man, this one with an English accent said, "Something odd is happening."

Fiona snorted. He had no idea.

"What's going on?" Claire asked. "Is the woman who fainted in there?"

That made Fiona's ears perk. What were the singing voices doing with her mother?

"Yes, but we don't know what's happening to her." This was the first one. "She didn't seem febrile, but she was experiencing tachycardia. Then something pushed us out of the room."

"What sort of something?"

Fiona quietly cheered for this Claire person's calm demeanor and logical questions. At least she thought she did so quietly.

"What was that?" Footsteps approached, and Fiona curled herself yet tighter. "Did you hear something squeak?"

"I hear something in the bedroom," the first man said. "It sounds like the squeaking of a large mouse."

"Mother!" Fiona tried to cry, but her mouth wouldn't make the word.

"Claire, do you have a mouse in your reticule?"

Fiona's satin prison lifted and dropped slightly as though with a sigh. *Oh god, oh god, they're going to find me and... Something was trying to catch me.* But her little spot grew tight.

"I found it in the ballroom. It didn't act like an ordinary mouse."

"No, I fear it isn't."

The purse shrank around Fiona, and with the ripping of seams and cold air, the singing crescendoed, and she found herself curled up in a ball on the floor of Devon Meriweather's hallway. Naked.

HENRY HAD SEEN a lot of strange things on his various assignments as special investigator for the queen, but the sight of a large mouse popping out of the side of Claire McPhee-Radcliffe's reticule and then growing and turning into a young woman with copper-colored hair and milk-pale skin—Fiona Telfair—ranked up there with the oddest. Thankfully Chadwick Radcliffe had already been unbuttoning his dinner jacket, and he slung it over the confused girl, who crouched on all fours and looked up at them with wide green eyes.

"Is my mother here?" she asked, then passed out. Henry caught her before she hit her head on the floor. He wrapped her in the inadequate garment as best he could and hoisted her into his arms, trying not to look at her exposed limbs and barely covered other parts.

Claire retrieved the remains of her reticule from the floor. Only the outer layer had torn, and she gathered up the inner pouch.

"Thankfully I don't think anything is broken," she said. "Perhaps we should get her into a room before someone comes along and the poor girl's reputation is ruined?" She inclined her head toward the door through which they'd brought Mrs. Telfair.

"Let's try the next one," Henry suggested. He didn't know what lay in that room.

They found another bedroom similarly decorated, this one in warm golden wood and dark green. It felt somewhat nautical to him. He laid the girl on the bed after Claire pulled the covers down. Then, once they'd covered the girl, Claire waved the smelling salts vial she'd retrieved from her husband's jacket under the unconscious young woman's nose. Her eyes fluttered open.

"Oh? Oh!" She clutched the sheet and duvet over her. "Where am I? Where's my mother?"

Claire smiled. Had she found a kindred spirit in the girl's inquisitive nature? Many young ladies he'd known would have screamed or hidden. Or fainted again, as useless as that was.

Claire spoke gently. "I'm Doctor Claire Radcliffe. The gentleman over there is my husband, another physician, Doctor Chadwick Radcliffe. And this is Inspector Henry Davidson. Who are you?"

The girl acknowledged each of them with a small nod, then said, "Yes, I remember you now. I'm Fiona Telfair. A guest at this ball. And I'm concerned about my mother. She fainted downstairs." Then her eyes glittered with the precursor to tears. "When she saw me."

Claire patted her hand. "It must have been quite a shock for you. What had happened before that?"

Claire's touch seemed to have a calming effect. Fiona told her story without much emotion, but her face betrayed her shock at her own words. "I went into the library for some quiet, and I found a book I was interested in. I'd just sat down to take a look at it when I heard singing. It seemed to come from the book?" She scrunched her brows together. "I don't know how. But then I became smaller and smaller and shrank into my clothing." She paused. "No, that's not right. Something else happened. Then I went downstairs to find my mother, and..." She spread her hands, but continued to frown. "That didn't make much sense, did it?"

"No, but that's all right. We'll sort it all out. You said your clothes are in the library?"

Fiona looked down, then at Claire. "They must be." Her face reddened. "They're not here, so they must be there. Or am

I having one of those awkward dreams where you wake up naked in a public place?"

"I'll get them," Henry volunteered.

"No, you stay here and guard her," Claire said. "I'll try to find a maid to fetch them, and if not, I'll get them myself. It will be less scandalous for a woman to be seen fetching clothing than a man."

"Less scandalous than a young woman being left alone with two men?" Henry asked.

"One of whom is a physician," Claire argued.

"A Negro physician," Chadwick said. "As her mother pointed out."

"Very well, both of you stand outside the door. Fiona, we'll need to leave you alone for a few minutes."

Fiona nodded. "I'll be fine. If you find my mother, please send her in."

"We will," Claire promised. "Just try to rest." The three of them walked out of the bedroom.

"I'm not sure what to think about all of this," Claire said, "but at the very least we need to get the girl some clothing. Do you know where the library is?"

"Just beyond the powder room for the ball, as I recall." Henry had walked through the house several times, as had the other members of the "security team," but of course Claire hadn't since they'd been stationed separately. "You can get to it without going through the ballroom if you take the back hallway and servants' stairs."

"Do you need help?" a maid asked. She approached the room with some linens. "I need to go in for a moment, gentlemen."

"I'm afraid the room is closed for now." Henry showed his inspector badge. He didn't know if that would work here in the States, but it seemed to have the desired effect. The maid nodded and backed away, her eyes wide.

Claire stepped forward. "But can you show me to the library? Through the back way?"

"Yes, ma'am. Follow me." When she passed, the maid practically squeezed herself against the opposite wall. With a shrug, Claire followed her.

"What did Meriweather say about you?" Chadwick asked with a grin.

"Who knows?" Henry rubbed his right temple. He'd been clenching his jaw again, a habit he thought he'd broken but which always returned. "Perhaps we should check on Mrs. Telfair."

"If we can get the door open."

When they tried, the door to the green bedroom opened easily.

**22**

---

T*erminus, 23 December 1871*

After he looked for—and failed to find—Therese with her medicine case, Devon returned to the party. Perhaps his sister was there? He attempted to assure the guests who knew her that Margie Telfair had just become overheated and rested well in the care of a physician in the company of her daughter. At least he hoped Fiona had turned up.

Not that he had been keeping track of her or watching for her copper hair among the guests that thronged about him. He had been trying to figure out how to ask her to dance. And then he'd noticed her continued absence, well, that of her red hair, always easy to spot in the crowd.

He attempted to focus on the comments of the senator he spoke with, but he had to tuck a corner of his mouth in so he wouldn't smile. The feathers had been her mother's doing, he was sure of it.

Layla Bollington pushed her way through the crowd, and the senator Devon had been talking to excused himself so quickly as to almost be rude.

"Is the woman who fainted all right?" she asked.

Devon checked to see if Bollington had her ubiquitous pencil and pad of paper out, but she didn't. She only looked up at him with concern.

"She's resting comfortably under the care of Doctor Radcliffe."

"Oh! You know him?" Now the familiar inquisitive expression came to her face.

"We were introduced by a mutual acquaintance. I understand he has started good work in the city."

Bollington nodded. "Yes, he's training former plantation healers in modern medicine. Effective, but not efficient. Now if only someone would endow a school or some other way for more Negroes to be trained..." She gave him a sly grin.

Devon laughed. He wanted to be annoyed with her, how pushy she could be, but he found her attitude charming. How could he not admire someone who went after what they wanted, especially when their intentions were for the betterment of their people?

But she would make an even less acceptable wife than Fiona.

A maid beckoned to him from the far end of the ballroom, and he stifled a groan. Now what?

"I'm sorry, but I must go."

He bowed and made his way toward the maid, hurrying once he saw who she stood with. His sister Therese had a perplexed expression on her face.

He shoved aside the worry he didn't have time for and hoped his attempt to entertain the Terminus elite wouldn't end in flames like his parents' last airship ride. Devon dodged hopeful mamas and their daughters with what he hoped were charming smiles and compliments. Once he reached Therese and the maid, he wiped his forehead with a handkerchief and said, "I swear the room stretches in the heat."

"And the determination of the debutantes," Therese

added. "I'm sorry to bother you, but I think you need to see this." She lowered her lashes and her voice. "It's quite scandalous."

Swallowing another groan, Devon followed her and the maid to the library, which was just beyond the powder room and lounge the female guests had been using. A royal blue dress lay crumpled on the floor, and atop it, a hairpiece with a peacock feather.

"Do you know whose those might be?" Therese asked with a sideways glance after dismissing the maid, who had found them.

Devon shook his head, but ruefully rather than to say no.

"Has anyone seen Fiona since before the speech?" he asked.

"Some of the other girls said she freshened up in the powder room and then pleaded a headache, saying she wanted to go lie down for a moment."

"Did she get disoriented and undress herself?" Devon asked, both alarmed and intrigued.

"No." Therese picked up the dress. "Everything is laced, including the corset. Oh, and the ties on her underthings. No, it's more like she vanished from within them."

"How could that possibly be?" Devon held out a hand, but Therese pulled the dress away.

"Mama said the only times a man should see a woman's corset and other underthings are on their wedding night and in their marital chamber. Whatever happened to the poor girl, let's give her some privacy."

Instead, Devon picked up the peacock feather hairpiece. A few copper-colored strands clung to the hairpins that had secured it in place. How could someone just vanish?

"Oh!" A gasp brought Devon's attention to the door. At first he thought the woman was Fiona since their coloring was so similar, but then he noticed her hair was lighter, more reddish-blond, and she wore a lighter colored blue dress. He recognized her as Claire Radcliffe. He'd wanted to introduce her to Therese since she specialized in disorders of the mind.

"Lady Doctor Radcliffe, this is my sister," he said.

"It's nice to meet you." She took Therese's hand and looked into her eyes. Her own brows drew together in an expression of concern. "Are you feeling well?"

"As well as one can," Therese replied and pulled her hand away. "I'm worried about one of our guests, Fiona Telfair. Have you seen her?"

"Unfortunately, yes. She's in a somewhat awkward position. Are those her clothes?"

Therese nodded and piled all the garments into the female Dr. Radcliffe's arms. "What happened?"

"That I'm afraid we don't know. But I need to bring these to her. And Mister Meriweather, please be advised there is something strange in the guest room you loaned to Mrs. Telfair. It's probably best that you not open the door."

"Right. Wait, what?"

But she'd already left.

Devon turned to follow her, but then reflexively checked on Therese, who had sunk into one of the chairs. He'd come to associate every degree of paleness in her skin with a necessary action or intervention. In the current case, her pallor indicated she likely needed to take some laudanum for the stomach pain that flared when she'd pushed herself too hard.

"Do I need to get your case?" he asked, referring to the leather satchel that was never far away and that contained her medicines. Indeed, it leaned against the chair beside her.

"No, I just need to rest."

"Do you mind if I take a couple of laudanum vials, then? Doctor Radcliffe asked if I had any pharmaceuticals. Someone fainted in the ballroom."

"That's fine. Go," Therese said. "Find out what happened to Fiona. I'll be fine."

"Are you sure?" Devon took her hand and tried to feel her pulse.

She jerked her arm away. "Yes, go. This is yet another mysterious and interesting thing that's happened here this winter. Don't miss it." And with a smile that appeared to bring some color to her cheeks, "And then come tell me all about it."

Vinni barely paused in the office beyond the doorway, her ears still attuned to the commotion behind her. Men shouted, and she moved as fast as she could while being careful not to knock into anything that would give away her position. She guessed they would figure out sooner rather than later that they should look past the network of catwalks and ladders above the aether cloud, and she had no intention of being found when they did.

She only hoped Cat had gotten out when the catwalk crashed. Of the two of them, Vinni, although she looked less threatening, held up to torture better. Or had when they'd been in training in the cult, and then in boot camp in the Airship Service. She trusted Cat not to give her away—well, not to the men who searched for them—but she didn't need their mission compromised. They'd done what they were supposed to do— discover and confirm the source of the aether disturbance.

Vinni grabbed a couple of documents off the desk and stuffed them into a pouch at her waist. Perhaps they would give her an indication as to who owned the facility, which had been rented under an alias, and what they were up to. Besides building automatons that had something to do with excessive aether use.

The area beyond the office led to a hallway. Vinni had just reached the corridor when doors opened on either side, and automatons with glowing red eyes emerged. Vinni ignored her first impulse, to attack. Instead, she flattened herself against the wall and remained as still as possible. As she hoped, the false men, all of whom had strange grimaces and facsimiles of soldiers' uniforms, looked around and then retreated back into their rooms. She waited a few heartbeats and then slunk along the hallway. A familiar voice complained, "No, that's not right. They're supposed to patrol, not retreat. Why are they not following orders?"

*Uncle Dross was right.* But somehow she'd known Paul Farrell would pop up at some point. After he'd left the site of what could only be called a disaster in Boston, he'd disappeared. But he couldn't resist the chance to show off his talents. So what was he doing here with his automatons?

The hallway led to a set of stairs, and Vinni went up rather than down. She hoped Cat would give up and leave her. If not, it promised to be a long night of hiding and being hunted by multiple people. At least the weather hadn't turned cold yet.

Footsteps on the stairs above her drove her through the nearest door, which brought her into a large storage space. In spite of her good night vision, she couldn't see more than a few feet in front of her, so she had to move cautiously. Visibility remained minimal even when the door opened behind her and gas lamps flickered to life throughout the room. She scrunched between two crates, barely breathing so she could listen for the sound of anyone approaching.

"See? I told you no one was here." a man said, his accent lilting as was typical for the region. The words rolled into her ears rather than stabbing at them like the dialect from her home airship base of New York.

"Don't matter." This one had gravel in it, and Vinni hoped she wouldn't have to encounter the man it belonged to face-to-face. "The boss wants us to check everywhere. Catwalks don't just fall. There was someone up there."

While relieved they apparently hadn't found Cat, Vinni prayed they wouldn't come farther into the room. She waited, but the lights didn't go off. Nor did the men say anything else until, "Hey, you!"

Now she scrambled toward the door, but a dark-skinned man blocked the way. She pivoted and went down the next aisle between the crates. A skinny white fellow with pockmarked cheeks almost intercepted her, but she pushed a stack of boxes on him. She didn't wait to hear whether he was hurt.

Shots whizzed over her head before the first man who had spoken yelled, "What do you think you're doing? Do you want to get us all killed?"

"He's getting away."

"Nowhere to go but out the window, and there's no fire escape. Let him figure that out the hard way."

Vinni gritted her teeth. There was no way she'd give herself up. If she had to go out of the window, so be it.

The dark glass rectangle came into view, and she sprinted toward it. She paused long enough to shoot a hole through it, then leaped at the spiderweb-cracked glass, left elbow and knee poised to break it, and crashed through. She braced herself for the fall, but instead found herself caught in a net that dipped precipitously with her weight before lifting her higher. Glass shattered and tinkled on the ground below.

Pain stabbed through her elbow, and a dark liquid dripped into the air below her. Her blood. Dizziness made her grip on the net falter.

"Hang on," an oddly familiar female voice said, and Vinni looked up to see a woman with white-blond hair returning her shocked gaze. A woman Vinni knew. Vinni almost laughed at her predicament—out of the globe and into the aether sphere.

"Why, Mrs. Bailey," Vinni said. "Fancy meeting you here."

IT TOOK a moment for Henry's eyes to adjust to the dim light in what he'd started to call the light green bedroom. A dress lay on the bed, empty and flat except for the shape of the corset and underskirts. The skirt itself lay askew, half draped off the side of the bed. A strange smell permeated the small space, like the air just after a spring rain, but somehow not fresh.

The scratching noises had stopped when they'd opened the door. Weapons drawn, Henry and Chadwick entered, closing the door behind them. A lamp flickered on the mantle, and Henry lengthened the wick to give the room more light. Chadwick walked around the bed and gestured for Henry to join him.

The paint in the corner of the room by a clothes-press had been scratched away to reveal the plaster underneath. Deep tooth and claw marks indicated whatever had done it was larger than the typical rodent. So where was it?

They turned to the bed at the same time.

"It must be under there," Henry mouthed. Chadwick nodded. They bent at the same time and lifted the bedskirt. Two eyes about five inches apart stared back at them above large whitish teeth.

It was the biggest rodent Henry had ever seen, and it was not happy to see them, judging from the sound that came from it—a combination of hiss and growl. They dropped the bed skirt and straightened before moving back toward the door.

"What now?" Chadwick asked so quietly he almost whispered.

Henry gestured for him to follow him, and they exited the room.

"I suppose we'll have to advise Meriweather to trap it but not kill it." Henry said. "I'm sure Mr. O'Connell can come up with something."

"Trap what?" Claire arrived from the other direction, her arms full of clothing. Henry caught himself clamping his jaw shut when Devon Meriweather turned the corner behind her.

He knew he'd have to explain the difficult situation to their host; he just hadn't counted on having to do it so soon.

Chadwick excused himself to return to the ball since someone needed to keep an eye and ear on things, and Johann couldn't do much from his position with the musicians. Henry doubted the rest of his team, who patrolled the city in a small airship or the grounds with the security detail, were having as eventful a night.

"I'll help Fiona dress," Claire said. She ducked into the other bedroom, leaving Devon and Henry in the hallway.

"How is Mrs. Telfair?" Devon gestured to the closed door Henry stood in front of. "Has she recovered from her shock?" The thin line of his lips indicated he hadn't forgiven her for her rudeness.

"In a sense." Henry, typically not at a loss for words, struggled to find the ones that wouldn't make him sound like he needed a visit to an asylum. "Perhaps you should sit down." Of course there was no place to do so.

"Just tell me." Devon raised his eyebrows. "Please don't say she's dead. I'd never forgive myself."

"No, she's not dead."

Relief made the host's color return. "Good. Then what's happening? Does she need to go to a hospital? A sanitarium?"

"Not exactly. There is, ah, a very large rodent in the green bedroom."

"Oh my god! The poor woman." Devon moved toward the door, but Henry stopped him. "What? You're not keeping her in there with it, are you? I've got plenty of bedrooms we can move her to."

Henry sighed. He couldn't think of a better way to say it, and from what he knew of Devon Meriweather, he'd appreciate directness. "Mister Meriweather, I'm afraid to say that Mrs. Telfair has somehow become a large mouse."

**23**

---

*T*erminus, *23 December 1871*

When someone knocked on the door, Fiona pulled the covers up to her shoulders and said, "Come in."

She'd managed to convince herself she'd dreamed of the ball and the library, and now she had made a nocturnal journey to a bedroom where she could enjoy wiggling her feet and running her fingers over the soft, high-quality linens. The sheets she slept on at home had become close to threadbare, the blankets adequate for the mild Southern winter so far. She dreaded the cold that often came in January and February. But that didn't matter in this wonderful, delicious...

The lady doctor Claire Radcliffe entered, and the weight of reality crashed over Fiona. Or did it? She thought she'd recognized Claire from somewhere, but the name had thrown her off. But here stood one of her heroes, a woman with a talent for tinkering who had helped invent La Reine, the gun that had ended the long War Between the States. And she was a physician, so she'd had formal education.

"How are you feeling?" Claire asked. Fiona, hoping they

could be friends, already called her Claire in her mind. She watched as Claire put the clothing on the bed before placing a hand on Fiona's forehead. "You don't seem to have a fever."

Now Fiona blinked away the sting at the back of her eyes. When had her mother last touched her with such care? Not since she'd become of marriageable age. Her father had stayed the kind parent. Before he'd disappeared.

But Claire had asked her a question. "Better. Please tell me, was I really a mouse?"

Claire laid out Fiona's garments so they'd be easy to put on quickly. Well, as quickly as one could with all the layers society required a woman to wear.

"My torn reticule says so." But Claire didn't seem upset. In fact, she grinned, and Fiona did as well. They must have similar minds if they saw an intriguing puzzle where others would perceive something strange and frightening.

"Oh, I'm so sorry. I'll mend it for you."

"That's quite all right. What do you remember about the experience?"

Fiona reached for memories, but they'd disappeared, hidden behind a foggy curtain. "As for what I recall, it all seems like a strange dream. Giant shoes. Moving fabric walls. Tunnels under tables."

"Spilled morsels?" Claire stood back. "There, I think that's everything. Here's your shift."

Suddenly shy, Fiona asked, "Would you mind turning around?"

"It's all right, I'm a physician." But she complied. "You don't have a maid?"

Fiona hopped from the bed, noticing how much colder the air felt now that she'd warmed herself in the cozy sheets and since she didn't have fur. Her mother's voice popped into her head—*"Don't go telling people outside the family about our problems. You'll never catch a husband if people realize how poor we are."*

Fiona pulled the shift over her head, careful not to muss her hair before she remembered it must be in a hopeless state. She spoke through the fabric, like it could filter her evasion. "What happened to my mother? Have you found her?"

Now she had the feeling Claire dodged the question. "In a sense. Are you sure you don't need help?"

Fiona had put on her stockings, garters, and pantalettes under her chemise, but then she got to the corset. Her mother had helped her with the laces earlier, but she didn't know if she could do them herself.

"I think I may." Fiona's skin heated. "My corset..." She loosened the laces, then put it on and fastened the hooks in the front.

"Don't worry, I won't pull too tight," Claire told her. Indeed, after a couple of firm pulls that made Fiona straighten but not uncomfortably, Claire tied the laces.

Fiona caught a glimpse of the two of them in the mirror. They could have been sisters, Claire's hair lighter and her face wiser, but they had similar haunted expressions in their eyes. Fiona looked down before Claire could notice and ask more, but it was too late. Claire walked around Fiona and tilted her chin up.

"I'm sorry to hear about your father. Whatever is happening, we can help."

Fiona caught the words—whatever *is* happening, not whatever happened. Which meant her mother was still in danger. And she'd wasted too much time already. Fiona started toward the door, but Claire caught her by the laces. "Not without your dress."

"Right." She'd already shown enough of herself.

Claire helped Fiona with the petticoats and then the dress itself. Then Claire helped her put her hair up with some pins she pulled from her reticule. Had those been some of the sharp things Fiona had felt?

"There. You look beautiful."

"Not like a mouse. So about my mother?"

Claire sat Fiona on the bed. Did she expect her to faint?

"This is going to sound like a strange question, but considering what you've just been through, maybe not. Has your mother ever turned into a mouse before?"

THE AIRSHIP ASCENDED out of reach of the warehouse with Vinni still hanging in the net. Just as she thought she was going to faint, they landed on the rooftop of a nearby building. Well, Vinni landed. She used the last of her strength to scramble out of the way before the small dirigible's gondola crushed her. Except it didn't touch down but hovered a couple of feet above the surface.

"Are you all right?" Iris Bailey's dark blue eyes were wide, Vinni hoped with concern.

"I... I think so." Vinni had crawled out of the way, her left knee and leg screaming, and now her left arm stinging with the touch of the air through the tattered remains of her sleeves and gloves. When she tried to stand, warm liquid ran down her left leg. She swayed, and Iris had to rush to prop her up. Vinni had forgotten how petite she was, but she was grateful for Iris's strength. Wasn't there a saying about surprising things and small packages? Vinni's mind whirled. She needed to get away, but she couldn't. She needed medical attention, but she didn't know where to find it.

She needed to get away from the neo-Pythagoreans, but not jump into the hands of her enemies. Well, it was too late for that now.

Iris helped Vinni into the airship and guided her to recline in the cargo area behind the two pilot seats.

"Edward, do we have bandages in here?"

"There's a kit back there. Look to your left."

Vinni almost laughed. Of course the fastidious Edward Bailey would know where everything was.

"Are you all right?" he asked, but Vinni could tell he was more worried about his wife.

"I'm fine, but she's in a bad way. Lost a lot of blood." Iris found the box with the supplies and wrapped Vinni's arm and leg as best she could. "Sorry, don't have anything to clean your wounds with, but this is the best we can do. We'll let Chad and Claire have a look at you."

Vinni nodded. Of course they'd all be there. She almost asked about Henry Davidson but stopped herself. When she'd pictured meeting him again, this was not how it had happened. She'd imagined rappelling down into the garden of a stuffy tea house, startling the overly proper patrons and bringing a true smile to the spy's face. Not being brought in like a trussed chicken.

Edward had only watched the two of them, and once Vinni was bandaged, he increased the power to the engines. Iris stowed the net and sat beside him.

"Is that...?" he asked.

"Lieutenant Crow." Iris shrugged, her gloved hands palmup. "Remember? From Boston?"

Edward and Vinni snorted simultaneously, and he said, "I don't think I can forget Boston. That awful party. What was she doing in there? The aetherometer—"

Iris interrupted him. "I don't know. What *were* you doing in there, Lieutenant?"

But Vinni didn't respond. The sound of the engine, which had a strange noise, distracted her. She wanted to identify it, but her attention kept slipping. Nothing serious, she thought, but it could become so. The English accents of her two captors soothed her, and she drifted in and out of consciousness.

She didn't wake until the gondola bumped while landing, but it thudded on something soft like grass, not hard like stone or brick. When Iris opened the door, Vinni smelled crushed leaves and grass, and music drifted through the air from somewhere not too far. Strings, mostly. A party?

"What have we here? Did you catch something good?" Irish accent. Must be Pat O'Connell. "How did the—" But someone cut off the question. The tones of a quiet but intense conversation hissed around Vinni, but she couldn't make out the words over the ringing in her ears.

"Uh, Professor and Mrs. Bailey? Mister O'Connell?" Vinni called, or tried to, but her voice came out strangled like in her nightmares when something awful chased her, but she couldn't move or scream. "I'm going to need that medical attention sooner rather than later." Then the ringing crescendoed, and she blacked out.

THE DOOR beside the room Devon had left Margie Telfair in swung open with a bang, and he barely jumped out of the way before it hit him. Fiona Telfair, a fiery ball of worry and anger, burst into the hallway from the next room.

"Where is she? Where's my mother?" Her voice cracked on the last word. Devon reached for his handkerchief in case she burst into tears, but she stepped back when she saw him, then curtsied. "Mister Meriweather." When she straightened, the track of a tear glistened on her cheek.

Devon handed her his handkerchief. "Please don't be distressed, Miss Telfair. Your mother is safe, although she may not be exactly as you remembered her."

Fiona's lips puckered like she tasted something bitter. "You mean she's turned into a mouse."

Devon hadn't expected Fiona to say that, but the others exchanged a look that reminded him of when he'd been in the foreign service and his commanders had been keeping something from him. "That's what I've been told, yes."

"And you believe it's impossible."

Devon recalled the state of Fiona's clothing when he'd found it. She certainly seemed to fill out her dress nicely now, her breasts two pale mounds above the bodice of the royal blue gown, the shade of which set off her hair and skin beautifully. He couldn't imagine her turning into something as repulsive as a rodent. Her mother, on the other hand...

"I have seen too many things on my travels to deign anything as impossible. Improbable, perhaps, but not impossible."

Fiona put her hands on her hips, and Devon could tell his answer hadn't satisfied her. "So, about my mother?"

"She's in there." Davidson gestured to the other bedroom. "Would you be willing to help us capture her?"

Devon wanted to object, but in truth, he didn't see any other way, so he allowed the others to take the lead.

"I promise we can help you," Claire said as though she repeated the assertion. "But we need to catch your mother first."

Fiona sighed. "Very well. But then I'm counting on you to figure this out." She looked at Devon. "I apologize for the inconvenience my mother and I have caused you."

He missed the easy rapport they'd shared earlier that week, albeit briefly. He almost said, "Not at all," but having one's guests turn into mice during a party made for a rather large— but intriguing—inconvenience, so he only nodded and replied. "Thank you. Please know I'm happy to assist you in any way possible."

A blush crept to her cheeks, and his own face heated in response. He hadn't meant what he said to come out suggestive, but he had been staring.

This was too much. Thankfully Davidson directed him and Chadwick Radcliffe to stand on either side of the door before Devon could say anything else stupid.

"I'll go in first," Davidson said. "Then Fiona. Then the others. Mister Meriweather, Mister Doctor Radcliffe, hold a sheet between the two of you and use that to capture the creature."

"I'll get one," Claire said and went into the room she and Fiona had emerged from.

"My mother," Fiona said, "she's not some creature, although her conduct isn't always ideal. Perhaps this will teach her a valuable lesson."

Her distress caused Devon a pang of grief for his own parents. They'd been far from perfect, but he missed them just the same. And he hadn't made any progress in finding her father.

"How are you holding up, Miss Telfair?" he asked.

"I'm as well as could be expected." She didn't look at him.

"Here." Claire handed a bed sheet to Davidson. "I'll stay out here in case she runs past."

"Good," Chadwick said. "She may need medical attention, and she'll accept it from you better than from me."

Fiona closed her eyes for a moment, her mouth tight. "I'm sorry." She opened her eyes. "For whatever she may have said."

"Perhaps this is an opportunity for her to learn something different." Claire put a hand on Fiona's arm. "Are you all right with this?"

Fiona nodded. "Let's get this over with."

They got into position, and Davidson opened the door. The first thing that greeted them was a blast of air smelling of autumn leaves and grass. The door to the balcony hung open, and a quick search told them they'd dallied too long.

Margie Telfair had escaped.

**24**

———

T*erminus, 23 December 1871*

When Fiona saw the door to the balcony swinging in the slight breeze, the sinking in her gut dragged her to sit on the bed, upon which lay her mother's empty clothing.

"Not again." The moaned words escaped from her mouth before she could catch them.

"I'm so sorry." Devon looked down at her. "I've failed you again."

Fiona squeezed her eyes shut. She wouldn't cry, not in front of him. But she wouldn't disagree with him, either.

"Devon!" A familiar man's voice called from the hallway, and something about it shot a jolt of anxiety through Fiona, but she couldn't remember why. It continued, "Where the dickens are you? The guests are starting to worry that you or Therese has been taken ill."

Devon cursed under his breath. "I'll be right there, Pierce." He took Fiona's hand, and his touch through her glove made a little shiver of pleasure snake up her arm. "It's apparent to me that you're in danger. Please accept my invitation to stay here under the protection of my household. You can become Therese's companion so there won't be gossip. Well," he amended. "Not too much."

Fiona snatched her hand back. She could only nod, and she hoped she heard the words he didn't say, that they could work on the puzzle of the disappearing tinkerers together. Now the weight of relief held her to the bed. Devon walked into the hallway, and the tones of two men in intense discussion faded as they walked away.

"I'll check the grounds," Mister Doctor Radcliffe said.

"Don't bother," Fiona told him, and she didn't try to keep the bitterness from her tone. "She's probably long gone. Like my father."

THE BED BESIDE FIONA DIPPED, and she tried to blink away the blur of the tears she'd been trying so hard not to shed. She saw that Claire sat beside her.

"It's all right to tell him—us—anything." Claire gestured to the two men. "We're used to strange things and interesting puzzles."

Fiona cocked her head. She liked interesting puzzles, but she preferred to not be a piece of one of them.

"Had anything unusual happened beforehand?" Davidson asked. "Even the smallest thing could be helpful. A change in routine, a visitor..."

"I know you think my father is somehow involved, but he simply can't be."

"It can be difficult to find out something about someone you care about," Davidson said, and Fiona found herself clenching her jaw as she did when her mother did or said something particularly condescending.

"No," she said, "please listen to me. My father would never do anything to put me in harm's way. And I found this at

Tinkerer Hall." She pulled the button she'd found from her reticule, thankful that nothing had gone missing.

He examined it, and she held her breath. Would he see it?

"It's a Prussian design," he said. "Solid brass."

"Yes." She almost slumped with relief. "It's a unique alloy, and not something that any of the tinkerers here would have access to. Toward the end of the war, such things had been melted down."

"So you're saying a button proves your father is innocent?"

"It proves that more than he and Thaddeus Lillet are involved. Please look wider." She blinked through the blur of tears. "I believe they could have been coerced."

"Was he aware that other tinkerers had gone missing?" Claire asked.

Fiona nodded. "Yes, which is why he hadn't left the house in several weeks. Only to take me to the ball." She clenched her fists. She'd been so selfish. "But he's talented enough that people come to him."

Davidson continued to scribble. "What is his specific field?"

Now Fiona lifted her chin with pride. "Aetherics, specifically applications in devices. After Professor Bailey's brilliant discovery about how to stabilize it, he started experimenting with aether as a way to animate devices, specifically to motivate them with different frequencies to do one goal-oriented, albeit repetitive behavior."

The male Dr. Radcliffe chuckled. "She sounds like you when you get wound up about something, Claire."

"There's no good reason for a woman to not show off her knowledge," Claire replied, but in a similarly teasing tone. Fiona sighed, happy for her idol, but also jealous. Would she find someone who admired her mind like that? And who would see her as worthy?

A wave of fatigue overtook Fiona, and she plopped on to the bed again. "I'm sorry. I'm exhausted."

Davidson closed his book. "Doctors, you should probably return to the party in case there's anything else. And allow Miss Telfair to rest. I'll be asking more later." He looked toward the balcony door. "And I'll alert my team outside to look out for a large rodent, and to capture it without harming it." He left, and the two doctors held a quick whispered conversation before Mister Doctor Radcliffe left the room.

Claire gestured to the dress on the bed, which looked like a deflated balloon. "What would you like us to do with your mother's clothing?"

"I... I don't know." And would it matter? Her parents had disappeared, leaving Fiona alone. Would she eventually become a rodent and run away or be taken, too?

"This is a lot for you." Claire put her hand on Fiona's shoulder. "I understand, but I don't think it's good for you to be alone right now."

Fiona almost clutched Claire's hand. "No. No, don't leave me alone."

"All right." Claire's voice took on an almost hypnotic, soothing tone. "I want to check on Devon's sister Therese. Would you like to accompany me? I don't know her—or you—very well, but I think you'll get along."

Fiona nodded, and they left the room. Fiona decided not to worry about her mother's clothes. She needed to try too hard keep herself together. Literally. What would bring on another rodent change?

Before she could say anything else, a commotion made her look toward the hallway.

After Devon entered the hallway, he found himself face-to-face with the last person he expected—Layla Bollington. He'd noticed that Therese had put her name on the list, her handwriting evident in its extra slanted double-L, and hadn't objected. If Therese wanted to entertain the press, that was fine with him, especially if it meant the ball would get good publicity.

"Can I help you, Miss Bollington?"

"Mister Meriweather, I need to talk to you. Now. Is there somewhere we could speak in private?"

Devon wanted to sigh with exasperation—he wanted to know what Henry Davidson would do next—but acquiesced. He suspected Bollington was not the kind of woman who would deliberately waste his time, and she might have information. "Come into my office."

"That woman," the reporter said. "Will she be all right?"

"I can't say." He couldn't tell her what had transpired. They reached his office, and he poured himself two fingers of brandy. His ankle ached, but he dared not take laudanum. Hopefully the brandy would take the edge off.

"Is something wrong, Miss Bollington?"

She drew herself up to her full, albeit not intimidating, height and pronounced, "Mister Meriweather, I recommend you end the ball early and send everyone home until we find your cousin and see what he's been up to."

"That's a big request. What makes you think he could present a danger to my guests?"

"I did some digging into the Tinkerer Guild's rolls, as we'd agreed upon." She gave him a look that said she was all too aware of his failure to share his discoveries with her.

"My contact turned out to be suspicious," he told her. Well, not as suspicious as her father, but still... He didn't know what to think. The brandy left a nice warmth in its wake but didn't touch his ankle pain. He put the glass down. "But you seem to have found something."

"Your cousin has had some interesting financial dealings with the Tinkerer's Guild." She withdrew an envelope from her reticule. "I made some notes, and I just received confirmation from a contact at the bank that these are accurate."

Devon rubbed his eyes. "And who is your contact?"

"I can't say. But I can vouch for their legitimacy."

She handed him the papers, and he looked through them. Names were listed in one column, figures in another, and a total on the bottom that made him raise his eyebrows.

"What does it mean?" he whispered.

"It looks like your cousin was making 'donations,' specifically to certain projects. If you look at the names, those were the men who were taken, along with some of their families."

Including Thaddeus Lillet and Bryan Telfair. Devon shook his head. "You can't think Pierce has anything to do with this. My cousin wouldn't hurt anyone, not deliberately."

"Do you know what your cousin was doing while he was away?" She crossed her arms, and Devon suspected with a sinking feeling that she'd not finished her revelations.

"He went to school up north, then came home to run the family's business."

"And did you go to his graduation?"

"No, I was abroad."

"Did your parents?"

"No, they'd been killed in an airship cr—" His knees gave way. "You can't be serious. He can't have had anything to do with that."

"You know the reason for the accident's never been solved." Her tone had softened. Devon's head spun.

A soft knock at the door heralded the arrival of Henry Davidson. "I may have something to add to Miss Bollington's information, if it is as I suspect. A telegram just arrived for me from one of my contacts up north."

Devon shook his head. "These things she's saying, they're impossible. Pierce has never been anything but loyal to my family. Look, he even arranged to buy this beautiful house..."

That Devon hadn't wanted. And that had a mysterious door off the laboratory. Could Pierce have been lying about not being able to open it? Did he have more sinister experiments lying under the bluff the house sat upon? "But what were you about to say about his time at school?"

Davidson pulled a piece of paper from his jacket. "I received a communication from Harvard. He was dismissed for unsavory conduct during his second semester."

Devon read through the missive, which looked official. "What did they mean, 'unsavory conduct'?"

Henry spoke, and like Bollington, his voice carried only sympathy. "I sent a message for clarification. They said he got mixed up in some strange religious group up there and was expelled for fighting, breaking campus rules about curfew, but mostly for trying to recruit others into his group."

"What was the group?" Devon couldn't reconcile this picture with what he knew of his cousin, the boy he'd grown up with and the man he'd come to depend on.

"The neo-Pythagoreans." Henry shook his head. "They're a dangerous fringe cult, supposedly descended from the followers of Pythagoras, and invested in protecting their secrets at all costs, including deadly actions."

Devon stood. "I need to talk to him. I understand what you're telling me, but the connection to the Tinkerer's Guild is all circumstantial. And as for that...cult... If he was so invested in it, wouldn't he have tried to convert me and Therese to it?"

But he had been trying to marry Therese... To convert her? Or to get his hands on more of the family fortune?

"We don't know what mission he came back with," Henry said. "But it sounds like he was invested in aetherics development, although I'm unsure as to what end. We do know the neo-Pythagoreans have a strange relationship with aether and are experts at manipulating it through nontraditional means." He held up a hand before Devon or Layla Bollington could ask for clarification. "And that's all I can tell you. The rest is protected information."

Devon didn't care. "I'm going to talk to Pierce. He'll have an explanation for all of this."

But when they went to Pierce's chambers, he found them empty and many of Pierce's things gone.

"What in the devil...?"

A moan caught Devon's attention, and he opened the armoire to find Hollowell curled up in there. They helped him to stand, then sit on the bed.

"He took her. They took her."

"Who?" Bollington asked.

"Caprice."

"The little girl." Devon looked around. "Where?"

Hollowell wrapped his arms around his stomach and swayed. "I don't know. They said if I told you anything else, they'd kill her."

Some of the pieces from the previous day's conversation clicked into Devon's brain. "You lied to us about Telfair and Devine. You were trying to deflect suspicion away from..."

"Your cousin." Hollowell looked up at him. "And you see what I got for my trouble. I shouldn't've lied to you, Mister Meriweather. But they said they'd do awful things to her..."

"And now you have more reason to fear for her."

"I shouldn't've trusted them."

Bollington stepped forward. "How did you end up in the armoire?"

"They stuffed me in there. I pretended to be unconscious and breathe shallowly so they'd think I was about to die." He grimaced. "They're not the only ones with tricks."

"Well, we need to find them." Devon rubbed his face.

Henry put a hand on his arm. "I'll get my team on it. If Pierce suspects we've figured out his involvement, he may do something desperate."

**25**

---

Terminus, *23 December 1871*

Henry walked through the party to make sure everything at least felt normal. He didn't have much hope of finding Margie Telfair. He hadn't mentioned it to the others for fear of upsetting Miss Telfair, but there had been scratches on the floor and baseboard, barely visible in the dim lamplight, that showed evidence of a struggle. He hoped the team outside had captured the mousenapper.

The ball seemed to have returned to normalcy. Some people danced. Many chatted and sipped at punch. No one screamed or fainted.

How tiresome. Now that the monotony of the previous two weeks had abated, Henry wanted something else to happen. He'd forgotten—made himself forget, perhaps—the rush that came with the witnessing of a strange and unusual occurrence. But it wasn't as though such things dropped out of the sky.

He'd take a turn outside. Escape from the stuffy ballroom. Be head of security and check on his team.

He was just at the door leading out to the balcony that overlooked the house's broad lawn and gardens when he encountered Patrick O'Connell coming the other way.

"Good, you're just the man I wanted to see," Henry told him. "I need you to alert the security teams to look out for an unusually large rodent and to capture it without injuring it. In fact, it would be better to let it escape than to harm it in any way. Oh, and we're also looking for Pierce Meriweather, so please detain him if you find him."

O'Connell looked at Henry like he spoke gibberish. Rather unfair, Henry thought, considering Patrick had been privy to many forms of the strangeness aether could generate. A large rodent shouldn't be that surprising.

"I need to find Chad," Patrick said. "Edward and Iris are back with a guest, who is badly injured."

Chad must have seen them talking because he came to join them in the shadows. "Is everything all right?"

"You're needed. Someone's badly hurt."

"One of the team?" Chad's forehead tightened.

Now Patrick grinned at Henry. "Not yet."

Henry recalled the Irishman's love of a good tale—and the possibility of one. "Who is it?"

Patrick affected his Irish brogue as they walked. "Are ye remembering of a lass called Lieutenant Crow?"

Henry's leg hadn't bothered him much that night. In fact, he'd forgotten about it in the excitement of the women who turned into mice, but it twinged when the mention of Davinia Crow made him stumble. "What in blazes is she doing here?"

"Iris and Edward used the aetherometer to find a large concentration of stabilized aether. I didn't get the whole story, but she got caught in their net when she came out of a window."

"What are the injuries?" Chad asked, bringing Henry back to the problem at hand.

"They said her elbow and knee are torn up pretty good from breaking through the glass."

Henry shook his head. "What must have been after her to make her take such a risk?"

"You can ask her yourself. Here we are." Patrick opened the door to their quarters and then melted back into the night. They found Davinia Crow with Iris sitting beside her, pressing a bandage to her left elbow. Crow held a rag to her left knee with her right hand. Edward stood nearby, presumably in case Iris needed help. A cursory glance told Henry they were fine, and Davinia was not. She looked very pale, and she watched Iris through slitted eyes, her head lolling occasionally like she fought to stay conscious.

Chad leaped to action. "Status?"

"She's lost a lot of blood," Iris said. "I can't clean the wounds because I can't let up pressure on the bandages."

"Just hold them. You, too, Henry. Lieutenant, are you in pain?"

"I'm torn up like I've just fought a tiger bare-handed. What do you think?"

Her humor made Henry suspect she was covering up just how badly she hurt. Indeed, she started shivering.

"Blankets!" Chad looked up. "Edward, get blankets. We need to keep her warm, stop the bleeding, and then once she's stable, I'll clean the wounds."

They wrapped Crow in blankets, and Chad had her lie down on the rug. Iris and Henry continued to apply pressure to the wounds, and Edward made some sort of herbal tea at Chad's instruction and helped Crow drink when it had cooled enough. Finally some color came back to her face.

"There," Chad said. "I'll do what I can, but it's not going to feel good."

"Do what you need, Doctor."

Henry could tell Chad had been in an active military fort

with the speed and efficiency with which he cleaned, bound, and stitched the wounds. He had to force himself not to look away from the lacerated tissue and skin.

"You're lucky you didn't sever any tendons or major blood vessels," Chad told her when he was done. "It will take time for you to recover, but you should regain most of the mobility in your hand and arm. Now, drink this." He tried to hand her a teacup with laudanum mixed with herbal tea in it, but she pushed it away.

"No, thank you, Doctor." Crow attempted to stand, but the others had to catch her and guide her to a chair. "No laudanum. I should be on my way."

"Not so fast. Or slow," Henry told her. "You're not going anywhere. You're too hurt, and I have too many questions for you."

She favored Henry with a coy look. "You're presuming I have answers, Inspector."

Chad cleared his throat. "She needs to rest. You can question her in the morning. Presuming she's up for it." He gave them both a stern look.

Patrick returned. "Party's slowing down," Patrick said. "And no signs of—" He bit off the next word when he saw Crow sitting there. "You're looking much better, Lass."

"Yes, I hear the gauze elbow look is in this year." She held up her swaddled left arm. "The debutantes will be jealous."

Chad looked at the ceiling and then down at his now bloodied formal attire. "I should find Claire so we can head back to our apartment. I'll let you know if I hear anything else."

"Thank you," Henry told him. "For everything."

"Never a dull moment with you 'round, Inspector." And with that, Chad was on his way.

Iris helped Crow to stand, and Henry was once again reminded how he tended to underestimate Iris's strength despite her petite frame.

"Where were you?" Henry asked.

"I'll give you the address of the warehouse she jumped from," Iris said. "She needs to sleep. And it's not proper for an unmarried young woman to be in the company of so many men. She can stay in our room with me. Edward will sleep out here."

"Nonsense," Henry told them. "I have a perfectly good bed in my room that's not being used. He can share with me."

They didn't mention that Iris and Edward's room was situated in the middle of the hallway, which meant should Crow somehow manage to slip past Iris, she'd have to pass by either Patrick and Johann's or Henry's and now Edward's room. But Henry guessed she'd figure it out. He'd noticed her looking around, presumably for an escape route.

No, he wouldn't let this crow get away, not this time. He had too much to ask her, and there was one question that couldn't wait.

"Lieutenant Crow," he said, placing a hand on her arm. She looked up at him, and he could see the laudanum fog descending over her. Someone must have given her some before she'd realized it.

"Yesh, Inshpector?"

"What was chasing you?"

She shook her head. "Men. And since you won't believe it anyway, nutcrackers."


Fiona followed Claire to the library, which was empty. She glanced at the book she'd been reading when she'd turned into the mouse, and which now lay on a small round wooden table. She didn't touch it again. While she might desire to learn more about *Aetherics and the Music of the Spheres*, she didn't want to risk another transformation. Well, not unless it could be under controlled and not embarrassing circumstances.

"Is that what you were reading?" Claire asked.

Fiona nodded.

"Did you touch it with your bare hands or with gloves on?"

Again, the moments before and during her time as a mouse dissipated like candle smoke when Fiona tried to grab them. "I don't remember. I like the feel of books, especially ones with soft leather covers."

Claire smiled. "Me, too." But she didn't touch the book, either. Instead, she laid another one on top of it. "There. Hopefully no one will bother those."

A maid came in carrying a tray and picked up an empty glass from another table. "Can I help you, Misses?"

"Yes," Claire said. "We're looking for Miss Meriweather. Also, please make sure no one disturbs these books."

"Yes, miss." The maid raised her eyebrows but didn't ask why. "Miss Meriweather is in the gallery. I'll show you."

She brought them through the hall and then up some stairs. As they traveled, the music from the ballroom grew louder, and the undercurrent of murmurings and conversations found a sympathetic thrum of sharp anxiety in Fiona's breast. Were they talking about her? Her mother? Had they even been missed? She couldn't remember much of the ball before turning back into a human, only that she'd already felt off and had a headache when they'd left the house.

At the top of the stairs, the maid paused on a small landing and knocked softly at a wooden door. "Miss Meriweather? You have visitors."

Fiona thought she heard rushed footsteps, or perhaps she only sensed the frantic beating of her heart. She shouldn't have been able to hear, anyway, through the din.

The words, "They may enter," spoken with quiet authority, somehow floated through the door and cut through the other noise.

The maid opened the door and stepped back, still

balancing the tray with the single glass. Again, Fiona waited for Claire to take the lead and walk into the wall of sound, which lessened once they entered the chamber. It somehow seemed quieter in the middle, the sound a vibrating ring that shielded the center of the room in a cushion of relative silence. Fiona could hear her own breathing again and attempted to slow its rate. Anxiety, or a leftover from being a smaller mammal with naturally faster respiration? Could that explain her moment of acute hearing? Oh, where was her notebook when she needed it?

At home. Where her mother had insisted she leave it.

Fiona fought the frustrated frown that tried to crease her cheeks. But even the octagonal room, which some might find homey, failed to set her at ease. They stood in the room behind the balcony that overlooked one end of the ballroom. Art in ornate frames lined the red damask wallpapered walls, a different painting on each of the six sides that didn't contain the door through which they had entered or the balcony itself, which was wide enough for a small chamber ensemble. Comfortable but masculine furniture in dark wood and leather lay about the room. Fiona could picture her father and his colleagues here sharing brandy and smoking pipes, but she found it stifling. The scents of the ball—perfume, candle, sweaty bodies, salty food—mingled with the sweet tangs of leather and tobacco and made her stomach turn.

No, she couldn't have heard footsteps. There was only one door to the room, and Fiona doubted that Miss Meriweather had caused them.

Therese Meriweather sat in an armchair that seemed to swallow her and showed no sign of recent exertion or activity.

"Miss Meriweather, may I present Miss Fiona Telfair." Claire said.

"Yes, it's good to see you again." Therese rose and took Fiona's hands. "Are you well?"

"I...I think so."

"Yes, it sounds like you've had a rough evening, although you must tell me the trick to disappearing out of one's clothing. Getting undressed can be extraordinarily tiresome. So many layers."

Fiona's cheeks heated. It seemed improper to discuss *un*dressing with Therese even though she'd recently thought something similar. "I would tell you if I could determine how I did it, Miss Meriweather."

"And she is currently without a guardian," Claire broke in.

"Oh." Therese Meriweather sat back and folded her hands on her lap. "That is unfortunate. What happened?"

Not the expression of the sympathy Fiona had hoped for, but Therese acted oddly. "My parents have gone missing, and I have no relatives from whom I can seek shelter. It would be improper for me to stay at my house by myself."

"Did they disappear under mysterious circumstances?" Therese asked. "I do love a good mystery."

Fiona and Claire exchanged a look. Perhaps that's why Therese hadn't debuted—she was an eccentric, and a macabre one at that. But Fiona also sensed a certain forlornness, a despair of being understood. Because of her affair with Bollington?

"Very," Fiona said. "My mother was my chaperon tonight."

"Ah, so you're on the husband hunt." Now Therese looked at Fiona and pressed a finger to her lips. "And I suppose my charming brother has stepped in and offered to take you into his protection."

Fiona looked at Claire, who stood to the side and observed the two of them but didn't interfere. Fiona got the message— she needed to stick up for herself, even if she didn't like being pushed.

"I didn't ask him to." Fiona straightened her spine.

"Oh? Why not?"

Now Fiona felt toyed with, and the fatigue from the evening hovered behind and above her like a thunderhead ready to crash down on her with a drenching of fat raindrops that would soak her in an instant. "Because I don't want to marry. I want to study. And be like Doctor Radcliffe and make things and help people and..." The raindrops threatened to well up in her throat.

"I see." Therese steepled her fingers. "Then you must stay, at least until some other arrangements can be made." She picked up a bell from the table and rang it. "I'll have one of the maids show you to the rooms next to mine and find you something to wear. Unless you'd rather return to the ball?"

Fiona wrinkled her nose before she caught herself. Such an unladylike expression! "No, ma'am."

Therese laughed. "I don't blame you." A maid came through the door, and Therese shooed Fiona off.

"Go on, then. You must be exhausted. Ah, Doctor Radcliffe, I imagine you want to have one more look before you go. I assure you I'm feeling quite well in spite of all the excitement."

Fiona followed the maid and tried to examine the feeling of unease she had over the arrangement. Therese appeared content in her situation, and if she wanted a companion, it wouldn't be Fiona. But why had she acted so oddly? Oh! Fiona put a hand to her mouth. Had she and Claire interrupted something?

So many mysteries... Fiona hoped that nice British inspector would come speak to her again, if only to give her an update on the search for her mother. Perhaps he and his team could succeed where she and Devon had failed. The sooner she found her father, the sooner she could return to her old life, at least what was left of it.

.  .  .

Henry gathered Patrick, Edward, and Johann from the ball, which was winding down. He gave them a quick debriefing, and soon they were on their way to downtown Terminus to the address Davinia Crow had escaped from to look for clues. He shook his head—how did she always drop into his life at such interesting times? He suspected the fantasies that popped into his brain about settling down with her were just that—fantasies. Was that why he was so attracted to her—she represented adventure?

He dragged his mind back to planning how best to approach the warehouse. But when they arrived, parked the steamcart two blocks over, and approached, they found the doors unlocked and the place abandoned, apparently quickly. He stood in the main laboratory area, where the aetherometer flashed to tell them that there were still traces of it. Although the air lay thick and silent in the space, the occasional scratching sound in the walls told him that they were not completely alone. The question—were those real rodents or transformed ones?

"Let's say that the process Miss Telfair went through today was forced," Henry speculated. "How much aether would that require? And at what concentration?"

"I don't know, but there was a lot of it," Patrick said. "If it's reacting without any of the active stuff still here."

Edward nodded his agreement. "That's an interesting development—it leaves a residue."

"You didn't know that before?"

"No." Edward grinned. "No one's managed to make so much in one place." Then his face sobered. "We're dealing with a very clever scientist."

"More clever than you?" Johann teased. He held something in his handkerchief, which he handed to Henry. A button like the one Fiona had found in the ballroom lay nestled in the white cloth.

"Of course not," Edward scoffed. "But it's going to be tough to get at him. I'm sure he has some clever traps laid."

"Regardless, we need to rescue those poor people." Henry tucked the handkerchief and button in his pocket. They walked through the warehouse and offices, not finding much. A scurrying in one of the large rooms that was filled with empty crates caught Henry's attention, and he looked down to see the skinny tail of a rodent disappearing between two bricks. Something bright green lay on the floor where it hadn't been before. He bent down to retrieve a piece of grass.

"That's out of season," Johann commented.

Henry put it in the handkerchief with the button. "Well, then. Another clue matching what Miss Telfair observed."

"What do you think of the lass?" Patrick asked as they walked out. His tone didn't betray what might be behind the question.

"She's clever and resourceful, like one would expect of a tinkerer," Henry replied. "But still innocent."

"D'you think she'd fit on our team?"

Henry raised his eyebrows. He stopped himself from giving the first reply that came to mind, that he wanted to spare her the tough choices he'd already forced on the rest of them. "I believe we have enough tinkerer brainpower for now."

"And Devon Meriweather would probably object," Johann pointed out. "You can't have missed how he looks at her. I'm surprised, Patrick. You're the romantic of the group."

Patrick's cheeks turned pink above his red whiskers. "T'would be nice to have another Irish person around, that's all."

A laugh escaped Henry. "I'll see if I can find one for you."

They stepped into the dim light of the flickering street lamps, and Henry buttoned his coat against the breeze that the alleyways and narrow roads concentrated into a moving wall of cold. A movement in his peripheral vision made him hold up a hand, and they all stilled.

A dark-skinned man approached them. He wore the rough clothes of a laborer, and when his and Henry's gazes met, he nodded.

"Glad to see you here, Sir. Do you know what's going on in that place?" he asked.

"No," Henry said. It wasn't a lie—he didn't know exactly what was happening. "What can you tell me about it?"

The man rolled his shoulders, his hands still in his pockets. Henry gave his men a hand signal—*watch for weapons*.

"Well, now, not much. Only that there were strange comings and goings." He glanced up.

Henry noted the look. "What do you mean by strange?"

"They typically used an airship, but a black one, and only at night. But that's not the weirdest thing." He cleared his throat. "I'm only telling you this because you look like a lawman, but not one of Blair's men."

Henry removed his credentials from his pocket and showed it to the man, who nodded.

"Mind you, I know such things can be faked, but you have an honest face." He lowered his voice. "Once this place opened up, people started disappearing. And suddenly the neighborhood had a mice infestation."

Henry's stomach turned. "What did you do about it?"

"Couldn't do nothing. The mice were too smart to catch, and something didn't feel right about trying. And then one night, they all disappeared."

"Disappeared?"

The man nodded and looked up. "It was one of the nights the airship came."

That made sense, although Henry wasn't about to tell the man why. "And what about this building? Do you know who owns it? Who was renting it?"

"It's a Meriweather Rail warehouse, but before a couple months ago, they hadn't used it. And those weren't Meriweather Rail men. Those of us here know each other."

"Did you recognize who it was?"

"Yankees brought in. And one time I recognized one of Jim Blair's men." Anger briefly flickered over his features, and Henry guessed that the man shared his sentiments about Jim Blair, the racist sheriff of Terminus.

"Thank you, this has all been very helpful. Is there anything else?"

"Just one thing. If you see my wife Cora, pretty woman about my age with light skin and gray eyes, please send her back to me. She's been missing since..." He jerked his head toward the warehouse, turned on his heel, and hurried off.

Henry exhaled. "It sounds like they've been experimenting on the neighbors."

"Aye," Patrick growled. "Let's figure this out, and we'll catch the bastards."

"Right. And all signs point to Pierce Meriweather. Again." Henry sighed. "As much as Devon disagrees, it sounds like we'll be heading to his hunting lodge in the mountains."

*erminus, 24 December 1871*

A clap of thunder followed by a whoosh of rain against the side of the building woke Henry the next morning from the hour's doze he'd allowed himself. The wind whipped around the quarters, and a damp cold seeped through the cracks in the thin walls. When he turned to look out of the window, his leg throbbed its objection to the morning's sudden cold turn to the weather and to the amount of standing he'd done the night before.

Winter had come to Terminus.

The other bed stood empty. Henry must have slept unusually soundly to not have heard Edward rise.

Henry rolled out of the bed and stood with his weight mostly on his good leg before gingerly testing the other. No good. It felt like someone dug a finger into the muscles of his thigh beneath the divot of the puncture wound's scar. He limped to the wardrobe and dressed as quickly as he could in his normal daytime suit. He fingered his formal attire, which hung on the side of the door in anticipation of a valet coming to take it for cleaning, and smiled at the memory of the previous evening's events. But then he pulled the corners of his mouth into a frown. No, he couldn't allow himself to be seduced by the strangeness of the situation. And he certainly couldn't give in to the desire to rescue Fiona Telfair from both her horrible mother and the disaster that had befallen her family. He'd made his mind up to retire, and his leg agreed with every step that it was time. After this job, he was done, no matter how fascinating he found the odd powers of aether or the beautiful Lieutenant Crow.

When he walked into the hallway, he heard the sounds of two women talking. While the clever Mrs. Bailey lacked the soft approachability of Claire Radcliffe, Henry suspected that Iris and Davinia would connect in other ways. Both women had a certain single-mindedness when it came to seeking solutions and obtaining what they desired. And both were dashedly clever and of a scientific bent. And...

He stopped himself from cataloging the aspects that attracted him to both women. He didn't need to cause trouble for himself, heartache about what he couldn't have or shouldn't want. Besides, his job made him unsuitable for the domestic life, and there was no guarantee a normal household would be his even if he managed to leave his organization on good terms.

After Henry descended the steps—carefully—he found Edward and Johann in the kitchen area. Edward had a steaming cup of tea in front of him, Johann coffee. Evidence of their late night showed in the dark circles under both their eyes. Johann looked particularly rough, but then, he'd done the most work, both playing a challenging program and serving as Henry's eyes on the dais, and then his assistant in the warehouse. He would have to get both men's formal reports later, especially the details of Edward's and Iris's catching Lieutenant Crow in their net. But as interesting as the story might be, he dreaded the inevitable paperwork he'd have to do as a result of their bringing Crow to their headquarters.

"Good morning, gentlemen." Henry tried to sound more chipper than he felt. "Is the water hot?"

"Hot enough for Johann's bean water, but I'll reboil it for you to have a proper cuppa." Edward rose and re-lit the stove. "Do you know if Iris is up yet?"

Henry sat while he waited for the water to boil. "I heard her and Lieutenant Crow talking. I'm sure she'll be down soon."

Edward nodded. Henry exchanged a sympathetic look with Johann, who had remarked to Henry how Iris steadied his friend and kept him out of mad scientist obsession mode. So what steadying influence were they missing on Johann with his wife Marie being back in Boston with their child? A knock on the door brought Henry's thoughts back to the situation at hand.

"I'll get it." Johann inclined his head toward Henry's leg, which Henry realized he'd been rubbing. "You're looking sore this morning."

"Thank you." Henry stretched his leg in front of him and grimaced at the pull of the old injury. He shouldn't have overdone it the night before, but now that he thought back, he couldn't remember it hurting after women started turning into mice.

Johann walked into the living room, opened the door, and the smell of something fresh and buttery preceded his return to the kitchen.

"Biscuits from the main house. American biscuits," he clarified. "With butter and jam."

Edward sighed. "What I wouldn't give for a proper scone."

Henry didn't respond. During the brief time the door had been open, the sound of the rain and its fresh smell sprouted a sprig of homesickness in his chest. Odd, since he'd lacked a true home base for most of his adult life and had hopped from country to country with various missions. The longest time he'd spent anywhere had been Paris, but that was due to him having been stuck during the Franco-Prussian War. Unfortunately, the events of the previous night meant they likely wouldn't be returning to Boston or England any time soon. As for a return to England... Henry's contacts were still working on clearing the charges against Edward in the previous year's demise of Lord Jeremy Scott, who had died in an unfortunate aether destabilization incident. At least that's how his organization had tried to spin it.

"American biscuits and scones have the same ingredients," Johann said. "Don't be so picky, Edward. Oh, and Henry, the maid said that Mister Meriweather would like to speak with you when you have a moment."

"I'm sure he would." Henry nodded and kept himself from smiling at the paperwork reprieve.

"Make sure Lieutenant Crow doesn't go anywhere," he told them and stood. "I should see what Mister Meriweather wants."

"At least have breakfast," Johann said. "The water for your tea is almost ready."

Henry thought he heard footsteps in the upstairs hallway—Iris and Crow. He wasn't ready to face the Lieutenant quite yet, so he said, "I'll eat breakfast at the main house. I'm sure there's plenty of food." If anything, he'd found the Meriweather household to be more than generous with victuals, a sign of how well the family had fared after the war. He grabbed his Mackintosh from beside the door, donned it, and walked into the rain.

DEVON WOKE to a pounding in his head that echoed the thunder outside. His mouth felt as dry as the conversations he'd had the previous night, and when he sat, he tasted acid at the back of his throat. Thankfully, the headache only signaled that he'd drunk too much alcohol and too little other liquid, not that another sick headache stalked him. Although the one could turn into the other. Did he sense a sharp pain behind his right eyeball?

He swung his legs over the side of the bed and sat for a minute with his elbows on his knees and his head in his hands until the room stopped spinning. A quiet knock on the door heralded the appearance of Crenshaw, who carried a tray laden with coffee and a small glass that held a teaspoon of laudanum.

"I thought your head may be bothering you, Sir," he said, but without any smile visible on his lips. Still, Devon suspected the butler might be secretly amused.

"You're looking hale," Devon grumbled. "How? You were up later than I last night."

Crenshaw shrugged, and the tray remained level. "I don't need much sleep, Sir."

"Please set the tray over there." Devon gestured to the low bench by the window. "I'll be down for breakfast momentarily. I don't need help dressing." He didn't need Crenshaw to see his wobbly steps or his shaking hands.

He sent Crenshaw out and stood slowly. Once the rush had subsided, he crept toward the window bench that held the coffee and medication, determined for his steps to be firm if not fast. He mixed the laudanum into the coffee with some sugar and cream, which he managed to not spill in spite of his trembling hands, and drank the lot while still standing. He closed his eyes. After several deep breaths, the watery light from outside faded from obscene to normal, and his headache diminished to a dull and manageable ache. His steps and motions while dressing also smoothed and firmed to be his typical confident movements.

But his spirit... Each time he thought about Pierce's betrayal, he quivered inside.

Devon looked in the mirror at himself as he tied his cravat. He would need a shave—his dark stubble stood out against his still pale face—but as he'd had one the previous evening just before the party and didn't have any social plans for the day, he decided to wait. He couldn't meet his own gaze, however. The guilt at needing the laudanum lurked at the back of his eyes. How much had he taken the day before to ensure he could stand through the ball? His ankle no longer pained him, but the cure seemed to have turned into another problem. And another secret.

He found Therese and Fiona in the breakfast room. After the first whiff of eggs, sausage, and biscuits almost sent him to the water closet, his stomach settled, and he was able to greet the two young women. Therese looked tired, but Fiona appeared fresh and lovely in one of Therese's light green gowns. He helped himself to small portions and a half biscuit and sat across from Fiona. The footman poured coffee into the delicate china cup.

"You're the first lovely thing I've seen today," he told her. "I trust you slept well?"

Fiona's cheeks and neck turned pink.

"Devon," Therese scolded, "you're still in party mode. There's no need to charm anyone here. Fiona, maybe you could talk to me?"

"Oh?" Devon arched an eyebrow.

"I slept very well, thank you," Fiona said with a smile, and she only looked at Therese. "I was wondering—is Inspector Davidson going to come by this morning? I have some things I'd like to discuss with him."

Devon tamped down the unexpected spike of jealousy. He supposed the dour inspector could be considered handsome by some, if they liked the sallow, freckled narrow-faced English look.

"I don't know, but we can send for him if you like. He and his team are staying on the plantation."

"Please do." Fiona looked down. "I mean, if it's not too much trouble."

Devon and Therese exchanged an amused glance. The girl had spirit and knew what she wanted. Or, to be more exact, she desired something other than to find a husband. But what, exactly? He couldn't resist a puzzle, especially not one as charming and pretty as Fiona Telfair.

Why couldn't she be the daughter of one of the businessmen or politicians he courted to support his railroad rather than a poor tinkerer's child? She'd likely not be open to an alternative arrangement to marriage. Nor would he insult her with one. He respected her too much and, if he were to be honest with himself, didn't want the complication.

He motioned to the footman. "Please tell someone to fetch Henry Davidson. Oh, and please have them bring some of this food down to the quarters. Our guests likely haven't got anything nearly this good to break their fast with."

"Yes, sir. I'll ask Cook to pack them a basket." The footman bowed slightly and left.

"What's going on?" Therese asked.

Devon rubbed his eyes, which stung. "Pierce... He's gone."

Therese and Fiona looked at him, their mouths o's of surprise.

"Gone? When?" Therese asked.

"Last night. During the ball. Layla Bollington and Henry Davidson both had evidence linking him to the kidnappings. I suppose he decided to leave before he was arrested."

At the mention of Bollington's name, Therese's cheeks turned pink, and Fiona looked down at her plate. Anger stabbed Devon through the gut.

"Why was she here the morning after the ball, Therese? I thought someone may be giving her information. Was it you?"

"No, nothing like that." Therese held out her hands. "Devon, please believe me, I kept our family confidences to myself." Then he saw an answering spark of annoyance in her eyes. "As much as you've allowed me to know, which isn't much.

No, Devon." She dropped her voice. "Layla Bollington and I are lovers."

Vinni woke to throbbing in her hands and right elbow. Or was it stinging? A stinging throb? Or three. Plus her back and leg muscles cramped and tensed. In fact, there wasn't a part of her that didn't hurt.

Well, maybe her brain, but that was shrouded by a fog. What had happ—?

Oh. The falling catwalk. The chase through the warehouse ending in a leap through a broken window and capture by an airship. All of it crashed through her mind, and she opened one eye to see a cracked plaster ceiling. It wasn't the apartment she and Cat had shared in downtown Terminus. She'd memorized that pattern, the spreading spiderweb of age and decay. The fissures here were deeper, the ceiling stained darker, but the place lacked the musty odor of her previous accommodations. And the room was warm.

"Are you awake?" A woman with an educated English accent asked from across the room to Vinni's right.

"I... I think so. Mrs. Bailey?"

"Yes. How are you feeling?"

Vinni opened both eyes and turned her head to see Iris Bailey sitting on the room's other narrow bed. "Where am I?"

Iris shrugged. "I don't know how much I'm at liberty to tell you. Can I get you anything?"

Vinni ran her tongue over her teeth, her mouth dry. The herbal tea from the night before had fermented into an odd taste. "Water. Or something stronger."

"How about some tea?"

"That would be great. And..." She shifted, noting the pressure in her lower abdomen. Her face burned at having to ask, but the sling that cradled her left arm kept her elbow bent, and she'd need both hands to... "Can you help me with the water closet?"

"Of course."

The deed was done with British efficiency, and Vinni laid back down, her head spinning from the exertion, while Iris went to fetch some tea and breakfast for her. How much blood had she lost? Her heart pounded after even that small effort. Or, if she were to be honest with herself, her pulse raced with the realization of just how helpless she'd become. When she closed her eyes, she saw the image of Uncle Dross leering over her. He'd revel in her incapacitated state. And Cat... Vinni hoped she'd escaped. What would she think when Vinni didn't turn up? Would she go looking for her? Report back to the neo-Pythagoreans that she'd been lost?

Vinni knew they had strict orders when on a mission to not do anything that could compromise it, even if that meant leaving your partner in the hands of the enemy rather than expose yourself and the group's aims. But Vinni wasn't in the enemy's hands... Was she? She'd thought of Iris and her colleagues as adversaries, but that had also been when they'd worked toward opposite ends during the Cobb affair. Now...

Iris returned with a tray bearing tea and biscuits with jam and butter. "I'll help you eat," she said. "Don't worry, I've washed my hands. The Doctors Radcliffe have drilled us in proper hygiene, especially when it comes to food and wounds. Speaking of which, one of them will be by later to check on your injuries."

"Thank you." Vinni couldn't say more because Iris held the cup of tea to her lips. She wanted to drink the warm liquid faster, and she stifled her frustration at not being in control. When Iris removed the cup from her lips, Vinni asked, "Is Inspector Davidson downstairs?"

Iris cut the biscuit in half, and then put butter and jam on each side. "No, he's gone up to the house." Then, when she realized what she'd said, "Bollocks."

"So I'm in a place where there's a main house." Vinni smiled at the small victory. "An old plantation, perhaps?"

Iris didn't take the invitation to elaborate. "This has to be hard for you. I would hate not knowing where I am. Biscuit?"

"Oh? Yes please."

Iris handed Vinni a biscuit half, and she took a bite.

Once she chewed and swallowed, Vinni said, "This must be tedious. I'm sure you have more important things to do."

"Clever," Iris told her, "but I'm not saying anything else. Only that so far you're an easier patient than Edward was after our airship accident. How is your stomach doing with the tea and food?"

"Fine. I'm famished. Tell me about Professor Bailey." It would give her something to do while she ate, and she could suss out Iris.

"We'd been on an airship that was being attacked by the Clockwork Guild—a staged attack, mind you, but we didn't know it at the time—and one of the chutes on the escape compartment didn't deploy." Iris shuddered but held the plate steady. "Edward took the worst of it. Had a cracked rib and a concussion. Poor dear." She shook her head. "But it turned out to be a good thing. It made him let go of some things he'd been holding on to too tightly."

Vinni didn't react outwardly, but she wondered if Iris was trying to tell her something. But she'd already decided to let go of the neo-Pythagoreans. What else could she mean?

By the time Vinni finished her breakfast, her eyelids felt heavy. Iris helped her to lie back down and covered her up. "I'll check on you in a bit."

"Thank you, Mrs. Bailey."

"Of course, and please, call me Iris. If we're going to be roommates, we may as well use our Christian names."

Iris's words sparked an unexpected warmth, and Vinni nodded. "Please call me Vinni."

"I will. Try to get some rest."

Vinni didn't voice the reply that came to mind, which was, "Only when I'm safe. Or dead." But blackness overtook her as she had one final thought—could a woman who'd lost her faith find help with the people she'd been indoctrinated to trust the least, scientists and tinkerers?

**27**

———

T*erminus, 24 December 1871*
    A soft knock on the door roused Vinni from dreams of being chased through air that allowed her to breathe, but that also felt like water she could dart through like a fish. She never saw her pursuers, only knew something big and predatory followed her, seeking and searching, uncovering clouds and separating trees she tried to hide behind.

She almost resisted inviting whoever knocked in. Could her inner sense be trying to warn her? Eventually she did murmur, "Come in!" through a throat tight with nightmare fear.

When Doctor Claire McPhee Radcliffe entered, Vinni sagged with relief. She knew from the society's dossier on Claire that of all the members of Henry Davidson's team, she posed the least threat. Vinni admired a woman who only wanted the best for others...and who didn't fear to seek it for herself. Another commonality between her and the women on Henry's team. And, if she were to be honest, the men. They all had stepped out of traditional society to...what? She would have to observe and find out.

"Good morning, Doctor Radcliffe," Vinni said.

"Please, call me Claire." She placed her bag on the desk and removed bandages and a suture kit. "How are you feeling?"

Vinni shook her head. "Hungry. Tired. Trapped." She hadn't meant to let that last word slip out, so she pressed her lips together so she wouldn't say any more.

Claire gave her a small smile of understanding. Right, she'd essentially been kidnapped by her own family. "I'm sure we'll get everything straightened out soon. Henry—Inspector Davidson—will want to talk to you, but he shouldn't have a reason to hold you."

"I hope not." But did she?

"Hungry is good. Did you eat breakfast?"

"Yes. Mrs. Bailey helped me eat." She grimaced when she tried to move her left arm, but it hurt much less than it had before. "I had a biscuit, but I'm starving again." She suspected why... It had only happened to her once before, when she'd been thrown by a horse at the neo-Pythagorean compound. Would her peculiarity be unmasked again?

"I'll find something else for you to eat after I examine you again."

Again, the urge to escape and hide her strangeness battled with the desire to see what would happen. Not that she had a choice. Or maybe she did. If she asked Claire not to examine her, would she acquiesce?

For a moment, fog clouded her vision, and she saw her guide. It beckoned her forward, so she took a deep breath and said, "May as well get this over with."

"I'll be as gentle as I can," Claire promised.

Vinni declined to argue that that's not what she meant. Instead, she held out her hands and allowed Claire to unwrap the bandages starting with her left elbow, which had gotten the worst of the injuries as she smashed through the glass.

"This is healing very well," Claire said, her eyebrows raised. "I recognize Chad's sutures." She smiled, and the fondness on her face made Vinni look away, both in envy and to respect the strength of the loving feelings evident there. She and Cat had felt that for each other...she'd thought. But she couldn't imagine the intense Dr. Chadwick Radcliffe allowing his wife to go into harm's way. No, he'd sacrifice himself first. She swallowed against the sick feeling in her throat at the memory of what Cat had led her into.

"Are you all right? Does it hurt?" Claire asked, bringing Vinni back to the present.

"No, not badly." She wasn't ready to share her emotional injuries.

"Now let's look at your leg."

Again, Claire gently unwound bandages, which came away stained with dried blood. Vinni forced herself to look at her left knee. Instead of raw lacerations, only red lines remained.

"These aren't bad at all. In fact, we can leave the bandages off." She shook her head. "My husband is very careful, as you probably guessed. How is your range of motion?"

Vinni bent her leg and elbow and felt the cuts pull, but nothing came open as they should have if the wounds were as bad as she remembered. "Fine. They pull a little, but not bad."

"If you can, try to wear breathable materials so they can heal." She manipulated Vinni's injured joints, and a frown line grew between her eyebrows. "I'm sorry, I know you said this happened last night, but these injuries look days, not hours old."

Vinni shrugged in what she hoped was a nonchalant manner. "I heal quickly. It's a special talent."

Claire looked up from her examination, curiosity evident in her blue eyes. "Special talents are good, Lieutenant."

"If you say so. Sometimes they set us apart." She couldn't help the bitterness in her tone that leeched through from the memories of how she'd been teased for not having any kind of aether-related sensitivity, only her freaky ability to heal. She'd never told anyone of her guardian spirit.

To Vinni's surprise, Claire smiled with understanding. "It depends on who you're with. Hopefully you'll find your team soon. Now, I'll clean and rebandage your elbow, and we'll go downstairs and find you some food. It's best to be up and moving, although be careful. I heard you lost a lot of blood, so you may get faint easily."

Vinni nodded, too stunned at the sense of camaraderie that had appeared between them. Her inner guide told her to trust Doctor Claire McPhee Radcliffe, but while her external wounds healed, her internal ones still chafed. Would she be able to trust again? Even more, could she trust Henry Davidson's team, at least some of them? There was only one way to find out.

"Once I eat, I'd like to talk to Henry Davidson," she said. "I need to know what he has planned for me."

Claire smiled like Vinni had just said she'd help however she could, which she hadn't—had she?

"Do you feel up for a walk to the house? Some fresh air may do you good. I'm guessing you're in the dark about what's been happening, but I have the feeling you're an important piece of our puzzle."

Again, an image of belonging, of fitting. If only she could trust that to be true...


THE NEWS of Pierce's disappearance didn't surprise Fiona. She had vague memories of him attacking her, but they weren't clear enough to know whether it had happened or if she'd dreamed it. Or if it could be a mouse memory. She forced herself to go into the library even though fear tightened her chest at the thought of returning to the room. However, instead of bad memories that felt like dreams, a pleasant surprise greeted her.

"You!" Fiona didn't know whether she wanted to run up and hug the woman, shake her hand, or curtsy to her. All three would be a bit much, so she stuck with the curtsy.

"Yes, me. Your security team plucked me from the air in the nick of time." She gestured to her left elbow. "And patched me up."

"What happened?" Fiona temporarily forgot her hunger, which had been gnawing at her.

"Long story, but we found the warehouse where they're testing automatons. It's downtown."

"So close?" Where had the bright green grass stain on the non-automaton's trousers had come from, then?

She sighed, wishing she'd managed to get more useful information and feeling like she'd failed Devon. She hadn't seen him since that morning, when he'd stalked out of the dining room after Therese's revelation. How was he dealing with all the surprises?

A petite woman with white-blond hair entered the dining room followed by Claire Radcliffe.

"Lieutenant Crow, you know Iris Bailey," Claire said. "Miss Telfair, this is Mrs. Bailey."

Lieutenant Crow—so that was her name! And Iris Bailey. Fiona dropped into a curtsy and tried not to trip over her own excitement over meeting another one of her heroes. "You're the famous archaeologist, the one who discovered the Pythagorean temple in Rome." She'd read the story in one of the history/archaeology journals her father had been subscribing to. Another clue she'd missed that he'd become interested in combining the softer sciences with aetherics.

"I'm pleased to meet you," the petite woman said. Fiona thought she read curiosity in the woman's eyes, and she couldn't blame her. Fiona would look at anyone the same way if she'd known they turned into a mouse on occasion. She hadn't yet discussed the events of the previous evening with Devon, and she didn't know if she could. His words from their initial tea, which felt like it had been months, not days before, still hung in her mind, that he had no intention of marrying her. Now she supposed no one could. She should have been relieved at the thought, but...

She watched Claire Radcliffe and Iris Bailey pour tea for themselves and chat as they filled their plates. Both were married, and both maintained their professional identities and roles as part of Henry Davidson's team. Fiona had a million questions about the mysterious group of people, none of whom seemed to have anything to do with enforcing laws except for the dour Davidson. What had happened to make him so serious? She'd seen the same expression on returning soldiers, that faraway look that said their pasts had caught them, at least for a moment. Then the look of regret when they emerged in the present, which was the same as they'd left it.

Could Fiona have what Claire and Iris did—supportive husbands who encouraged them in their careers and intellectual pursuits? But what would happen when they had children? Surely the situation would change for each of them. There were responsibilities, after all. She wished she could ask them.

"Penny for your thoughts?" Lieutenant Crow asked.

Fiona shook her head. "It's not important."

"Are you all right?" Now Claire went into doctor mode. "You had quite an evening last night."

Fiona's face flashed hot when all eyes turned to her. "I'm fine."

"No strange sensations?" Claire persisted. "Hot or cold flashes? Itching?"

Fiona paused. Was that an itch, or did she feel it because Claire suggested it? "I don't think so. Please don't make a fuss over it. It's nothing."

"A young woman who can turn into a mouse, and whose mother became one, is not nothing." Iris Bailey put her plate on the table with such emphasis her rashers bounced. "We're here to determine what sort of energy caused it."

Claire shook her head. "I wish you'd said something sooner."

Fiona arched an eyebrow, but she tried to choose her words so as not to be disrespectful to her idol. "I don't know that anyone would have believed me. I didn't know it was more than dreams until the ball last night. And then Pierce..." She shuddered, the memory coming back with clarity. "He made me change. With another doll."

"Another doll?" Iris Bailey asked. "There is more than one?"

"Yes," Fiona said with another shiver. "Inspector Davidson said they'd go back to the house and look."

"No," Claire told her. "Someone broke in and stole it. Nothing else was missing, according to your maid."

"Tessa!" Fiona half-rose. "Is she all right?"

"Yes, they brought her back here. And set someone to watch your house, although I doubt anyone will enter it now."

"Good." She sank back into her chair. "Although we don't have much to steal, someone always wants something."

"Isn't that the truth?" Lieutenant Crow muttered. "But enough rehashing what happened. We need to figure out what to do moving forward." She stabbed a fork at Fiona. "This one has been the closest to the force, but she doesn't know what it was."

"Just that my father was studying aetherics and emotion/motivation." Fiona put in. "So the motivation for the doll was to stay put and expose me and my mother to the aether vibrations that caused the changes."

"Right." Iris gestured with her fork. "Mice were once associated with the neo-Pythagoreans. I've seen the statues. Apollo, specifically, wasn't it?"

Lieutenant Crow nodded. "Yes, the legend is either that the god protected the army from mice or used the mice to protect the army. Either way, he could control them. But what if the legends got it wrong? What if the mice *were* the army?"

Fiona wanted to disagree, to say it was impossible, but her experience made her say instead, "Pierce tried to capture me. He knew he couldn't control what I did."

"They haven't gotten that far yet," Lieutenant Crow told her. "They're still working on it." She sighed. "I can't believe I was so stupid as to miss the connection."

"Which was...?" Iris prompted.

"That the talented apprentice, Mister Bon Climat, was Pierce. Bon Climat—good, or merry, weather?" She put her head in her hands. "I should have figured that out as soon as I heard the name."

"Sometimes we miss what's right in front of us," Iris said. "You have no idea how long it took us to figure out how to stabilize the aether in spite of all the clues we had. Or that it could influence people's emotions. We still don't know how."

"It seems," Claire added, "that it can cause changes on a level smaller than the animalcules that make up living things. Perhaps it travels through the substance that holds us together just as light travels through it."

"But then how can it change one thing into another?" Iris persisted. "Alchemists have been trying to do that for centuries, perhaps even millennia." Then she became quiet and got a faraway look in her eyes.

Lieutenant Crow shifted as though prepared to say something, but Fiona put a gentle hand on her bandaged arm, a request for her to wait and give Mrs. Bailey the space to figure out her thoughts. Instead of looking angry, Crow nodded, and Fiona smiled her thanks.

"Perhaps scientists did at one point know how to make changes like we've seen," Iris continued. "So much was lost in the flood. All the alchemists in the middle ages had were bits and pieces of the history. Wouldn't being able to change, to shift, into someone or something else be more valuable than gold to some?"

Claire smiled, but it was sad. "I've spoken with many people in my work as a neuroticist who wished they were someone else or something else. They felt it would help them to escape their problems. Of course it wouldn't—some problems follow us no matter where we go." She sighed, and Fiona wondered what she was remembering.

"I recall a ritual," Lieutenant Crow said, "that had that particular thing as its aim. It was reserved for the highest level priests in our cult, and Bon Climat—I mean Pierce Meriweather—wouldn't have had access to it, but he may have heard something about it and managed to duplicate or imitate it."

Fiona shivered. "He was muttering something under his breath when he wielded that stupid doll."

"All roads lead back to Pierce," Claire said with another sigh.

"I was afraid of that." Devon stood in the doorway, and Fiona clenched her knees together so she wouldn't go to him. His unshaven face, red-rimmed eyes, and unkempt hair spoke of his distress at his cousin's betrayal. Fiona's heart swelled with sympathy. She knew that sting from thinking her father had turned against their family. She would always feel guilt for doubting him, but it was nothing compared to the pain of knowing a loved one wasn't who you thought they were.

"Come sit down," Claire said as she rose. She pulled a chair out for him, and he plopped down. Claire wrinkled her nose. "Have you eaten?"

Devon rubbed his eyes. "A little. I need some coffee."

"I'll fix you some tea." Claire and Iris exchanged a look Fiona couldn't interpret, and Claire poured a cup of tea and added generous amounts of cream and sugar.

Devon sat with his head in his hands until Claire put the cup in front of him.

"Are you in any pain?" she asked.

"My ankle." Devon blinked, and he pulled one corner of his mouth back into a half-frown. "And my family pride."

Fiona wanted to reach out and squeeze his hand. She knew he had dreams of marrying into a good family, but after everyone found out about Pierce—and they would—he would find himself shunned. No one would want to be associated with such a scandal. But where would he and Therese move? They couldn't stay here.

Unless they managed to find the tinkerers and save them. Then Devon could be a hero, the man who salvaged his family's reputation and undid the damage his cousin had caused.

Fiona shoved aside the thought that had dared wiggle into her brain, that if he were as much of a disgrace as she, they might have a future together. There was still the mouse problem. And that it was a problem allowed her to speak.

Or was it? No, she couldn't consider that right now. She'd go mute again.

"We need to get into that chamber in the basement," Fiona said. "The one off the laboratory."

Devon shrugged. "I've been trying to figure it out, but Pierce"—his mouth twisted like he tasted something awful —"hid his tracks and any clues to it well."

"But you could figure it out if you see it from inside." She took a deep breath. "I can. Or at least my mouse self can." Saying the words 'mouse self' made her want to giggle, but she kept her expression serious. If she had this odd ability, she might as well use it.

Everyone at the table exchanged looks.

"Is it safe?" Lieutenant Crow asked. "I haven't saved this girl's bu—er, bustle—to have her risk herself by turning into...a mouse?" She gave Fiona a doubting look. "I've heard of attempts, but no one's succeeded."

"What choice do we have?" Fiona pressed. "We need to find Pierce. And my father and the others. This is our best lead."

Henry Davidson entered the room followed by three men, one of whom Fiona thought she recognized as a musician from the night before. He introduced them to Fiona, then said, "Patrick and Edward have looked at the door, and as you guessed, it's locked with some sort of tool that we don't have, and there's not enough time to fabricate one."

"Miss Telfair has an idea," Claire said.

Fiona relayed it, and Davidson nodded. She didn't know whether to be relieved or surprised at his lack of protest. "It seems the most efficient way. Claire, you and..." Then he stopped. "Lieutenant Crow. It's good to see you up and about." A slight smile loaned a hint of softness to his features.

"Inspector." Crow dipped her chin.

Fiona pressed her lips together so she wouldn't grin. Was that a blush? She could almost taste the attraction between the two of them.

"Well." Davidson cleared his throat. "Miss Telfair, if you're willing to help, I welcome your assistance. As I was saying, Claire, please accompany her. You, too, Lieutenant Crow. I suspect you have some knowledge of these things."

"Perhaps a little." She sounded reluctant.

"And you, too, Devon, since it's your house. We'll wait nearby."

Fiona admired how Davidson took command and folded everyone into his team. She stood. "Well, I suppose I should get this over with."

**28**

———

Terminus, *24 December 1871*

Fiona followed Devon into the basement of the house. As though her brain knew she considered turning into a mouse, she began to smell in more detail. The musty odor of the wooden steps told her they must be old and would need to be replaced soon. The earth said it hadn't wanted to relinquish space for the house and its invading humans, and it still held secrets. The air, chill and dry, seemed to swirl around her, curious as to what she was doing. And as she descended, her eyesight became dimmer until she again saw things in black and white and shadow and light. She needed to hold on to the rail so as not to lose her footing.

Or perhaps she felt she was about to change because of the experiments she could sense behind the door. Devon didn't need to point it out to her. She would have been able to follow the vibrations if she'd been blind.

"Are you all right?" he asked, and his fingertips touched her hand.

She jerked her arm away from his touch. She couldn't bear the thought of him reaching for her and finding that fur had begun to grow in anticipation of her turning into a little monster. For wasn't that what she'd become—a vermin?

At least she could be a useful one. "Don't look," she gasped, but again, her dress ballooned around her, the shrinking taking place more quickly, the cloaking with fur almost instantaneous. She heard, then felt, his footsteps backing up, and she slid out of the dress, darted out of the way before it toppled. She'd hoped for more warning, but her concern melted away as she became more comfortable in her new skin.

"My god," Devon said. "That's incredible."

If Fiona could have blushed, she would have. He would never look at her romantically now. But it didn't matter—she had work to do.

First she ran along the base of the door, her whiskers quivering for any eddy of air, her nose twitching as she investigated the smells along the bottom to see if they seemed stronger in some places. Devon stood behind her, watching, and she had to fight her instincts to run and hide.

*He won't hurt me, he won't hurt me... At least not like that.*

She made a note to tell him she was grateful he didn't have a cat.

Next in her investigation were the sides and top of the door itself. What had seemed like crumbling mortar and brick in a flat plane to her human self became a wall with footholds, and she scrambled up it along the crease that had been almost hidden to human eyes but which now presented as an airy gap to her nose. She found a spot where she could fit through and squeezed into the space, following it until she came to the knob mechanism, which stuck into the rock. It would be a simple turn from the other side to unlock it. Fiona paused. Did she want to turn into a human again to open the door? Then she would be naked. But she didn't know if she could manage to trip the opening mechanism as her mouse self.

Well, she'd try. She stuck her paw into it, but the tumblers were too stiff to respond to her attempts. Then she tried twisting it, but she was too light to make a difference.

"*A little girl's life is in danger,*" someone whispered to her—through the aether? The voice that vibrated through her soul sounded like the strange woman's—Lieutenant Crow, as she now knew her to be. That explained the airship corps uniform Fiona had seen her wearing that first day. "*Do what you need to do.*"

Fiona made her way to the ground, which was dustier on this side, and sneezed. She focused on fighting against the influence of the aether, but it was too strong, like trying to walk upstream in a river. The vibrations beat her into her mouse shape.

"*Help me,*" she sent to the disembodied voice. "*Can you do something?*"

"*It's a high-level protocol, but I can try.*"

Fiona sat and waited. The aether vibes pressed against her sensitive ears and nose, disorienting her. She feared she wouldn't be able to do what she needed if she couldn't fight them. She'd just lie down and sleep.

A light pressure descended over her curled-up form, like a hand that cupped her and protected her. The pressure eased, and she uncurled, then kept uncurling until she stood in her human form. She twisted the knob, then collapsed into her mouse form again. She barely maintained enough awareness to sense the door swinging outward and the air from the basement and cave laboratory mixing.

Gentle hands—real ones—picked her up. "I need to bring her away from all this," Crow said. "It was too much for her."

"Will she be all right?" That was Devon. Fiona smiled to think he was concerned about her.

"Yes, she just needs to rest. All those changes are tough on a body. That's why only our most advanced priests and priestesses attempted it. This one is special to have managed it so many times."

"Yes, she certainly is."

Fiona barely had time to register his words before she passed out.

DEVON WATCHED Lieutenant Crow take Fiona in mouse form out of the laboratory followed by Claire Radcliffe, whose face displayed her concern. He wanted to go with them, to make sure Fiona was all right, but he needed to find his cousin and Hollowell's niece. And the tinkerers. Could they have been hiding at his estate the entire time?

He ignored the worktable and shelves that had been set up in the cave. He'd leave them to Henry's tinkerers, who had entered the basement along with Henry when the women left. But he grabbed one implement—a pistol with an experimental silencing device. He made sure it was loaded. Then he found a lantern, lit it, and started down the tunnel.

"What are you doing?" Henry Davidson asked.

"Following the tunnel," Devon said. He glanced over his shoulder to see Edward and Patrick murmuring over the cave's contents and Henry watching him.

"It could be dangerous," Henry pointed out.

Devon refrained from a snide comment. "We don't have a lot of time," he reminded the inspector. "And it's my property. I want to see what's down there."

Henry paused, and signs of an inner argument flickered through his expression. Finally, he nodded. "Go. But yell if you run into any trouble." He sighed and bent to rub his right thigh.

"I will." The red clay walls appeared sturdy enough, but they seemed to try to smother Devon, especially once he'd rounded a bend and gone out of sight of the laboratory. With each step, he grew more confident that nothing would go wrong. Then a pressure under his right foot made him look down. He'd stepped on a wire.

He paused. Nothing happened, but he didn't know what would occur when he released it. Would it trigger something? Should he call for help?

"Trouble, Cousin?" The glow of a lantern from the other end of the tunnel preceded Pierce's appearance. "Oh, I see you've found my security wire. A pity. As soon as you release it, this whole section will collapse on top of you."

"Why are you doing this?" Devon asked. "I thought you were my helper, my family. That we were in this together."

"In what, dear cousin? Your family business with your family money? I knew that as soon as you'd gotten your influence, established your legacy—" Pierce's laugh held something Devon hadn't heard in it before—bitterness. "You'd kick me to the side."

"It would have been your legacy, too," Devon said, but Pierce shook his head, and Devon knew his rationale was weak. He'd only been thinking of himself. And Therese.

"You and I both know it wouldn't have. I would have always been the cousin your father took in on charity, your helper and friend, but nothing more. Nothing meaningful."

With a pang, Devon recognized he and his cousin wanted the same thing, but he hadn't seen it. Hadn't considered it. He'd followed his father's lead in treating Pierce as a treasured family member who had fallen on hard times, but there had always been that feeling of doing him a favor. Of him being there because of their kindness. No wonder it had grated on Pierce.

"Look, Cousin, I understand. And I won't treat you like that anymore."

Pierce crossed his arms and shook his head. "No, now you'll treat me like a criminal and the man who tried to kill you. Or perhaps you won't treat me as anything at all."

He grabbed a lever on the side of the wall, which Devon

hadn't noticed. Devon raised the pistol, aimed it at Pierce, and tightened his finger on the trigger.

Pierce raised his eyebrows. "You don't have the guts."

Devon's hand trembled, and he tried to force himself to fire, but he couldn't. With another bitter chuckle, Pierce pressed the lever down.

With each inch it descended, a rumbling noise above Devon grew. Devon didn't know if stepping off the tripwire would accelerate the reaction, but he decided it didn't matter.

And if it took both Pierce and him with it, then at least he wouldn't have been the one to kill Pierce—the crush of earth would.

He spun around and dashed down the tunnel. A roaring sound punctuated with explosions and crashing noises followed him, and dust choked his lungs, but he kept moving.

A lessening of the gloom told him he was close to Pierce's secret laboratory, but a panel descended, cutting off the light. He ducked his chin and rolled, reaching the other side just before the metal slab met the ground with a clang. He stumbled into the lab.

"Everyone, get out!" He slammed the door to the basement behind him. A wave pounded against the bricks, sound and pressure as one, and he realized too late that standing there holding it wouldn't keep it from exploding inward. It propelled him into the lab, and the last thing he recalled before blackness crushed him was that he wished he could have told Fiona how much she meant to him.

FIONA MOUSE FOLLOWED the voice out of the dark tunnel she'd fallen into. A woman's voice, soothing and rhythmic, sang a melody with lyrics she couldn't understand, but soon its repetitiveness made it familiar and gave her the strength to keep moving forward. She clawed through layers of thick wool that gave way to cotton, then something lighter and fluffier, and her eyelids fluttered open to a smooth plaster ceiling. She lay on the bed in the room they'd brought her to when she fainted at the ball. When she turned her head toward the source of the song, Lieutenant Crow stopped chanting.

"You brought me back," Fiona said. "I heard you. Your chanting drew me out of wherever I was."

Lieutenant Crow nodded. "You changed back into human form, but you didn't wake. I had to do something." She placed a hand on Fiona's forehead, and Fiona tried to flinch away from the light pressure. The Lieutenant's hand felt like a block of ice.

"You're burning up." Crow frowned. "You've had too many changes, and I don't know what sort of experiments Pierce Meriweather—Bon Climat, as I knew him—was running, but you don't need to go back down there."

A rumbling noise shook the house, and one of the pictures fell from the wall and broke with a tinkle of glass and cracking of wood. Crow stood.

"What was that?" Fiona asked and scrambled to a seated position, attempting to keep herself covered. If only she could figure out how to keep some sort of clothing when she changed...

"Nothing."

But Fiona knew the other woman was lying. "No, really."

"It seems that Mister Meriweather found a security feature in the tunnel. It's a series of explosions set off by a tripwire." She rubbed her eyes. "I should have realized Bon Climat would copy what Uncle did at the compound."

"Devon," Fiona whispered. She had no doubt he'd gone into the tunnel and... Now she shrank again, but just her insides, at the thought that Devon Meriweather had just been crushed to death. Her vivid imagination supplied the terrible images, and her brain recalled the smells of the earth and chemicals in the laboratory, one of which had been the dusty tang of gunpowder. "I should have said something, but I didn't recognize it."

"Mice can't be expected to remember everything. Their little brains don't hold much."

Fiona swung her legs over the side of the bed and wrapped the sheet around her as best she could. "I have to go see. I have to know."

"No, you need to stay here. I'll find out what happened."

She left the room, and Fiona collapsed back on to the bed. She felt wrong, physically and emotionally. Her skin alternated between feeling too loose and too tight, and she made herself stop running her tongue over her teeth, which ached. Twin pains sat in the middle of her brain and her solar plexus, and she wondered if those were the places where the change started. She tried to catalog her sensations, mostly to distract herself from worry over Devon and whoever else had been in the tunnel—were the tinkerers down there?—but her mind kept wandering back to it. Was he all right? Was he hurt? Had he make it out? He had the athletic build that said he could put on some speed when necessary, but Fiona didn't know if he was a runner, and how fast would someone have to be?

And she realized something uncomfortable, something she'd hidden from herself all along. Something she didn't know could be possible until she saw the female members of Henry Davidson's team interacting as equals with their husbands and colleagues. Devon hadn't seemed shocked or judgmental. Could he be as open minded as they? Could something grow between him and Fiona, a relationship built on mutual respect? Friendship, she told herself, but she knew that to be a lie. Could they be more? Would he be willing to in spite of her mouse problem? Would it still be an issue after they'd found and defeated Pierce?

Defeated him. Fiona almost laughed. With what? He'd

outsmarted them at every turn. And Devon could be... No, she wouldn't allow herself to think it.

But she knew herself to be a good tinkerer, and she'd had the best apprenticeship anyone could have with the Guild. Pierce had dropped out of school and taken up with a pseudo-religious organization that eschewed science for superstition. Well, they obviously knew something considering they could make people turn into mice and manipulate aether so it defied the laws of physics. But she had confidence in her own abilities.

And she had to have confidence in Devon, that he'd survived.

Lieutenant Crow burst in through the door. "He got out. A pressure wave knocked the laboratory door off and flattened him, but his injuries are minor. He's asking for you."

*erminus, 24 December 1871*

Claire Radcliffe entered with her arms full of clothing. "This is starting to feel familiar," she said, and Fiona smiled back at her in mutual relief that no one else had been hurt.

Fiona sat again, and Lieutenant Crow slipped out. Claire helped her to dress. With each movement, Fiona felt stronger, and she felt the pressure of questions building in her middle. When she sat at the dressing table—again—and Claire helped her with her hair—again—Claire paused, her hands resting on Fiona's shoulders.

"You're practically bursting, Dear." Claire met Fiona's eyes in the mirror. "What do you need to know?"

Fiona caught the words—*need* to know, not *want* to know—and she blinked back tears as her heartbeat accelerated in her throat. Dare she ask? She knew Claire would be honest, and Fiona couldn't stand the thought of being disappointed... But her scientific side asserted itself.

Yes, she *needed* to know what could be possible, not only in general, but for her.

"You and Mister Doctor Radcliffe," Fiona said. "You have a relationship that's, well…"

"Unusual?" Claire finished, her lips tightening.

"Yes, but not in the way you think I'm asking. I mean, you and he, you're both doctors. And he doesn't seem to want you to be anything other than what you are. And it's the same for Mrs. Bailey. And…" She stopped to breathe, the words clogging her throat.

"And you want to know if that's possible for you?" Claire finished for her, her tone gentle.

"Yes." She didn't have the courage to ask what made tears shimmer in Claire's eyes. "Yes, is that possible for me? I never thought I wanted marriage, and I still don't know if I can…" She gestured to herself. "Turning into a mouse isn't the most attractive thing."

Claire swiped her wrist across her right eye. "I believe it's possible for you, Fiona. But sometimes it doesn't come easily." She shook her head. "If I'd had a sister, I would have wanted to tell her what I'm telling you. Smart women have to fight for everything because we're not what society expects. And when you find someone who loves you for who you are, that's even more worth it."

"But how do you know?" Fiona pressed. "It's not like you can measure it, like Mister O'Connell and Professor Bailey with their aetherometer."

Claire squeezed her shoulders. "Sometimes you don't for a long time, but when you do, you do."

Fiona heard the weight of a story in Claire's words and wanted to know more, but she would have to ask later. It seemed Henry Davidson's team had lots of interesting tales, and with another jolt, she wondered if hers could be one of them. But first, she needed to see Devon.

"But I can't talk to him." She sighed. "Only when I'm solving a problem or a puzzle."

"It seems to me that your situation is the biggest puzzle of all." Claire spoke as she plaited Fiona's hair in a simple braid that she then wound around her head and secured with pins.

"Is that how you see people as a neuroticist?"

Claire smiled. "Sometimes. But we're talking about you. Perhaps Devon is your puzzle to solve, and you need to stop being afraid of the solution."


WHEN FIONA ENTERED Devon's room, she found him lying on his bed attended by the other Doctor Radcliffe and with Henry Davidson standing nearby.

"Fiona..." Devon held out his hand to her, and she approached him and took it. "I was worried about you."

Puzzle, puzzle, puzzle... "You were worried about me?" she asked, and a little thrill shimmied through her chest, excitement that he'd been thinking of her and that she could speak. "I'm not the one who just escaped from a collapsing tunnel."

"I've been told the entire hillside collapsed." He shook his head. "I can't believe I didn't see it. Didn't know what Pierce was really like."

At the despair in his voice, Fiona's knees weakened, and she sat on the side of the bed.

Claire Radcliffe cleared her throat. "I think these two have some things to talk about. I'll stand outside the door to make sure nothing, ah, happens, but everyone needs to leave."

Davidson looked like he was about to argue, but he acquiesced when Chadwick Radcliffe took him by the arm and led him through the room.

Once they were alone, Fiona looked down at Devon, who gazed at her with something in his eyes she hadn't seen from a young man before—admiration? Or was there more to it?

"Are you badly hurt?" she asked, although she suspected he wouldn't tell her the full truth.

"Not too much, but it knocked the wind out of me." He grimaced as he wriggled to his elbows and then to seated. She helped to arrange pillows behind him and used her movements around him to examine him. Although someone had washed his face to attend to his wounds, red dust gave his neck a ruddy sheen. He'd been stripped down to his shirtsleeves, leaving bare his neck and the upper part of his chest. For some reason seeing the line of dark hair that disappeared below the shirt's opening made her own face flash hot.

"Am I so ugly?" he teased, but she thought she heard a note of insecurity.

"No, not at all." She returned her attention to his face. A narrow cut ran along one cheekbone, another along the jawline opposite. They made him look somewhat rakish, and the thought of that word made her own cheeks heat again.

"Are my wounds disfiguring?" He put a hand to his cut cheek, then winced. "They sting like the dickens."

"No, you're still quite handsome."

"Handsome? You think so? Wait—you don't have to answer that."

Fiona realized she'd been conversing with him normally. And flirting! Did that count as puzzle-solving? She felt the stiffness come to her tongue again—no!

*This situation is a problem to solve*, she told herself with as much sternness as she could muster. *I will not let it defeat me.*

THAT WAS A STUPID QUESTION... Devon hurt in places he hadn't known he had, but he dared not shift positions again lest he spook her. She had a certain ease he hadn't noticed before, but she seemed to stiffen and retreat to wherever she went when her nerves took over. How could she be so brave as to turn into a mouse, but so unsettled around him?

"Are you comfortable?" he asked. He wondered if he'd been

too bold with his previous questions, but she'd been looking at him frankly for the first time. But as he'd teased, the guarded look he'd come to associate with her expression had returned. Right. She'd been talking to him, but now she shook her head. The block, whatever it was, had returned.

"What is it?" he asked. "Why can't you talk to me?"

She bit her lip and looked down at her hands. In a voice so soft she almost whispered, she said, "Because I didn't want to marry. Because I didn't think anyone would want to marry me. And then you teased me. Oh!" She looked up. "That wasn't you. It was your cousin."

Devon didn't want to think about Pierce. Devon could only hope he'd been buried in the same collapse that had injured Devon, but he guessed not. Pierce was too clever to get caught in his own trap. But he had to ask. "Pierce teased you?"

"About what I was reading. I remember now. I thought it had been you until he said something about it in the library. Because you kept asking."

"He'd told me you liked Poe." And had almost ruined Devon's chance with her. Then his brain caught up to what she'd been saying. "You were talking about marriage?" And he'd gone and been a cad when he'd seen her after the party.

She nodded. "As we worked together, something made me want to when I talked to you, so I had to stay quiet."

Warmth flushed through him. Something made her, the intelligent Fiona Telfair, want to marry him? Or at least consider it when she spoke with him?

"And what about now?" He took her hand and rubbed his thumb over the backs of her fingers. "What do you feel now?"

She lifted her head, and tears glazed her eyes. "I feel confused. I feel sad that you're hurt and that I turn into a mouse and that my father is still missing..."

Guilt stabbed through Devon. Sure, he'd been working to recover the tinkerers, but he hadn't made much progress. Had he known on some level that Pierce was behind it and sabotaged it to protect his cousin? Or had he done something to push Pierce to act as he had?

"I'm sorry," was all he could say. Tears choked his own throat, but he wouldn't cry in front of her. He wanted to say, *sorry that I somehow caused this, sorry that my cousin kidnapped your father, sorry that things are all mixed up now.*

"I..." She shook her head. "I don't know what to say."

He didn't, either, and he couldn't, so he tugged her until her face and his almost touched. He angled his head and brushed her lips with his, then waited for her to draw back. She didn't, so he tried again, this time with a firmer kiss, and she leaned into it as well. He nudged her lips apart with her tongue, and then they kissed in earnest, communicating with each other with their mouths like they couldn't with their words, not yet.

He kept her left hand captured in his right one, but he ran his other hand over her shoulder and into the stray silky curls of her hair, which had escaped the pins and the braid. He'd heard the expression "spun gold' used to describe a woman's hair, but Fiona's didn't remind him of cold metal in spite of its copper color. It was more like flame, or a sunset—something alive and warm and comforting.

She broke the kiss first, and he took satisfaction in seeing her cheeks aflame and her eyes shining. He again dared not shift lest the evidence of what she'd done to him become too prominent beneath the sheets, and he reminded himself she was an innocent. He doubted her dragon of a mother had prepared her in any way for what could and did happen between men and women. But he'd be damned if he would apologize for kissing her.

He waited for her to speak first, almost holding his breath lest she went mute again.

Finally, she asked, "What now?" This time her question was a challenge.

"We find your father."

"I'll go prepare. As much as I can." She stood and took her hand back. With a nod, she walked out of the room, and he watched her go.

"Stupid, stupid, stupid," he said and covered his face with his hands.

"For what, dear brother?" Therese had slipped in when Fiona left. "If you'd been in here alone with her any longer, I would have had to interrupt. Please tell me you didn't take that girl's innocence in spite of your battered state."

He peeked out. Therese stood with her hands on her hips and frown on her face. Now another level of heat came to Devon's cheeks. He'd been stupid more than once that day. "I owe you an apology," he said. "For this morning. I shouldn't have run out when you told me—"

"That Layla and I are lovers." She crossed her arms but he caught the worried expression around her eyes. For him, or for what he'd done with Fiona? Or for herself? Could she doubt that he'd still love her as a brother?

"For ignoring what was right in front of me because of my damn ambition." He didn't normally curse, but it released something for him. His heart sank at the thought of how she must feel about their cousin's betrayal. Or was she relieved? At least now he knew why she'd never been interested in marrying.

"You mean Fiona?" Therese rolled her eyes. "Anyone with eyes could have told you that. Money comes and goes, as does influence, but intelligence? That sticks around and is infinitely more desirable."

"Right. I recognize that now. And I've been stupid for not recognizing what Pierce was up to." *Or you*, he wanted to add. Had she made herself sick so he wouldn't pressure her to marry?

"Oh?" She sat on the bed in the spot vacated by Fiona, and

Devon scooted over so her voluminous skirts would have room. Was that why he'd missed Fiona's charms for so long? He had become accustomed to Therese's presence, which, in spite of her illness, could fill a room.

"He's gone." And he didn't mean physically. He meant their idea of Pierce. "Therese, he betrayed us. He almost killed me."

He expected Therese to show some sign of shock, like a gasp or covering her mouth in horror. Instead, she nodded.

"You're not surprised," he said.

"I knew there was something off about him." She shook her head. "I thought it was because, well, because I'd decided not to marry a man, and so his pressing his suit rubbed me the wrong way."

"Always?" Devon whispered, not missing her qualification. How much about the people closest to him had he refused to see?

"No, since he returned from school. He'd changed. I can't explain how. Maybe he'd become more distant, less warm." She scratched her temple. "No, less genuine. Like he had a secret, but it was such a deep one there was no point in asking him to share it."

"Why didn't you tell me?" But now that she'd said it, he recognized he'd seen the same thing—that the Pierce they interacted with had become like a shadow or side of a different person.

"Would you have believed me?" She spread her hands. "You were so focused on making a good match for yourself so you could continue father's legacy and establish your own."

"Not that that's an option anymore," Devon sighed. "No one will look at me for their daughter now that Pierce has brought us into scandal." And his heart sank to join his stomach when he said, "I can't bring Fiona into this. She would be ruined along with us."

"She's already in this, dear brother." Therese patted his hand. "Whether you like it or not. What is your plan?"

"We have to find Pierce—assuming he's still alive—or find out where he was based and rescue the tinkerers." He rubbed his eyes. "But Therese, I can't imagine putting a bullet through his head or his heart. He's our *cousin*. The only family we have left." And wouldn't that compound the scandal—cousin killing cousin? There had been times during the war, stories of cousins being on opposite sides during battles. When one came home and the other didn't from that particular engagement, people had talked, speculated. No matter the context, killing family did not sit well with people. And again, he couldn't drag Fiona and her family into it by association.

Therese started to say something, then shook her head. "You'll do what you need to do when the time comes." She stood. "I believe the others are gathering in the dining room. Do you need help getting up?"

"Can you help me with my shoes?" Devon couldn't imagine bending down to tie them.

"Anything for you, dear brother."

**30**

---

*erminus, 24 December 1871*
Vinni returned to the dining room, where she found Iris Bailey poring over maps.

Iris looked up. "What happened?" she asked. "We heard the explosion. Is everyone all right?"

Vinni took a deep breath. The women on Henry Davidson's team had always intimidated her, although she'd taken pains never to show it. But she'd typically had the advantage over them aside from when Iris and she had had the encounter at the museum the previous spring. And then the Cobb party, where they'd all been tossed by the figurative whims of the gods. She had nothing but admiration for Irish McTavish Bailey, the titan in the tiny frame.

"Mister Meriweather—Devon—was hurt but sustained only minor injuries."

"Claire and Chad will take care of him." Iris smiled. "It's all right, Lieutenant, I won't bite you."

"I'm not sure you'd be able to catch me to do so," Vinnni said. "I've the longer legs. But please—call me Vinni. I owe you for rescuing me."

Iris laughed. "You don't owe me anything. You've increased our knowledge of what's going on by a great deal in a way we couldn't have done for ourselves."

Vinni didn't add she was now essentially a prisoner. If she'd escaped before, she could do so again, but now she felt an odd responsibility to solve this situation that their rogue priest had caused even though she was no longer a member of the neo-Pythagoreans.

The thought caught her off guard, but it rang true—she had left them mentally when Uncle Dross had attempted to rape her, and then physically when she'd sent Cat away from her on the catwalk.

Devon and Fiona entered, followed by Claire. Vinni smiled at the younger redhead. Her admiration for the girl had grown since knowing her. She had a lot of—what did the Southerners call it?—gumption. She had gumption. And sass. And she could turn into a mouse, which was brilliant, if dangerous. Vinni had known priests who claimed to be able to shift forms, but after doing it too often, they had become shells of themselves. Perhaps they'd left bits and pieces of their bodies and souls in the aether when they changed into smaller things? With the difference in mass between Fiona and her mouse self, she had to be shedding something, but what? The girl looked exhausted, and she kept touching her lips.

Uh, oh. Vinni knew that gesture. She'd done it herself often enough after Cat had kissed her for the first time.

*Ah, Mister Meriweather, you cad.* She swallowed the irrational anger that rose like a scalding wave. *Don't you dare turn your back on that sweet girl. Don't you dare put her in danger.*

"Are you all right?" Iris asked, and Vinni came back to herself.

"Yes, sorry, bad memories."

Iris nodded with a smile that didn't illuminate her eyes. "We all have them at this point, don't we?" She put a hand on Vinni's elbow. "If you ever need to talk, you can trust me. I'm good at keeping secrets."

Vinni almost laughed at the idea. After the spring, she'd sworn never to trust Henry Davidson or any of his associates again, but then, she'd also been part of the neo-Pythagoreans. She could understand Iris Bailey and the others better now. They'd all shared the horror of watching the gods take their revenge on Parnaby Cobb and the fear that they'd do something to the people assembled in the ballroom.

Henry Davidson himself appeared, and Vinni's gaze snapped to his face. He looked tired. No, weary, a familiar look. Captains who were holding on to their careers just long enough to get their pensions had that soul-exhausted appearance, like the thought of one more flight, one more landing, one more insolent crew member or demanding passenger would break them. Poor man. She wanted to go to him, but she sat there, her hands aching as the air healed her wounds, and watched as he took his place at the head of the table. Devon Meriweather sat to his left, and Fiona beside him. The others arranged themselves accordingly. When all had arrived and were seated, their number included Davidson, Fiona, Devon, Claire, Iris, Vinni, and the rest of Henry's team that he'd brought with him—violinist Johann Bledsoe, doctor Chadwick Radcliffe, and famed aetherist Edward Bailey, Iris's husband. They shared a smile when they saw each other, and Vinni had to look away. Would seeing others in love always be so painful?

When she glanced up, she felt someone watching her, and she looked to the head of the table, where Henry sat. The corners of his mouth lifted into a small, understanding almost-grin, which she returned. So he understood heartbreak as well. Perhaps she would allow him to talk to her later.

"Now that we're all here," he said, "let's discuss how to first find Pierce Meriweather and then take him down."

"Where's Patrick?" Iris asked. Vinni realized that the brawny Irishman, who had come with Davidson, was absent.

"He's following Pierce in the small dirigible that Miss Telfair flew away from Tinkerer Hall," Claire said. "He took to the air as soon as he could after the tunnel collapse and spotted him leaving on horseback. Patrick's the best pilot of any of us."

"You all know how to fly?" Fiona asked, her eyes wide and hopeful.

"Yes, in case we're in situations like you were in," Claire told her. "Some of us aren't talented with mechanics like you are."

"Oh, she's a good pilot in her own right," Vinni said, then smiled to see Fiona blush under the praise. What had the poor girl been kept from doing? Or, worse, how had others treated her? Again, a wave of protectiveness came over her.

"How is Pierce managing to ride with an injured shoulder?" Edward Bailey asked. "Wasn't he shot?"

"Sometimes people heal fast," Claire said and winked at Vinni. "He may be one of them. Or is taking enough opiates to numb himself."

"He certainly has a supply," Devon muttered.

Chadwick Radcliffe cleared his throat. "Right. I received a message from Patrick a few minutes ago. He telegrammed from north of the city that he lost Meriweather somewhere around Dahlonega. We need to pinpoint his exact location."

"I'm guessing it's somewhere near my family hunting lodge," Devon said. "He goes up there often."

Chadwick Radcliffe spoke again. "There's a lot of uninhabited land up there. We need a way to confirm his location."

"We can use the aetherometer," Edward Bailey told them. Vinni didn't miss the scientist's glee at getting to use his new toy.

"But will it work if the laboratory is underground?" Vinni asked. "You said your signal doesn't go through walls. I do remember that much."

"She has a point." Iris and the others murmured their agreement and frustration.

No, they couldn't be stuck. Vinni spoke before she could lose her courage. "I know someone who can help." She tried to clamp down on her lips, but they kept going. "My associate Catherine O'Day can sense large aether concentrations." She didn't want to bring Cat into it—and risk being sucked back into the cult—but what choice did they have?

"Through what means?" Edward asked.

"Through, well, she does it somehow. She closes her eyes and gets a feel for it."

"Will she cooperate?" Claire asked and looked at Vinni's elbow. "No one has come looking for you as far as I know of."

"I believe she will if we explain the situation to her." But Vinni wasn't so sure. Cat hated Davidson and his team more than Vinni had after the events in Boston the previous spring. "We have to try."

"Meanwhile, we'll get to test our devices to defeat the aether-driven automatons, if that's what they've invented." Edward grinned.

Iris and Vinni exchanged an indulgent look. The degree to which Iris loved Edward and all his quirks, including his boyish excitement over getting to invent, made her wonder if she would ever find anything similar. Vinni again tamped down her jealousy—how often could she do so before it exploded outward? And now she would have to talk to Cat again.

"Right," Henry said. "It's mid-morning. I want to leave mid-afternoon at the latest. I'm sorry, I know this isn't how you intended to spend your Christmas Eve, but we know this group moves quickly. Lieutenant Crow, if you please." He tilted his head, and Vinni nodded. She knew she wouldn't be able to avoid him forever. She found she no longer wanted to.

.   .   .

"Lieutenant Crow?"

Vinni had gotten distracted looking out over the front lawn, where Patrick O'Connell had just landed the small dirigible they'd taken from tinkerer hall. She admired how he and Edward Bailey checked it over and addressed small problems before they could become big ones, an important procedure she also performed on her larger machines. Why hadn't she done the same in her relationship? If she'd cultivated it more, taken Cat for granted less, then maybe she wouldn't have betrayed Vinni.

Or was that just wishful thinking? It didn't matter now. She turned, wondering whether she should make an excuse to not be alone with him. But her inner guide nudged her toward him.

"I'm coming."

She followed him into an office that likely belonged to Devon Meriweather. She'd seen Devon standing on the lawn looking lost and awkward while the others talked tech-speak around him, as far as she could tell. He seemed to have taken a sudden interest in tinkering and engineering, but he looked lost. Poor guy. She recognized in him the qualities of a leader, or at least the potential to become a good leader, and one of them was a thirst to understand. Or maybe he wanted to increase his knowledge base because of the Telfair girl. But she dragged her thoughts away from Devon and Fiona and back to the man who stood in front of her.

Henry Davidson, with his combination of mystery and danger, had always fascinated her. When she'd been given that initial assignment to intercept his team and then him, she'd jumped at the chance. For some reason, Uncle Dross and the rest of the neo-Pythagoreans hated him. Vinni had heard that he'd been investigating their reach across the globe and had exposed some of them, so she could understand their enmity, but not the depth of their emotions toward him. That had always seemed excessive to a group of people that preached self-control and moderation.

She scoffed internally. She'd found out the hard way how hypocritical Uncle Dross could be. It shouldn't have surprised her that that would extend to his enemies as well. And then, with a shudder, the question occurred to her—had she now made an enemy of him? And did she care, beyond risking the safety of those around her?

"What can I do for you, Inspector?" she asked since he hadn't said anything, just gestured for her to take a seat and then did so as well. The large desk loomed as a wooden wall between them. How disappointing. She'd always wanted to sit with him by a cozy fire and trade stories. He must have some good ones.

"I wanted to speak with you privately since I understand that your position within the neo-Pythagoreans likely condemns you to secrecy."

She pondered whether to mention that her position no longer existed, that she had run away, but she kept her mouth shut on that topic. "I appreciate your understanding my need for discretion."

"Right. I also hope you appreciate how we need your knowledge to defeat this foe. Men's, women's, and children's lives are in danger. I am aware that as part of the Airship Corps, you swear an oath to protect your passengers and others entrusted to your care. I hope that extends to the current situation as well."

"You don't need to remind me of my oaths, Inspector." She tilted her chin toward him. "I am aware of my responsibilities, thank you very much."

"I mean no offense, Lieutenant." He held up his hands, then sighed and placed them on the desk in front of him. "You are, to be frank, quite the enigma to me."

"Oh?" She sat back. This could be interesting.

"Yes. You drop into my life and my mission last spring, help my team in a tough situation, but then keep me from capturing Paul Farrell, and vanish."

"My vanishing wasn't all that mysterious. I had to get back to the corps." *And normal life to recover from all the strange stuff I'd seen.* She wasn't ready to tell him that quite yet, but wondered how he'd managed after everything.

Or had he seen so much that strange things no longer bothered him? Impossible. To remain unaffected would mean that he would be a machine, an automaton. Not a man.

"You take your duties seriously." It wasn't a question. And she caught the thread of exhaustion that ran through his words.

Vinni studied him. He was still the handsome Englishman, thin of face with a smattering of freckles and with sandy brown hair, but she now saw in the curve of his neck and shoulders the tension that said he held himself up and kept himself going through sheer force of will.

What *had* he seen? Or done?

"As do you, it seems." She walked around the desk and sat on it so nothing stood between them. "Tell me, Henry, what is this interview really about? I've been forthcoming with your team about what I know that can help you."

"I can't help but feel that you and I have more in common than we've let on," he said. "May I call you Davinia?"

"My friends call me Vinni."

He smiled, and for the first time, she saw the expression without any reserve. It made him look decades younger. "Vinni? That's charming."

She nodded, not wanting to do anything to bring back his typical stern expression. It hurt her heart to think that no wife or child had had the benefit of that grin, that moment of delight. But the shutters closed, and she sighed.

"May I call you Henry?"

"Please do."

They looked at each other. The giving of their Christian names seemed to have unlocked something, opened some door closed with formality, and Vinni found herself at a loss for what to say next. She'd flirted with a few young men in the cult, but nothing serious had happened with anyone until Cat, when them both being women seemed to not violate the injunction of the cult against unauthorized romantic relationships between members. What Vinni felt for Henry... Fascination, yes, but also admiration. She'd long had a great respect for strong leaders, even now that she'd seen how one could so easily abuse his power. What drew her to Henry was his integrity. She knew without any doubt that he'd never put any of his people in a position of harm without a damn good reason.

"What now, Lieu—er, Vinni?" he asked, and his smile returned, but it was a ghost of its former self.

"I believe you were about to tell me the real reason you called me in here to speak with you."

He ran his hands through his hair in an uncharacteristic gesture of uncertainty, and she felt a thrill of female power. How could she throw him off like that?

"You and I seem to have similar problems," he said. "Although you've done better with addressing your difficulties than I have mine."

"How so?" She enjoyed watching his lips as he spoke, his every word precise.

"I don't know why, but I feel I can trust you with this. Although first, allow me to ask you something. You've been here for several hours, and you've made no move to escape."

"You've had me watched the entire time."

He arched an eyebrow. "You're an incredibly resourceful woman. You could have figured out a way away from our surveillance. My team is good, but they are as yet untested as a team, and they are not trained in keeping prisoners in houses."

"So I'm a prisoner," she said, disappointment flattening her tone. "Is that all you see when you look at me... Henry?"

He ran his finger over hers, which rested on the desk, and his touch thrilled her. "Not at all. But tell me, Vinni, why have you not tried to run? Even injured as you are, I'm sure you could have found a way."

So there it was. She could invent no good reason to lie, and indeed, the small hope that he could help her sprouted into a larger one. "I was already making plans to leave the neo-Pythagoreans," she said, "and when the opportunity presented itself, I took it."

"And were you so desperate to leave that you shot out a window and jumped with no concern for how long the drop would be?"

Vinni looked at her hands, which she'd moved to her lap and clasped without realizing she did so. "I am ashamed to say it, but yes. I hope you will not consider me weak."

He shook his head. "No. Sometimes one must risk one's life for freedom. I am well aware of this."

"And so that is why I haven't tried to leave," she pressed on. "I am hoping that you, with all your resources, can help me to disappear. I don't think the neo-Pythagoreans will let me go easily, and I am truly sorry for the danger my presence puts all of you in."

"And is that why you've stayed?" He tilted her chin up with one finger and made her meet his gaze. "For a chance at freedom?"

She swallowed around the knot of anxiety that had bloomed in her throat. She'd trusted Cat with her heart, and that hadn't turned out well. "First tell me what you meant, that you could trust me with something. With what?"

He took his hand back, leaving a cold spot on her chin. "As I said, we have more in common than it seems. As much as I respect my organization, I, too, am seeking a way out."

"Why?" She realized how unfair it was since she hadn't given a reason for her own decision, but she had to know.

"Because I'm tired. That's all there is to it. I'm tired of death being two steps behind me and those in my charge. I'm tired of facing the evil in the world in a way that most people have no idea exists. I'm weary of the weight of responsibility and the unending impossible tasks. Of Faustian bargains and continued compromise, all in the name of a larger good that I perceive the barest glimpses of." He pressed a hand to his lips and took a deep breath. What else had he been about to say?

"I understand," she said.

"But do you judge?" He took her hands, and she didn't snatch them back, although the drilling she'd gone through in the cult screamed at her to do so. Why did that come up now?

"Not at all. No man or woman is supposed to have to carry that sort of weight for their entire lives." She did remove one of her hands from his, but to cup his face. The beginning of stubble pricked her fingertips, making their touch more intimate. "How long have you carried it, Henry?"

"I ran away to the city to become a policeman when I was seventeen." He closed his eyes and leaned into her hand, then planted a kiss on her palm. Her heart pattered like raindrops on pavement. If he continued, she'd have to deal with the storm.

"You were very young."

"And how old were you when you joined the neo-Pythagoreans?"

She almost snorted. Like it had been a choice. "I was abandoned near their compound when I was four or five. I was very young and don't remember the details."

He held both her hands again. "You were a small child? Do you know who your parents are?"

"No." The tears that gathered at the corners of her eyes surprised her. "I have the barest of memories. Being here has brought some of them back, but nothing useful."

"So you are a woman of many mysteries." He stood, and she looked up at him. Something about the angle made her heart double its already frantic beating, and she snatched her hands away. She pressed one to her chest and tried to make sense of the flood of conflicting emotions, the desire to be closer to him and the need to get away from him and his allure.

*He's not going to hurt me*, she tried to tell herself, but she couldn't shut down her reaction.

"Are you all right?" he asked and leaned closer. "Did I do something?"

She shook her head. "No, just please step back." She hadn't noticed the weather before they started talking. In fact, it had been a cloudy but calm day. Now wind howled outside the windows and rattled the latches.

Henry backed away as she asked, then glanced toward the noise, and his stoic mask resumed its place for a moment, to be replaced by the hardness of anger. "What did they do to you, Vinni? Did they hurt you?"

She closed her eyes, better able to breathe without him so near. "They tried. He tried." The wind calmed.

"Who? Paul Farrell?"

"What?" She opened her eyes to give him a puzzled look. "No, our leader, Uncle Dross. He likes young women. He likes to take advantage of the ones in the organization. And he tried to do that to me." The wind picked up again, but not as strongly.

"Vinni, please believe me when I tell you I will never do anything to hurt you."

She nodded and stood. Now that she'd resumed her stance, her anger and panic drained away, leaving her hollow and sad. She thought she'd evaded Uncle Dross, but the effects of their encounter—and the thousand small ones before it—had followed her. "I do believe you, but I don't know what I can do to control my emotions. It happened to me not so long ago."

"Sometimes we can't escape what happened in our pasts, but we can move beyond it." He reached out, then shook his head and drew his hand back. "Take as long as you need, and please let me know if there's anything I can do to help."

She looked at the hand that hung by his side, the one she wanted to reach for, but fear kept her own rooted in place. "Thank you, I will. But I need to do some thinking."

He walked to the door and opened it. The dismissal stung, but she'd already ended their encounter with her words.

"Let me know what you need to keep you safe during your conversation with your colleague."

"I don't think I'll need anything. Just... Am I free to go?"

"Yes. You were never a prisoner here."

She heard the lie in his words. But her captivity at the Meriweather estate remained nothing compared to the prison Uncle Dross had created around her heart.

**31**

———

Terminus, *24 December 1871*

After Henry watched Vinni leave, the butler informed him that Devon wanted to speak with him. Henry found Devon at the desk in the library. Stacks of books, some of them open, surrounded him. Others had bits of paper and ribbons marking places in them.

"You wanted to see me."

"Oh. Right." Devon rubbed his eyes. "I'm sorry. I'm not handling the news very well."

Henry made a sympathetic noise. "It's hard to find out someone isn't who you thought they were."

Devon looked at him, his expression one of surprise, but then he nodded. "Right. Yeah. Pierce." Devon waved Henry in and cleared off a spot on a chair. "Any luck finding more evidence against him? Enough for a legal case?"

Henry took a deep breath. "Yes, from the evidence my team has gathered and observed, the masterminds behind the disappearances and the nutcracker automatons are likely your cousin and a rogue inventor named Paul Farrell."

Devon crumpled back in his chair like Henry had shot him with a pistol. "The evidence, please."

Henry handed Devon the portfolio he'd made up from Layla Bollington's evidence, his team's, and the papers Davinia Crow had grabbed. The folio contained the financial documents that linked Pierce with the warehouse, including evidence that he'd been conducting business from it such as signed delivery receipts. Then there were notes. Scientific calculations in Farrell's hand with Pierce's comments. At least Henry assumed it was Pierce.

Devon flipped through the papers, and when he looked up, denial danced with despair in his eyes.

"I trusted him." Devon said and tossed the portfolio on the desk. "I trusted him with my *sister*." He rubbed his eyes. "She said she couldn't make herself love him. I almost wanted her to marry him, which would have been a mistake in so many ways. This monster..."

"Sometimes the worst monsters are hiding in plain sight." Henry leaned forward. "Mister Meriwether, you can't blame yourself for this."

"Oh, can't I?" Devon stood and paced behind the desk. "I can't blame myself for ignoring the little signs, for allowing them to make a fool of me?"

"Them?" Henry asked.

"Him." Devon gestured to the books on the desk. "I've been looking into engineering texts trying to figure out how to disable these metal creatures or at least to change their instincts so we can turn them to our cause. What if these were the same texts he looked at and got his ideas? What if I aided his dastardly cause?"

"Then you learn not to make the same mistake in the future." Henry spoke to himself as well as to Devon.

"But I'm not you. I'm not the great Inspector Davidson, favorite of the queen, hope of two countries." Devon punctuated his words with a flourish. "How can I even think I'll get to the point where my instincts are as good as yours? How can I protect Therese? Or Fiona?"

The man's pain, naked on his face, stoked Henry's own. The wall he'd built between his past and his present cracked, and words that he'd never told anyone before escaped. "You'll learn," he said again. "My trust of others in the past cost me dearly. My fiancé in my youth." He had to swallow the grief that still wanted to overwhelm him. "And then, as a young inspector, I unwittingly aided a criminal. A murderer. But through these mistakes I learned who I could and couldn't trust."

"And you trust your team? The Professors Bailey? The Doctors Radcliffe? Maestro Bledsoe?"

Henry surprised himself by answering without hesitation, "Implicitly. I trust each and every one of them with my life."

Devon plopped in the chair again. "I need such a team. And I don't have one. I'm afraid I'm going to have to step back from your mission, Inspector. For as much as I trust you and your team, I'm afraid I cannot trust myself." He clenched his hands. "Pierce tried to kill me, and I still couldn't pull the trigger."

Henry nodded in spite of the crush of disappointment in his abdomen. "Will you at least give us access to your hunting lodge?"

"Yes, I'll come with you as far as there."

"Good. We will miss you and your sharp-shooting skills. They would have been invaluable. As much as Miss Telfair's inside knowledge of the world of the mice."

"You'll be fine without me. As for Miss Telfair..." Devon shook his head. "As much as I would love to protect her, she is her own woman, and she will make her own decision regarding whether she will help you."

Henry raised his eyebrows but didn't say anything. Perhaps Fiona Telfair would be the key to getting Devon back on board. Meanwhile, Henry would sort out his own notions.

"I trust in your discretion," Henry said.

Devon dismissed Henry's concern with a wave of his hand. "You can trust me on that. I will not reveal your history."

"Thank you."

Henry left the library but stopped the next maid he found. "Do you know where Miss Telfair is?"

WHEN VINNI ARRIVED at the flat, she had to knock since she'd lost her key. She hoped Cat was still there and hadn't gone back to Massachusetts. Or elsewhere.

After enough time had passed to make Vinni question whether she should knock again or leave, the door opened. Cat stood there in her Airship Corps uniform. The red rims around her eyes and bags underneath them said she'd been crying and not sleeping.

"Thank Goddess!" Cat pulled Vinni into a tight embrace. Vinni closed her eyes against the familiarity and now-familiar panic, but she stayed for a few moments before pulling away.

"Where have you been?" The question came, inevitable and unanswerable, at least when it came to the entire truth.

"The automatons—and men—chased me through the warehouse, and I had to go out a window. A private airship pilot rescued me."

Cat frowned. "You could have been killed."

"I know. I was lucky." She didn't say she'd prefer death to continued captivity to the cult. There was no point in starting an argument. "What happened to you?" She followed Cat into the kitchen, where she sat at the table, and Cat resumed her tea preparation, which Vinni had apparently interrupted.

Cat ladled more water into the kettle from a bucket on the counter. "Water's out. This place is a dump."

Cat hadn't asked if she wanted tea, merely assumed. Vinni took a deep breath to quell the rising irritation. Sure, she wanted tea, but it would have been nice to be asked. But she needed to have her questions answered. "Where did you end up after you retreated from the catwalk?"

"I watched you cross, then go through the door. I went out the way we came in and waited."

"For how long?"

"Long enough to hear the crash. Then I looked for you."

"And you couldn't find me."

Cat put the kettle on the stove and lit the burner underneath. Her decisive actions revealed more than her facial expression. "At least there's gas. No, I couldn't find you. I've been worried sick."

Vinni noticed how Cat wouldn't meet her gaze. "What did you do?"

"Waited. Worried. You could've sent word about where you were."

Vinni pointed to her left elbow. "I'm injured. I couldn't write."

Cat shook her head. "You know what I mean. You could've sent someone with a message."

"I wasn't in a place where I could do that." She didn't want to mention Davidson, Meriweather, or... "Oh! But I discovered something relevant to our mission. Remember the rogue priest Bon Climat? He's down here. He's behind the aether surge."

"Bon Climat?" Cat's eyebrows rose. "Uncle Dross will be interested."

By the tone of Cat's voice, Vinni guessed something more was afoot. "Yes, you can send him a telegram to let him know. Perhaps he can send someone to help."

"No need. He's on his way."

A jolt of panic drove Vinni to her feet. "What? When?"

"I had to send word to him after you disappeared, Vinni. It's protocol."

"Why didn't you wait?" Vinni swallowed, her throat thick. "I can't... I can't see him. Can't bear the thought of being in the same room as him."

"It's protocol," Cat said again. "As much as you hate it, the neo-Pythagoreans are your family."

A wave of dizziness overtook Vinni, and she plopped back into the chair. She blinked, but another memory forced its way into her consciousness. Of sitting and looking up at a younger Uncle Dross, who smiled at her without warmth.

*"We're your family now, Davinia. Yes, that's what we'll call you. Our little David, fierce enough to take on Goliath."*

What had that meant? And what had she been named before?

"They're not my family. They stole me." As soon as she said it, she knew it was true. She hadn't been found wandering. They'd done something to her real family and stolen her. But why?

A rattle made them both jerk. The wind had picked up again. Vinni had experienced the vagaries of Southern weather, but it dawned on her that the wind could be connected to her emotions. Was that why she always had favorable flying conditions, because she was always happy in the sky?

"Don't be ridiculous." But something in Cat's demeanor, a certain stiffness, said she knew more than she let on.

"What do you know, Catherine?"

At the sound of her full name, Cat crossed her arms and narrowed her eyes. "Why did you come back, Davinia? You're eager to escape. I know this. What brought you back?"

Vinni sighed and rubbed her eyes. "I need your help tracking Bon Climat. He's cleared out of the warehouse, and we think he's gone to the mountains, but not sure exactly where. Since innocent lives are involved, we need to find him quickly and confirm the location before going in with weapons."

"'We'?" Cat's voice took on an unfamiliar high pitch—fear? "Who's 'we', Vinni?"

"The people who are helping me. That's all I can tell you." A small stab of satisfaction poked Vinni—see? She had important secrets, too. But more than her own future was at stake. "Please, Cat. He's got children up there, and there's no telling what lengths he'll go to ensure their parents' cooperation."

The kettle whistled, and Cat poured the contents into a pot, to which she added a second tea bag. She moved slowly, almost meditatively, and Vinni kept quiet to allow her to think. Cat cogitated best when moving.

Finally Cat said, "Fine, I'll help you."

"Thank you."

"But—" She held up a hand. "I need a promise from you first."

"What?" Vinni tried to calm the flutter of her heart in her throat. Whatever Cat wanted, Vinni wasn't going to like.

"I need you to promise you'll return here. To me. Once you find him."

"Why?" Vinni asked. "Why are you asking this?" Returning to Cat would mean returning to Dross.

"Because I love you. We'll figure out a way to fix this together."

Vinni thought she'd be happy to hear Cat say that, but she knew from their long association that Cat spoke of emotions to ensure her cooperation and her promise. But what could she do? She needed to know the location of the missing tinkerers.

"Fine. I agree to return to you after Bon Climat is captured and the tinkerers and their families freed."

"Good." Cat put the teapot and two cups on the table. "I'll meditate after we have our tea and see if I can locate Bon Climat, at least give you some coordinates."

"Thank you. By the way, when is Uncle Dross arriving?"

Cat glanced up at the clock. "His airship lands in about an hour. Don't worry—you'll be gone by then."

But he'd be here when she returned. Or he'd surprise them at the location of the kidnapping victims. If Vinni was supposed to be the brains and Cat the brawns of their partnership, how had she been outsmarted? But she'd figure out a way out of it. She had to.

When Vinni hadn't returned by the time he and his men returned, Henry started to worry. He'd had faith she would come back, but what if her associate had prevented her from doing so? Or, worse, what if she'd decided not to help them after all? He allowed his irritability to show with Devon, who now avoided him.

Henry watched the men and women load the lightweight wagons they'd be driving to the mountains. A light drizzle fell, frosting everyone's hair and hats with sparkling mist, but the cold damp made his leg ache. Made him ache.

A laugh brought him out of the gloom he'd almost descended into. Fiona Telfair helped Claire and Chadwick with the medical wagon, and she and Claire shared a laugh. Fiona would fit well on his team, but he couldn't stand the thought of something happening to her. Not that he'd have a choice. Well, he always had a choice, this time a difficult one. She wanted to be included, to have the chance to find her father. But he couldn't make himself allow her.

The sound of hooves pounding up the drive alerted him to Davinia Crow's return, and some of the tension eased in his chest. He helped her to dismount.

"Do you have the coordinates?"

"Yes." The word sounded like it would be followed by a *but*, so Henry waited, but she didn't volunteer anything else.

"Can you show me?"

"Yes."

He wondered at her sudden reticence, but he didn't have

time to ask. "I was worried that your colleague wouldn't help or allow you to return."

"She did. But..." She shook her head. "It doesn't matter."

They went into the library, where Devon had spread a map of the mountains on the table. Vinni took her instruments and marked off a location. "That's where Cat—my colleague—says the biggest concentration of aether is."

"Do you know what's in that spot?" Henry asked.

"A series of caves under the mountain." Devon rested his finger on a spot not too far away. "And here's the hunting lodge. I suspect there's another tunnel between that cellar and the caves."

"Right, then we're headed to the right place." He looked at Vinni and resisted the urge to take her hand. "Will you come with us?" he asked. "It may be dangerous."

"Dangerous is perfect."

**32**

_______

Foothills, *24 December 1871*

Fiona tried to remember to inhale, but she caught herself holding her breath. She'd never been part of anything so exciting. Or dangerous. Sure, Inspector Davidson had told her she couldn't come with them into the cave, but she could at least see them off and wait with Claire to help.

She caught herself looking around for Devon, but he held back. He'd decided not to go after Pierce, and so they'd wait together. She could understand why—what would she do if she got to the end and found her father had helped to mastermind the whole thing?

Davidson emerged from the stables and waved them in. "As you said, Devon, there's a tunnel leading from the cellar into the mountain. There's no one in either tunnel or house."

They headed for the basement, where the secret tunnel lay cracked open.

"Did they leave in such a hurry that they left it open?" Fiona whispered.

"No, it's more likely a trap." Davidson frowned. "And why are you here? Go upstairs."

Fiona cursed her big mouth. She'd ruined her chance to sneak along. She retreated to the stairs and watched.

Henry raised his hand. "Be on alert, all of you. And lower your goggles. Even you, Miss Telfair."

They all did so, and the place took on a dreamy quality through the lenses of Fiona's eyewear. Patrick O'Connell put on thick leather forge gloves and moved toward the cave. He swatted at something that flew at his head, and it nicked his glove, taking one of the fingertips off. Someone shrieked, and Fiona hoped only the glove had been damaged.

A swarm of tiny glistening white clockworks flew from the opening. One of the men that Davidson had brought with them swatted them, and he cried out when his hand came away bloody.

"They're razor-sharp clockwork snowflakes," O'Connell called. "Don't try to swat at them. Just duck." He grabbed a cast-iron skillet from a nearby table and swung at one.

"Retreat," Henry Davidson said, his quiet voice cutting through the chaos with its urgency. Fiona didn't need any other encouragement to dart back up the stairs.

She flattened herself against the wall as the team and the rest of the men Inspector Davidson had brought reconvened in the kitchen. All had made it out, although several sported cuts, some worse than others. Fiona swallowed—she'd never seen so much blood.

Fiona simultaneously wanted to help but not get in the way as the Doctors Radcliffe tended to the wounded. She hadn't been hurt, but Devon had another cut on his cheek. Thankfully the goggles had saved their eyes, but surrounding flesh had been lacerated.

"What are they?" one of the men asked.

"Small clockworks," Edward Bailey told them. He held up the one O'Connell had swatted with the pan. Fiona went over to see.

"That's the lass's specialty," O'Connell told Edward. "Let her see it."

He handed it over, and Fiona lowered a magnifying lens over her right goggle lens to take a better look. The contours of the wires had a certain familiarity... "This is very similar to the clockwork brooches I submitted for a Guild contest last year," she said. "Looks like someone copied my design. And improved on it," she admitted grudgingly, but a smile escaped. Yes, it irked her that someone had copied her work, but it also thrilled her that someone had thought her work good enough to base their own on.

Henry Davidson joined them. "Do you have any insight as to how to disable them?"

Fiona looked closer. "Something is telling them to attack. Ah, here we are. There's a tiny wax cylinder in the middle. Sometimes they're used to capture sounds via wires that scratch on them. Other times, they can be used to manipulate the action of clockworks by moving wires as they turn in certain patterns. The easiest way to disable them is to melt the wax."

"We need to melt the snowflakes?" Edward asked.

"Yes, essentially."

Since they'd gathered in the kitchen, it didn't take long for some of them to start boiling water on the stove in large shallow pans to use steam to melt them, as Iris Bailey said she had seen someone do in Paris with a spy clockwork. Others found what they could to fashion some sort of covering for the men who would take the pans into the laboratory and attempt to herd or lure the snowflakes over them.

When the water was boiling, four men who wore other pots and pans, and who looked like a quartet of kitchen knights, took the pans down the stairs. Fiona got a peek into the area, where the snowflake clockworks lay on surfaces in a glittering, albeit uneven, coating. As soon as the first man reached the bottom of the stairs, they rose. Fiona watched as they swirled over him, then slowed as they met the steam from the pan. The others had similar success, and soon the snowflakes lay on the tables and ground, and some in the pans, for good.

"Nice work, Miss Telfair," Davidson said. "And this confirms the link we suspected with a guild member."

Fiona looked at Devon, who appeared stoic, but underneath miserable.

"Thank you," she said. "But it's also because I am in the Guild—or as much as I can be—that I'm able to help. Please don't think we're all like the mastermind." She crossed her arms and hoped he would get the hint.

"Noted," Davidson said. "All right, you may accompany us."

"No!" Devon said and started forward. "Fiona, please stay with me where you'll be safe."

"Devon, as long as tinkerers are being taken and turned, no one is safe." She stepped back, hoping he'd follow her, but he shook his head and turned to go back into the kitchen.

"Right then," Davidson said, "Everyone, look alert. We have no idea what other tricks these bastards have up their sleeves."

AFTER THE SNOWFLAKE ALMOST-DISASTER, Henry found himself hesitant to enter the underground laboratory.

"Watch out for tripwires," Devon Meriweather had warned. "That's how he almost got me at my estate."

Henry again wished he'd had the foresight to watch over Meriweather more closely. He'd underestimated the man's foolhardiness. Or perhaps had dismissed him as another rich young man who would stumble into trouble but not of the serious kind.

The underground laboratory stretched around and behind another wall, where they found something unusual—well, unexpected. The whole situation could be described as unusual at a minimum. A gate stretched before them, and a sugary smell filled the air.

"Is it made of candy?" the Telfair girl asked.

"Don't touch anything." Henry held up a hand to command them to halt. "We don't know what trickery this could be."

"Do we look like Hansel and Gretel?" Patrick O'Connell grumbled, but he didn't move forward.

Henry approached the gate, which sported a powdered sugar-covered crown of something that looked like hard icing. The pillars seemed to be constructed of caramel made bumpy by nut-like objects embedded in it. As he stirred the air, some of the powdered sugar wafted toward him and lodged in his nostrils before he could cover his nose and mouth. A strange taste filled the back of his throat, like bitter fruit candy, and he waved his hand.

"Get back. Cover your airways. Don't breathe it in."

As he spoke, the words appeared in front of him in thick wooden block letters and seemed to float away from him with a lightness that belied their apparent density. He shut his mouth before more sound could escape. Who knew what damage he could do?

The hands that grabbed at him passed through him as though he was a wisp of some sort, a ghost that could move through and among the living without being caught up in their petty ways and disagreements, and not limited by their boundaries and spaces. He glided through the gate and into a forest. A river of lemonade flowed past his feet, and the plants and trees grew candy on them. Thick grass carpeted the ground, and Henry recalled something about the automatons having grass stains on them. Well, that explained that.

"Don't eat anything, no matter how delicious it looks," he warned whoever was around him, although he didn't know for certain who that could be. His words again left his mouth, their block letters landing one by one in the lemonade river with splashes and floating away. Dolphins with golden scales frolicked with them, playing with the capital *D* from his red warning and bouncing it back and forth. He shook his head. Silly creatures.

He moved away from the river and farther into the woods. The tinkerers had to be in there somewhere, although at this point he moved on instinct. Then he came to a clearing and found his old steamcart. He almost ran, the memory of its explosion flashing through his brain, followed by the stabbing pain of grief and the shame of being ostracized for his unwitting role in Polly's death. But the vehicle stood there, quiet, and docile, and he had to approach it.

"It's a beautiful machine," said the voice he thought he'd never hear again. He turned to see Polly, her dark hair up in the simple bun she favored, and her green eyes twinkled with mirth. He noticed her resemblance to Davinia Crow, although Polly had an innocence that Davinia lacked. Or had had stolen. Polly was also younger, seventeen, and as beautiful as he'd ever seen her.

"It caused your death," he told her. "Don't go near it." This time, only the *D* appeared and floated away, suspended by tiny ropes from little airships. *D* for don't. *D* for Davinia. *D* for Davidson.

*D* for what the hell was happening to him? *Wait, that doesn't start with a D.*

"The machine did nothing wrong," Polly told him. She moved toward him, and although they'd been the same age when she'd died, he now felt the years that separated them.

"I shouldn't have trusted anyone else to do the maintenance work on it. They messed up the boiler gauge. It exploded, and the shock killed you—don't you remember?" *Don't don't don't.*

Polly put a finger on his lips. "My heart killed me. I was already weak and sick. That's why I couldn't marry you. Don't *you* remember?" Her *D*, made of white lace like her favorite collar, floated straight up.

"I didn't care. I would have taken any time with you I could get."

"Henry, Henry, Henry." She took his hands as she had when they were younger. "Look at what you've done. You weren't destined"—another *D* tumbled away—"to be a farmer. You were meant for bigger things. Are meant for them. You can't let these memories continue to veil your perception of your work."

"But if I couldn't save you, I could at least help others. Or thought I could." He frowned at the thought of Paul Farrell's escape. Who knew how much harm the man had caused since his flight from Boston?

"And you focus on your one failure rather than your many, many successes." She pressed the crease between his brows, another remembered and beloved gesture.

"There has been more than one failure." *Like being unable to extricate myself from this vision.* Henry hoped his rational mind was asserting itself over whatever strange effects the powder had had on his brain. And were the others having bizarre daydreams as well?

"Of course. You're human."

"And you're a memory." Henry pulled her hand from his forehead and kissed it. "A beloved and cherished memory. But nothing more."

She cocked her head and smiled at him. "Henry, come back."

"What?"

Her features blurred, as did the forest around them, and Henry blinked to clear the wiggling outlines of whatever he tried to look at. He found himself standing on the other side of the gate in a room painted to look like a forest, and he held Davinia Crow's hand.

"Are you back yet?" she asked.

"I... I think so." He rubbed his eyes. "What happened?"

"You breathed in some of whatever is on the gate. It made you see things."

"Did I say anything bizarre?" He hoped his conversation had been internal rather than external. He didn't want to have to explain Polly to Vinni. No matter what the Polly of his imagination had urged, he would always blame himself for her death, even if he'd hastened it rather than caused it outright.

"I couldn't hear much. You were mumbling." She cocked her head, and now Henry realized where his mind had dredged it up from. How odd that she and Polly had the same favorite gesture when they wanted to ask something but weren't sure how. Or perhaps not.

He didn't want to consider what it might mean, that his attraction to Vinni stemmed from her resemblance to his dead almost-fiancée.

"That's good. I don't know that it would have made any sense." He glanced over her shoulder, half expecting to see the *D* floating away, but his words stayed were they were supposed to.

"Something about poly. As in many?" She winked, and Henry's face heated. So he had said something, but she wasn't going to ask him about it here.

"Was anyone else affected? And how did we get to the other side?"

"You walked through, and I covered my nose and mouth and followed you. The men are washing whatever that stuff is off the gate. The professor is itching to study it, as is his wife. They think it's similar to something they found a formula for in the Ottoman Empire."

"Good, I'm glad it's being de... I can't remember the word." He realized he still held her hand and dropped it. "What other surprises do you think Pierce Bon Climat has in store for us?"

"I don't know, but you're not going first. I don't want to lose you like that again. It was quite frightening."

If he'd been in her shoes, he would have been angry at her for taking a stupid risk, but she looked more scared than anything.

"I promise I won't do anything stupid."

"Good. Looks like they're about done. Shall we see what's in the next chamber?"

"Just because I said I wouldn't go first doesn't mean that you should. Lieutenant? Vinni? Wait."

———

*nderground Near Foothills, 24 December 1871*

    Fiona fiddled with the Krakatuk nut pendant she wore. So far neither of the menaces they'd encountered—the killer snowflakes and hallucinogenic powdered sugar—had been specialties of her father's. She hated that she doubted, even though Hollowell had said he'd been forced to lie. But hadn't her father driven her family to ruin? How could that be the action of a sane man?

Lieutenant Crow led the way through the room painted like a forest with a yellow strip along the floor. Fiona didn't have much time to examine it, but when she looked away, the patterns seemed to move like the undulations of water.

A large mouse blocked the door, which had been built to look like the entrance to a fortress, completed with studs and iron strips over the wood.

"*Don't go in there,*" the mouse warned. Fiona didn't want to think about why she understood it.

She had to ask, though. "Why not?"

"*There are large dolls, and they're hungry.*" With those words of warning, the mouse scampered off.

"What did it say?" Henry Davidson asked.

Fiona swallowed against the fear that rose in her throat. "That there are dolls. And they're hungry."

"A talking mouse?" Patrick O'Connell asked. "Did you breathe in some of the sugar, Lass?"

"N-no. I don't think so."

"Right, then," Davidson said. "Considering what we've just been through, caution is imperative. Look out for traps, either above or below. And be careful when you fight the dolls. Sometimes automatons aren't."

Fiona made a note to ask him about that story later. As the previous doors had, this one swung open easily into the largest room they'd encountered yet. A single candle flickered in the gloom, casting the limp figures along the walls into shadows.

Henry put a finger over his lips, and Fiona nodded. Perhaps they could get through the room without waking anything. That hope lasted for all of ten seconds before something in the corner stirred, and a low laugh reverberated through the chamber.

"Welcome to the Land of Sweets," a deep voice said. "You can try to bite them, but they want to dance."

Two automatons rose, a man and a woman in red embroidered clothing, and their faces blank except for drawn-on mustache and lips.

Henry shoved Fiona behind him as Patrick stepped forward. He moved to the door on the other side of the chamber and tried it, but it was locked.

A tug at Fiona's hem made her look down, and she saw a gray mouse, larger than the usual species. She swallowed her revulsion and bent to pick it up. More the size of a rat, it sat heavy on her palm and pointed to her locket and then to her shoulder, where the strap of her violin case lay.

"Papa?" she mouthed, not even daring to whisper.

The mouse-thing nodded, then pointed downward. She placed it back on the ground, and it scampered off.

What had it been trying to tell her? Something about the locket and her violin. Did he want her to play something? She dared not repeat the sequence that had turned her into a mouse.

The tinkling of notes from an unseen music box made her look up, and the automatons bowed to each other and began to dance with jerky movements. There was something beautiful, if lacking in grace, in their motions. The "man" twirled the "woman," and when she flung out a foot, something went flying, striking one of Henry's men in the stomach. He doubled over, then fell to the ground. Blood poured through his hands, which clutched a dagger protruding from his belly.

"Take cover!" Henry yelled, but there was nowhere to go. The Spanish automatons flung two more daggers, which the members of the group ducked, then went still.

"Status," Henry barked.

"Ferdinand's badly injured," someone told him.

"Look alive. Patrick, you and Edward work on that door."

The next two automatons moved forward. They wore costumes of embroidered turquoise satin in what Fiona recognized as an Arabian style.

"Perhaps you would like some coffee?" the disembodied voice said.

The music started again, this time a melody in a minor key, and the automatons began to dance, more smoothly and with sensual moves that made Fiona look away with heated cheeks.

With each twist and turn, the dolls scattered what looked like coffee beans, and indeed the rich and mouthwatering smell rose around them. Henry motioned for everyone to move away from the beans, which, when the dance ended, sparked and flared. Someone yelped, and several of the group members beat out flames on their trousers. The poor man who'd caught the dagger in the stomach lay still and Fiona choked back tears of fear, anger, and sorrow. Were they to be cut down one by one?

Still unsure of what she was supposed to do, Fiona placed her violin case on the ground and opened it. She removed her violin and bow and moved the instrument into position.

"What are you doing?" Davidson asked.

"Did you not see the mouse?" she asked.

"No, I was too busy watching the automatons."

"There's a musical key." She swallowed. "I'm afraid of what it will do to me, but I have to try."

Henry nodded. "You're a clever girl."

Fiona managed a small smile. "Thank you."

Now a group of small automatons moved out from the wall wearing brightly colored and embroidered costumes from the Far East. "Tea time!" the voice said with a chuckle.

The music that played had grown in complexity, and Fiona recognized the series of parallel intervals as coming from China, which made sense considering that's where tea had originated. She closed her eyes and listened. She had just raised her bow when someone threw her to the ground. She curled around her violin to protect it, and her bow bent, but it didn't break.

Spouts of boiling tea came from the small automaton's mouths and arced over Fiona's head. Someone behind her yelped, and the mist that fell on her face stung the cuts that had been made by the snowflakes.

"Using tea as a weapon?" Henry asked once the streams ended. He stood and shook a fist at the automatons, which backed up and resumed their places on the wall, as the others had. "I'm offended now. Status?"

"Two with severe burns," Chadwick Radcliffe said. "Peter and Phil."

"Door's still stuck," Devon called. "Edward's working on the lock now."

"Can we shoot them?" someone asked.

"No, they're metal, and there's too little space in here."

The largest automaton yet came forward. Fiona had thought it was part of the wall, but no, what she'd thought was a shelf along the wall turned out to be a large dress standing about ten feet high. The dress opened down the middle, then spread like a theatre curtain to reveal small wheeled automatons shaped like gingerbread cookies, which zoomed out. Each held a bow and arrow, and they notched the arrows and pulled the strings taut.

"Now, Miss Telfair," Henry said.

Fiona lifted her bow and played the series of notes, which she improvised into a sort of Scottish jig, the kind of bawdy music her mother forbade her to play. She repeated the note sequence often enough but with space between the repetitions, hoping that would keep her from changing into a mouse.

The gingerbread archers put down their bows, cocked their heads, and seemed to listen to her, as did the other automatons that moved forward—a shepherdess with a nasty harpoon at the end of her staff, sheep, and mechanical wolves with sharp teeth.

Fiona kept playing, and the automatons continued to come forward, making for a strange audience.

"We can turn these into weapons," Patrick O'Connell said. "Fiona, keep playing."

She did, paying more attention to her internal state than to what was happening around her. She watched O'Connell and Edward Bailey moving around the machines, doing something to disable them. Finally, O'Connell said, "It's safe now. We've disarmed them."

"Good." Henry looked around, and Fiona could almost see the mental calculations happening as he assessed the damage.

"Doctor Radcliffe, please attend to the injured. Do what you can for them. Tinkerers, please see what you can do to turn these automatons into something we can use. I suspect that the next task will be our most difficult yet."

Johann Bledsoe had moved to the side of the cave where the large automaton had sat and disappeared behind it. "Henry?" he called. "You need to see this." He pointed to an iron ladder, which the large creature had concealed. It led up the wall to a wooden door that stood ajar.

HENRY CLIMBED THE LADDER, went through the door, and scrambled on to a ledge, which overlooked a large vaulted space. He crawled to the edge, which was guarded by an outcropping, and stopped to rub his leg. It had been behaving up to this point, but the day's activities—especially the ducking and landing on the floor in the last chamber—had angered it.

"Are you all right?"

Henry bit back the short reply when he saw the true concern—but not pity—on Vinni's face. Of course she'd followed him. "Yes, at least I think so. I don't think we'll be running through that." He gestured below. At first what had seemed to be a large multicolored carpet that covered the space moved and undulated, and Henry's stomach and throat met somewhere in his chest.

That was no carpet.

Vinni seemed to have the same string of realizations because she said, "Those are the mice, aren't they? The tinkerers and their families."

Henry nodded. They couldn't send just any automaton in there. Nor could they go in with weapons blazing. They'd kill or crush the innocent citizens of Terminus.

Another movement across the chamber caught his eye— light moving behind a dark curtain on a raised stone platform.

The warm peach color that flickered through the small holes in the fabric and the tingling across his skin said one thing—active aether.

"Do you feel it?" he asked Vinni.

"Yes." She wrinkled her nose. He resisted the urge to tap it. "It's how they're keeping the mice in thrall. And as mice."

"Then we need to disable it, but we have to do so without hurting them."

They moved backward through the tunnel and met up with the others, who still disassembled and catalogued the pieces of the last group of automatons they'd met. The place looked like a sadist's toy shop. Which, he supposed, it was.

"This is it," Henry said. He sketched out a rough map of the chamber in the sand on the cavern floor. "These are our entry points. Here's the dais with the device that's keeping all this going. I presume that's where Farrell and Pierce Meriweather are holed up as well. There's a curtain."

"To keep the mice from seeing what's happening?" Claire asked. "Their brains aren't so far changed that the cleverer ones would lead a revolt."

"Quite possibly." Henry nodded to acknowledge her quick thinking. "So Edward, I need you and Vinni to figure out a disabling counter-frequency. Patrick, you modify the ginger-bread mother to be a Scooper that will gently"—he held up a finger to emphasize the word—"capture the mice that try to escape through the one main tunnel. We don't want them to end up in a small space when they turn back into humans. Doctor Radcliffe, are you ready for any medical emergencies?"

"Yes," Chad said. "It will be chaos down there."

"Is there some way to separate the men and women?" Fiona asked. Her pale cheeks had gone pink. "When they turn back, they'll all be naked."

"She has a good point," Claire said. "And with their brains

transforming back more slowly, we don't know what will happen."

Henry rubbed his eyes. "I will leave that question to our engineers." He checked his watch. "We have four hours until midnight. You have three to figure all this out. Let's get these people rescued by Christmas."

**34**

———

Underground Near Foothills, 24 December 1871

At eleven o'clock on Christmas Eve, Henry and Vinni stood on the overlook, this time with contraptions on their backs that looked like the wings of bizarre Christmas angels. Golden halos around their foreheads held optic devices. Henry wished he could check and re-check that everyone was in position. Vinni bounced on her toes, barely containing her excitement.

"Don't you love this?" she whispered, gesturing to the panorama below. The mice seemed to be moving more, which would make sense since, as rodents, they'd be more active at night.

"Love what?"

"The chase." She struck a dueling pose. "The battle. The knowing that you're doing something to set the world right."

He started to say no, but he didn't want to crush her spirits. And he remembered back to his own youth and his early time on the force when he thought he'd been doing just that. Before he realized he'd helped a killer to get away with a crime spree.

He'd eventually brought him to justice, but he'd never forgiven himself.

But could he do so now? Hadn't he saved enough lives, done enough battle, to stop beating himself up?

"Yes, I suppose I do." He smiled, but wearily, and he read her disappointment in how she looked away.

Henry's watch clicked to 11:11, and he adjusted his optic to bring the stage into better focus. "Ready?"

Vinni's grin was back, and he allowed himself to catch it. Half his own mouth lifted in response.

"Yes." Before he could give the command, she ran to the edge of the outcropping and flung herself into the air, the wings of her mini-glider taking her on an angle to the stage. He rushed to follow.

When his foot left the stone, his stomach seemed to stay behind, leaving him with the sensation of hollowness as he followed just to the left of her path. She touched down on the stairs in front of the curtains and ran to the right. After a landing that jarred his leg, he limped to the left.

The aether device's frequency filled Henry's ears and brain like the hum of an excited airship. He lowered the two earpieces from the halo and plugged his ears and hoped Vinni had remembered to do the same. He depended on her to execute the plan. His job was to wait, watch, and jump in if necessary.

A commotion filled the back of the room, and a large device that resembled one of the clockwork snow scoopers came into view. It was followed by two remanufactured automatons from the last chamber. The larger machine captured the bulk of the rodents. The other two caught the remainder and placed them in giant net bags woven from a stretchy fiber that would expand but not break under their skirts. They looked like they scooped the mice up and put them in their bowls for some monstrous recipe.

"What is this?" The surprised voice belonged to the hand that pulled aside the curtain, and Henry had to hold himself back from lunging at Paul Farrell. The inventor's dark hair stood mussed, and he removed the eyepiece he'd been wearing. "Pierce! We have visitors."

As Henry had hoped, the two of them focused on the fray at the back of the cave. Mice lunged toward the front but stopped as though they encountered an invisible barrier, making a wave of furry bodies.

Henry gave the signal by raising his hand, and resonant low notes from two violins filled the cave. Fiona and Johann played —Fiona on the outcropping where she would hopefully be safe and Johann in the cave behind the rodent-capturing devices. The mice stilled as the new frequency battled that of the device on the stage.

Pierce Meriweather, Devon's beloved cousin, pushed through the curtain and removed his magnifying goggles. Henry wondered what they'd been doing back there. Now that both of them had emerged, he held his breath and waited for Vinni to disable the mouse control device.

Where was she?

When Vinni landed on the steps leading up to the stage, she darted right according to their plan. She shed the glider wings and leaned them against the cave wall so they wouldn't get in the way. The noise of the aether device threatened to disorient her, and she lowered the guards from her halo. However, the plugs were too big for her small ear canals.

She drew on her training from her days in the neo-Pythagorean temple and hummed a note that was discordant to the harmonies of the machine. The pressure lessened, and she kept her own noise going as she slipped behind the heavy canvas curtain.

Vinni caught her breath when she saw what Paul and Pierce had been up to. Nutcracker automatons lined the stage in a circle three deep around the aether device, a column of glass that glowed with a peach light. Vinni squinted to make out the swirling aether donut. Something about the cylinder magnified it and drew her toward it.

"Keep humming," she sang to herself in that discordant note and broke the compulsion. Something picked up the discord, and the notes from the two violins thrummed through her bones. She wasn't the only one to notice. The heads of the automatons swiveled toward the back of the cavern, and their eyes glowed yellow.

"Oh, big hairy ox's bollocks," Vinni sang and made a mental note to tell Iris that she'd picked up her expression. She flattened herself against the cavern wall and tried to make her way behind the giant nutcrackers so she could get closer to the mechanism.

"Ah, there you are, my dear," said a voice Vinni had hoped never to hear again. She looked to her right and saw Uncle Dross standing about ten feet away. But no Cat.

"Where's Cat?" she asked, afraid that somehow her former lover was caught up in all this.

"Out there." Dross pointed to the sea of mice and laughed. "She had no idea." He moved toward her. "But you're the one I'm more interested in, Davinia. Have you discovered anything...interesting...about yourself since being here?"

Vinni forced herself to maintain a relaxed posture. Otherwise he'd see her attack coming. She pulled a knife from the sheath at her thigh with her left hand while brushing her hair, which had come loose from its pins in the landing, with her right. His gaze followed her dark hair as it tumbled around her shoulders, and he licked his lips. Lizard lips, she thought with a shudder that didn't stop. Their last meeting flashed through her mind, the knowledge of what he wanted to do to her twisting her stomach.

"You know where I come from," she said. It wasn't a question. The sounds of the battle raged around them, but she kept her focus on him. The aether drew her to it, and she used that distracting feeling to keep her rage in check. At least she'd learned something useful from the cult.

"Yes, and I'm willing to give you all the answers you want... for a price." He stood close to her now and traced a finger along her cheek with one hand and trapped her against the wall with his other forearm against her chest.

Nausea rose through Vinni's gut. The survival training she'd received in the cult and then in the Airship Corps kicked in, and without thinking, she brought the dagger up behind him and into his lower back. Blood gushed over her hand, and she let go of the knife. He arched, her kidney stab true, and crumpled to the ground. She raised her other hand to her face in horror.

"Oh, bollocks," she whispered. While she'd fantasized inflicting violence upon him, she hadn't thought it would go like this.

As he writhed, he laughed, his grimaces alternating with mad glee. "Oh, you stupid girl," he gasped. "Now you'll never find out what happened to your family. What—who—you are."

"What do you mean, 'what I am?'" She knelt beside him, but as she watched the pain move over his face, she couldn't find the regret she knew she'd feel later.

"Something no one will expect."

"What do you mean?" She caught him by the shoulder, her hand leaving a bloody smear on his white robe.

"You'll. Never. Know." And with a final cough, he died.

She straightened, cold anger covering her like a cloak. She wouldn't let him hurt her anymore, no matter what he claimed to have known. And now he wouldn't harm anyone else, either. She kicked him one more time, just to be sure.

"That's for all the other women."

Then she wiped as much of his blood from her hand as she could before she turned her attention back to the battle and put her hair back up. A breeze caressed her cheek, and she caught something that looked vaguely human-shaped in her peripheral vision, but it disappeared before she could look straight at it.

She shivered. Now that she literally had a man's blood on her hands, what would the consequences be?

DEVON HAD PACED in the kitchen until one of the men had come back and told Claire Radcliffe that her help was needed to tend to the injured.

"Is Fiona all right?" he asked. The man turned to Devon, and Devon caught a flicker of disdain before the man's features recomposed themselves into polite neutrality.

"Yes, she's fine."

The first time Devon had seen the man, it had been dark, but his voice brought familiarity back. "You're Thom. From Tinkerer Hall."

"Yes, I volunteered to join the inspector. To find my family." The edge to his tone reminded Devon of what others thought of him—a coward, and now what?

"I'm ready," Claire said and lifted her bag. "Go on ahead, Thom. I'll be there shortly." Then she turned to Devon. "Will you be all right?"

He nodded, his throat too full of shame to speak.

"Look," she said. "I understand you've been through a lot. But think carefully. Do you want to become old and bitter, stomping around on your bad leg and fearing to take risks because it may destroy what you've built?"

He thought about Henry Davidson, reserved and aloof. And alone even though he'd built a team.

"You're young, Devon. You don't have to choose legacy over what really matters to you."

Her words loosened something in his gut, and he inhaled the first full breath he'd taken since they arrived.

"You're still limping. Here." She took a small glass vial of laudanum and placed it on the coarse wooden table. "It will help the pain."

Then she walked out, leaving Devon with not just one, but two choices. Should he follow and risk having to make the decision he feared the most? And should he take the comfort the laudanum would give him?

FIONA PLAYED the one note on her violin and watched the scene below. A tall, lanky man with a mop of dark curly hair had just emerged. The mad inventor Paul Farrell? Henry had mentioned him several times. And he had the right hair and physique to be the person who had come to the Tinkerer's Holiday Masquerade Ball as the Masque of the Red Death.

Fiona tried to concentrate on her music, but this close to the aether device, her skin crawled and her guts twisted, compelling her to change. She imagined the relief it would be to give in and race down the wall to rejoin her mother and her other family, mingling her soft fur with theirs, her warmth with—

"I am me, I am human," she sang along with the violin note, sometimes changing the pitch of her voice to match the other violin, sometimes matching her own. Maybe Devon had been right. Maybe she shouldn't have come, should have left the heroics to the others, but she couldn't abandon them.

Tears made the cheek pad on her violin wet, but she didn't

stop to wipe them off. Devon hadn't been able to take his cousin's betrayal. She understood that. But she thought they'd had something. Or had their stolen kiss been meaningless? She was just a tinkerer's daughter, after all, and he one of the most powerful men in the city, perhaps the country. Maybe she should give up, run down the wall, join the—

Pierce Meriwether joined Paul Farrell in front of the curtain.

"It turns out we have an audience for our performance," Paul said. "Shall we show them what we have?"

"Most assuredly." Pierce grinned and pulled on a cord. The curtain fell in a pool of black cloth, and Fiona hoped no mouse bodies had been crushed under its weight. She gasped but kept playing. Nutcracker automatons lined the stage, and Fiona swallowed her terror. Vinni was pressed against the wall behind them, but there was no way she'd be able to get to the aether device. Fiona couldn't see the inspector.

Farrell walked back to the aether device and turned a lever. The color darkened to red, and the wasp-buzz of anger filled Fiona's chest. The mice below also felt it.

Pierce laughed, a sound both gleeful and terrifying. "Nutcrackers, dance! Mice, attack!"

Fiona moved to the edge of the precipice, her violin silent, her fists clenched. She needed to murder them, all of them, and her fingernails lengthened into claws. A pressure at her tailbone threatened to become a tail, and her spine curved in preparation for folding.

Tears streamed down her elongating face, and she tried to yell through a mouth that no longer wanted to form the words, "I am me, I am human. I am me, I am human!"

"And you're beautiful." Strong hands caught her just before Fiona tumbled into the seething mass of teeth and fur below. "D-Devon?"

He stroked her hair, and the desire to change receded. She straightened and contracted and lengthened back to her human form as he held her close.

"Yes, I couldn't leave you." He handed her the violin and bow. "Now play as though your life depends on it."

She nodded and resumed, this time a different note. But nothing happened.

She looked back at Devon, who fingered his rifle strap. He watched the tableau at the front of the cavern, his lips pressed tight. What sort of argument was he having with himself?

"This isn't enough," she told him. He blinked, and he looked back at her.

"What do you mean?"

"Someone needs to disable the aether device!"


DEVON NODDED. Somehow he'd known it would come down to him. Now here they were, the choice unavoidable. He unslung his rifle from his back. He'd have one, maybe two shots, and then he and Fiona would have to duck back into the cave behind them. But he still waited to see if Inspector Davidson and Lieutenant Crow could defeat the mad tinkerers.

The thought of his cousin having turned to the side of the planters still devastated Devon, and worse, now he stood between Devon and his target. If Devon took the shot, he would risk killing his cousin. But if he didn't, he put the city in jeopardy.

He glanced at Fiona. Tears and sweat dripped down her face, and her clenched jaw told him she struggled to maintain her form. Her determination to keep playing while she fought such a battle internally made his decision less difficult. Pierce had done that to her, to her and a thousand other innocent souls. Devon couldn't save him. Indeed, he never had been able to.

What had Henry said? That sometimes one had to pull the trigger and let God sort it out.

Devon raised the rifle to his shoulder, took aim, and shot.

## 35

_____

Underground Near Foothills, 24 December 1871

Henry found himself in hand-to-hand combat with one of the automatons. The others had leaped off the stage toward the threat at the back of the room. Farrell and Meriwether simply watched and laughed as the mice and machines went after Henry's team, who, truth be told, held their own with the aid of the automatons they'd reconfigured and reprogrammed, but barely. Finally, Henry managed to shove the automaton hard enough back on to the stage that Vinni, who had just defeated her own, was able to take off its head. Without the optical input, the machine thrashed around and then lay still.

Johann and Fiona had changed their notes, and the mice stood still, listening and confused. Henry and Vinni rushed to the aether device and found themselves with pistols pointed at them by the two inventors.

"Nice try, Inspector," Paul Farrell said. "But you're too late. If you come one more step, we'll give the command for the automatons to attack the mice as well as your crew. I happen to know you don't need any more innocent blood on your hands."

"Nor do you," Henry told him. "You can stop this."

"And go to prison?" Farrell snorted. "I haven't managed to escape the authorities for this long to give up now."

Two shots echoed through the chamber, and Henry and Vinni ducked under a shower of shards.

Henry used his wings, which he had never shed, to cover himself and Vinni. When the shower of hot glass had ended, he looked up to survey the damage.

Pierce lay on the floor, a bullet through his head, and Farrell... Paul Farrell was gone. Of course he'd prepared an escape route. But Henry couldn't chase after him now. He hoped that one of his team had caught the sneaky inventor.

As Claire had warned, the mice turned back into humans, slowly at first. The scene resembled a bizarre garden of furry seedlings sprouting into human plants that uncurled from fetal positions on the floor. Henry signaled for his team to move forward to make sure everyone was safe and to release the mice the automatons had captured.

To Henry's relief, while plenty of blushing occurred, no one became violent. Indeed, the place erupted into small, then larger celebrations as families found each other and embraced. The Doctors Radcliffe and the rest of Henry's team moved through the crowd offering blankets and words of comfort and direction. Men and women covered themselves as best they could, and children clung to their parents' legs.

Claire joined Henry on the dais.

"What do you feel?" Henry asked. If anger simmered beneath the celebrations, she'd know.

Claire closed her eyes and took a deep breath. "Mostly happiness for the reunion and freedoms, relief at no longer being mice, and sadness over what happened. Some regret." She gestured to a portly gentleman who stood and spoke with Margie Telfair, who recounted something with as many dramatic gestures as she could manage without her blanket falling off.

"That must be Bryan," Henry murmured. "Yes, I'm sure Fiona will have some things to say to him."

"Speaking of whom..." Vinni nudged Henry and pointed to the precipice they'd been watching the scene from. There Devon stood, his rifle on his back and his arms around Fiona, whom he kissed so passionately her precious violin hung limp in her hand.

The sight made Henry smile.

"The corners of your eyes are crinkling," Vinni said. "Be careful, or that dour face of yours will get laugh lines."

For the first time in decades, Henry laughed, truly laughed. He took Vinni in his arms and gave her the best kiss he knew how.

# EPILOGUE

*erminus, 27 December 1871*

"Well, I never would have thought it suitable to celebrate Christmas on December 27." *Sniff.*

Fiona and her father exchanged exasperated and amused glances in the back of the steamcart. Margie Telfair seemed to have recovered her normal—that was to say, irritable—humor upon returning home. They'd found the dirigible moored in a large cavern on the other side of the Mouse Hall, as Fiona thought of it, and Henry Davidson's team had spent the rest of Christmas Eve night ferrying everyone back to Terminus. Fiona had insisted on being last, not least of which was so she could help and spend more time with Devon.

She didn't kid herself that he'd be hailed the hero of the rescue even though Davidson's team had done most of the work. As had she. And she had no doubt he'd need time to mourn his cousin. As much as she might want to be there to comfort him, she didn't know if he needed her. Yes, they'd kissed, but then they'd gotten swept up in the rescue, and she didn't know—had he been caught up in the moment? She supposed she'd find out. He'd invited her family as well as the others who'd been taken to a delayed Christmas dinner and celebration.

When they arrived, Bryan helped his wife and daughter out of the carriage. The house blazed with candles in every window, and evergreen garlands festooned the windows and columns of the lovely estate. Fiona wondered what it would eventually be named, not that it was any of her business.

Crenshaw took their coats and smiled at her. "It's good to see you again, Miss Telfair," he said with a wide grin.

"Thank you. It's good to see you, too."

"There she is!"

Fiona turned to see Therese standing with Layla Bollington. She looked to her parents for permission to go to them, and her mother nodded. Crenshaw touched her father on the shoulder and leaned down to say something, but Fiona couldn't tell what. She rushed to Therese and Layla.

"Are you quite recovered?" Therese asked. "You must tell us everything."

"Yes, everything," Layla echoed.

"I..." Fiona shook her head. Where to start? "How's Devon?"

The other women's expressions sobered. "He's happy to be entertaining, I think," Therese answered. "It takes his mind off..."

Fiona nodded. She wasn't going to force Therese to say, "Killing our cousin."

"But the rescue seems to have done his social standing some good." Layla inclined her head to where Devon stood by the punch bowl, surrounded by the men who'd called him a coward. He said something, and the rest of them laughed. Fiona picked out the ones who had eligible daughters. Ah, yes, the proud papas made up most of the crowd.

She turned to greet Lucy and Posey, and when she glanced back, Devon had gone.

"How could you go without us?" Lucy demanded.

"We waited in the yard for hours after the ball," Posey added. "Then one of the servants found us, and we had to go home."

"And then you rescued everyone on your own." Lucy pouted.

Fiona laughed. "It wasn't just me."

She, of course, ended up telling the quartet who surrounded her what had happened. Except for the kiss, of course. And she left out the deaths. They all knew that one of the stable hands and Pierce had been killed. But they thrilled at the descriptions of the mice and the nutcrackers and other strange contraptions.

She also left out the part about her turning into a mouse. That shouldn't be an issue moving forward, and she knew they'd ask more questions than she could answer.

Coils, she hoped her rodent-shifting abilities wouldn't return. She glanced around for Devon, who remained absent, and her parents, whom she couldn't find. Something told her they were together. Planning her future? Surely Devon and her father knew her well enough to recognize she wouldn't appreciate having no choice in the matter.

WHEN FIONA HAD WALKED into the house, Devon had immediately been aware of her. He nodded to Crenshaw, who, with a small grin, returned the gesture.

It was time for Operation: Mouse.

First he needed to get the Telfairs alone. Crenshaw would do that. Then he had to convince them... Well, the true convincing would be Fiona, but he needed to make sure they'd approve. The part of him still ragged from what he'd done—had to do—to Pierce couldn't handle any more family conflict.

Once Bryan and Margie Telfair joined him in the library, he found himself tongue-tied. Had that been how Fiona felt around him? And how had she gotten over it? Right, treat it as a puzzle, and he found in Fiona the most intriguing puzzle of all.

The words broke free. "I have a quandary," he told them. "I would like to court your daughter, but I'm not sure how receptive she'll be. She made it clear she's not interested in marrying." Well, she'd said the thought of marrying him made her shy, but that wasn't exactly a ringing endorsement.

To make matters worse, her mother, whom he'd thought would be excited for the potential match, frowned at him.

Bryan spoke. "I'm willing to help you, assuming Fiona is open to it, but why now? I've been aware of your attitude toward those who aren't high up in society. We don't qualify, and I'll be honest—I've been concerned about the attention you've shown Fiona."

"I mean her no disrespect, Mister Telfair. Nor you. If this experience has taught me anything, it's that social standing and money don't mean much when things go bad. Loyalty, intelligence, and persistence do." Indeed, the night after he'd shot Pierce, the thought of Fiona's steadfastness had kept him anchored as the waves of grief and sorrow over Pierce's betrayal tossed him around. He'd reached for the laudanum and had drawn his hand back more times than he could count.

"And what of her having turned into a mouse?" Bryan asked.

"Bryan!" Margie shrieked. "That's all over now."

"Even if she turns into a mouse, I'll love and cherish her," Devon promised.

"Well, then," Bryan told him. "If she gives you permission to court her, I'll not stand in your way."


THE WEIGHT of someone's hand on her shoulder made Fiona turn, and she saw her parents.

"Fiona?" her father asked. "Can we have a word?"

She nodded, flushed with shame, although she didn't know why. Was it not ladylike to relay one's adventures, even when asked? The flush passed. Even if it was, she didn't care what others thought. She'd survived more than Meribelle Blair or most of the women there.

She followed her parents into the library, where Devon stood. He smiled when he saw her and took her hands.

"How are you?" he asked, and she found herself caught up in his hazel eyes.

"I'm doing well, thank you." None of the previous fear remained, only uncertainty and curiosity over what they'd been discussing.

"Good. I've asked your father a question." He released one of her hands, and they turned to face Fiona's parents.

"Mister Meriweather here has something to ask you, Lass," her father said.

"Oh?" She looked up at him. Her heart beat at what felt like mouse-rate.

"Yes, may I court you? It will take time to recover from the events of the weekend, but you were magnificent."

Although relief washed the anxiety from her chest, she couldn't let his heart run away with his head, even if she was sorely tempted to do so. "But I turned into a mouse."

"It doesn't matter. I'm falling in love with you, and I want to make sure you're fine with that. Since you haven't been sure about wanting to marry."

She nodded, and this time if she had a lump in her throat, it was for a good reason. "Yes. Somehow it's not so bad if I'm being asked if I want to."

"Not so bad, huh?"

He bent down and kissed her, and she closed her eyes, savoring the feeling until her father cleared his throat.

"Oh, let them kiss," her mother said with a sniff.

Fiona almost opened her eyes in surprise, but Devon chuckled and pulled her closer.

The thought briefly crossed her mind that she hoped Henry Davidson and his team felt as happy as she did in this moment, but the sensations swallowed her awareness again.

"WHAT ARE you going to do now?" Henry asked Vinni as they stood on the balcony and watched the Christmas celebration.

She sighed. "Everyone keeps asking me that. I don't know." She wanted to find out what Uncle Dross had been referring to and who the shadowy figure in the cave had been. "I need to find out who I am, Henry."

He squeezed her hand. There had been a few touches, a few more kisses since the rescue, but they'd agreed to take things slowly, to figure out if they could have some sort of relationship. If Cat had been in the cave, Vinni hadn't found her, and she suspected that Uncle Dross had lied. When she'd returned to the flat, she'd found it emptied out and Cat gone. But Vinni sensed Cat wasn't out of her life.

For the first time in a long time, she felt untethered.

"I still have a few weeks of leave left," she told Henry. "I may do some digging around, some investigating. Maybe something will jog more memories loose."

"Do you need help?"

"I... don't know." The breeze picked up and blew a stray wisp of hair into her mouth. "Will you be sticking around long?"

"Perhaps. Perhaps not. I'm still awaiting orders."

"Aren't you going to retire?" She turned to face him.

"Not yet. My team isn't ready to be on their own. Maybe after a few more missions, they can go on without me."

"Then maybe this should be goodbye."

He tucked the stray wisp of hair behind her ear. "Let's make it an *au revoir* rather than an *adieu*, shall we, then?"

"Yes," she whispered. "Until I see you again, then."

"*Au revoir*, Vinni."

When Vinni closed her eyes, she saw her guide give her a thumbs-up, so she figured she'd be seeing Henry Davidson again. They kissed, and unlike the kiss inside, this one held more questions than promises.


*THANK you so much for reading* Mission: Nutcracker! *I hope you liked it. I'm so happy to be following Henry Davidson on further adventures, and he and Vinni will continue to be a focus of the series. I'm curious about Vinni's past, and you may be as well.*

*Please consider leaving an honest review at the site where you bought the book. Reviews help us authors to know what you did and didn't like, and they inform readers as to what books are worth their time.*

# WANT TO READ MORE?

More Inspector Davidson Mysteries will be coming in 2020, but meanwhile, why not check out the Aether Psychics – the series where Inspector Davidson and his team first appeared – from the beginning with *Eros Element*? You can search for it at your favorite online store or order it through your local physical bookstore with the following ISBN: 978-1945074363

About *Eros Element*:

*An ancient energy. A daring expedition. Two misfit scientists in a race against time...*

Iris McTavish always wanted to follow in her father's footsteps. But when his sudden death leaves her household on the brink of ruin, she may have to choose an unwanted marriage over her passion of archaeology. To save her house and prove her worth, she embarks on a mysterious and dangerous expedition...

Edward Bailey's strict scientific code holds back his anxiety and heartbreak. With his professorship and his department in danger, however, he realizes he'll need to find the secret to turning unstable aether into limitless power to keep himself afloat. And for once, Edward can't do it alone...

As Iris and Edward seek out hidden clues, they're hunted by clockwork spies and a shadowy society. During their dash across Europe, the misfit explorers must work together to crack a worldwide energy crisis and discover the truth if they want to stay alive.

*Eros Element* is the thrilling first book in Aether Psychics, a series of Victorian-era steampunk adventures. If you like puzzling mysteries, incredible inventions, and a touch of magic, then you'll love Cecilia Dominic's high-spirited series.

Buy Eros Element today to embark on a charming clockwork adventure!

# EROS ELEMENT PREVIEW

G *range House, 10 June 1870*

On the day of the journey, Iris woke to a quiet house and the sense something had gone terribly wrong. Concern she'd forgotten something important had made her toss and turn until exhaustion claimed her.

But a different kind of anxiety had awoken her this time. With a sigh, she rolled out of bed to check everything one more time.

In the dim room, she touched her trunk, valise and reticule in turn, then moved toward her maid Sophie's luggage. Instead of leather-covered wood, air met Iris's questing hand, and she hurriedly lit a lamp to reveal that Sophie's trunk was gone. She ran into Sophie's room, a small bedroom off Iris's, and found it to be empty of Sophie and all of her things. Iris's sleep-fogged mind told her Sophie had been taken by whatever had made the strange symbol on the office window.

"Sophie?" Iris called. "Sophie, where are you?"

She dashed down the stairs and found Cook in the kitchen. Her eyes were red from crying.

"Cook, where is Sophie? She's been kidnapped with all her

things." As she said it, Iris knew how silly it sounded, and her brain put together Sophie's strange absences and distant looks of the past weeks.

"Yes, Miss, but not in the way you think." Cook gestured to a letter on the table. Iris picked up the folded sheet of vellum with trembling fingers and sensed regret and fear but also joy and excitement.

*The emotions must be intense for a material as flimsy as paper to hold them.*

*Dear Miss Iris,*

*I am sorry to leave you like this, but I can't bear to go on a journey. I've been seeing the Scotts' footman and was hoping you'd accept Lord Jeremy's suit so we could be together, but since you're determined to go on your adventure rather than being sensible and marrying him, I had to take matters into my own hands. With Lord Jeremy's help, we've run off to Scotland to be married. I will see you when you return and would be happy to resume my position as your lady's maid.*

*Best, Sophie*

*Accept her back after she's run off like that? Hardly. Cheeky wench!* Iris's cheeks burned, and she crumpled the vellum. What was she going to do now? She couldn't go on the journey without her maid, her chaperon. What would become of her reputation?

"Miss, begging your pardon for bothering you at such a time because I know how much Miss Sophie meant to you, and I'll miss her too," Cook said. "But I need to buy eggs today since our chickens aren't laying, and I need money for the market."

"Of course," Iris said, the reality of her situation crashing down around her. "The hens seem to know when something is amiss."

"Yes, Miss. Are you still going on your journey?" Cook shot her a concerned glance, but unlike Sophie had never voiced her opinion of Iris's actions.

"I need a moment to think."

Iris went into the office, where she fetched the key for her late father's strongbox, and she opened it and counted the money remaining. Even if they were down to a household of two—and Iris would need another maid if she were to maintain the appearance of her social class—she needed to bring in an income. She closed her eyes and thought about her options—stay and accept Lord Jeremy's offer of marriage or go on the journey by herself. The thought of his shocked look when she turned him down and the idea of looking across the breakfast table at him every morning made her stomach turn. But he wanted more than just Iris... Thinking about how he would desecrate her father's study and steal his work made up her mind.

*I cannot marry him.* The thought asserted itself with unarguable certainty. *There's no other option. I'll go on the journey unchaperoned. If I return with my reputation ruined, it will be with enough income that Cook and I can go somewhere and start over. And if I don't return...*

She refused to consider the possibility.

A line from Sophie's letter came to mind—*with Lord Scott's help.* What if the maid had revealed the plan for the journey to her lover's employer?

The grind of wheels on the stones outside made up her mind. Iris grabbed enough money for two months of household expenses for Cook, some for herself for the journey—in case of emergencies—and slam the lid of the box. She locked it, hid it and the key and ran into the kitchen. Three loud booms echoed through the house, but Iris couldn't tell whether it was the front or side door.

"Cook, go to the door and see who it is," she called. "If it is Lord Scott, please tell him I am not at home. If it is a porter for my trunk, send him in."

"Yes, Miss."

Iris dashed upstairs and finished her toilette. She attempted to pin her hair up and hoped her buttons in the back weren't askew, but there was little she could do about either. Her fingers trembled too much.

Cook appeared in the doorway followed by a tall young man whose eyes took in everything about the bedroom including Iris herself. The look he gave her made her stand straighter and lift her chin to show she wouldn't be intimidated. Instead of bowing or looking away, his lips peeled back into the sort of smile one expected to see on the patron of a naughty peep show.

"These your things, Miss?" he asked, his tone respectful unlike his expression.

"Y-yes," Iris said. The whole situation seemed ill put-together, so she asked, "And who are you?"

"Name's Lamar. I work for Mister Cobb. Your train's in fifteen minutes. We better get a move on."

Once again, the sound of the knocker on the front door echoed through the house. Iris went to her window, where she saw the familiar lines of the Scott coach with its matched four chestnut geldings in front of the house. *Bollocks!* She couldn't remember what the itinerary had said about who would pick her up, but Lamar seemed close enough.

"Yes, we should. Take the trunk down, and I'll meet you by the back gate. Don't argue, just do it."

He complied, again looking more amused than anything else. What did he find so funny?

She embraced Cook, who grasped her upper arms.

"Oh, right." Iris pressed the household money into her hands. "This should be enough to take care of you for a couple of months."

"I don't like the feel of this, Miss." Cook's face, which looked like it had been fashioned by a pastry chef to resemble the holiday dough-dolls children received on Christmas morning, fell in lines of concern. "You're going to go off with that strange gentleman?"

"It's either that or be forced to marry Jeremy Scott. He's lazy but clever, and I have no doubt he will trap me in a compromising situation such that I will have to wed him or suffer my reputation ruined." And doom herself to a life of misery. Regardless of what her mother had said, Iris couldn't consign herself to that fate. Not without a fight.

She pecked Cook on the cheek, grabbed her reticule, traveling hat, and valise, and rushed down the stairs. "Wait five minutes and then answer the door!" she called over her shoulder. "Stall them so they won't follow me. If he catches me, he'll make me miss the train."

"Yes, Miss." Cook huffed down the stairs behind her. "I've fresh scones. That's always good for stopping a man."

*Especially that one.* Iris smiled, rushed through the kitchen, and into the garden. Her trunk was loaded onto an open carriage, where Lamar sat behind... Not horses, but a long cylinder that puffed out plumes of white steam.

"An open steamcoach," Iris sighed. She would have been more excited—only the wealthiest had smaller vehicles good for racing as well as driving, and she hadn't had the chance to ride in one—but she wasn't sure it could outrun the Scott team. No matter, it was better than waiting to face her doom. She tossed her valise and reticule onto the seat and climbed in before the driver could get down to hand her up. He handed back a set of goggles instead. She tried to tie her hat on while he drove away but found herself having to hold on to the side of the carriage for balance with one hand and grabbing her things with the other.

"Can you take it easier?" she asked. "I'm about to lose everything."

A whinny behind her told her that they had been spotted.

"On the other hand, hurry," she said.

"Doing the best I can, Miss. The train in front of us is more important to me than the coach behind us." He shot her a look of mixed amusement and irritation. "You were supposed to be the easy one to fetch. Those gentlemen have no idea what they're getting into with you, do they?"

Iris spared another glance behind her, where she swore the Scott coach was catching up with them. How far away was the train station? She'd often gone with her mother and the footman when they had one to drop her father off before his expeditions, but this man was taking a different route. A hard bump made her lose her grip and bang her elbow when she grabbed again for the side.

"Careful," she hissed around the pain that radiated to her collarbone. She got a hold on the carriage door handle, her fingers tingling. "Do you know where you're going?"

"I'm taking the smaller streets a steamcoach can manage better than a coach and four," he said. "Don't worry, they're falling behind."

Iris looked behind her, but a sharp pain in her neck made her have to take his word for it. After what seemed to be hours when they alternated evading their pursuers and seeming to almost fall into their clutches, the bulk of the train station rose in front of them, the train itself there. It huffed and hissed, and Iris hoped it was settling in after stopping, not getting ready to depart without her.

~

Two days earlier...

*Aetherics Department, Huntington University, England, 08 June 1870*

Of all the things about the college Edward Bailey liked, the ivy was his favorite. It clung to the buildings, climbing up their stone faces, sending leafy tendrils along window edges as if peering in on lectures. On foggy days, it served as a green veil over the facades and provided a sense of decorum and discretion. He much preferred its jaunty green leaves and steadfastness through all seasons to the flashy color and riot of spring flowers with their pretty lies and false promises.

On this Monday morning, Edward tipped his hat to one particularly long tendril that hung over the door of his department building. He then ascended the cozy stairwell with its wooden rail smoothed to softness by generations of eager, curious students and gave a nod to the three discolored splotches that stood guard around the window in his office. He'd nicknamed them Hickory, Dickory and Doc due to their shapes. A fanciful notion, to be sure, but he considered them to be his guardians as he worked through the puzzles inherent in his profession.

They had not, however, prevented the department secretary, an eager young woman named Miss Ellis who eschewed sensible spectacles for a frivolously fashionable pince-nez, from putting a note on his desk about a meeting he'd neither scheduled nor desired. It was to happen in the department conference room at ten o'clock that morning, which would disrupt his routine abominably and abdominally because he timed his taking of tea such that it would provide a needed urge for a mid-morning break right around ten. Now he would have to make his tea a half hour earlier so he wouldn't end up squirming during the meeting with his chairman and his dean. They'd given him enough to squirm about in the eight years he'd been at the University.

"Well, this is most unacceptable," he muttered before his door opened to reveal the tall blond figure of Johann Bledsoe.

"Usually people talk about my unacceptability after I leave, not before I arrive," Johann said. He sat without being invited and crossed one ankle over his knee.

Politeness kept Edward from saying what he really thought about yet another interruption to his routine—goodness, what was next, a surprise visit from the queen?—but he did give his friend an exasperated look. It was quite rude of him to come in and sit without being invited.

"And to what do I owe the pleasure of this visit?" he asked, although his tone conveyed it was, indeed, not a pleasure.

"I got a note saying there would be a meeting here at ten that required my attendance. Knowing your habits, I took the liberty of coming early and having Miss Ellis make your morning tea so you wouldn't experience any awkward moments while speaking with your supervisors."

Edward's gut simultaneously twisted at the thought of having to leave the meeting to attend to bodily needs and the horror that his friend knew his habits so intimately he could plot to interrupt and adjust them to the whims of others. Underneath, he had a premonition the meeting would be the start of a life-wide disruption, perhaps an upheaval. It was time to put a stop to this nonsense.

"While I appreciate your consideration, Johann, I will not allow a meeting I neither called nor desired to interrupt this morning's important work or make a shambles of my carefully orchestrated routine, which has been developed through years of study and experimentation for maximum productivity."

"Too late, old boy. Here's Miss Ellis with your tea, twenty-three minutes early. That should give your stomach time to process it before the chair and dean arrive."

Indeed, Miss Ellis walked in carrying a tray with Edward's favorite teapot, cup and saucer set along with a half cube of sugar—she had instructions as to how he liked them split— and two teaspoons of cream in a little pitcher that had been warmed to exactly one hundred and forty degrees. Alongside were two small lemon strawberry scones, their tart fragrance mingling with that of the strong black tea to make for a siren song of scent. Brilliant, now his mind was so confused it mixed up its analogies. He'd never get anything done now.

"Your tea, Professor Bailey."

Edward put his head in his hands. Was everyone conspiring against him? His stomach growled at the aroma, and he glared toward his abdomen. He'd eaten breakfast at the normal time— why did these savage impulses betray him?

"Look at the poor gentleman," Johann said. "He's overcome with sentiment at how well we care for him."

"He's overcome with something all right, sir," Miss Ellis said, a flirtatious edge to her tone. Johann tended to do that to the fairer sex. As for his insouciant secretary, Edward didn't have the heart to reprimand her. Indeed, its caged animal beating— tea twenty-one minutes early—warred with his growling stomach.

"It's okay to emerge from your shell. She's gone. I'll pour the tea."

Edward peeked through his fingers. Johann poured two cups.

"You put the cream in first, right?"

"I've known you for how long? Yes, I fixed it the way you like it." He passed Edward the fixed tea, and Edward almost dropped the saucer on his desk, his fingers trembling.

"Thank you." He would not allow this disruption to turn him into an impolite savage, after all. "What are you doing here? If the meeting is with my chair and dean, what use could a musician be to them?"

"Perhaps they want to talk of a collaboration between our departments?"

Edward stared open-mouthed at his friend. "A collaboration? With musicians? What is this University coming to? I'm a serious scientist."

"Studying something no one seems to understand but you, and that barely."

"I am an accomplished aetherist in my field." Edward drew himself up and gestured to the stack of journals on his desk. "I have articles in all of these volumes."

"As you remind me every time I visit," Johann remarked. He set his teacup on top of the stack.

Edward drew in a gasp. "Move that at once! What if you spill?"

"Then you'll make another pile from among the dozens of spare journals you keep in your closet over there. Now tell me, how are the Duke, Duchess and ducklings? How many do they have now?"

Edward sighed. He knew Johann tried to educate him in social niceties like inquiring about family—his friend had two siblings and two parents, but Edward didn't see the point in asking about them since he never spoke with them outside of mandatory holiday gatherings—and bit his tongue so he wouldn't snap that they were irrelevant to the destruction of his morning.

He filled Johann in on what he knew of the family, but he couldn't focus. When his chair had a chance to inflict an interdisciplinary project on him, trying to stop him would be like keeping an airship from lifting once the gases were heated —it would take more than his measly efforts. Edward hoped that, like an airship, this disruption would float away and disappear, preferably before lunch.

~

Department of Archaeology, *Huntington University, 08 June 1870*

"Perhaps it's time for you to settle down, Miss."

Iris McTavish wrenched her mind into the present and away from the fascinating story the file in her hand told her, of frustration with academic strictures and lack of collaboration. "Not you too, Sophie." She shook her right hand, which one of her dear departed father's files had graced with a paper cut, and stuck her newly lacerated thumb in her mouth.

"I know it's not my place, Miss, but without your father bringing home his salary, how are you going to keep up the household? Cook and I are worried."

Iris rubbed her eyebrows before remembering the dust on her hands. Now she was sure she sported smudges to make her look like a stage actor or some sort of urchin. "I'm working on that."

A knock on the door forestalled the rest of the conversation, thank goodness. Sophie opened the door to reveal a messenger boy.

"Cor," he said and took off his hat with an admiring look at Sophie. "They din't tell me Professor McTavish were a ghel."

Iris stood and drew the urchin's gaze to herself. "Professor McTavish isn't—" The words stung her throat with waspish ferocity, and all she could choke out was, "available." She swallowed the sensation that tried to erupt through her chest and make her burst into tears like a schoolgirl with a broken heart. Yes, her heart was broken, but she couldn't afford silly displays of emotion.

"Oh, well, are you his secretary? Ent no one at the front desk."

"That's because it's summer," Iris's grief burst through as irritable words. "Most of the faculty are off on trips, and the department secretary's mother is ill, so she's gone to care for her." Which worked out well for Iris. Otherwise, the secretary would have breathed down her neck while she cleaned out her father's office. *She never had much use for me.*

"So who're you, Miss? Meaning no disrespect, but I got this urgent message to deliver to Professor McTavish, and if I don't, I won't get paid and we won't eat."

His voice cracked on the last word, and a tendril of tenderness curled in Iris's heart. The poor boy sounded as desperate and panicked as she felt.

"I'll take it," she said.

"How do I know you'll get it to him? My instructions were to give it to him or his assistant."

"Well, then you're in luck. I'm his assistant." Iris ignored the look Sophie shot at her and put on her gloves before she took the message from the boy. "Here's a halfpence for your trouble."

He didn't hide the disappointed look on his face, but he bobbed his head and disappeared.

"Miss..." Sophie said.

"Sometimes the universe drops things in your lap that you don't recognize as gifts at first," Iris told her. "That's what Father always said." She unfolded the slip of paper and read it, then looked at it again slowly, word by word. It was in English, and the words familiar, but the meaning didn't hit her brain until she read it out loud:

*Dear Professor McTavish,*

*Word of your illness has reached us, and we are saddened to hear of your sudden incapacitation. However, we have a project which you will likely find interesting. If you are well enough, we have funding for you and an assistant to undertake a multidisciplinary summer expedition in search of a treasure, the likes of which has never been found. Please join us for a meeting in the Aetherics*

*Department this Monday June 6 in the conference room on the fourth floor at ten o'clock a.m. You will be well-compensated for your time and trouble with bonus once the treasure is located and delivered.*

*Sincerely, Dean Hartford*
*College of Sciences*

"IT'S FOR YOUR FATHER, MISS," Sophie said. "Not for you. Too bad, it would have been a good opportunity."

"It still might be. What if we tell them that my father is too ill to travel, but I'm his assistant and would be willing to undertake his duties instead?"

Sophie's mouth disappeared into a disapproving line. It reminded Iris of her mother, who would make the same expression whenever Iris would accost her father when he came home to ask about what he'd found on his expeditions, and had he brought anything for her. She later discovered the true reason for her mother's frown, but she pushed those thoughts to the back of her mind as irrelevant.

"But you're not a trained archaeologist, Miss."

"I would be if the University recognized the apprentice system, which was good enough until administrators got hold of academia. Besides, if I acquit myself well on this journey, the University may accept me as an archeology student in the fall. Then I could get a scholarship, which would help support the household beyond the money we'd get for our duties. It sounds like we'll get paid even if we don't find this treasure."

"And what if they find out your father has died?"

Iris patted her hidden skirt pocket, where she held the telegram from France. He'd gone there to see if the warmer climate would help his lungs and passed away at a sanitarium on the coast. She shared it with his chairman before he left for Bulgaria to research the symbolism of the bull in ancient European pottery, and from the department secretary's reaction when she'd shown up the previous week, she was sure the chair hadn't shared the sad news with anyone before he left, likely to keep the fallout from delaying his trip. Everyone knew he had a Bulgarian mistress. The note from the dean confirmed her secret was safe.

Had the death of Professor Irvin McTavish happened a week earlier, Iris wouldn't have been able to work the deception. But now...

"I doubt they will. Circumstances have aligned in our favor." Her shoulders hunched around the guilt sprouting in her chest at having to lie, but what else could she do? If she continued with things as they were, she and her servants would be turned out of their house in the dead of winter, or at the latest in the heat of the following summer if she could manage to sell her father's most precious artifacts. Now determination replaced guilt.

"Get ready, Sophie. You're about to become the assistant to Miss McTavish, assistant archaeologist."

Now Sophie's plump lips hopped to one side. "All right, Miss, but only because I know we need to do this. But if we're discovered, you're on your own with the punishment."

"I will do my best to protect you should that unlikely event happen." Iris moved to wipe her hands on her skirt, then stopped and looked at her gloved fingers. "Would you mind bringing me some water to wash with? We have a meeting to attend in twenty minutes."

# ABOUT THE AUTHOR

By day, clinical psychologist Cecilia Dominic helps people cure their insomnia. By night, this USA Today bestselling urban fantasy and steampunk author writes fiction that keeps her readers turning pages past bedtime. She prefers the term "versatile" to "conflicted" and has published both short story and novel-length fiction. She lives in Atlanta, Georgia, with her husband and the world's cutest cat.

You can learn more about her at her website:

ceciliadominic.com

Sign up for Cecilia's newsletter and get a steampunk novella at the following link:
the following link:
Newsletter

We hate spam and promise to keep your email safe!